LP GRA
Graham, Heather
Phantom evil

Willimantic Library Service Center
1320 Main Street, Suite 25
Willimantic, CT 06226

DEMC

D1531367

PHANTOM EVIL

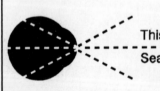

This Large Print Book carries the
Seal of Approval of N.A.V.H.

PHANTOM EVIL

HEATHER GRAHAM

THORNDIKE PRESS
A part of Gale, Cengage Learning

GALE
CENGAGE Learning

Detroit • New York • San Francisco • New Haven, Conn • Waterville, Maine • London

Thorndike Press, a part of Gale, Cengage Learning.
Copyright © 2011 by Slush Pile Productions, LLC.
Krewe of Hunters Series #1.

Thorndike Press® Large Print Core.
The text of this Large Print edition is unabridged.
Other aspects of the book may vary from the original edition.
Set in 16 pt. Plantin.

LIBRARY OF CONGRESS CATALOGING-IN-PUBLICATION DATA

Graham, Heather.
    Phantom evil / by Heather Graham.
        p. cm. — (Krewe of hunters ; 1) (Thorndike Press large print core)
    ISBN-13: 978-1-4104-3712-9 (hardcover)
    ISBN-10: 1-4104-3712-4 (hardcover)
    1. Supernatural—Fiction. 2. Murder—Investigation—Fiction. 3. New Orleans (La.)—Fiction. 4. Large type books. I. Title.
PS3557.R198P48 2011
813'.54—dc22   2011006200

Published in 2011 by arrangement with Harlequin Books S.A.

Printed in the United States of America
1 2 3 4 5 6 7 15 14 13 12 11

Dedicated to the Hotel Monteleone,
and the wonderful staff there,
and to everyone who has helped me all
these years to keep Writers for New
Orleans up and about — and our
writers writing on for the beautiful and
historical city of New Orleans!

Dennis Hewitt, Jorge Cortazar,
Irwin Lee, Michael Montgomery,
Elsa Trochez, Wayne Crawford, Bertilla
Burton, Kathy Bass (Le Café),
Lucille Williams (Le Café),
Estefania Ramirez, Kelly Morgan,
"Albe" Hendrix, Ricky Jones, Al Barras,
Burt Robinson, Darren Carey,
Joseph Lecour, Ken Dillion,
Robert Kotish, Ruoal Vives,
Alex Olisevsci

Lawrence Williams, Keith Donatto,

Marvin Andrade, Grace Bocklud,
Bryan Isbell (Royal AV)

Chef Randy Buck (Executive Chef),
Chef Jose Munguia (Sous Chef),
Chef Ming Duong (Pastry Chef),
Fred Connerly, Jorge Melara,
Renee Penny, Hilda Henderson,
Thomas Joseph

At Fifi Mahoney's — the world's most
amazing wig shop

Brian Peterson, Marcy Hesseling,
Nikki McCoy, Jamie Gandy,
Bobby Munroe, Megan Lunz

And at Harrah's

Jordan Smith, K. Brandt

And . . . very especially, Sheila Vincent,
who has gone above and beyond for us,
so very many times!

writersforneworleans.com
theoriginalheathergraham.com
eheathergraham.com

PROLOGUE

The house on Dauphine

"Mommy."

She had dozed, Regina Holloway thought. Sheer exhaustion from the work she engaged in at the house on Dauphine Street. Sheer exhaustion had finally allowed her to drift off to sleep. The word, the whisper, was something she had conjured in her mind; she had been so desperate to hear it spoken again.

Waking, not opening her eyes, she listened to what was real. The sound of musicians down the street, and the spattering of applause that followed their jazz numbers. The deep, sad heartbeat of the saxophone. The distant noise of the mule-driven carriages that took tourists around the historic French Quarter. Sometimes, the sound of laughter.

She breathed in the smell of pine cleaner, which they had been using on the house. Beneath it — drifting in from the open

French doors that led to the courtyard of the beautiful home — was the sweet scent of the magnolia trees that grew against the rear wall. They'd finally gotten their home in the French Quarter, with its subtle and underlying hint of strange days gone by.

Some said that it was haunted by those days, by that history, certainly not always so pleasant. This house had been, after all, owned by Madden C. Newton, the killer who had terrorized many a victim in the years following the Civil War. The tour group carriages rolled by with tales of ghosts and ghastly visions seen by previous owners. But neither she nor David believed in ghosts, and the house had been a steal. Now, of course, she longed with her whole heart to believe in ghosts. If they existed, she might see her Jacob again.

But ghosts were not real.

The house was a house. Brick, wood, mortar, lath, plaster and paint. She and David had both grown up on the "other" side of town; they had dreamed of owning such a house. They had, however, never dreamed that they would live in it alone.

Yes, she knew what was real, and what wasn't. She was learning to live without the painkillers that had gotten her through the first months after Jacob had been lost. The painkillers had given her several strange visions, but none of them ghostly.

"Mommy."

But she heard the word, and she heard it clearly. She opened her eyes, and a scream froze in her throat.

A little boy stood there. A little boy just about Jacob's age, seven. He was dressed in Victorian-era breeches, a little vest and frock coat, knickers and boots.

And an ax blade cut into his skull, the shaft protruding from it. A trail of blood seeped down the sides of his face.

"Mommy, it hurts. It hurts so badly. Help me, Mommy," he said, looking at her with wide, blue, trusting eyes.

She so desperately wanted to scream. She had seen her son in dreams, but this wasn't her son. She knew the stories about the house, knew about the murders that had taken place here just after the Civil War. . . .

Yes, she knew, but at the worst of times, she hadn't had such strange and horrible visions.

He wasn't real.

Sounds emitted from her at last. Not screams. Just sounds. Sounds of terror, like the nonsense chatter of an infant. She wanted to scream.

"Mommy, please. Mommy, I need you."

It wasn't Jacob, and it wasn't Jacob's voice. And Jacob had been killed in a car accident six months ago; a drunk driver had nearly killed them all, veering over three lanes on I-10 late at night.

Jacob had died at the hospital, in her arms. He had been buried at Lafayette Cemetery, dressed in his baseball uniform, which he had loved so dearly. She wasn't hearing her son's voice.

Just his words.

Mommy, it hurts. It hurts so badly. Help me, Mommy.

Jacob's words, those he had spoken when she had held him at the hospital, just seconds before the internal bleeding had taken his sweet, young life.

This was not Jacob.

No.

She closed her eyes, unable to scream. She prayed that David would come home, Senator David Holloway. Her husband, handsome, even, lucid, rational, wonderful, ever there for her in their shared grief. David could hold her, and she would find strength. He was due home. Dusk had come. Dusk, and yet, there had still been pink-and-yellow streaks remaining in the sky, casting light upon the dust motes that had danced in the

10

room. Dust motes that became the image of a murdered child.

He would go away. He wasn't real. He was the result of the local lore about the house, that was all.

"Mommy, please, I need you. Please, just hold my hand."

She opened her eyes. He hadn't gone away. He was standing there, anguished eyes on her, reproach and confusion in them. The boy was wondering how she could ignore him, stare at him with such horror in her own expression.

"Mommy?"

"You're not . . . not there," she whispered.

"Mommy, don't leave me! I'm scared. I'm so scared. Take my hand, hold it, please, I'm so scared!" he said.

And then, the little boy reached out. She recoiled inwardly, sheets of icy fear sweeping through her with the rage of a storm. And then . . .

She felt the little hand. That little hand, reaching for hers. It was warm, it was vital, and it seemed so alive.

The fingers squeezed hers. She squeezed back.

"I need you, Mommy," he said.

She didn't scream. She managed words.

"It's all right," she said.

Suddenly the twilight became infused with dust motes that sailed on pink-and-yellow ribbons of light, a palette fueled by the dying of the day. Soon, the harsh neon lights of night would take over on Bourbon Street, and the rock bands would reign over the plaintive drumbeat of jazz. Soon, David would come home, and she would hear some psychobabble about her imagining the ghost of a long-dead child to take the place of Jacob.

No one could take her son's place.

But suddenly she wasn't frightened. She needed to reassure a child.

"It's all right," she said again.

"It's going to be dark. See, outside, in the courtyard, it's going to be dark," the little boy said.

"There are lights everywhere. In the courtyard, on the gates," Regina said. "I'll turn on the room light. I won't leave you in darkness."

She sat up, still feeling the cling of that little hand. She walked to the French doors; it was spring, and the air was so fresh and beautiful, as if newly washed, and the scent of flowers was in the air. The inhabitants of the Quarter loved to twine vines and set flowers out on their patios and balconies.

For a moment, Regina inhaled deeply.

Yes, she was desperate. In so much pain. They would say that she was seeking a companion to make up for Jacob, not replace him. That sounded insane. She would never make up a little child with an ax sticking out of his head.

"I love the courtyard, Mommy," he said, leading her.

"Yes, it's so pretty," she said. Hysteria started to rise in her again. She was thirty-five years old, and now she had an imaginary friend.

He looked at her again, leaning against the railing. Suddenly, it seemed that the light hit the child's great blue eyes strangely. There was a look of cunning in those eyes.

She thought she heard something behind her. She turned and frowned with confusion.

And then shock.

She was dimly aware of being pushed.

She was fully aware of falling.

Her scream tore from her lips at last, until it was cut off abruptly.

Skull shattered, neck broken, Regina lay dead with her eyes wide open.

CHAPTER ONE

Jackson Crow sat staring at the pile of dossiers before him. This was his first meeting with the man on the other side of the desk: Adam Harrison, white haired, dignified, slim and a taste for designer suits. The office was modest, nicely appointed, but far from opulent. Plate-glass windows looked over row houses in Alexandria, Virginia, and other companies with shared space in the building had names such as Brickell and Sons, Attorneys-at-Law, Chase Real Estate and B. K. Blake, Criminal Investigation.

Adam had just handed him the folders. "Jackson, do you have any idea of why you're here?"

He'd returned to his old Behavioral Sciences Unit in D.C. to discover that he was being given a new assignment. His leave of absence, it seemed, was somehow permanent.

His last assignment, despite the excellent

work done by him and his colleagues, had ended with three of them being dead. Yet if it hadn't been for his intuition, two other fellow agents might have died as well. Local police had not responded to the call sent out, and there was no way to blame himself.

Naturally, he did.

Maybe the empathy of his superiors had caused them to give him a new assignment, in a different place — behind a desk.

He'd heard things *about* Adam Harrison. He'd worked solo over the years — and for the government where the government could not act officially. Adam went in where others did not.

It wasn't because of extreme danger. Rather, it might be considered that he went in because of extreme *weirdness.*

"No," he said simply.

"First, let me assure you, you are not being let go. You will still be working for Uncle Sam," Adam told him. "The assignments will come from me, but you'll be heading up the team. A new team."

A cushy job somewhere behind a desk that didn't involve serial killers, kidnapping or bodies discovered beneath concrete.

Jackson wasn't sure how he felt; numb, perhaps.

"Take a look at this."

16

He hadn't had a chance to look at the files yet, but Adam now handed him a month-old New Orleans newspaper bearing the headline Wife of Senator David Holloway Dies from Fall into Courtyard.

He looked up at Adam.

"Read the full article," Adam suggested.

He read silently.

Regina Holloway, the wife of beloved state Senator David Holloway, died yesterday in a fall from a balcony at their recently purchased French Quarter mansion on Dauphine Street. Six months ago, the Holloways lost their only son, Jacob, in an accident on I-10. While there is speculation that Regina cast herself over the balcony, David Holloway has strenuously denied such a possibility; his wife was doing well and coming to terms with their loss; they were planning on building a family again.

The police and the coroner's office have yet to issue an official cause of death. The house, one of the grand old Spanish homes in the Quarter, was once the killing ground of the infamous Madden C. Newton, the "carpet-bagger" responsible for the torture slayings of at least twenty people. Less than ten years ago, a teenager who had broken into the then-empty house also perished in a fall; the coroner's office ruled his death accidental. The alleged drug dealer had raced into the vacant house to elude police.

An uneasy feeling swept over Jackson, but he calmly set the newspaper back on the desk and looked at Adam Harrison.

"That's a tragic story," he said. "It sounds likely that the poor woman did commit suicide, and the senator is in denial. I'm afraid I've seen other instances in which a woman could not accept the loss of her child."

"Many people are insistent that the house is haunted," Adam said.

"And that a ghost committed this murder?" Jackson asked. He leaned forward in his chair. "I'm not at all sure I believe in ghosts, Adam. And if they did exist, wouldn't they be things of mist and imagination? Hardly capable of tossing a woman over a balcony."

"The senator has friends in high places, though he's still only a state senator. He absolutely insists that his wife did not commit suicide," Adam said.

"Does he suspect murder?" Jackson asked.

"The house was locked, no lower windows were open, and the gate to the courtyard was locked as well."

"Someone could have crawled over the wall or gotten through the gate," Jackson suggested.

Adam nodded. "That's possible, of course. But no witnesses have come forward in the past month to suggest that such a thing might have happened. The death was determined to be a suicide fairly quickly. Are you familiar with the city of New Orleans, the French Quarter or Vieux Carré, specifically?"

An ironic smile curled Jackson's features. "Land of vampires, ghosts, voodoo and fantasy. But some of the world's best cooking, and some truly great music, too."

"All right then. You work in behavioral science. Don't you agree that people's beliefs can create actions and reactions?"

"Yes, of course. Son of Sam . . . Berkowitz believed that howling dogs were demons commanding him to kill. Or, it was a damn good defense."

"Always a skeptic," Adam said. "And yet you're not really, are you?" Now, Adam smiled.

"I am a skeptic, yes. Am I open to possibility? Yes," Jackson said carefully.

19

"You know, both of your parents were amazing believers," Adam reminded him.

Jackson hesitated.

Yes, they had been believers, both of them, always believing in a higher power, and it didn't matter what path someone took to that power. Jeremiah Crow had been born a member of the Cheyenne Nation, although his ancestry had been so mixed God alone knew exactly what it was. He had loved the spiritualism of his People, and his mother had loved it as well. Nominally Anglican, his mother had once told him that religion wasn't bad; it was meant to be very good. Men corrupted religion; and a man's religious choice didn't matter in the least if it was his path to decency and remembering his fellow man.

But his maternal grandmother had come from the Highlands of Scotland, and her tales of witches and pixies and ghosts had filled his childhood. Maybe that's why it had been while he was in the Highlands, and not on his Native American dream quest, that he had found himself in a position to question life and death and eternity, and all that fell in between.

"You're here because you are the perfect man for this team, Jackson," Adam said. "You're not going to refuse to investigate what seems like the impossible, but you're also not going to assume a ghost is the culprit."

"All right. So you want me to go to New Orleans and find out exactly why this woman died? You do realize there's a good chance that, no matter what the husband wants to believe, she committed suicide."

"Here's the thing, Jackson, most people will believe that she committed suicide. It is the most obvious answer. But I want the truth. Senator Holloway has given his passion to many critical committees in our country. He has made things happen often when the rest of the country sits around twiddling its collective thumbs. He is a man who can weigh the economy and the environment, and come up with solutions. *He* wants the truth. He's young in politics, barely forty, and if he doesn't bury himself in grief, he will continue to serve the American people with something our politicians have lacked heavily in the past fifty years — complete integrity. People in Washington need him, and I'm asking that you lead the group."

"If it's my assignment, I'll take it on," Jackson paused. "But . . . do I really need a unit?"

"I believe so. I'm giving you a group to

dispel or perhaps prove the existence of ghosts in the house. They all have their expertise as investigators as well."

He was quiet, and Adam continued, "When several members of your last unit were killed, you got to the ranch house quickly enough to save Lawson and Donatello. No one knew where the Pick-Man was killing his victims. No one knew that he had arranged for your agents to be at the ranch house."

Jackson felt his jaw lock, and despite the time he had taken for leave, he swallowed hard. They'd lost good agents. Among them Sally Jennings, forty-five, experienced, and yet vulnerable no matter how many years of service she had seen.

He'd felt that he'd seen Sally; dreamed that he'd seen her, standing there at the house.

And it had been that *dream* that had brought him to the ranch house, and there he had discovered that she had been the first to die.

"I shot the Pick-Man," he said. "He's dead."

"That was the only chance Lawson and Donatello had, since, had he seen you before you warned him and fired to kill, he'd have put that pick through Donatello's chest," Adam said. "Trust me, I've watched you for years, Jackson. I actually knew your parents."

That was surprising.

Adam might well have known about the event when Jackson had been riding near Stirling, Scotland, and been thrown. His friends had gone on, thinking that he had left them; that he'd won the race and the bet. He'd encountered a stranger after, one who had saved his life. And then. . . .

It had been long ago.

And yet, hell. He'd spent his life debunking ghost stories and dreams like the one he'd had. Finding the truth behind them. Proving that the plantation in Virginia was "haunted" by a cousin of the owner who wanted him out of the estate. Proving that there were no ghosts prowling the Rocky Mountains, that a human being named Andy Sitwell was the Pick-Man, even if he supposedly believed that the ghost of an old gold-seeking mountaineer was causing him to commit murder.

Six months had passed since he had shot and killed the Pick-Man. Six months in which he had tried to mourn the loss of his coworkers. He'd been back to Scotland to visit his mother's family, and he'd spent a month with his father's family — helping

23

them organize their new casinos and hotels.

But he was ready to get back into the kind of work for which he knew he had a talent. Digging. Following clues. Whether it meant studying history, people, beliefs or a trail of blood. He was good at it.

He had the mind for it, and the mind for the kind of unit Adam Harrison was putting together.

"I'm open to possibilities," he said to Adam. "Possibilities — there are a lot of people out there manipulating spiritualism and making a lot of money off the concept of ghosts."

Adam smiled. "That's true, and I actually like your skepticism. As far as believing in ghosts, well, I do," he said. "But that's not important. I've got you scheduled for a flight into Louis Armstrong International Airport at nine tomorrow morning. Is that sufficient time to allow you to get your situation here in order?"

His situation here?

The apartment in Crystal City had little in it. All right, a damn decent entertainment center because he loved music and old movies. A closet of adequate and workable clothing. Pictures of the family and friends he had lost.

He nodded. "Sure. What about these?" He

lifted the file folders, the dossiers on his new unit. "When do I meet the crew?"

"They'll arrive tomorrow and Wednesday," Adam said. "You've got the dossiers; read up on them first. I figured you might want the house all to yourself for a few hours. Angela arrives first — she'll get in tomorrow evening around six. You'll know who they all are when they arrive if you've done the reading." Adam stood, a clear sign that the interview had come to an end. "Thank you for taking this on," he said.

"Did I actually have a choice?" he asked with a rueful grin.

Adam returned the grin. Jackson was never really going to know.

He started out of the office. Adam called him back.

"You know, you have a gift for this, Jackson. And you can really take on anything you want."

Jackson wasn't sure what that meant, either. "I'll do my best," he promised.

"I know you will. And I know that we'll all know what really happened in that house on Dauphine."

X-Files. The thought came to Jackson's mind as he finished with Adam Harrison.

He went down to his car, still wondering

exactly what it was he was getting into.

Yeah, it was sounding like the *X-Files*. Or Ghost-files.

And he was going to have Ghost-file helpers. Great.

In his car, he glanced through the dossiers, scanning the main, introductory page of each. Angela Hawkins, Whitney Tremont, Jake Mallory, Jenna Duffy and Will Chan. The first woman, at least, was coming from a Virginia police force. Whitney Tremont had started out life in the French Quarter; she had a Creole background and had recently done the camera work for a paranormal cable-television show. Jake Mallory — musician, but a man who had been heavily involved in searches after the summer of storms, and been called in as well during kidnapping cases and disappearances. Then there was Jenna Duffy. A registered nurse from Ireland. Well, they'd be covered in case of any poltergeist attacks. And Will Chan — the man had worked in theater, and as a *magician*.

It was one hell of a strange team.

Whatever, Jackson figured; it was time he went back to work. There was one thing he'd discovered to be correct — the *truth* was always out there, you just had to find it.

■ ■ ■ ■

The house seemed to hold court on the corner. It sat on Dauphine, one block in back of Bourbon and three or four blocks in from Esplanade. The location was prime — just distant enough to keep the noise down in the wee hours of the morning when the music on Bourbon Street pulsed like an earthly drum, and still close enough to the wonders of the city.

The actual shape was like a horseshoe; a massive wooden gate gave entry to the courtyard, while the main entrance on Dauphine offered a sweeping curve of stairs to the front downstairs porch and a double-door entry that was historic and fantastic in its carvings.

Jackson turned the key in the lock. As he stepped in, the alarm began to chirp and he quickly keyed in the code he had been given.

"Straight out of *Gone with the Wind*," Jackson murmured aloud as he surveyed the house. "Tara meets city streets." The front room here served as an elegant reception area, perhaps even a ballroom at one point in time. He could almost see Southern belles in their elegant gowns swirling around, led by handsome men in frock

27

coats. A piano sat to the far end near an enormous hearth with tiled backing and a marble mantel. A second, identical fireplace was at the other end of the wall. Midroom was the grand, curving staircase.

What furniture remained was covered in dust sheets.

The hallway on the second floor led to the right and left as he headed up.

He moved on around an ell and came to a long hallway of bedrooms. Here. At the end.

This was the room.

He turned on the light. It seemed to be completely benign, a pretty room, one that had already been prepared for occupancy — or that *had been* occupied. A beautiful four-poster canopy bed sat on a Persian rug, covered in white. Handsome deco dressing tables sat to either side of the room, and large French doors, draped in white chintz and lace, opened out to the balcony that wrapped around the house as it faced the courtyard. Would he feel anything? He did not.

He walked over to the French doors and threw them open, stepping out on the balcony.

The courtyard below explained why a house that came with such a tragic history could still win over buyer after buyer. It was paved with brick, and in the center, typical of New Orleans, was a fountain and sculpture. A beautiful crane spread its metal wings above the bowl and the water splashed melodically below it into a large basin.

There was a car park to the side, and elegant little wrought-iron tables, shaded by colorful umbrellas, sat across from them. He realized that the kitchen and dining room were behind the round tables, and that food could easily be passed out from the kitchen through a pass-over counter area. He wasn't sure that had been part of the original house. He was going to have to study the blueprints again.

The only thing that marred the beauty stretched before him was the chalk mark down on the bricks where Regina Holloway had lain after she had fallen.

And died.

The blood stain had been cleaned, and yet it seemed to remain.

The courtyard was closed in by the house itself, and by a nine-foot brick wall, and the double wooden gate, large enough to let a car in. But the gate was locked, and it had a key-in pad the same as the main entrances to the house. Senator Holloway had never been a fool; the alarm had gone in the second his signature had been dry on purchase papers. All this Jackson knew because he had read the police reports on the "suicide."

He noted, though, that it would be almost impossible to reach the wall from the end of the house. There was a good four feet between the end of the balcony and the wall; a statue of Poseidon with a trident was positioned there, so it would be a pleasant fall if one were to attempt a leap — and not make it. But, again — not impossible.

Just so damn improbable.

Maybe it was a good case for his first back in the working world; it was incredibly sad to think about the death of Regina Holloway, but he could hardly begin to imagine the loss she must have felt. He'd seen it before. Parents weren't supposed to outlive their children. Any loss of a child was unbearable.

He heard the doorbell ringing and grimaced, thinking that the house had definitely been built at a time when the third floor housed a number of servants; the main entrance was a good distance from this wing. But he was expecting Detective Andy Devereaux, so he left the balcony and the room, pausing one minute in the doorway. Still, he felt nothing. The room was just a room. He hurried on back to the front door.

30

Andy Devereaux was a tall man, light mahogany in color, with powder-blue eyes that testified to his mixed heritage, if the attractive shading of his skin did not. He was bald, clean-shaven, fit and trim and tall. He wore a baseball cap to protect his pate, jeans and a tailored shirt beneath a casual, zip-up jacket. He offered Jackson a firm handshake when they met.

"Detective Andrew Devereaux, Andy, to my friends," he said briefly.

"Jackson — first name, not last — and that's what I am to my friends," Jackson told him. "Thanks so much for meeting me here."

Devereaux nodded grimly. "Hey, I'd do anything I could for the senator and his family. It's a crying shame about Regina. A sweeter woman never drew breath."

"Come on in, and just give me the lay of the land, will you? I got as far as Regina's master bedroom at the end of the horse-shoe," Jackson told him.

Devereaux stepped into the house, removing the Saints cap that had shielded his eyes and sticking it into his jacket pocket after unzipping it. When the jacket front moved, Jackson could see that the man was on duty — and armed.

"You know the history of the house,

right?" Andy asked him.

"Basically, the 'ghost' stories began back after the Civil War. And, apparently, there have been a number of suicides, or murders made to look like suicides, since then," Jackson said.

"Yep. You'd never know it, though, standing in this parlor," Andy said. "Rich folks keep buying the place. It's usually a good deal. One time, it went higher than a kite — folks were *trying* to buy places like this, chock-full of stories. Though before Senator Holloway bought the house, it had been empty for several years. Before that, it was bought by some hotshot New York banker. The fellow wanted to make a haunted bed-and-breakfast out of it."

"Yes. And one of his first guests wound up dead — in the courtyard — and he sold out, right?" Jackson asked. He hadn't read all the material on the house — that would have taken several years. But he'd gotten the gist of what had gone down.

"That one was cut-and-dried, too, I'm pretty damn sure, though I was still a kid in high school when it happened. Apparently, the banker was expecting all the people who oohed and aahed over a good ghost story. What he got was a fellow who had just had his life seized by the IRS. Man's wife left

32

him, and his kids disowned him. Guess he figured it would be a good place to check in — and check out. There was lots of whispering when it happened," Andy said. "But, from what I understand, the police work that was done was solid back then, too. That was about fifteen years ago, now. Place was sitting around, mostly all renovated but covered in dust, when Senator Holloway bought it. His son was killed in an accident soon after, which set them back on the renovations, for want of a better way to put it. He and his wife had just started fixing up the place until a couple of weeks ago."

"The senator is absolutely convinced that she didn't commit suicide," Jackson said.

Andy grimaced, angling his head to the side. "And what do you think?" he asked. "That a ghost pushed her over the balcony?"

Jackson shook his head. "No."

"Then?"

"We're just here to explore every possibility. I don't believe that ghosts push people to their deaths. I do believe that people do."

"The alarm never went off. No one tampered with the locks. Maybe Mrs. Holloway let someone in, but how did he get out? I suppose it's possible that someone scaled the wall, but hopping down? He'd have surely broken a few bones," Andy said.

"Unless he had help from the outside," Jackson said.

"I don't say that something of the kind is impossible, but I can tell you that we searched this place up and down and inside out. There was just no evidence, no evidence whatsoever that anyone else was ever in the house."

"I believe you," Jackson said.

"But you're still here."

Jackson shrugged and grimaced. "I work for the man. I go where I'm told," he said. And it was pretty much so the truth. The last thing he wanted to do was offend a good officer who had probably made all the right moves. Hell, he wanted the police on his side — and because they wanted to be, not because they had been told they had to be.

"Thing is," Andy told him, "we all wish to hell there was something that we could tell him. Senator Holloway is a fellow who isn't all talk, air out the backside, you know what I mean? Not many can keep their souls once they get into politics. He's rare. He's one of the few representatives the people have faith in these days."

"But he must have enemies," Jackson said. "What about the people around him? Any-body have arguments with his wife? Someone who wanted something from him, and she might have been the naysayer?"

"Not that I know about. David Holloway insisted it wasn't anybody close to him," Andy said.

"What about household staff?" Jackson asked.

"There were two maids. They were employed full time, nine to five, but they're not working anymore. I'll get you the files on them," Andy told him. "And those closest to the family. That would include the chauffeur, a fellow named Grable Haines, and . . ." He was thoughtful for a minute, scratching his chin. "Well, most importantly, the senator's aide, Martin DuPre. He can help you with other things you might want to know. He's with the senator all the time. Then there's Blake Conroy. He's Senator Holloway's bodyguard. I've got those files all set for you." He studied Jackson for a minute. "I've got two shootings and an apparent drug overdose right now, but I'm here to help you anytime you want. You get top priority. I can even drop the files by."

Andy Devereaux was telling the truth when he said that he liked the senator; Jackson wasn't sure that investigating what had already been investigated and ruled a suicide was more important than the other cases in his workload.

"I'll bother you as little as possible," he promised.

"You bother me when you need to. I understand there are others coming?" Andy asked.

"Five," Jackson said. "They're here to inspect the house, more than anything else. A woman named Angela Hawkins is due tonight. She's good at talking to people, so she'll probably have a few conversations with the senator and those around him. I —"

"What's inspecting the house going to do?" Andy asked. "I'm telling you that our forensics people are damn good."

"And I don't have a problem in the world believing that," Jackson assured him. "And that means you know this house."

"Yes, I do," Andy told him. Hands on his hips, he looked around. "It sure is a beautiful place. No one mucked it up too much, modernizing it. Back before the 1880s, the kitchen was on the outside. They attached the place after that point, according to the plans. Added the second two stories over there, and added it all on together. It became an academy for young ladies in the 1890s, but . . ."

"But there was a suicide. One of the girls

went out a third-story window," Jackson said.

"You've done your reading," Andy said approvingly. "Some say there was just an evil presence in the house, and it caused people to do bad things. The local rags picked it up at the time. There's rumor the girl was pregnant, but there wasn't an autopsy on her. The parents wanted her interred right off, and they were rich and they got their way. The records still exist, they just don't say much," Andy told him. "I've got copies of all the old stuff at the station — the house has become a bit of an obsession for me." He paused for a minute, and then said, "I guess that history is why you ghost people are here, right?"

"We're not ghost people," Jackson said.

Andy shrugged. "Sure. But it's odd, I'll say that. It all goes back to Madden C. Newton. He was pure *evil,* and evil doesn't just go away."

CHAPTER TWO

No one answered Angela Hawkins's knock on the door. She'd arrived at twilight. For a moment, she appreciated the fine lines of the house, and the size of it. She'd been in New Orleans plenty of times before, and she had always loved the city and the architecture.

But Jackson Crow was supposed to have been there.

She had a key, but she didn't want to take him by surprise. He had been an ace agent who had brought down one of the country's most heinous serial killers of recent times.

He might be quick on the draw.

Hopefully, a member of the Behavioral Science Unit of the bureau would have the sense not to shoot her, but she did know that he'd been out on leave, and she really didn't want to die that way.

She knocked again, saw the bell and rang it, and waited, and no one came. He was in the city, she knew, because she'd received a terse text from him. *At the house.* She hadn't even known how to reply. *Good? Good for you, hope you're comfortable?*

About to board the plane, seemed the simplest response.

She checked her phone. She had received another text from him. *At the station.*

What station? She had to assume he meant the police station. Wherever, he wasn't here. She used her key and entered the house.

She paused in the entry, the door still open, hoping that the atmosphere inside wasn't overwhelming. It wasn't. It wasn't depressing. The room was simply beautiful, huge, and when she flicked the switch by the door, a glittering chandelier dead center came to life, casting glorious prisms of light about the room. Amazing that something so beautiful could have remained so for almost two hundred years. People had a tendency to destroy the old to make way for the new, something that was sometimes necessary. But that progress had kept the house so pristine and so unchanged it was just short of miraculous.

She left her luggage and carry-on at the door, pausing to delve into her bag for the book she read on the plane. It was a little out-of-print bargain she had managed to acquire from a show with which she traded frequently. One nice thing about her side job was that her antiques business created a network of friends with strange and awesome things — including books. Might as well find a place to wait until Jackson chose to show himself.

Departing the entrance hall was like entering a different home; the foyer might have remained in limbo for centuries, while here the modern world had burst in hard. An entertainment room caught her eye. She didn't have a good sense of dimension, and could only think that the TV screen was *huge;* it was surrounded by cabinets that offered all manner of audiovisual equipment. Here, too, there was plenty of space for visitors; there was a wet bar — just in case the kitchen, right around the corner, she believed, was too far — a refrigerator, microwave station and a half-dozen plush chairs, recliners and sofas. Entertainment had definitely been done right.

Moving into the kitchen, she was met with a pleasant surprise. The room was absolutely beautiful, remodeled and state-of-the-art with an enormous butcher-block workstation in the center with rows of pots and pans and cooking utensils above it on wire stainless-steel hangers. The sink and counter area had a large window that was a bypass to a counter outside on the courtyard. There was a massive refrigerator-freezer combination, dishwasher, trash compactor, microwave, all manner of mixers, and all was shining and immaculate.

The senator's wife had intended to entertain, so it seemed.

There were eight chairs around the kitchen table, and Angela drew one out and took a seat. She opened the book she had found — her true treasure trove of information on the house.

In 1888, Jack the Ripper terrorized the denizens of White-chapel; in 1896, the man known as H. H. Holmes was hanged, having confessed to the serial killings of at least twenty-seven victims before he was hanged. Before that, New Orleans had its own monster, Madden Claiborne Newton. While the mystery of the identity of Jack the Ripper makes him one of the most notorious fiends to find his way into the pages of history, Holmes far surpassed his body count — as did Madden C. Newton.

41

Angela paused. She looked around the kitchen and felt nothing. It was so modern. Yet, this was still the home in which the atrocities had taken place.

She flipped a few pages.

Newton's first murder (in New Orleans, at least) was suspected to be that of Nathaniel Petti, the bankrupt planter from whom he had purchased the property. Nathaniel Petti was a desperate man, selling his New Orleans "townhome" to Newton for whatever he could. He had already lost the family plantation on the river, and while Lincoln's plan after the Civil War had been that the North should "forgive their Southern brethren," the death of the strong and humane leader left many in the country in a mood for vengeance, and the laws during Reconstruction were often brutal on the native inhabitants of the South. Such was the case in New Orleans. Nathaniel was being taxed into the grave. He disappeared after the sale to Newton, who was newly arrived from New York City. Petti's wife and child had died during the war years, and the official assumption — if there were such a thing at the time — was that Petti had left, unable to

42

bear the pain of being in New Orleans. While martial law became civil law, politics created almost as much of a war as that which had been fought. While the Freedman Act became law, the "old guard" of the South rose, and organizations such as the KKK came to life. Race riots in 1866 cost more than a hundred souls their lives, and there could be little worry given to the fact that one disenfranchised man had disappeared.

This set the stage for Madden C. Newton to begin his reign of terror.

To this day, it is not known whether or not he killed Petti; what is known is that Petti disappeared, and the motto of the day for the Reconstruction populace was, "Good riddance!"

Angela twisted the book to read the old, fraying dust jacket. It had been written by a man named James Stuart Douglas, born and bred in New Orleans in 1890, when the Civil War, and the era of Reconstruction, would have been fresh in historical memory. There was definitely a bit of skew in his telling of the story.

According to Douglas, the killer, Newton, found those who had newly arrived in the city, and offered them a place to stay. He also found those who were suddenly homeless — apt to leave the city and look for an income somewhere else. The first known murder had been of the Henderson family from Slidell. They had been about to leave for the North, searching for a place where Mr. Henderson could find work. His son, Percy, had been twelve; his daughter, Annabelle, had been ten. All four of the Hendersons had perished after accepting Newton's offer of hospitality. The children had been brutally killed with an ax in the room where they had slept; Mr. and Mrs. Henderson had died after being tied to chairs in the basement, cut to ribbons and allowed to bleed to death. Newton had found watching people bleed to death particularly stimulating. Before Newton's execution, twenty-three known victims later, he described his crimes, and told police where to find most of the bodies.

Angela stopped reading again. No wonder the house was on all the ghost tours in the city.

Darkness had come. She reminded herself that she wasn't afraid of the dark.

Maybe that wasn't true — here. The house suddenly seemed to be alive with shadows. It was probably a bad idea to read the book when she was alone and night was coming on. She wasn't really afraid of the dark, but she didn't want to start seeing things in her mind's eye that weren't there.

She sat still for a minute, thinking about the past. She could recall the day of the plane crash she had survived — but which had killed her parents and everyone else on board — at any given time.

So clearly.

She was incredibly lucky to be alive.

Alive and still so aware of the strange events that had occurred when she had opened her eyes with flames and sirens all around her . . .

A doctor had told her once that strange things could happen when the neurons in the brain were affected, causing such things as the "light" so many people with near-death experiences saw, so, according to him, she hadn't seen the "light" of spirits leaving their mortal forms; she had experienced neurons crashing in her head. After her sessions with the doctor, she had learned to keep quiet. Nor did she ever explain why it seemed that sometimes she had more than intuition. She'd always had a good grip on the world — in many ways there were very thin lines between the truth and insanity. People's perception of the truth was often the difference between leading a normal and productive life — and having someone lock you up for your own welfare.

Adam Harrison seemed to be different, as had many of the officers she had worked with at the police force in Virginia. She had become known for her use of logic, careful study of a crime scene and the victim, and the possible personality of the perpetrator or perpetrators. Police officers tended to believe in intuition; good detectives always seemed to rely upon gut instinct.

Sometimes, she had almost been frightened of herself. But she had to tamp down the fear; good could come when she allowed the thoughts and "instincts" to run through her.

Take the Abernathy case. The one in which she had really made a difference. The baby had been kidnapped by kids just wanting to make money. Two teens, seventeen and sixteen. They'd easily managed to steal the baby from the babysitter. But they'd buried the little boy, and if she hadn't come to the house, if she hadn't added it all up — no break-in, no signs of disturbance, no prints or even smudges on the windowsill — and felt certain that the child was close, they might never have found the baby, buried in the crate right in the backyard.

She would never forget the joy in the mother's face when they had dug up that baby, and she had heard her awaken at last and cry. . . .

She had entered the mind of the Virginia Stalker, and found the remains of Valerie Abreu, allowing the courts the evidence to put the man away.

There were battles, of course, that she couldn't win. Life was full of them.

She had lost her parents. And she had lost Griffin.

Griffin, her fiancé, had died in her arms, with his mother softly sobbing at his side. Cancer was as cruel as any enemy she could ever face and she had been helpless against the disease. Griffin, who had seemed to understand her and love her for all that she was.

But Griffin had found peace, and Griffin had loved her. He told her that she had a special gift, and that she should always use it to the best of her ability.

Yes, she had a gift. And now she had knowledge and experience. The police academy had saved her and she'd served with the force as an officer just before the call had come from her superiors, informing her that she'd been asked to meet with a "Federal" man named Adam Harrison.

Thanks to her time with the police, she now dared to take chances she might not have before.

She stood up, determined to know, now, while she was in the house alone, why the area was driving her so crazy, making her feel so uncomfortable. Some of the houses in the French Quarter actually had basements, she remembered. Getting a better sense of the physical place would definitely be the *logical* move to make now.

The French Quarter was barely above sea level, but it was "high ground" for the area. The basement was only halfway below the ground, and its roof was the floor where she stood now. She still needed to spend time studying the original blueprints of the house first.

But she felt a draw she couldn't withstand.

Angela walked toward the door and turned the handle.

The door opened, and darkness stretched before her. The basement.

Andy Devereaux appeared to be easy and low-key, something that probably served him well when interrogating suspects. His voice lulled. He was soft-spoken. Everything about him seemed easy — except that he had the sharpest gaze known to man. And like a lazy-looking, tail-twitching great cat, he could move in the blink of an eye. The uniformed officers at the station seemed to like *and* respect him.

Jackson stayed at the station long enough to meet some of the district personnel with whom he might come in contact when exploring all angles of the Holloway case, and then Andy drove him back to the house on Dauphine. Jackson realized that he was lucky; Devereaux seemed to like him.

Andy loved the city of New Orleans, and he loved being a cop. He wanted Jackson to understand the city, and the police force. "This department is a damn good one, and believe me, it's had its ups and downs, and we still go through some hell now and then — God knows, things that test a man's patience to the core. Katrina, the oil spill — we just get on our feet again and get knocked down, so you've got destruction, desperation and poverty, and all of them clashing together. Some folks love the city, some folks just sweep down to make a living on the misfortunes of others. We had a force down here early on, early 1800s, and then just like now, some years were good, the city was organized and reorganized — the French Quarter, Vieux Carré, that's the original city — but the Marigny came in on it early, just like the area we call the CBD now, Central Business District. And the Americans came in to form the Garden District — or the 'English' area. Anyway, they get a police force going, but along came the Civil War. By 1862, the Union had taken over and you have military rule. Then, the war ends, and carpetbaggers sweep down. Lincoln is dead, and Johnson isn't really sure he wants black men to be equal with white men, but the ball is rolling. For years, that ball bounces up and down, equality — kill the upstart Africans — equality, no not really, just don't own the man." He glanced sideways at Jackson. "I don't have any chips on my shoulder. History is history," he said.

"Amen," Jackson told him. "Remember when we were talking earlier and you asked me if I believed that a ghost had pushed Regina Holloway over the balcony? Well, I said no, and I meant it. But I think that people can play on the emotions of others with the power of suggestion, and the history of the house is tremendously important in that respect. And the history of the New Orleans police force fits right in there, because everything written about Madden C. Newton suggests that he managed to get away with all those murders because the city was in such a knot — emotionally, socially and governmentally — when he was committing the killings."

Andy nodded and pulled the car to a stop on the side of Dauphine in front of the house. "Best hamburgers in the world about three blocks from here on Esplanade," he said. "A place called Port of Call. Seriously, best burgers anywhere, and best potatoes, go figure."

"Thanks again," Jackson said, exiting the unmarked police car.

Andy drove off.

Shadows had settled around the house. Though it was in excellent shape, it carried a poignant hint of the decaying elegance that made up so much of the city.

He walked up the steps to the porch — Angela Hawkins should have arrived by now. He unlocked the front door, calling out, "Hello," as he did so, not wanting to startle anyone with his presence. He stepped into the grand ballroom or parlor. The great chandelier was lit, casting a haunting glow over the sheet-draped furniture.

"Hello?" he called out.

The woman was here; a big shoulder bag and a carry-on suitcase sat by the door. She traveled like a cop, he noted. Light.

"Miss Hawkins?" he said, his voice loud and strong.

Still, there was no answer. Of course, the place was huge.

He went up the stairs first, following the horseshoe, thinking she might be choosing a bedroom for the stay. But she wasn't upstairs, so he came down to the kitchen. "Miss Hawkins?" he said again. She wasn't there either, but she'd left a book on the table; an old one. He looked at the title. *Madden C. Newton: The True Story of New Orleans's Own Jekyll and Hyde.*

He leafed through it. Interesting, and surely, almost impossible to acquire.

Where the hell was she?

The courtyard caught his eye, and he looked out, for a moment dreading the possibility that he might see a body smashed and broken on the ground. But there was no one outside — no bodies lay on the bricks.

"Miss Hawkins?"

As he spoke, he heard a *whack.* The sound was hard. Like an ax hitting wood, or . . . a pickax slamming into hard ground.

He hurried to the nearest door and threw it open, once again, strange and deadly visions coming to his mind despite his perpetual search for rationality.

She found the ghost of the ultimate evil in man. Madden C. Newton. And the ghost had taken form and shape, and was hacking up the elusive Miss Hawkins . . .

Whack, whack, whack.

"Miss Hawkins!"

Wooden stairs led down to a shallow basement. Someone indeed had a pickax, and looked as crazy as all hell.

Angela Hawkins was attacking the floor with a pickax and a vengeance. The dry dirt floor just beneath the staircase.

CHAPTER THREE

"What the hell are you doing?" He might have been a fool to race down the stairs to accost her — she knew how to hold an ax. The basement held an incongruous sight. Angela was about five foot eight and slender, though shapely. Despite her height, she was almost fragile in appearance. She paused for a moment, staring at him with enormous, bright blue eyes that belonged on an anime character.

Ah, great! He was being given the nut-job assignment. He should have said no. He should have just resigned, and headed off to work the casinos.

Angela remained frozen for a second longer, obviously a bit disconcerted by being discovered at her task.

"Um — hi! I'm Angela Hawkins. You must be Jackson Crow." Maintaining a grip on the pickax with her left hand, she offered her right in a strong handshake.

"Yes, hi, nice to meet you." The words seemed a bit ridiculous. At least she wasn't swinging the ax at him.

He hoped he betrayed nothing in his expression. Did she know about him? That he had taken down the Pick-Man? *Was this a test?*

He tried not to sound as hard and angry as he felt when he spoke.

"I'm Jackson Crow. And — sorry, excuse me, but what *are* you doing?"

She shrugged ruefully. Her soft-knit, cap-sleeved dress completed the perfect picture of sensuous femininity, which seemed so opposed to the strength of her handshake — and her prowess with a pickax. But then, she'd recently gone through the rigors of a Virginia police academy, so she must be in excellent physical shape. She'd been through a lot, the death of her parents, and the death of her fiancé. Maybe she had been through too much.

There didn't seem to be a crazed light in her eyes. Which was a positive sign.

"I'm looking for a body," she said.

"Dead — I'm assuming."

She nodded. "Yes, or bones, I guess. I'm not sure what would happen to a body buried down here for over a hundred years."

"And there's a reason you think you're

going to find a body buried down here? The house has gone through a great deal of construction over the years. The bodies buried here were discovered over a hundred years ago," he told her.

"Ah, some, but not all," she said. "I'm looking for the body of a man named Nathaniel Petti."

"Petti — the fellow Newton bought the house from?"

"Yes."

"No one knows what really happened to him," Jackson reminded her.

"Yes, that's why I'm looking for him," she said. With a mighty swing, she hit the ground again.

Whack!

"We're not here to tear the place down," he said. "What makes you think that he's under the ground there?"

She hesitated. Just a split second. "Well, I've been reading, of course."

Whack.

"You've been reading, and that led you to a space beneath the stairs?" Jackson asked, trying to remain courteous while he cursed Adam Harrison.

They'd sent him a maniac.

"Please, I'm honestly not sure how to explain this, but I'm almost positive that

I'm doing the right thing," she told him.

She was destroying the floor of the basement.

"You do know that we're supposed to investigate the house — not tear it down?" he asked.

Once more, she shrugged.

"Well, I've gone this far . . ."

That was true.

Whack.

He was about to stop her. He was going to step in and tell her that he'd been charged with being the head of the team.

But the last whack did something.

She had managed to get down about three feet. And that was all it took.

He saw — a bone. A distinctive bone. A jawbone.

"Let me," he told her, taking the pickax from her.

"Wait! Careful," she warned.

He knew how to be careful. He used the pickax a bit away from the skull, and he used it with a strength it was simply biologically impossible for her to possess.

In a matter of minutes, he had most of the skeleton showing.

"It's Petti," she said. "It's Petti, and he was the first victim."

It was impossible to argue. It might have

been someone else, but what did it matter? She had managed to discover a skeleton — almost complete, he was certain.

"I'm going to call Devereaux — the local detective in charge of the case," he said. "We'll let him tend to the remains. Because, after all, actually, they are his."

Jackson eyed her as he dialed. Her discovery after being in the house a little more than an hour seemed uncanny.

It made him think about his own experience as a boy. Made him think about the men in the Cheyenne Nation, the ones who talked about the things they had seen on their dream quests. Made him . . . damn uneasy.

"I have a book," she said, as if reading his mind. "A book on the murders. It was only logical to think that Newton had killed Petti, the man he bought the house from. He would have put him here, under the stairs, where it was unlikely that future digging might be done, just because of the awkwardness of the stairway."

"The stairway is wood, it's surely been repaired many times over the years," Jackson said.

"But not moved, because there's the doorway," she pointed out.

Andy Devereaux came on the line. Jackson told him what had happened, staring at Angela Hawkins all the while. She looked back at him, never flinching.

There were no sirens. Devereaux and a team of crime scene specialists and pathologists from the coroner's office arrived quietly. Jackson watched while Angela gave her flat and logical explanation again, and then, as they stepped away to allow the crime scene unit and then the pathologists take over, she excused herself to wash up.

He stared after her, shaking his head. The woman was a witch. She had been pleasant, serene and completely at ease, certain of herself as she had spoken to the detective. She was certainly beautiful enough with her golden hair and crystal-blue eyes, lithe figure and easy poise.

That didn't make it any better. She was calm now, but she'd been wielding a pickax with a vengeance.

With an inward groan, he wondered what the hell it was going to be like when he met the rest of the team.

The bones had been taken by a pathology team that had been called in along with the crime scene unit, and after a great deal of discussion on exactly who should be collecting the bones. They were planning on sending the bones on to another team at the Smithsonian, a team that specialized in bones that were over a hundred years old.

Frankly, Angela didn't need any team to tell her a simple truth; the bones were those of Nathaniel Petti, the man who had owned the house before selling out to Madden C. Newton. But the exact cause of Petti's death might be determined, and the man with such a sad life and death might be put to rest at last.

Angela wondered if it was wrong to be starving after she had just found the remains of a human being. But she was alive herself, and being alive meant that the machine must be fueled. She couldn't wait for the last of the police — even though she really liked Andy Devereaux — and the crime scene unit to leave.

Of course, it was a bit uncomfortable, having Jackson Crow watch her throughout the proceedings as if he was studying a strange and foreign object — or meeting an alien.

Her hunger was going to have to wait. When the other officers had left, Jackson asked Andy about the police shooting range. Andy arched a brow. "It's getting late —"

"Can we still get in?"

"I'd like a little target practice," Jackson said. Angela felt her cheeks color. He didn't want target practice; he wanted to see if she was really capable with a weapon.

Andy looked at his watch. "Come on, then, let's get the house locked up, and I'll take you."

Jackson stared at Angela. "Shall we get our weapons?"

Yes, she thought. She was being put on trial. Fine; she'd go to target practice.

It was quiet when they arrived; two men were down the row, earmuffs stifling the constant sound of the explosions.

Andy wasn't practicing; he set up Jackson and Angela.

Her gun was a Glock and she knew how to use it. Somehow, she'd been blessed with twenty-twenty vision, and the ability to utilize it and her weapon properly to aim. Her stance was steady, and comfortable, and she used both hands in a grip known as the Weaver position, her weaker hand — her left — supporting her grip. She was stronger than she looked, and ready for the powerful recoil on the gun. She didn't let Jackson's presence disturb her, and in a matter of seconds, she'd removed the entire heart area from her target.

She turned and looked at Jackson, who hadn't fired a shot yet. "Satisfied?"

He had the grace to grin. "I just want to

make sure you're ready for whatever comes."

"My dossier must have told you that I can shoot," she said.

"Some things are best viewed in the world," he said with a shrug. He turned away from her. "Andy, this was great. Thanks."

"Yep. I'll get you back. It's getting late."

Andy brought them back to the house. Angela's stomach had begun to ache. She couldn't help it; she was feeling resentful and irritated. She was being judged.

At last they closed the front door on Devereaux, and Angela noted that although she had taken out her weapon as requested, she hadn't taken her suitcases, small as they were, anywhere yet, and she should probably pick a room before going out.

"I'm just going to throw those somewhere and find a place to eat," she said to Jackson, whose gaze remained on her.

He nodded. "I'll go with you. I haven't had dinner, or, anything that really resembled lunch, for that matter."

Not an emotion in sight. Jackson Crow was an interesting and arresting man. She'd assumed that his surname, Crow, definitely meant something of a Native American background. His eyes, however, were an extremely deep shade of blue — not black at all, as she had first imagined. A strong contrast with his black hair. He seemed excellent at concealing his thoughts and emotions, but she had seen a look in those deep dark eyes a few times that seemed to judge her as being certifiably insane. Then again, of course, given the way he had found her, she supposed it might be quite logical that he'd look at her as if she was a bit askew.

If she quit on the first day, would they let her back on to the force?

She wasn't going to quit. No matter how he looked at her.

"Did you pick a room?" she asked.

"I thought I'd take one that's straight up the stairs and to the left. I put my bags there. Some of them need sheets and a dusting, but there are three rooms on the level just above us that have apparently been kept up . . . I'm assuming the senator and his wife were prepared for company, live-in help, and probably, the senator's aide, chauffeur and bodyguard."

"But it's just us now?" she asked him.

"Just us. And the others will be in tomorrow."

"Have you met any of them?"

"Nope. We're all a surprise to one another," he said.

She was pretty sure that she'd been quite a surprise to him.

"All right, I'll just run these bags up. You're in the last bedroom on the left-hand side once I'm up there?" she asked.

He nodded. "I can take your bags up for you," he offered.

"It's okay. I never travel with what I can't carry. I'll be right down."

She felt his blue gaze on her as she grabbed her carry-on and her shoulder bag. As she reached the landing, she saw that there were three rooms to her left; the first seemed the easiest place, and so she deposited her luggage on the floor by the foot of the bed. The room was handsomely designed with a black-and-gold motif, almost à la the New Orleans Saints. Angela imagined that Regina had carefully planned it as a guest room, which, definitely, did not sound like the act of a woman contemplating suicide. In fact, from what she had seen, the grieving mother had been dedicated to making the house the perfect home for a man-of-the-people politician.

Angela wasn't an expert on the depression that led to suicide, so she couldn't really be sure how people might behave before taking their own lives. A call to a few forensic psychiatrists was in order.

"Any particular cuisine in mind?" Jackson asked her as she came back down the stairs.

She gazed at him questioningly. "It is New Orleans," she told him. "Anywhere."

"Most places are open until at least ten. How about Irene's?"

"Lovely."

They locked the house and strolled two silent blocks down to Royal, passing the burst of sound that was Bourbon as they did so. Two mounted-police officers at the corner watched over the night, lest the revelers become a bit too happy. Come-on persons were in the street, hawking the cheapness of an establishment's drinks, the wonders of the band or the exotic talents of the dancers within a certain club.

Even when Jackson was approached by a slightly long-in-the-tooth woman urging him to an upstairs establishment to see Wicked Wanda on a pole, he seemed amused.

"Sorry, I'm with a friend tonight," he told the hawker.

"She can come, too!"

"It's okay — I know that I'd just love Wicked Wanda," Angela said. "But we're heading off to dinner."

"We serve food!" the woman told him.

"We have an amazing menu. Two amazing menus, actually. Spankings are five dollars a shot, pants up or down."

"And then the servers bring you your food," Jackson said, grinning. "Sorry," he lied, "we have reservations."

They managed to elude the persistent woman, and walk quickly on down to Royal where they reached relative quiet. Royal Street was known for its antiques shops and boutiques, and was more serene than the raucous Bourbon by night.

Arriving at Irene's, they were ushered past the first dining room to wait at the bar, where a pianist played and sang old tunes, nicely performing "At Last." Jackson asked her if she'd like a drink, and she opted for a cabernet.

"You know, I could get the drinks," she told him.

He grinned. "We're on an expense account. Let me use the company's money."

"I wonder what the taxpayers would think about that," she murmured.

"Actually, Adam Harrison funds the special unit. I believe he started off in a nice financial place at birth, and managed to parlay his inheritance into a tidy sum through investments and real estate. The last thing he would begrudge his people, I

66

think, would be drinks and dinner after digging up a corpse."

"Bones," she corrected.

"Dead man," he said with a grin and a shrug.

By the time he acquired the drinks, the hostess returned to lead them to a table. Angela had always liked Irene's; the food was delicious, there were fine white cloths on the table, and the noise level was at a gentle hum.

Angela couldn't help but note the way Jackson fascinated their server. She herself had set out to dislike the man, or, if not dislike him, set up a reserve against him. She knew that *he* knew a great deal about everyone on his team, while the team knew almost nothing about him — or each other. Though tall enough to stand just an inch or so above most men, he had an easy courteous manner and a slow smile that appeared to enchant everyone around him. Perhaps it was natural that he should attract attention.

"So, here we are, one day in. Body — discovered," he said, taking a swallow of his scotch on the rocks.

"It was only logical," she said.

He laughed. "Only logical. That man has been buried beneath the stairs since Reconstruction, and you found him in an hour."

"I'm an extremely logical person," she said, running her fingers up the stem of her wineglass.

"So, what's your story?" he asked her.

"You know *my* story. You have the dossiers. *I* start the questions."

"Okay, shoot."

"What's your background?" she asked.

He grinned. "Obvious, I'd say."

"American Indian. What kind?"

"Cheyenne."

"And what else?"

"English — well, Scottish, originally, but my mom grew up in London."

"Cool. Are your parents alive?"

"No. My mom died from cancer eight years ago, my father had a heart attack four weeks later."

"I'm sorry."

"So am I. And you?"

"My folks are gone. You know that. They died in a plane crash."

"And since the plane crash —"

"My turn," she interrupted. "Do you know your family — or families?"

"Yes, of course, very well. I like family. You? What is your feeling for your brother?"

"I adore him. My turn. Siblings?"

"No."

"Ah. You're an only child," she said gravely.

"Yes. I'm so sorry."

She shrugged, grinning. "I've met a few people who were an only child within their household, and they came out okay."

"Ouch. Preconceived notions."

"No, it's just that, rich or poor, a person who has siblings has had to share upon occasion. There will always be a time when what happens in a sibling's life is more important. That's all."

"Ah, but I'm Cheyenne," he said, a quirk of amusement on his lips.

"And that means?"

"We're all about community, and the People."

"I see. Leaning back on your pedigree," she said solemnly.

"Don't forget that part of me is clansman," he said.

"All for the good of the clan?" she asked.

He laughed. "We're big into standing up for one another in feuds," he said. "Actually and honestly, I do play well with others."

Their server arrived with their food orders. She opted for another glass of wine and Jackson decided on a second scotch. He laughed and teased the pretty girl serving them, pleasantly, and not obnoxiously,

Angela noted. He was still smiling when she left them at the table with their fresh drinks and plates of food.

"Do you see ghosts?" Jackson asked her.

She froze, startled by the sudden impact of the question. She had to force herself to swallow her bite of food.

"Do you?" she replied.

He took another sip of scotch, and his eyes met hers squarely. "I believe that the world is full of possibilities. Do I believe in ghosts like the ones on TV? No. I'm pretty sure that if ghosts exist they are around both by day and night, and that we don't need to see a lot of people with their eyes wide open — deer-caught-in-the-headlights — jumping at every sound."

"Logical," she told him.

"Pardon?"

"Logical. If they exist, they must exist in daylight as well as in the middle of the night."

"What about Griffin?" he asked her.

Once again, she froze. He had a knack for throwing in a tough question just when she had relaxed.

"What about him?" she asked dully. "He's dead."

"Do you ever 'see' him?"

She shook her head. "No."

70

"You two were together for years," he commented.

"Five, to be exact."

"You didn't foresee his death?" he asked.

She stared at him, every muscle in her body as tense as piano wire. "When they told us that the cancer had spread into every organ and riddled his bones, yes, I *foresaw* it."

"I'm sorry," he said. "I wondered if it made you — susceptible."

"Susceptible to what?" she demanded.

"Seeing ghosts. I just wanted to make sure that you were over it, and that you were standing on even ground."

"Am I over it? Do we ever get over the loss of loved ones? No — I have never managed to do so. My parents, and Griffin, are always alive in my heart. Do I accept the reality of it? Yes. And they are all gone. Gone. They don't come and take my hand and direct me to dead bodies — or to lost children, for that matter." She paused, needing to wet her lips. She didn't sip her wine, she chugged it. Most unattractive, she was sure; she didn't care. He could be so completely courteous. He could make her comfortable, he could make her laugh. And then, he could home right in for the kill.

"What about you?" she demanded more

71

heatedly than she had intended. "Do your lost field agents come and speak to you in the night? Do they ask you how you didn't happen to get there in time to save them?"

There wasn't so much as a crack in his expression, not a change whatsoever in the steady dark blue eyes that surveyed her.

"No. They are gone. Like you, I accept that they are gone. Like you, I do remain haunted by the lives they once led."

She flushed. He should feel badly for badgering her about the losses in her life. She was left feeling similarly — but she had phrased her words in a much meaner manner.

"I'm sorry," she murmured uncomfortably. Damn him! She didn't need to be apologizing to him.

"One thing is true — we can't undo the past. We can only do our best in the present, and hope to find the answers in the future. Dessert? Coffee?" he asked her.

She shook her head. "No, thank you."

"Want to split a bread pudding? It's out of this world here."

She sat back, still uneasy, and totally baffled by his ability to remain so unruffled. She had been tested throughout dinner, she realized.

"I'm fine, thank you."

"Another glass of wine?" he asked.

"Fine, why not?"

He ordered brandy and bread pudding, and she had another glass of wine. His conversation turned casual. He talked about his love for the city; he had worked here for nearly a year when he had first joined the bureau. "Things are always just a little bit different in these parts. Louisiana laws are still based on Napoleonic Code — French law — while the majority of the country is based on English law. It's not major, but there are some differences. You'll note they have parishes instead of counties."

"I went to Tulane. I know that," she told him. Inane. He had her dossier.

"And majored in history and philosophy," he said.

She nodded. "And you?"

He shrugged. "I spent six years in college. I liked it. I might have stayed a college student all my life, but it doesn't pay the bills. World religions, history and psychology."

Angela frowned. "Psychology, of course. You were with a Behavioral Science Unit. So, tell me, because I was thinking today that someone as involved as Regina was in preparing that home to be the perfect welcoming point for her husband wouldn't

73

have committed suicide. And to be honest, suicide had sounded like an entirely rational explanation to me before."

"It's hard to say. I didn't know her," Jackson said.

Dessert and drinks arrived. He was persuasive; she did try the bread pudding, and it was delicious. And it felt oddly intimate to share a dessert. She hadn't done so in years. Since Griffin had died.

He sipped his brandy. "It does seem as if she was devoted to her husband, and as if she had determined to put her life to good use. That speaks against suicide. But then again, the loss of a child might have made her snap."

"But that kind of snap? Going over a balcony?" Regina asked.

"That's what we're here to find out," he told her.

They left soon after. The walk back down Chartres Street was quiet; they took St. Peter's up to Dauphine and crossed Bourbon once again. They were at the more subdued end of Bourbon there, but distracted, Angela had been walking a few steps ahead.

"Hey, honey, wanna party?" someone asked.

He was a blond frat boy. He looked harmless. He was with other blond frat boys.

She could take care of herself, she knew. But Jackson stepped forward easily, slipping an arm around her. "Not tonight, but you all have a good time, and take care," he said pleasantly.

The frat boys waved and went on. Jackson's hold on her eased, but they walked next to each other.

He didn't say anything; neither did she. He knew she could have managed on her own; she knew that he had quickly defused the situation.

And then they were back. They'd left lights on, and the house on Dauphine stood white and dignified in the moonlight, captured in shadow and in a soft glow. The windows might have been eyes, and, Angela thought, the ghosts of dozens of lost souls might have looked out from behind them, gazing at the world they had left behind.

The *house* wasn't evil, but evil had lived behind the facade.

Angela was suddenly certain that Regina Holloway had *not* committed suicide.

CHAPTER FOUR

Before retiring for the night, Jackson had done a survey of the house, studying the alarm system.

He'd learned two things: every window in the house was properly wired; and though the gate to the courtyard was wired as well, only the gate was wired. It would have been possible for someone to climb the wall into the courtyard. However, once that happened, they'd have to have the code to get through the alarm.

Even so, it was possible and probable — no matter how excellent a police force might be — that someone had come over the wall. After that . . .

It had been twilight when Regina Holloway died. A time when someone might have slipped over the wall. A time when she might have had the alarm off, since she had been out on the balcony. She might have had the doors locked, but if she had opened her bedroom doors to the balcony — or if anything had been left open by one of the maids — there would have been access to the house.

The night, however, was uneventful.

Angela Hawkins was still asleep when he came down to the kitchen. There was little there, but someone had seen to it that some basics had been stocked, so he was able to brew coffee and munch on one of the English muffins that had been left in a package in the refrigerator.

He called to set up an interview with the senator. First, he reached a secretary, and then was put through to the senator's aide, Martin DuPre, and while he was asking DuPre if the senator would be available for an appointment, DuPre's protective hedging came to a quick halt when the senator himself came on the line. He assured Jackson that he'd be there that evening around five or five-thirty, and that their investigation was the most important issue in his life at the moment. He was glad to be in New Orleans at the moment, since the state legislature wasn't in session. He hadn't lived at the house since his wife had died; he had taken an apartment in the city.

Jackson was in the kitchen, working on notes for the investigation, when the doorbell rang.

Answering it, he discovered a young man with a guitar case strung over his shoulder and an overnight bag in his hand.

"Hi," the visitor said.

"Can I help you?" Jackson asked.

The young man extended a hand. "You have to be Jackson Crow. I'm Jake Mallory. I know it's kind of early, but I grew up in the Garden District, and I was awake — and here I am."

"Jake. Good to meet you. Come on in."

Jackson kept his tone level, his greeting polite.

But he wondered what the hell Adam Harrison had been thinking.

Jake Mallory was tall, probably half an inch short of his own height. He had auburn, slightly long hair, an angular, well-defined face and light green eyes. His build was more lanky than bulky, but he looked as if he was about to play guitar on the streets for money. It wasn't that he looked unkempt; he was fastidious and probably extremely attractive to young women. He just didn't have the look of someone about to become part of an elite investigation unit.

If this *was*, in truth, an elite investigation unit.

Then, again, maybe he looked exactly the

part, just because he didn't offer the customary appearance.

Jake walked in and whistled at the great entry slash ballroom. "Wow. I've heard about this place all my life. I've never been in it." He set down his bag and let the guitar case slide slowly to the parquet.

"It's quite a house," Jackson said.

Jake met his gaze. "Amazing. Huge, so it seems. How was your night?"

"Uneventful," Jackson assured him. "Want the grand tour? Or did you want to take it alone?"

"Either way," Jake said, shrugging and shoving his hands in his back pockets. He laughed. "We used to come and stare at the place when we were kids. Dare each other to go up close and all that. There were great ghost stories about it."

"I know what the ghost stories say, and I've got blueprints, but you might know a lot that I don't," Jackson said.

Jake laughed ruefully. "Yep. Forgot that you probably know just about everything about me, too. I have to admit, it's amazing to be here. To actually sleep here."

"So, you're not afraid of ghosts," Jackson said.

"I'm fascinated by the possibilities!" Jake said.

Jackson had read that Jake was a local boy by birth; he'd also gone to school here, and gotten a music degree from Yale. He'd returned to New Orleans and worked with a musicians' coalition in the city.

Adam had apparently found him fascinating because of his ability to find people. He'd been responsible for finding both survivors and those who had not survived after the summer of storms wrought their havoc on the city and its residents. Jackson wasn't sure just what his specialty was, beyond an uncanny ability to find the dead. There didn't seem to be a real investigator in his group, Angela's police training notwithstanding.

Jake looked at Jackson with a sharp and steely look in his eyes. "We're all being tested, though, I assume."

"Tested?"

"Look, I'm called frequently to find the lost. So, I have to admit, I'm curious about exactly why I'm here. Regina Holloway isn't lost, she's dead. Everyone knows where she is. But then, you found a body last night, didn't you?"

"I didn't find it. Angela Hawkins found it. And how do you know about that already?" Jackson asked.

"I don't believe you've turned on a television or read the local paper today," Jake said.

Jackson frowned. "Reporters got in on it?"

"Don't kid yourself. This is the Deep South, and it's Louisiana. Though we have a history of corrupt politicians, sweet tea and a slow, steady lifestyle, our reporters are sharks — just like everywhere else in the country. You had police and forensics experts in here last night. That kind of thing doesn't go unnoticed, especially when it's the second time it's happened. Detective Devereaux had the police spokesperson give an official statement. But . . . well, the speculation on what happened is far more intriguing."

"I'm going to need a newspaper."

"Don't worry . . . there's one in my bag," Jake said. "I'll call and get a paper delivered here every morning. That way, you'll know what we're up against as far as gossip goes."

"What's been written about us being in the house?" Jackson asked.

"Oh, just that the senator has brought in a team of investigators. People believe that he's so heartbroken, he had to do something to try to prove that his wife didn't commit suicide."

"Did you know her?" Jackson asked.

"No. But, I've seen her. She was really

loved here — just like the senator. Hey, he's like a breath of fresh air. Especially in Louisiana." Jake's wry grin deepened. "The people loved Huey Long because he shook things up and worked for every one despite his carousing. Senator Holloway, he's loved the same way. He wants big money to take care of big-money problems, and he wants to create work for everyone. *And* he was an honest-to-God family man."

There was a sharp intelligence beneath the laid-back exterior of the man, Jackson thought. He might prove to be a far greater asset than Jackson had imagined at first sight.

"Politicians, in one way, seem perfectly understandable, but then it's always hard to tell what is lurking in their minds, they're so accustomed to wearing masks," Jackson said.

"True, but I do know New Orleans, and a lot of the players here," Jake offered.

Conversation paused. Jackson had the curious feeling that they were being watched, and he turned to see why.

Angela Hawkins looked down at them from the second-floor landing. It struck him again that she was an exceptionally beautiful woman, far too angelic looking, really, to have been a cop. Despite last night, she retained a reserve that was no less daunting than a suit of armor. Though beneath it all, he sensed her capable of a smile that would light the world. Studying her personality was an intriguing and appealing concept.

"Hi, there!" Jake called to her.

"Angela, Jake, Jake, Angela."

"So, how did you sleep? Any ghosts prowling the halls?" Jake asked. He might have been asking her if a shopping mall had been busy.

"I was out like a light last night," she told him. "Welcome to the crew!"

Jake smiled at her. And Angela returned it. They seemed to have an instant, easy rapport. He was surprised to find himself envious.

"Thanks. It's good to be here."

"I can get Jake up to speed on what I know about the house," Angela offered.

"Sure." Hmm. He heard the tension in his voice. What he was feeling was ridiculous; they were peers. He knew better than to feel a macho, ego-driven need to be the divine leader, most respected and most admired — and liked. He found himself thinking about his last team; they had worked so well together for so long. Each member with his or her own specialty and all of them learning to work like a well-oiled machine. But, he had to remember, they'd been together five years. This was a new team; despite his lingering feelings of pain for his last coworkers, he had to make himself start fresh, and give each member of this new team a chance to fall in — just as he had to learn to lead again, as smoothly as he had in the past.

"Sure," he said again. "That will be great."

He almost managed to laugh at himself as he headed back to the kitchen, to finish the notes he had been making after his conversation with Andy Devereaux, and after they had discovered the bones of Madden C. Newton's probable first New Orleans victim.

Almost. It was one thing to understand the way the human mind worked. It was another to buck against it when you were the human in question.

"I play a lot on Frenchman Street," Jake told Angela. "Things have changed a lot since our season of storms. The demographics in the city have changed, and it's kind of like a movement for survival. Let's face it, the history here is great, but tons of the tourism comes because of Bourbon Street, for people to have a good time in the old Big Easy. So, now, you don't hear all the different stuff you used to hear — well, not as much. The bars on Bourbon mostly have pop — Journey, Bon Jovi, hard-hitting fast stuff. Of course, everything is a contradiction. Next thing you know, the best sax player known to man will show up working at one of the tourist places!"

"It's always been a city of contradictions," Angela assured him, liking the young man very much.

"You know it well?" he asked, arching a brow as she led them at last to the entertainment slash family room. He sat at the end of the sofa and she perched at the other, winding her legs beneath her as she faced him.

"From college," she told him. "I grew up in Virginia, but I absolutely love New Orleans, so it does feel just a little bit like coming home. Despite the gruesome reason."

"So, tell me, Miss Hawkins, what do you do?" he asked.

She hesitated. "I guess I'm a 'finder,' too. That's what you do, right?"

He nodded, shrugging. "I guess I have a certain sense for . . . finding people." He lowered his voice, looking toward the door.

"Do you?" she asked. "How do you mean?"

He hesitated a minute, then said, "Friends of mine almost went insane. Their five-year-old was kidnapped, and two boys had been kidnapped right before. One's body had been found. I had a dream about a child holding my hand, taking me down into an area of bayou near Slidell. I found the body of the second. And it was amazing, because when I found it, I also found the old swamp house where they were keeping my friends' little boy. He survived. I was so grateful, but the experience shook me up — that was for certain. But I didn't dwell on it. Knowing things, seeing events and people — it isn't always good. Some people turn away from you; they think that you're out to hurt them, or they want to put some distance between you and them, because there might be something really odd about you." He paused again. "I think I lost a best friend that way." He laughed softly. "Actually, the love of my life. But . . . well, if you have experiences like mine, you stay sane yourself by learning to use whatever talent you have, gift or curse, to do what you can to help stop some of the depravity and evil in the world. New Orleans is my home, so my talents came in handy when the city was in trouble."

"Do your ghosts come in dreams," she said.

"Sometimes. Yours?"

She found herself looking to the door as well. "I get feelings that seem almost like a divining rod — and yes, I get the dreams. I — I saw something when my parents were killed in a plane crash. I saw them walking toward the light, along with a lot of other people. The therapist who worked with me afterward told me that I saw what I needed to see in order to be able to bear the grief."

"But you never believed that."

"No, but my time with the therapist made me extremely careful about what I say to other people!"

He laughed, his green eyes still bright. "Well, I do know people who see them — ghosts — and see them easily."

"Really?" she asked.

"I'll introduce you," he said.

"They live here?"

He nodded.

"Does Adam know about them? Why wouldn't he have brought them in on this team?"

"Well, frankly, Nikki and Brent have three small children now. I'm sure Adam would have liked to have them on a team, but they're busy parents. I don't believe they would work away from the city, not with their children growing up. They have their schools, their church, their sports teams . . . they're good people, though. I met Adam through them, actually . . ." Jake paused in thought.

"I see. And I understand — I think. Adam wants a team that will stay cohesive for a while, a group that starts out together and learns to work together," Angela said.

"You think Regina Holloway committed suicide?"

Angela simply looked at him for a moment and admitted, "No."

"You think the house is haunted?" he asked her.

She laughed. Once again, she chose her words. "Say I believe that a house *can* be haunted. Perhaps things go bump in the night — or ghosts prowl the hallways. I don't think that ghosts pushed Regina Holloway over the balcony."

"Good conclusion."

The voice came from the doorway and Angela turned quickly to see that Jackson Crow had finished whatever work he was doing and stood there, watching them. She felt color flood her cheeks. Just how long had he been there?

"I wanted you to let Jake know that he needs to go ahead and pick a room," Jackson said, his blue eyes as enigmatic as ever.

"The rest of the crew will be arriving soon. You might want to get settled. The two maids who worked in the house when Regina was alive won't come back to work here, but they should be here in a few minutes to show us where the linen can be found, towels, cleaning articles, all that."

"All right, I think I'll go ahead and take that third room in the hallway where you two are," Jake said. "And I'm pretty good at picking up after myself. I can cook, too," he assured them.

"I'll help you," Angela said.

"I just have my guitar and my bag," he said.

"I'll get the guitar for you — and treat it like gold," Angela assured him. "You wouldn't want to drop it on the way up the stairs."

"Sure," he said, and they both walked past Jackson. Angela felt that he watched them, and she wondered why. She was equally curious as to why she was suddenly trying to avoid him.

Because the meeting over the pickax remained between them — and she didn't really want him knowing that, despite her credentials, she definitely still had her vulnerabilities.

She wasn't sure. She was confident, and she knew how to keep her own counsel. But there was something about the way that he looked at her . . .

She usually didn't care, she realized. She *wanted* Jackson Crow to like her.

"Hi!"

The fourth member of his team, Whitney Tremont, had just rung the bell. She'd been born and bred in New Orleans just like Jake, but with the difference that Jake came from an "English" background and Whitney was pure Creole.

She was, he thought, a compelling little bundle of energy. She was little, no more than five-two or five-three, slim, with curly hair and hazel eyes, and skin the color of amber. She had a smile that was infectious, and a soft, sweet voice.

They had sent him another child.

No, there was a keen intelligence in her eyes. She had been a straight-A off-the-charts student; she had studied ethnicity, religion, philosophy, modern and ancient beliefs, while also receiving her degree in film from NYU. Her maternal great-grandmother was a noted contemporary voodoo priestess, and owned a shop called As You Believe up near Rampart Street. She

90

had helped the local police crack down on a cult of would-be voodoo worshippers who had taken it upon themselves to bastardize the beliefs for the sake of human sacrifice — two young people had died during blood-drinking rituals. According to her file, she had a chameleon-like ability to slip into any group and be accepted as one of them — and somehow manage to film or video events and people who had never allowed such a thing before. Her expertise was cameras and film, and Jackson knew that she, like Will Chan, whom he had yet to meet, had been brought in for their work with cameras and sound.

"Hi," he said, reaching for her large, tapestry travel bag. "Come on in. Whitney, right? Miss Whitney Tremont."

"Jackson Crow. Love the name," she assured him.

"Thanks."

"So, you've already been digging up bodies — I'm late to the party," she said.

He grimaced. "A skeleton. Angela Hawkins found it."

"I'm impressed, and the majority of the people in the city are convinced that now all the ghosts who might not have been busy yet will be crawling out of the woodwork. Anyway, if they do, I'm hoping that we catch them on film. I have a lot of equipment out in the van."

He looked over her head. There was a fellow in the driver's seat who looked so much like her that he had to be her brother. The man waved to him; Jackson waved back.

"I'll open the courtyard gate. And call the troops to help. Well, the two who are here now," Jackson told her.

"Okay," Whitney said. "That's my brother, Tyler, over there. I'll get him to come around the corner," she said cheerfully.

Whitney went out; he called for Angela and Jake, and soon they were all in the courtyard, meeting Tyler and hauling heavy boxes out of the van. They decided to set up in the grand entry slash ballroom, so Jackson shut off the alarm entirely in order for them to open the middle courtyard doors and take the shortest route.

It didn't take them more than thirty minutes to bring everything in.

Tyler was as tall as his sister was short, ranging a good foot over her head. He was as pleasant with the others as if he had been leaving his sister at summer camp, but when he was actually ready to leave, he gave her a huge hug and said seriously, "You be careful, and you don't take any chances, and you don't go getting your nose in where it shouldn't be."

"I'm all grown up now, Tyler," she reminded him, but she hugged him in return.

"She has a tendency to rush in — right into people who have guns," he said.

Jackson grinned. "We'll watch out for her. I promise."

Tyler nodded. "Adam wouldn't have set her up with you if you weren't good people. And if she wasn't going to be safe." He paused, looking around. "So this is the Newton house. It doesn't look like a dark torture chamber, but . . . I'm sure it's creepy as hell at night. You all be careful, huh? I remember when the kid took a header when the cops were after him about a decade ago. Brought it all back. And now Mrs. Holloway . . . it's a shame, and it may just be that the place is bad."

"We'll all be looking out for each other," Jake said solemnly.

Hugging his sister and warning her to call him, Tyler left at last.

Jackson looked at the four members of his team and the mass of boxes in the living room. "Well," he said.

Whitney shrugged. "It's not bad, really! Somebody else is in film, right?"

"Will Chan, but he's not here yet," Jackson said.

"We follow orders well," Angela assured her.

"And I'm way brawnier than I look," Jake added, laughing.

"That's good. Because you can all start while I check the doors, windows and the alarm system again," Jackson told him. "Here are the rules — no one opens the gate without me knowing it. We're going to be opening the balcony doors from our bedrooms, so I'll have the alarm set during the day so that we can do that. Though it will sound if we don't key ourselves in and out of the front door — everyone understand?"

"Yes, and thank God! I can't imagine not going out on that beautiful balcony," Whitney said. She didn't seem the least disturbed by the house — simply fascinated.

"We'll dig on in and help Whitney start getting set up," Angela assured him.

"I won't be that long."

He was long, though. Longer than he intended.

None of them had been up to the third floor yet. After taking the grand stairway to the second floor, he briefly checked each of the rooms on the front end of the house, and came around to the middle section, and the stairway there. He went up to the third level. Thankfully, the middle section was one big expanse of space. With remnants from the decades that the house had stood.

No one had gotten up here yet to start on the cleaning. The area was rife with dust; it almost felt as if he took a step back into a different time. Dressmakers' dummies were along the wall, near one of the three dormer windows. Jackson checked them; the alarm wires were in place. Clothing on the dummies ranged from an antebellum ball gown to a World War II–era swing skirt.

A huge old sewing machine was in another corner, and a wire crate held toys from eons past, wooden soldiers, dolls that might have been collectibles, croquet mallets, balls and wickets. More — he couldn't discern everything in the container.

He walked through the low hallway at the one end, arriving at the area over the ballroom, and discovered that it had been set up as a row of dormitory-style rooms, and he assumed that the rooms had been slave quarters for the household staff at one time, and servants' quarters at another.

It was slow going, but he checked each of the dormer windows. He walked back through the main storage room and through the low-ceilinged hallway to the last ell; here, he found just two rooms, both of them large, and both of them empty. But the alarm wires were in place, and the windows were secure. He walked back down to the second floor and went through all the motions, finally reached the first, and checked that all the windows not facing the courtyard were secure.

The place was huge. Despite the fact that the police had searched the premises, and despite the alarm system, Jackson still wondered if there hadn't been a way for someone to slip in — uninvited, and unknown.

Back in the ballroom he discovered that his crew had been busy. There was a set of television screens arranged at the far end of the room, cables, cords, lights and more equipment aligned against the wall.

"We're trying to decide which rooms should get the cameras first," Angela told him. She stared at him peculiarly.

"What?" he asked.

"You look like a ghost yourself," Whitney said, giggling.

"Like you've been playing in a pail of plaster," Jake added. "You went up to the attic? I'm guessing there hasn't been a cleanup crew there."

He groaned and looked at his arm. The sleeves of his cotton shirt were white.

Once again, the doorbell rang and he walked to the door, expecting the remainder of the team.

A tall, slender woman of African descent stood there as straight as a ramrod, and as ancient as one. She frowned, seeing Jackson, and murmured something that seemed to be a prayer against curses.

Angela swiftly came running to the door, catching the woman's hand. "Hi, I'm Angela. Jackson is just dusty — can we help you?"

"Gran-Mama!" Whitney cried. "You're early."

Jackson spun back to look at the old woman. Angela had reached out a hand to invite her in.

"Who are you?" Jackson demanded.

"I am Mama Matisse. Whitney didn't tell you that she asked me to come?" the woman asked. "Whitney, child! I don't come where I'm not invited!"

"Gran-Mama," Whitney began, her face chalky, "I just haven't had time to talk to them yet."

"No, she didn't," Jackson said. "You're a priestess? A voodoo priestess?"

"Yes. But I am also Whitney's great-grandmother," the woman explained.

Jackson wasn't sure whether or not to be

indignant at her demeanor. But he had the feeling that this woman could help them, and that the wisdom in her eyes ran deep. He bowed his head slightly. "Whitney didn't mention you, but, please, yes, stay, help us." He cast Whitney a frowning glare; she lifted her hands helplessly.

"Gran-Mama — Mama Matisse — was friends with both the maids who worked here. And she knew Regina and the senator. I thought you might want to hear what she can tell us," Whitney said.

Jackson nodded at her. "I'll run up and take a two-minute shower. Mama Matisse, Whitney will take you into the kitchen and get you some coffee or water or whatever. Please?"

"I am here to help you," Mama Matisse said with tremendous dignity. "I will do my best. You see, the police have not much cared for what I've had to say, but I can tell you this — the very day that Regina Holloway died, her maid, Rene, came running over to tell me that there were ghosts in this house. There were ghosts, and there is tremendous evil, and whether or not they are one and the same, that you must discover."

CHAPTER FIVE

Mama Matisse drew a long bony finger down her teacup as she sat at the kitchen table. "Whitney asked me to come here today because of the maids — and because I was here, and worked with Regina Holloway," Mama Matisse explained.

"You worked with her?" Angela looked from Mama Matisse to Whitney.

"Regina Holloway was very fond on my great-grandmother, and believed in her wisdom," Whitney explained.

Mama Matisse nodded gravely. "The maids will not come back in this house, Trini or Rene," she assured Angela. "They are afraid. They have taken money from the senator to live on while they look for new positions. They need to keep working in this city, so if you were to try to call them and ask them questions, they would not come to you with a ghost story. They don't mind if I speak to you in their stead. If you question them, if the police question them again, they will not speak about the ghosts, and that is all that there is to it. But they have talked to me, and I don't believe they care that I talk to you."

"Thank you," Angela said.

"They are afraid that people will think that they are crazy," Mama Matisse said. "*Loco,* as Trini says," she added.

"My great-grandmother is considered to be extremely wise," Whitney said. "Many, many people come to her. Whether they are voodooists, Jewish, Buddhists, Christian or whatever."

"I promise you, we're not going to repeat anything that you say," Angela assured her.

Mama Matisse looked at her. "If you were to repeat what I say on behalf of the maids, it wouldn't matter. I have said it, and not them."

Angela nodded. Mama Matisse did not easily trust people, but Whitney had asked her to come, and so here she was.

"The women, both Rene and Trini, worked here the day that Mrs. Holloway died," Mama Matisse said.

"Did they tell you that they saw something?" Angela asked.

"Yes, they saw a ghost. Or they thought they saw a ghost. He was in the hallway,

Trini told me. They saw a man, and then he disappeared. They didn't tell Mrs. Holloway. She had said that she didn't believe in ghosts. And the man disappeared, so he couldn't have been real. Mrs. Holloway had told them that she was going to lie down. They later heard that she was dead, that she had killed herself, going over the balcony. They were very upset."

"Of course," Angela murmured.

"I didn't believe it," Mama Matisse said. "I didn't believe it a minute when they said that she committed suicide. Neither did her maids. She was Catholic. She went to church every Sunday morning, and sometimes, during the week. Her faith was strong. To a Catholic, it's a grave offense to God for us to take our own lives."

"But she was very upset about the loss of her little boy, right?"

"She was sad, yes," Mama Matisse said. "So sad — I was here when the senator told his wife that they always wanted more children, and that they would try again, that they would have several. Mrs. Holloway told him that they couldn't replace Jacob. The senator said no, they would never try to replace him. But they had always wanted more children and they would try. And she said that yes, she loved children, and she loved him, and that she would fix up the house, and that one day, they would have a family. And they talked about all the needy children in the world, and maybe they would have a child, and adopt a child."

"That doesn't sound like someone about to commit suicide," Jackson said from the doorway to the kitchen.

He had showered away the dust, and appeared clean, striking and confident as he came in to join them. He was casual, pausing to pour himself a cup of coffee before taking a seat across the table from Mama Matisse. "She sounds like the nicest woman imaginable. What about the other people in their lives? Those closest to them? What about their day-to-day lives?"

"I don't know about their day-to-day lives, Mr. Crow," she said. Angela didn't remember that Jackson had ever introduced himself, but Mama Matisse knew who he was. "I haven't been here before on a day-to-day basis. I can tell you this — Mrs. Holloway had many friends. But she needed time to be alone — because people kept telling her how sorry they were about her son."

"We really need to speak with the maids," Jackson reminded.

Mama Matisse merely stared at him.

"I'm sorry. I'm grateful that you're here."

"The maids will not speak to you. They will not speak to anyone anymore. They talked to the police, and they have nothing more to say. They are afraid. They have their lives to live."

"If this case ever goes to court —" Jackson began.

"Do you think that everything is solved in a court, Jackson Crow? I think that you know differently," Mama Matisse said.

Jackson stared back at her. Angela was certain that he had reacted inwardly, but, as usual, she saw nothing change in his expression.

"You are right. You can't always force the truth in court," Jackson agreed. "So, please, tell me, who was closest to them. Tell me what you can. David Holloway is a politician, so his life is full of people, but tell me what you know about his relationships."

"Let me think about those around him . . . There is Mr. DuPre, and Senator Holloway's secretary, Lisa Drummond. Lisa Drummond protects the senator at his office. Martin DuPre tries very hard to be the go-between. He protects the senator's time. The senator still appears to be reeling from what has happened. He is dependent on those around him. He must have an aide. He is proud of Mr. DuPre, and thinks that one day he will step into politics on his own."

"Actually, I'm curious. The government is in Baton Rouge. Why was the senator so determined to have a wonderful home in which to entertain in New Orleans, do you know?" Jackson asked.

Mama Matisse smiled. "That is no mystery. New Orleans is their home. There need be no other explanation. They had an apartment in Baton Rouge, of course," she said.

Jackson said, "Well, of course. I'm sorry. Of course. And Baton Rouge isn't so far, right?"

"It's just eighty miles," Mama Matisse said. "But that's why Senator Holloway has a chauffeur. He works in the car when he drives there and back."

"But he must have stayed over in Baton Rouge often enough," Jackson said.

"Yes, I suppose so."

"Did Mrs. Holloway stay here alone when he was gone?" Jackson asked.

"Yes, many times. Of course, the senator was home a lot. The first week they moved in, the state legislature wasn't in session," the old woman told him. "You must understand, while I knew Mrs. Holloway I was not her spiritual adviser. She had her priest, but she did have me do a banishing spell."

104

"A banishing spell?" Jackson asked.

"Yes, as a precaution against all evil," Mama Matisse said. "But you must remember that Regina Holloway clung strongly to her own faith. Father Adair came and blessed the house. However, this is New Orleans, and she was part of the fabric of the city. A banishing spell is not black magic. Black magic is when you wish someone ill."

Whitney cleared her throat and told them, "My great-grandmother does banishing spells often. And when you do a spell, it has to be done the right way. You are always careful not to wish anyone ill. If you wish a ghost to leave, you wish that the ghost finds peace, and you hope that leaving is what will bring the ghost peace."

Mama Matisse nodded solemnly.

"I see," Jackson said.

Angela wasn't sure that he really "saw" anything, but she didn't say so. Instead, she asked, "So, she wasn't afraid of the house?"

Mama Matisse shook her head slightly. "No, I do not believe that she was afraid of her own house."

"What about the chauffeur, Grable Haines? Is he still with the senator, and did he drive for Mrs. Holloway as well?" Jackson asked.

105

"To the best of my knowledge," Mama Matisse said, "Mrs. Holloway never drove, and she only got into a car when she was going someplace with the senator. Friends picked her up sometimes, but otherwise, she did everything in the French Quarter. She liked a hat shop on Royal Street . . . She bought groceries just down on Royal, too. She liked to walk to Jackson Square, and go sit in the cathedral. She didn't like to leave the area . . . She hated cars."

"Because her son was killed in a car?" Angela asked.

Mama Matisse lifted her hands with a shrug. "So one might think. She didn't own a car. She just rode with the senator when he wanted her with him. So, that means, if she had to go somewhere, she went with the senator — and Grable Haines. Oh, I believe she liked Grable. Everyone likes him. He is a handsome man," Mama Matisse said. She leaned closer across the table toward Jackson. "But, sometimes, a man can be too handsome. Too many things in the world come too easily to him."

"I understand," Jackson said.

Mama Matisse smiled. "You understand, but you don't accept many things," she said.

Jackson smiled at her; they were challenging one another, Angela thought, and yet, it also seemed that they respected each other innately.

"Do you think that a *ghost* killed Regina Holloway?" Angela asked.

Jackson flashed Angela a quick look. "I'm asking," she said quietly. "Just asking. Do *you* think that a ghost might have killed her?"

"I told you, I wasn't here the day she died," Mama Matisse said.

"But what do you think?" Jackson persisted.

"This is what they told me — Rene yelled for Trini. She was in the laundry room." She pointed. The laundry room was a small area next to the kitchen, but the two rooms didn't attach. "Trini said that she came quickly, and she *thought* she saw a man, vanishing into thin air. She made a cross on her chest and they both prayed to the Virgin and came into the kitchen, but there was nothing in here then."

"You're still not telling me what you think," Jackson said, smiling.

"I think that evil can exist, that's what I think," Mama Matisse said. "I can only tell you what they said to me. If it's true or not, I don't know. But, soon after this happened, it was time for them to leave for the day. Mrs. Holloway came to the door with them, and they left. They were very frightened. That's why they talked to me."

"They never told Regina Holloway about the ghost?" Jackson asked.

"She said that she didn't believe in ghosts — the maids would not have told her that they had seen one," Mama Matisse said flatly, staring at Jackson.

"What about the alarm?" Jackson asked.

"They heard her set the alarm. She was always careful when she was alone." Mama Matisse hesitated. "But . . . she didn't like the basement. She never went there when she was alone. She locked the door that led down to the basement."

Jackson looked at Angela. She kept staring at Mama Matisse.

"Did she say why she was scared of the basement?" he asked.

Mama Matisse shook her head. "She just said that basements — and attics — were inherently strange places. They were like depositories for the past, and she just didn't like them."

Jackson mulled that information over for a moment.

"She did believe, I'm sure, that she and the senator lived with a certain amount of danger and uncertainty because he was a politician."

"Yes."

Jackson then asked her, "Tell me about Senator Holloway's bodyguard, Blake Conroy."

Mama Matisse sniffed.

"He should have been guarding Mrs. Holloway, maybe," Mama Matisse said. "The girls told me that he was always eating. Making a big mess in the kitchen, and thinking that he could make a big mess anywhere that he went. He is a big man," she added.

"Was he mean, or rude?" Jackson asked.

"It's rude to make a mess of a clean kitchen."

Angela smiled; she saw that Jackson did, too.

"Did Mr. Holloway have a bodyguard just because he was a politician?" Jackson asked.

"Well, there are some people — and some groups — who don't like the senator," Mama Matisse said.

"Do you know who? Can you tell me about them?" Jackson coaxed. He apologized. "You see, we love New Orleans, but you know so much more than we do."

"Senator Holloway said all people did was fight when what they needed to do was figure out a solution. To live in our world, we had to learn to compromise. Senator

Holloway likes to give speeches. He says that he believes in New Orleans and the state of Louisiana — it's a place for everyone to live, and to live together, and to remember the past so that we never repeat it," Mama Matisse said.

"You don't sound as if you believe all that," Jackson said.

Angela was surprised; she hadn't heard anything out of the ordinary in Mama Matisse's voice.

She shrugged. "He is a politician."

"So, who disliked him? Who would want to hurt him?" Jackson asked.

"The Aryans, for one," she said.

"Have they become a political group in this town?" Jackson asked.

"They are bigots, that's what they are," Jake Mallory, who had been leaned against the counter, said irritably.

"They're Louisiana based, but they're an offshoot of a group that formed up in North Dakota. Most people around here ignore them," Jake said. "They could make Archie Bunker look like a bleeding-heart liberal."

"Archie Bunker?" Whitney murmured.

"Hey, don't you ever watch TV?" Jake asked her. "Archie Bunker, *All in the Family,* a major television show in its social honesty, reflecting the changing times."

"Hey, we can do television history at another time," Jackson mimicked.

"Right. The Aryans do hate Senator Holloway," Whitney said. She was next to Jake, and she lifted a hand dismissively. "They have a campaign against interracial marriage. Ridiculous." She made a face. "I'd be a poster child for what not to do! They are convinced that we've diluted America, and that all mixed babies should be aborted."

"They sound charming," Angela said dryly.

"There's another group, too," Mama Matisse said. "The Church of Christ Arisen."

Jackson waited, and Whitney explained, "They are like the Baptists, the Catholics and the Presbyterians all rolled into one."

Jake sniffed. "That insults the Baptists, the Catholics and the Presbyterians!"

"They don't believe in anything but early to rise, early to bed. No dancing, no drinking, no sex before marriage. Adultery means you're banished from the church," Whitney explained. "They believed that Haiti got what it received — just like New Orleans — when nature swept in and killed people. That was God taking vengeance on sinners. They campaign against Senator Holloway because he's a huge believer in social reform. He opened a home for unwed mothers. They were horrified."

Jackson frowned, confused. "But — they don't believe in abortion, I take it. Why wouldn't they want to help unwed mothers?"

"Unwed mothers shouldn't exist," Whitney explained.

"I see," Jackson said.

"That's why the senator needed a bodyguard," Mama Matisse said, nodding solemnly. "I believe that the senator spent time investigating the groups, trying to find out what they might be up to next. But it was all very hush-hush, so I can't really tell you much. He was worried that they might mean to take physical action against him."

"So, they do believe in assassination?" Jackson asked.

"There was a doctor who came down from New York City and opened a clinic — a family-planning clinic. He was on a lot of the local talk shows. He denied that he had come because they call New Orleans the Big Easy," Whitney said. "He was a smart man, from what I could see. He said that it was better for a confused young woman to abort a child early than to give birth in a ladies' room and flush the living child down the toilet."

"What happened to him?" Angela asked.

Whitney looked at her with a sad grimace. "He died in a hit-and-run accident just outside his clinic. It was over in the CBD — the Central Business District. Unrelated to their son's accident."

Angela could see that Jackson seemed to have acquired all that he wanted from Mama Matisse.

"You have been so kind to come and talk to us," she said. "We thank you so much."

Mama Matisse rose. She looked at Whitney. "You know where I am. Come to see me, and we can talk more if you wish." She turned to Jackson, studying him. "You have the ability to find all the answers — if you let yourself do so."

"Well, thank you for your faith. I'll see you out," Jackson offered, rising. "Do you need a ride anywhere? It would be the least we could do."

Mama Matisse shook her head. "I am nearing ninety. I am nearing ninety because I walk the French Quarter every day. But thank you. You do have courtesy."

"Well, thank you," Jackson said. Angela was surprised when Mama Matisse offered him her hand. Jackson took it. There was an interesting exchange of gazes between the two. Mama Matisse smiled. They walked

113

out together.

"This is so, so sad," Whitney murmured.

"Yes, and it was good of your great-grandmother to come. Especially because she's right. We can't make the maids talk to us."

"Because Rene thought that she saw a ghost. And she won't tell anyone — but my great-grandmother. Neither was here when Regina died," Whitney said. "But I knew that they had spoken with Gran-Mama."

"Ah, but was it a ghost? A trick of the light, or her imagination — or was someone really in the house?" Angela asked reflectively.

"I'd say that we opened a can of worms," Jake said, shaking his head. "Now it doesn't just seem like someone might have been responsible, it seems that way too many someones might have been responsible."

"Way too many someones," Angela said. "Whitney, I love your great-grandmother. She's fascinating. I hope to see her again."

"Yes, she is wonderful. She has so much wisdom — and kindness in her heart. But she's not a fool, and she doesn't like people easily." She laughed suddenly, looking to the door. "Our fearless leader is a skeptic, and she knows it. But I think she's seeing something deeper inside him. Something that makes him special."

Angela wasn't sure about that. Jackson Crow was courteous, and he knew how to be completely stoic.

Except for the fact that he didn't seem to think much of her. She winced inwardly; oddly enough, she felt a great deal as Mama Matisse did.

There was something deep in him that he didn't give away easily. And more oddly still, she wanted to know what it was, wanted to know more about the real man beneath the facade. Why had he been chosen to lead their team?

Firsthand knowledge and work with human behavior, she told herself dryly.

But she did have a certain gift, whether he wanted to acknowledge it or not.

She rose. "Excuse me, you all. I'm going to run upstairs for a minute."

"Do you want us with you?" Jake asked.

"Not right now," she told him.

Leaving them, she hurried up the stairs to the second floor — and to the room where Regina Holloway had been.

Right before she had died.

She paused for a minute, and then she lay down on the bed as Regina might have done that fateful day. She closed her eyes.

She imagined the woman who had been

Regina Holloway. Her life had so recently been perfect. She'd had a loving husband. And a child. A son.

She had lived in this house; she hadn't been afraid.

She had been lost and hurt.

Angela let the pain sweep into her, and she opened her eyes. . . .

She could see them. Two children. They were adorable. They were near the foot of the bed, and they had a game of jacks. The little girl had blond pigtails, and she wore a calico dress that probably ended at her ankles; the little boy was in breeches and a bleached cotton shirt and gray vest. They were both seated cross-legged, facing one another as they played.

She lay very still on the bed, never sure if she was imagining, or if there was a place somewhere deep in the human soul where one could "see" what had gone on in the past.

"Annabelle!" the little boy said. He sighed and leaned over to catch the bouncing ball. "You have to drop it right where you are, or it will roll away. Look, watch me."

The little boy dropped the ball, collected a number of jacks and caught the ball again. "See?" he said.

Annabelle nodded and took the ball from

him. But her lower lip trembled. "I'm so scared, Percy. I'm so scared. I don't like it here."

"You don't need to be scared. Mommy and Daddy are here; that nice man, that Mr. Newton, he's helping us."

"I want to go home."

"We don't have a home anymore, Annabelle. We don't have a home."

"Daddy said we were going away."

"We will go away, unless Mr. Newton can give Daddy some kind of work. Then Daddy can work, and we can buy a house again, and we won't have to leave our friends."

"Our friends are all gone," Annabelle said. "They've been gone since the war."

"The war is over, Annabelle." The little boy's voice hardened. "We lost. So now we all have to start over again."

Annabelle started to cry.

Percy took her into his arms, soothing her.

"There, there, Annabelle. It's going to be all right. . . ."

"What the hell are you doing?"

Jackson Crow's deep voice interrupted her; the children vanished.

Angela bolted to a sitting position.

"Were you napping?" Jackson asked her, incredulous.

"No, thinking," she told him. She rose. "What's going on?"

117

"We're going to lunch." He might have realized that she was about to say that she would just stay in the house while they went, because he thwarted her attempt before she could make it. "It's important. I want everyone to have a chance to connect away from here, to get to know one another as much as possible."

She nodded. But when he turned away, she paused.

This room. She had "seen" the children here, and Regina Holloway had been here before walking out on the balcony.

And then dying.

"Angela!"

Jackson Crow was waiting for her.

"I'm going to move into this room," she told him.

"Oh, no," he said.

"Oh, yes. It's going to be important that I do."

"I don't know if that's a good idea," he said. "I respect your abilities, but it's just not a good idea for anyone to sleep in here. Especially not you."

She set her hands on her hips. "I'm not depressed or crazy, and I'm not going over the balcony. I'd like to be in here. I think I may find something."

"This is the room we're investigating," he

said curtly.

"That would be the point," she said.

He stared at her, irritated. "If you move in here, I'll have to come over to this wing," he said.

"No, you don't have to. Adam Harrison brought me in on this for a reason," she said with a shrug. "I think that I need to make this room my own. I think it's important."

"Dammit, I'm not leaving you in this part of the house alone."

"I was a cop," she reminded him.

"Good for you. *I* am the head of this team."

"And, as such, you should use whatever talents Adam Harrison has given you. Jackson, really, I'm not mentally deficient. We are taking serious care with the alarms and the locks, and if you move over to this wing, you'll be there to rescue me — if I need rescue. I'm not a piece of blond fluff," she reminded him.

He looked at her for a minute. "We're all vulnerable. Weapons don't really change that. The most accurate shot in the world is vulnerable —"

"You're vulnerable. Yes, I know," Angela said.

He was quiet for a minute, studying her with his deep, intense blue eyes. She thought he was going to deny her again, insist that he was the head of the team again, and it was his way or the highway.

But he didn't.

He let out a deep, aggravated sigh.

"All right, fine. When we get back, we'll settle the rooming situation."

She smiled. "That's great. I'll be glad to have you near," she said.

He arched a brow. "What a smile you have when you get your way," he noted.

"Honestly, I think it's important," she said.

"We have a lot that's important on the agenda now," he said. "Come on, let's head out and get lunch, because the senator is due himself this afternoon. And before he gets here, I want to find out what our ghost-hunting 'children' intend to do with all the photographic equipment."

Still smiling, she preceded him out the doorway.

The ballroom was empty when they reached it; she looked at Jackson.

"The kids have gone on," he said.

Angela laughed. "They're not all that young!" she said.

"Mid-twenties," he said.

"Right, and how old are you — Methuselah?"

"Thirty-four." A small smile curved into his features. "It's not the years, kid, it's the mileage."

"Amen," she murmured, waiting as he set the alarm and then locked the house. "Where are we going?"

"Maspero's — you know it?"

"I do," she told him.

As they walked, she said, "You think that Mama Matisse gave us a lot of good information this morning, right?"

"I think she gave us a great deal. I think Whitney might have mentioned that she was coming."

"I think that Whitney would have done so — had she actually had a chance," Angela said.

"Perhaps," he acknowledged.

"The police must have interviewed the maids after Regina was found. Do you think the cops are trying to hold out on us — that they just want it to be a suicide?"

"No. I think the police believe that they came to an end on possibilities. They did interview the maids. You heard Mama Matisse. What could the maids have told them — since they weren't going to talk about seeing a ghost? So, as far as it appeared, the house was locked up. Tight. The alarms were on. There was no sign of a struggle on Regina Holloway's body."

"But do you believe that one of these cults or groups or whatever that hate the senator might be involved?"

"It's possible. But Regina Holloway didn't open her door to anyone, I'm certain."

"What do you think about the 'ghost' Rene saw in the hallway?" Angela asked.

"Might have been a ghost in her mind. Or there might have been someone in the house," Jackson said.

"But she said that the 'ghost' vanished," Angela said.

"It's really the 'locked room' mystery. What do you believe about the power of suggestion?" he asked.

"I think that it can definitely have power," she told him.

"A tremendous power," he said. "Take a fortune-teller. The fortune-teller says something — and the prophecy can be self-fulfilling."

"In other words, say that a house is haunted, and you'll find a ghost?" Angela asked.

"Something like that."

"So you don't believe in a haunting at all?" Angela asked.

"I never said that — I believe that we're all *haunted* in one way or another," he said.

"To the left, to the left, Miss Hawkins. You're wandering off on me. The restaurant is right over there."

Maspero's was open and easy, right off the square and popular with tourists. The food was reasonable and good, and the kids had already gotten them a table. The two were seated together on one side, leaving Angela and Jackson the two chairs on the other.

They'd already ordered appetizers and passed around plates of shrimp and onion rings and boiled crawfish. Angela realized she was starving and helped herself to the offerings. The group ordered the rest of their meals, and when food arrived and they'd started eating, their conversation turned back to the task at hand.

"What's next?" Jake asked.

"This afternoon, we're expecting a visit from the senator," Jackson told him. "And, sometime tonight, Jenna and Will are going to arrive, and our team will be complete."

"What do Will and Jenna do?" Angela asked him.

"Jenna is a nurse — Irish," Jackson said, shrugging. "And Will is an actor and a musician — an illusionist."

"How interesting," Angela said. "You were a profiler, working in the field. I was a cop.

Jake is a musician —"

"And a computer wizard and sound engineer," Jackson interrupted.

"Ah," Angela murmured.

"And now we'll be getting an illusionist — and a nurse," Whitney said. "And, then, of course, you have me. An expert with cameras, film and what's fake on them and not."

"The nurse must be coming in case we injure ourselves — tangled up in film or sound equipment," Jake said, grinning.

Jackson kept quiet. Angela thought that there had to be another reason they were getting a woman who was a nurse. She looked at Jackson, but he just said, "Will has gained a tremendous reputation for his illusions. He was asked to do a show for one of the paranormal TV networks. He turned it down."

"That's interesting," Whitney said. She looked around at them all, and then sighed. "Jackson must know this — I was working for a cable program — and I was accused of doctoring the film to create an effect. And I didn't, and I was furious that anyone would think that I had. Anyway, I probably should have just said that I did it, let everyone have a laugh and gone on to get back to work. But I didn't doctor the film, and the film wound up disappearing, and I quit before I could be fired."

"What was on the film?" Angela asked.

"It looked like the ghost of a floating woman. We were out at one of the planta- tions. All kinds of companies have filmed out there, and you know, when it's going to be on television they reenact the 'haunting.' The thing is, we hadn't even started work- ing on the images yet — and there she was. I don't know how they think I pulled it off — minus an actress, lighting, editing equip- ment — but, supposedly, I did."

"Intriguing," Angela said, looking at Jack- son.

"There's usually something that isn't what it appears, and it usually is manipulated," Jackson said. "Anyway, Will and Whitney are our film team, Jake is a computer whiz — he can, and has, hacked into many places." He smiled, staring at Jake.

"Nothing terrible. I just know my way around a computer," Jake said in his de- fense.

When the meal ended, Jackson suggested that he and Angela go back — just in case the senator arrived early — while the others went and did some grocery shopping.

They left Jake and Whitney at the corner store on Royal, and headed on up toward

Dauphine.

The house seemed just a house when they reached it again. Jackson opened the door and keyed in the alarm.

"You're still sure you want to sleep in Regina Holloway's bedroom?" Jackson asked her.

"Absolutely," she said earnestly.

"Okay, then we'll pack up our things and move to that wing. I'll take the bedroom right next to it."

They set about the task. As they did so, Angela realized that once the other two arrived, all six of them could be in the house — and not even run into one another unless they descended to the kitchen or the courtyard at the same time.

She had just brought her belongings into the room and stepped out onto the balcony over the courtyard when the gate swung open and a black limousine drove in.

The driver stepped out. He was tall, dark-haired and handsome. He smiled, displaying deep dimples as he opened the back door. That had to be Grable Haines.

First out was a hulk. A true hulk. She assumed it was the senator's bodyguard, Blake Conroy. He was clean-shaven bald, and muscled like a Titan.

Another tall man, lean and almost elegant

looking, got out of the car. He seemed to be about thirty-five, and moved with a fluid grace — and darting eyes. More than the bodyguard, he seemed to be on the lookout. He had to be Martin DuPre, the senator's aide.

She'd seen pictures of Senator Holloway. He was a striking man, as tall as the chauffeur, solid and lean in build, with graying dark hair and a face that was well sculpted, but showing signs of strain and character. Sad in a way that she felt as if her heart tightened, watching him.

He looked up at the house and saw her looking down, and for a moment, his weathered features tensed; his hand came to his chest, tightly clenched.

She realized she was standing where his wife would have stood.

Before falling.

Before being pushed.

Before dying.

She winced, and perhaps her horror at her accidental faux pas was evident, because he smiled at her then, lifted a hand and waved.

Then Jackson stepped out from the dining room doors below to greet the senator, and she quickly stepped away from the balcony and back into the bedroom.

She paused for a minute, wondering if she

might feel anything of the woman who had lived here so briefly.

But there was nothing, and so she started to leave the room. And then, as she did so, she thought that she felt something. A touch on her cheek. A gentle touch. Something so light it might have been imagined.

"Regina?" she said softly.

But again, there was nothing. And so she hurried down the stairs, anxious to meet the senator — and the men who followed behind him.

CHAPTER SIX

"Good to meet you, Mr. Crow. You know, I'm grateful to Adam Harrison for setting up this team." Age became Senator Holloway. He was barely forty but looked more like fifty — a good fifty. His graying hair was left alone to gray. He had good teeth when he tried to offer a smile, and his handshake was firm.

"We're here to do everything that we can," Jackson assured him.

He turned. Angela, a little breathless, had come out the doors to stand behind him and to his side.

"Miss Hawkins?" the senator asked, offering a hand.

"Yes, I'm Angela," she said. "It's a pleasure to meet you, sir. And I'm so sorry. I saw the way that you looked up at me, and —"

"Not to worry," David Holloway told her. His smile was poignant. "I thought I saw an angel standing there for a minute. I understand you're here to investigate, and that's where you need to be in order to investigate."

"Senator Holloway, you did find your wife, right?" Jackson asked him.

Holloway looked over at Jackson. "You know that, of course. You've read the police reports."

"I'm sorry. I need you to go over everything again. With me," Jackson said.

"Why don't we go inside," Angela suggested. She looked at the senator steadily. "Regina had an amazing talent as a decorator and homemaker. The house was coming along beautifully."

"Yes, she was talented, wasn't she?" the senator said. He looked up at the house for a minute, as if he wanted to refuse to go in. But he said, "I like the kitchen."

"We'll go hang around the kitchen table then," Angela said.

"Let me introduce everyone and make sure I've got it right, but even without files . . ." Jackson said, smiling. "I'm Jackson Crow, and this is Angela Hawkins. You are Blake Conroy, bodyguard, right?" He said to the massive bald man. He didn't think that a man with so much bulk — even muscled bulk — might have scaled walls. "And, Martin DuPre," he said, shaking the man's hand. "We may be calling on you frequently, Martin." DuPre's Armani suit couldn't conceal his litheness. And he stood close to the senator, a protective barrier, despite the hulky bodyguard nearby. "And Grable Haines, you are responsible for getting everyone everywhere, right?"

"I go where the senator tells me," Haines said. "That's my job to serve Senator Holloway's needs."

"Let's go in and talk for a few minutes," Jackson said. He wanted to split them up. As they went through the courtyard doors, he said, "Senator, would you take a walk with Angela and tell her everything that you did the night you found Regina?"

Holloway's mouth was grim, but he nodded.

"Senator?" Angela said softly.

It was evident that she had struck a sympathetic chord with the man. They might not get new evidence today, but at least he could see the dynamics between the men who served Senator Holloway, and perhaps get a better sense of the man who had believed so fully in his wife that he would not accept a verdict of suicide.

Angela looked back at him gravely. He nodded, and she smiled grimly. It was a good communication. He may not like her and he might well be convinced still that she was a loon, but he trusted her with talking to the man; she knew it.

Maybe they were becoming something of a team.

"Did you come in through the front door that day?" Angela asked Senator Holloway. "Forgive me if I ask you to repeat too much. I know this is hard."

"Yes," he said. While Jackson had ushered the chauffeur, the bodyguard and the aide into the kitchen, she walked down the hall to the great ballroom with the senator. He stood there a minute, his eyes filled with sadness as he looked around the room. He frowned, noting the cameras and lights and screens set up, but then the frown faded and he just looked sad again as he surveyed the furniture, covered in dust cloths and shoved against the walls.

"It would have been beautiful," he said.

"You still own it," she reminded him.

He shook his head. "We really weren't fanciful people. We didn't believe in ghosts, and the house had been bought and abandoned, bought and abandoned over the years . . . its reputation had made it a deal when we bought it." Holloway studied her gravely. "But you dug up bones — right after you got here. I knew if I went to Adam

Harrison, he'd find the right people."

"I'm afraid the bones in the basement had nothing to do with your wife," Angela told him. "That poor man was a victim, like many others in Madden C. Newton's circle. Newton was a predator, swooping down on the misfortunes of others." She segued back to the present. "So you came in by the front door? Didn't your chauffeur let you off in the courtyard that day?"

He shook his head. "No, I wasn't in session. I have an office over in the CBD. I was working there, and I had Grable on call. I didn't need him to hang at my side all day, so I told him just to pay attention to his cell phone."

There was no alibi for the chauffeur at the time Regina Holloway died.

"So you entered through the front door?"

"I used my key, and then I tapped in the code on the alarm pad."

"The alarm was set, you're certain?"

He nodded. "At least, I think I'm certain. Yes, I'm certain. I remember hearing the little chirps that warn you to key in the code."

"What next?"

"I called out to Regina, but she didn't answer. Obviously," he added bitterly.

"And then you went up the stairs and

through the house?" she asked.

He nodded.

"Okay, let's retrace your steps," she said.

He walked toward the grand staircase and she followed. He traversed the hall, turned at the ell and turned again at the last ell.

Then he paused.

There was absolutely no doubt in Angela's mind that Senator David Holloway had truly loved his wife. He stood still, looking older than his years, his face a mask of grief and regret.

"Are you all right?" she asked gently.

He nodded and moved on. "I came to our room. I could see that she had been lying on the bed, resting. She loved this room. She was always so busy . . . she was industrious. That was why I wanted the house so badly. I knew she would work hard, embrace the project. And she did."

"What happened then? Did you go downstairs looking for your wife?" Angela asked. "Did you think she might have been in the kitchen, cooking, maybe?"

He shook his head. "I saw the doors open to the balcony. It was a beautiful twilight, and I figured she had stepped out to catch the night breeze. I walked out to the balcony, and I called her name again. And then I looked down."

Grief, poignant and fresh, had slipped into his voice. He covered his face with his hands. Angela touched him gently on the shoulder, and stood silent, waiting. Anything she might have thought of to say would have been inane.

He took a moment, and then looked at her, his features contorted with pain. "Her eyes were open," he said, his voice ragged. "Her eyes were open. She lay on her back, her head at an awful angle, and blood was pooling beneath it. But her eyes were open, and she almost seemed to be staring at me. Or . . ."

"Or what?" Angela asked.

"As if she had seen something as she died. Something so horrible that she couldn't bear it. Something terrifying. And, I'm afraid I know what it was."

Startled, Angela asked, "What?"

"A ghost."

Confused, Angela stood still and quiet for a minute. "You said that you and your wife weren't fanciful people. That you didn't believe in ghosts," she said.

"I didn't. Not until I owned this house."

"But — you believe your wife saw a ghost?"

He let out a breath, staring at her. "There were places in the house she wouldn't go when I wasn't home. She said that they just made her uncomfortable. And I don't really know what I saw, but when I was in the kitchen once, I felt as if someone was watching me. I looked at the door to the basement — and there was something there. I don't know what. It seemed like a big black shadow. It was there, and then it was gone. Was it a ghost? Hell, I don't know. I do know that I felt as cold as ice, and had rivulets of fear racing up and down my spine. I told myself I was being ridiculous, but, later, that night, Regina asked me if I believed in ghosts. I said no, and reminded her that neither did she. But, then, after she died . . . I started to think about it again. And when she died, people looked at me as if I had to be a monster — as if I had caused her suicide. I didn't. I believe now that ghosts caused her suicide, and you people need to find out if they're real — you need to prove it for me!"

Jackson sat on the counter, trying to remain casual and easy while questioning the trio that continually surrounded Senator Holloway. They'd chatted about the Saints and other local sports teams, and he learned that the hulk — Blake Conroy — had wrestled professionally. Grable Haines admitted to having done time in a juvenile detention center for petty larceny, and Martin DuPre had simply been in love with politics since he'd been a kid. "Politics and power, they go hand in hand. And the *right* people need to be in power. I'm lucky. I learn so much from Senator Holloway, it's like a miracle, a present from God," DuPre told him.

"Everybody loves the senator," Blake said, nodding.

"But he needs a bodyguard," Jackson pointed out.

"He's a politician — and no wishy-washy yes-man, either. He sticks to his guns. If he ever changes his stance on something, it's because he's received new information," Conroy said. He was drinking a soda — the regular-size bottle dwarfed by his mitts.

"Mostly, some of the really right-wing religious groups are against him," DuPre told him.

"I heard about a few earlier," Jackson said. "The Aryans and the Church of Christ Arisen."

"The Aryans are assholes," Grable said.

"Freedom of speech in this country — nothing we can do about them," DuPre reminded him.

"Yeah, well, thank God they don't have much of a hold here, not in New Orleans,"

Blake said. He slammed a fist against his palm. "They are neo-Nazis at their worst. Of course, it would be illegal to euthanize anyone with *impure* blood, so they use words as weapons. And they do it well. If God had wanted us to be all one race, we would have come that way, they say. God had separations in color for a reason."

"Um — we come as one single race at the beginning, as far as I understand anthropology," Jackson said.

"Yeah, go figure," DuPre said. "Thing is, the senator, he's *always* politically correct. No matter what those —" he stopped for a moment, glancing at Grable "— *assholes* do, the senator is calm and soft-spoken, just holding his own."

"What about the Church of Christ Arisen?" Jackson asked.

"Well, now, they're just really weird," Grable told him. "They have some secret rituals, like the Masonic Lodge."

"Don't compare them to Masons!" Blake protested. "My dad was a Mason. And a Shriner. Those guys got together and supported kids in hospitals. Don't even compare."

"Well, you have to be a member of the church to attend their meetings. There's a bishop, name's Richard Gull," Blake told him. "And there's a high council, with five members. They're protected by law, but I don't think they should be."

"Hey, there's an enormous church in this country where people worship *aliens*, for God's sake," DuPre put in. "It's a free country, with separation of church and state."

"You can have all the laws in the world — and that don't stop the Santeria groups from practicing animal sacrifice," Blake said.

"Or voodoo priestesses from torturing snakes!" Grable asserted, shuddering as he made a face.

"You feeling sorry for the priestess or the snake?" Blake asked him, grinning.

"Well, anyway, can you all tell me about the day Regina Holloway died?" Jackson asked. They'd been talking, the three of them, easily, coworkers who might not have a lot in common, except for their love for their boss.

But they sobered and went silent at the question.

"Should have been a good day," Grable said, shaking his head. "I was off most of the day. I gambled at the casino and won. Then the senator called me, and I picked him up and dropped him off. Wasn't half an hour later that I got the call about Regina. I got back here, but . . . by then, the coroner's office had been called in, cops and yellow tape were everywhere, and the senator was in the entertainment room, with DuPre."

Martin DuPre sighed softly. "It was horrible. Senator Holloway cried. Sobbed. I had to get him away from people."

"Why weren't you with him?" Jackson asked Blake. "Sorry — I mean, you are his bodyguard."

He shook his head. "He was just working in his office in the CBD that day. Going in and coming out. He said that he didn't need me."

"So where were you all day, Mr. Conroy?" Jackson asked.

"At home. I don't have much time to call my own, and it was like a picnic! I have a place uptown and I just worked out all day. But I came when I got the call, too. DuPre let me know what was going on, and I got here as fast as I could. I felt helpless as a baby, though. Never saw anything like the senator," Blake said. "The next week, it was like he didn't care if he died himself. I was working hard then, I'll tell you. Running after him, keeping up with him," the bodyguard said. "He'd start working, he'd want to walk. He'd start working again, he'd want coffee, he'd need something at the apartment — he was all over the place."

"Mr. DuPre?" Jackson asked. "Where were you that day?"

"Me? I was at the office most of the day. I was going to come back here with the senator, but he said that he didn't need my help, he wanted to try to have a nice night with Regina," DuPre said sadly.

None of them had an alibi, except for Du-Pre.

Blake Conroy was just about the size of a yeti — doubtful he had leaped down from any brick walls. Both DuPre and Haines were probably more agile.

Didn't matter. He needed to chase down the alibis on all three of the men.

He looked to the doorway. Angela was back down with the senator.

The senator handed Jackson a card. "My office address, and my business phone and cell phone are on that card. I've taken an apartment in the complex down on Decatur Street, overlooking the river. I'd just as soon we talk there from now on," he said.

DuPre, Haines and Blake stood, clearly aware that they were leaving.

"I know it was hard for you. Thank you for coming here today," Jackson told the senator.

"Thank you for being here," the senator

told him sincerely. "Find out the truth. Maybe I can let Regina rest if I can just know the truth." He was quiet for a minute. "I didn't believe in ghosts, dammit. But, I might have been the fool, and, of course, I couldn't say that to the police. There is something about this house. If I would have taken more time with Regina . . . but maybe that wouldn't have changed anything. Maybe there are ghosts. And maybe the ghosts were too much for her."

Jackson was startled by his statement, and looked at Angela. Her eyes widened and she subtly shook her head.

"You now believe that there are ghosts in here, Senator?"

"Don't you people confirm that sort of thing?" the senator asked. "I mean, Miss Hawkins was here one night, and she dug bones out of the basement. If my wife went over that balcony, something made her do it. God alone knows — maybe it *was* a ghost."

"Sir, I have a book on Madden C. Newton. Reading it led me to the bones," Angela said.

"When was this book written?" he asked, frowning.

"Years and years ago," Angela assured him.

"Why didn't the author find the bones?" the senator asked. "Because he didn't have a sixth sense," he said, nodding sagely.

"Actually, in the book, there was a mention of the fact that Madden C. Newton used to tell people that his basement was an amazing place, and that he loved the shadows beneath the stairs," Angela said. "So, I'm afraid it was the book that led me to the skeleton."

"Probably," Jackson said, a slight edge to his voice, "the author of the book didn't dig up the bones because he didn't have access to the house, and if he had had access, he might not have had Angela's ability to work inside the mind of a victim — and a killer."

"Of course," the senator said softly. "Well, I'll leave it all in your capable hands, and, of course, these gentlemen are at your disposal," the senator said. He offered his hand to shake with Jackson, and then headed out the kitchen door to the courtyard. His trio waved and murmured goodbyes, following him.

Jackson slipped down from the counter to follow them out. Angela came behind him.

It was evident that Senator Holloway was eager to find a killer — living or dead — as long as it meant that Regina Holloway had not killed herself. Grable Haines opened one side of the back door of the black sedan for the senator; DuPre entered before Blake Conroy, letting the massive bodyguard maneuver his bulk into the car last.

The gate opened; the car backed out carefully onto the street.

"There's a pecking order," he noted. "DuPre is the closest to the senator. Then Conroy, and then the chauffeur, Haines. DuPre considers himself highest in the senator's esteem, and he's very aware he's the most educated. Probably the only bright future among them."

"Do they get along?" Angela asked him.

"Yes. They seem to do well enough." He turned to look at Angela. "What made him suddenly turn to ghosts?"

"I was surprised, too," Angela said. "He talked about the way that Regina had died," she said. "He said that he could see that her neck was broken — or that her head was at an angle — and that her eyes were open. She was staring, wide-eyed, as if she had been in terror of something. And he told me that he'd seen a shadow in the kitchen that had given him the creeps, but that he had still denied it to his wife. He wants ghosts to have killed his wife. And he feels that people hated him after she died, because they believed that it was his coldness that had led his wife to suicide. I think he wants someone else to blame — and he wants it to be a ghost. If we can prove that there are ghosts in this house, he'll be vindicated."

"Ghosts don't kill people," Jackson said flatly.

"And I'm not sure how we'll prove — beyond the scientific eye — that ghosts exist. Maybe he believes that if he can get a crack team of paranormal investigators just to *say* that the house is haunted and there are ghosts here manipulating and terrifying people, that will be enough."

"I need to study the coroner's photos," he said, turning and heading into the kitchen. He opened his computer, still on the table from that morning, and accessed a number of the files he had downloaded.

She was standing behind him. He realized that he was drawing up a grisly death scene — and that he was still aware of the subtle and alluring scent of her perfume. He was seated; a strand of her wheat-gold hair fell on his shoulder. She didn't notice. She was looking at the screen.

He had looked at the various photos — Regina Holloway taken in death from several different vantage points — several times. Now he looked again, studying the dead woman's eyes.

"Once, science actually studied the eyes in forensics — believing the last thing a person had seen was preserved, like film, on the retinas," Angela murmured. "It does look as if she was terrified."

"Terrified — and looking at someone or some*thing*," Jackson mused. He moved the photos around and stood up, nearly knocking her over. He caught her by the arm, steadying her. "Sorry!" he said gruffly. "Let's get up to the room."

She was a distraction. He was concentrated on the position of a body, and he was still aware that touching her, he felt the softness of her flesh, and the vitality beneath it.

He gave himself a mental shake. They were becoming a *team,* he reminded himself.

And . . . and he didn't like the fact that though she didn't say so, she was convinced that ghosts walked around, and maybe even that ghosts would talk to her in Regina Holloway's bedroom.

He paused, gritting his teeth. Was he afraid, maybe just a little, that everything he wanted to deny was true?

No, reality and truth lay at the heart of this death. There was a human being out there responsible.

He took the center stairs up to the second floor, aware that she was following him. He strode straight to the balcony in Regina's room and looked down to the courtyard, envisioning the position of the body. "She didn't dive forward," he said after a moment. "She went over backward."

Angela walked to the balcony and turned around, placing her palms on the railing. "She was standing like this."

"Yes. Do you think that a suicide would have stood here, and flung herself over *backward?*" Jackson asked.

"It's not *impossible,*" Angela said.

"Right. But you agree with me. It's highly improbable."

"Yes, but remember the old Sir Arthur Conan Doyle slash Sherlock Holmes adage?" Angela asked him. "When you get rid of the impossible, what's left is the only answer, no matter how improbable."

"Conan Doyle believed in ghosts, and Senator Holloway sure seems to think we hunt them," Jackson said.

She stared back at him. "We do, don't we?" she asked quietly after a minute.

"I used to be with a respected Behavioral Science Unit."

She laughed. "And I was a cop, looking to eventually become a detective. Jackson, apparently there are people out there who believe ghost hunting is a respected talent. Adam Harrison put us all together because he believes in us. He believes in our ability to prove that ghosts *aren't* responsible, just as much as he does in our ability to let our minds discover what really was in the past. What is a ghost? To some people, a ghost is a memory. To others, a paranormal experience might be a way of dealing with a loss, or something else terrible. If we can open our minds to all kinds of possibilities, accepting the fact that *science* hadn't really even begun to discover the incredible machinations of the human brain, we strip away whatever it is about this assignment that's embarrassing you."

"I'm not embarrassed," he protested. He had been, he realized. He winced.

What were ghosts? Memories?

Face it. He'd seen a ghost in his mind's eye — or the machinations of his brain had brought a ghost to him — and he had saved two lives because of it. Angela, looking at him so earnestly, was right. As a child, he'd been saved by a ghost. A memory. Or a man who had become a ghost memory, because he'd seen a portrait in a hallway of a medieval warrior.

There were times, even now, when he

looked back and wondered. He'd been a boy when he'd been in Scotland, riding with his friends. Racing. All these years later, he could still remember falling from his horse — and lying on the ground in the middle of the woods, thinking that his friends had gone on, assuming he was way ahead of him. And then the man had come to find him, help him, bring him home and leave him on his doorstep. Then, later, he had wandered his mother's ancestral home, and he had seen the man in a painting. A painting he had seen before, but hadn't connected with the man who had saved his life. But it was him. Or someone who just looked like him. He had always clung to that explanation. Yet there was always that question at the back of his mind.

He knew that he could do what Angela did; stop, clear his mind, concentrate. And the possibilities of what might be were out there.

She laughed suddenly. "You've seen a ghost," she told him.

"You've seen ghosts," he accused her.

She was still smiling. "I don't know what I've seen, really. I believe that there's more to life than what we see. All right — I've *been* places when a parent senses that a child is in danger."

He stared at her, a bit annoyed; she seemed completely comfortable with her own beliefs, and confident in herself. She didn't run around broadcasting her talents, she just accepted them.

He smiled suddenly. "Some things, we'll just figure out as we go. This is new to all of us — I think we're an experiment Adam has wanted to orchestrate for a long time."

She grinned, and he thought that she moved just a step closer, maybe even beginning to like him. "Yes, and it's actually really intriguing to be a part of it. It's a good group. I like the others."

"Where *are* those kids?" he asked. "They should be back from the store by now."

"I'm assuming they'll be back soon," Angela said. She frowned, and he realized that she was still standing with her back to the railing, leaned slightly back. He visualized the body falling from her position, and knew that with a bit of impetus — a push or a shove — she would land on the courtyard, just as Regina Holloway had landed.

Despite himself, he reached out and pulled her closer to him, and away from the balcony.

"Sorry," he said huskily.

"I'm not going over," she told him, looking up into his eyes. She wasn't angry, and she didn't move away from him. For a moment, chemistry — animal magnetism — coursed through him. Maybe her parents had known when they'd named her that she was destined to grow into such a golden and elegant young woman.

He just wanted to stay close to her; to protect her, from herself, if need be.

She didn't seem to mind being close. She did seem a bit amused. "I'm actually quite competent at defending myself, you know?"

"I've seen a lot of competent people go down — I've seen cops go down, I've seen the most brilliantly trained men I knew go down," he said, an edge that he hadn't intended in his tone.

She touched his cheek with the pads of her fingers; it was a nice gesture, one a friend might make. "I know," she said softly. "I'm sorry."

He caught her hand, thinking that he might say more, thinking it was a surprisingly intimate moment. He'd known her a day now. Maybe the intensity of the situation made it seem they had known each other much longer.

Maybe animal magnetism was just that — he would have been attracted to her no matter where or when or how they had met.

He found himself caught in her gaze,

wanting to know more about her. "Are you ever totally honest?" he asked her gently.

"What do you mean?" she asked.

"I know about your work with the police — before and after you became an officer. But what happened before then? What's the real story on the plane crash?"

She stared back at him. He thought that she would brush him off with a casual remark. But she hesitated. "You already think I'm crazy."

"I know that the mind — that the human brain — is a frontier. Many things may be possible. Or the illusions that we create in our mind may seem very real. I'm serious. Please. Tell me. What happened with the plane crash?"

She took a deep breath and looked away from him. He knew that the memory was painful, but she had apparently decided to share it.

"The weather was bad throughout the flight, but our flight attendant kept assuring us that it was like bumping over the waves in the ocean. I was only twelve then, but even I knew when it went straight to hell. The flight attendant went rushing by us, white as a sheet, crossing herself. The plane began to heave and twist, and when it went to the side, I knew that something was really, really wrong. I was sitting next to my mom, and she threw her arms around me, as if she could protect me. The passengers started screaming. I can still hear the sound in my mind sometimes . . ."

"I'm sorry," Jackson said quietly.

"Some were pulling out their cell phones, trying to say goodbye to loved ones. Most were just screaming. Then it happened fast. The pilots struggled, I'm sure — but they were attempting to land against a terrible wind shear — I learned that later. The plane broke up as it hit the ground. Luggage flew, no matter how it had been stowed. A wing broke off. The plane spun around. The next thing I knew, I was sideways down on the tarmac, and fire was bursting all over in spurts along with the remnants of the plane. I managed to undo my seat belt and fall face-first to the ground. I shouted for my mother and father. I tried to crawl through the wreckage."

She stopped speaking. Jackson urged her on. "And what then?" He almost whispered the words.

"Games in my head? In my heart?" She looked at him. "I saw them. My fellow passengers. They had turned into yellow light, and they rose from the ground, heading for a greater source of light, and I wanted to get up and follow them. I saw my mother, and I shouted for her, but she was ahead with my father. They had found one another, and my father was looking at my mother with a pained expression that still held hope and love. I cried out for them both to wait. They didn't seem to hear me, but there was someone next to me. A man in some kind of white shift, so it seemed, and he hovered down by me. He smoothed back my hair and he said gently, 'No, little one, they have to go, and you have to stay. It's all right. If you look, you'll see all the light and the splendor, and you can know in your heart that you're always safe, for the light shines down upon you.' He touched my face, and I closed my eyes. When I opened them again, the sound of sirens blaring was all around me, and I was in excruciating pain. Luckily, I blacked out again. I spent weeks in the hospital. But Eamon was there for me, my brother. He hadn't been on the plane with us because he's three years older than me, and he was away at football camp."

"And so you made it," Jackson said. "And you believe that . . . you saw your parents walk toward the light — heaven? — and that you were told by an entity of good that you had to stay behind?"

She shrugged. "Yes, that's more or less the gist of it. And, so now, you think I'm crazier still, but maybe I have a right to be crazy?"

"You survived," he said.

"Yes, I survived. My broken bones mended, and my burned flesh peeled away, and thankfully, I don't even bear a scar."

"I don't quite believe that, but you went into law enforcement, and you've helped in many cases," he said. "Any connection?"

She smiled ruefully. "Not really. I fell in love, lost the man I loved to cancer, and knew that I had to use whatever I possessed to try to help others. I am not a particularly good soul or anything of the like — it was what was left for me to do that seemed important."

"Actually, I do think that you are a good soul," he told her.

He didn't want to. He liked her. Very much.

Despite the way he had met her. Pickax in hand.

They were caught there, in that intimate moment, not just physically intimate, but somehow, as a meeting of something that might be of the souls, though that sounded somewhat ridiculous.

"So what about you?" she asked quietly.

"None of us got to see your file, if you'll recall."

He was saved from having to answer her when they heard the doorbell ring, and shouts arise from the front, the sound carrying easily to them where they stood outside on the balcony.

"Hey, please! Carrying a heavy load out here, you know!"

That came from Whitney.

The doorbell rang again, insistently.

Jackson stepped back.

"Ah, gee, honey," he said lightly. "I guess the kids are home."

CHAPTER SEVEN

In the next few hours, bags of groceries were put away, and Whitney and Jake settled in.

Angela spent the time in her room — Regina Holloway's room — arranging her own clothing in drawers and closets, and pausing now and then to see if she could get a sense of the children again, and she wondered if finding them would really help the team in their quest to discover the truth. But she didn't see or feel anything; the room was just a room at that moment, a beautiful one. She kept the balcony doors open because the city had yet to grow hot and humid; spring was still in the air, the humidity was not at the eighty or ninety percent it could be and the breeze that came in was just beautiful.

She found herself wondering more about Jackson Crow. He had become human to her; she still couldn't believe that she had told him about the plane crash — and the man who had spoken to her, telling her that it wasn't time for her to go to the "light."

A tap at her open door interrupted her thoughts.

Jackson leaned against the door frame, his stillness so familiar despite their short acquaintance. Adam wouldn't have him heading up this unit if there wasn't a core of belief in life after death. She knew he had to be shaken up about his last experience in the field; people had died. Friends had died.

And despite the fact that two of the kids had only just arrived, making her the more senior team member, she could barely imagine what he had felt. She was certain that Adam had taken great care when putting their team together. They were people who were very different, but who had the talents and personalities that would complement one another.

"Are you busy?" he asked her.

She nodded at the open drawers. "Just finishing in here."

"I wasn't sure if you'd sensed more bones in the wall. I wanted to be able to duck quickly," he said.

"No, the pickax is in the basement," she told him, able to smile. He was actually joking. "You're safe."

He nodded and walked in. "Do you have a hang-up about people sitting on the end of your bed?" he asked.

"Nope."

He sat. "So, what was your take on the senator?"

"Well, you heard him — I think he really wanted ghost hunters."

"But what did you feel about him? About his emotions?"

"He's really devastated by his wife's death," she said. "And he *is* the one who found her. What did you discover in regards to his companions?"

"Every one of them is a possible suspect. The day she died, they were all in New Orleans. Senator Holloway was working. Blake Conroy was at his home gym, so he says, and Grable Haines was gambling."

"What about Martin DuPre?"

"He was at the office with the senator, but I doubt they were in clear view of one another all the time. You can walk here from the Central Business District. I'd say it would take someone twenty to thirty minutes, walking briskly. A cab would take a few minutes, depending on traffic. Perhaps he has his own car. I didn't want them all together when I got into specifics."

"Where do you want to go from here?"

159

she asked.

"Tonight? We're heading toward dusk, you know. I thought we should lie low, help set up the cameras and get started taking video or film or whatever they work with, and see if we have any surprises showing up on the screens."

"And are you expecting anything?" she asked him.

He shrugged. "I never say never."

"Really?"

"Really." He glanced at his watch. "It's almost seven, it's been a long day — I'm heading down for a beer. Oh, Jake Mallory is a sushi freak — and an expert sushi chef, so he claims. Do you eat sushi? He's doing up some noodles and stir-fry, too."

"I'm pretty safe on almost anything," she told him. "Well, I don't want to try monkey brains, or anything, but otherwise . . ."

He grinned, rising. "You coming down?" he asked her.

It was twilight. Part of her wanted to just go with him; a beer did sound appealing at the moment. But this was near when Regina Holloway had died, and if there were things that might be seen in the room, this was the time. She should be open to allowing the past to talk to her now, whether that meant ghosts, or just something that she did with her mind.

She remembered talking to Jake, though, and Jake telling her ardently that he *knew* people who saw ghosts.

Jake and his friends were crazy. That was all she'd allow.

"I'll be down in just a few minutes," she said.

"I'll keep your beer on ice," he said, leaving.

Sensations could indeed be strange. The room seemed empty when he left; drained of life. She tried to dismiss the thought, reminding herself that she had only known him one day. Last night, he'd put her on the defensive. But maybe that was what he had felt he needed to do as the head of the team. Today, she felt as if she had seen behind his facade. He was vulnerable, too. He knew that he hadn't caused the deaths that had befallen his last team. Yet, he still blamed himself.

And, it was possible that he still believed that he'd been assigned to some kind of slightly crazy unit, a babysitting unit — a unit not actually meant for the hundreds of serial killers active in the country at any given time.

Regina Holloway was dead. There was no saving her now.

Angela lay down on the bed and closed her eyes. She tried to imagine the children as she had seen them before, on the floor, playing jacks. It was horrible to think how the children had died, and she wondered how Newton had managed such horrendous murders without being heard. She was pretty sure many of his torture-killings had taken place in the basement, but she thought that the children might have been killed in this room. She thought about Percy, trying to be an older brother, trying to reassure his little sister.

It hurt to imagine the fear that must have seized them both when the man who was supposedly trying to help their father had come after them with an ax.

She found herself praying, so many years later, that somehow, they had died quickly, and that the pain hadn't gone on too long. And still . . . had Percy watched Madden C. Newton chop up his sister? Or had the older brother been the first to die?

Darkness was settling over the room. She hadn't opened her eyes, but she could feel it, just as she could feel the breeze that wafted in, and the way that it lifted the curtains by the French doors.

She opened her eyes slowly.

The little boy was there. He was watching

162

her sorrowfully.

She didn't move; she was afraid to blink. His face was old for his years, and his eyes seemed to carry the wisdom of the ages.

"Be careful, please, be careful," he told her.

Was she dreaming?

"Percy?" she asked softly.

But as if the breeze could dissipate illusion, he was suddenly gone.

She waited. She felt frozen. She realized that she was afraid, and yet she wasn't afraid of the little boy who had to be Percy.

She was terrified, she realized, because it hadn't been a dream. It had been real; she had thought about him, and he had appeared.

The mind; a scientist would say that she could do such things only through imagination.

Anticipation and dread rushed through her body and she closed her eyes. Fear followed hope. She opened her eyes, but there was no one, nothing there.

She sat up, and felt the darkness in the room, alleviated by lamps that had come on in the courtyard, and from the light in the hallway. The room was drenched in shadow. The closet door was slightly ajar, as was that to the bathroom. For a moment, she had a child's ridiculous fear that a monster would suddenly rush out of the closet and attack her.

She waited, determined she would not be frightened out of the room. She did believe that something *evil* — ill will? Something more tangible? — resided in the house. But, whatever evil might lurk in the minds of men had nothing to do with the appearance of the child. She wanted to see the little boy again, the little boy she was certain had to be Percy.

But laughter drifted up to her from the kitchen, and she heard the sound of a guitar being strummed.

Jake, the musician, and computer and sound expert.

It was time for that beer Jackson had promised to keep cold for her.

Jackson read the newspaper article on the discovery in the house, surprised to find himself comfortable on a stool near the counter pass-over to the courtyard. Jake was strumming his guitar while calling out orders to Whitney to do his prep work — insisting it would come out to be a feast.

He was adept on the guitar. The instrument he had brought with him was acoustic, and he kept his tunes low and mellow — but ridiculously bawdy at times — causing

Whitney to stop in the midst of her tasks that he had assigned to her and giggle. He had to admit, Jake made him laugh now and then, and it seemed like a good thing that, so far, they all seemed so easy and ready to get along with one another. But then, Whitney staged a revolt, laughing and telling Jake that she'd set the table, fixed his flipping rice balls, and it was time for him to get back in the act.

Jake sighed, set down his guitar and started to work, thanking Whitney for all her excellent preparation. Jackson looked at the newspaper again.

The article contained little more than the facts, but with, of course, the questions about the house being haunted being raised again, and the tragedy of Regina Holloway's death coming to the fore once again. He liked the spin in the article, though — the reporter had quoted Andy Devereaux's police spokesman as saying, "The investigation team that discovered the bones will be continuing to study the history of the house, and seek out any more such surprises, before Senator Holloway puts the house back up on the market. With its infamous past, it doesn't seem at all impossible that there may be more skeletons — literally — hanging in a few of the closets."

Thankfully, the article didn't even hint at the unit being ghost hunters — or, thank God, any type of sci-fi-driven team claiming that the aliens did it all.

"Jackson?"

He looked up. Whitney, smiling and cheerful, was offering him a bite of something off her tongs. He smiled, remembering Angela's earlier words. "It's not monkey brains, is it?"

She laughed, and Jake, standing over the range top, joined her. "No, I've never had monkey brains. And, as long as I'm in the kitchen, there won't be any, I promise."

"Salmon, avocado, tempura shrimp and cream cheese," Whitney advised him.

He took the bite. The little piece of roll was delicious. "Wonderful. We've found ourselves a cook," he said.

"Chef," Jake said in protest.

"Oh, no, not every night," Whitney said. "You're too bossy."

"Hey — you're supposed to be the assistant. I give orders, you assist," he said.

"Well, I guess I don't care who cooks, or if I have to follow a few orders — as long as you don't make me the main cook," Whitney said. She wrinkled her face, taking over from Jake to stir the vegetables. "I can prepare one delicious dish — jambalaya.

And it is good."

"Jambalaya sounds great, too," Angela said, entering the kitchen. "Wow. It smells wonderful down here," she said. "Are we eating in here? Or in the dining room? Hey, do people actually eat in their dining rooms, ever? Or is that an only-when-company-comes kind of thing for real these days?"

"I say the courtyard . . . it's gorgeous outside," Jake told them all. "Well, the dining room isn't for eating, we all know it's just for show. No, the dining room ain't for eating, just for company, just for show, just when you bring that Bourbon Street stripper-ho-ho home, oh, yeah, just for show!"

Whitney groaned.

"Hey, it's a good song!" Jake protested.

It wasn't a particularly good song, but Jake had an amazing musical ability. Jackson had a feeling that he sat with that guitar, strumming out solutions to his problems.

"Courtyard it is," Whitney said.

It all moved quickly with the four of them taking out the food, lights and all that was needed. They were all aware, of course, of the place where Regina Holloway had fallen, but then they were there to investigate the death — and therefore honor the life — of the woman.

"Hey, I'm pretty sure that Regina Holloway believed in spirits — in some form or another," Whitney said, passing out the sushi rolls.

"Why?" Jackson asked her. "Your great-grandmother said that she didn't believe in ghosts. What do you mean — spirits?"

"Well, Regina Holloway went to my great-grandmother's shop sometimes for advice, but I think she was doing things on her own as well. I found red candles in the lower cupboard. They're part of a banishing spell that's used frequently here in New Orleans. And my great-grandmother didn't say anything about Regina buying candles from her. I'm just curious as to what she was doing on her own."

"Good question," Angela said.

"I'll stop by my great-grandmother's shop tomorrow," Whitney said. "I wonder if she sold Regina the candles, and if she knows anything about it."

"She must — your great-grandmother is a wonderful contact, Whitney. Angela, I think it would be great if you were to go to the store and spend more time with Mama Matisse. She just might say something else that we haven't thought about that could turn out to be really important," Jackson said.

168

"I would like to go with you," Angela said. "If you don't mind. I don't know a lot about voodoo."

"It's not what you think," Whitney said.

Angela laughed. "You don't know what I think."

"True," Whitney admitted sheepishly. "But most people believe it's all about black magic and zombies. For some people, it's a very serious religion. And for anyone who really practices voodoo, well, you wouldn't dream of doing anything evil. It's like the Wiccan religion — anything evil that you do will come back at you. Take a banishing spell. I'm not sure how well we explained it earlier. You can't just wish that someone you don't like will disappear — that could mean that you wish a train would hit them, or that they would walk off a mountain, or, well, something bad. Say you have a pesky neighbor. You have to try to banish him by hoping that he gets a new job that will make him richer, and then he'll buy a new house. Or, you have to wish that he decides to go live with his sister in Cleveland, and that he'll be happy there."

Angela reached for the soy sauce and said, "In this instance, Regina wouldn't have been trying to get rid of bad neighbors. She would have been trying to banish ghosts."

"Right. So she would have had to have wished that they find peace, and leave her home," Whitney said. "I'm not saying that voodooism hasn't had its share of deviants — like any religion. In Haiti, there are penal codes for anyone trying to create a zombie. And plenty of men in power did do so — part of it, of course, is mind control. And part of it was by using the poison of a puffer fish."

"But the religion is practiced by about sixty million people worldwide," Jake put in, adding soy sauce to his sushi. He looked up. "It came heavily into practice in the 1700s, when the Europeans bought or captured Africans from the kingdom of Dahomey, which is now more or less Nigeria, Togo and Benin. The word *voodoo* comes from *vodu* in the Fon language, and means spirit, or God."

Jake was rewarded with an arched brow and a small smile from Whitney. But then she waved a hand in the air. "Jake grew up here — he should know something about voodoo."

"Hey," Jake protested.

"Well?" Whitney asked.

"Well, inquiring minds do want to know," he said.

"And," Whitney continued, "there's a

170

supreme god, or *bon dieu,* and a host of *lon,* other gods, and they relate to the Catholic saints."

"Movies have made voodoo priests and priestesses into monsters," Jake said.

"I'd really love to see your great-grandmother's shop," Angela said.

Whitney shrugged. "See the good clean living of a voodoo priestess."

"But you grew up Roman Catholic," Jackson reminded her.

"Yes, my dad's parents were both of Irish descent. My mom's dad was Brazilian, and my mother's family was originally from Haiti, though they've been in New Orleans for countless generations."

"Cool," Jake said, staring at her.

"I think we've definitely got that going as a plan for you two to go tomorrow to Whitney's great-grandmother's place," Jackson said. "I'm going to have Will and Jenna watching over the house — if they get here by then, and if not, you stay, Jake. Whitney, whether you're here or not when he comes, Will can find his way around all the equipment that you brought, right?"

"You tell me," Whitney teased.

"He majored in film at UCLA," Jackson said.

"He'll manage," Whitney said.

"And, Jake, you're coming with me," Jackson told the younger man. "I may need someone with local know-how and knowledge of the political ins and outs."

"Great. Where are we going?" Jake asked him.

"To the senator's headquarters in the CBD. I want to see the offices. I want to know exactly where the senator was, and where his aide, Martin DuPre, was, when Regina Holloway died," Jackson said. "We've also got to get the chauffeur, the bodyguard and the aide separated so that we can get them talking about each other."

"A gossip fest?" Jake asked.

"Exactly," Jackson told.

"I love it," Jake said.

Whitney looked at Jackson and asked, "You're certain that someone living had something to do with Regina's death?" she asked.

"I'd stake my life on it," he told her.

"So, you *don't* believe in ghosts, or anything outside the normal experience of life that can be scientifically explained?" Whitney asked him, perplexed.

"I didn't say that I didn't, and I didn't say that I did. In my mind, the jury is out. I wouldn't exclude the possibility that things out of what we consider *normal* might exist.

172

In this case, however — gut hunch, a knowledge of the devious machinations living men can come up with — I believe that there's a human being involved in what's going on." He turned to Jake. "When we're done at the senator's offices, we'll head out to find out more about the Aryans and the Church of Christ Arisen."

"I have a hard time thinking the Aryans would kill a woman by somehow forcing her over her own balcony," Angela said. "She wouldn't have opened the door to them."

"They're fond of guns, and they are pretty clear about what they want," Jake said. "A gun in your face can make you open a door."

"Well, they didn't get in here," Whitney said. "From everything I've seen and heard Regina Holloway was a smart woman."

"That's why I believe she was killed by someone close. Someone who knew her, knew her habits, someone she trusted," Jackson said. "Still, political enemies need to be checked out . . . Hey, I want to see what all those monitors are going to show us."

"Probably Jake sleepwalking," Whitney said, grinning.

"What? Are you hoping for something? Do I or do I not sleep in the nude?" Jake teased.

"Please!" Whitney protested.

Angela stood up and started to collect plates. "Regina Holloway wasn't killed by the ghosts in this house," she said.

There was silence for a minute.

"Are you saying there are no ghosts in the house?" Whitney asked her.

"No. I didn't say that. If ghosts are memory — the memory of pain and suffering — then this place is full of ghosts. I just don't believe that the 'ghosts' in the house would have hurt Regina Holloway. I think they would have tried to help her."

Angela headed back into the house.

"Well, let's finish picking up," Whitney murmured.

"We'll finish. You can go work with your monitors and cameras. I'd like to see if we catch anything overnight," Jake said.

Whitney set off to set up more of the equipment while the rest of them cleaned up from the meal, suddenly subdued. Angela wound up sending Jake off to help Whitney while she and Jackson put the last of the food away. When they were done, they went to see where the cameras had been set up.

"We don't have enough equipment, obviously, to monitor every area at once," Whitney said. "But we've chosen a few for the night, and we've decided that we'll take turns watching what we have here for a while, and when it's time for us all to crash for the night — which we'll have to do to be halfway productive tomorrow — we'll run tape. Right now, we've concentrated on this room, the hallways where all the rooms are, so that's four, and we've also done the downstairs hallway through the entertainment area — and we have one camera left that we want to set up in the basement tonight," Whitney said.

"Sounds good," Jackson said. As he spoke, there was a knock at the door. The other three froze, startled by the interruption of the sound.

"Another member of our team," Jackson said, smiling. He walked to the door and looked out the peephole first, not wanting to be the cliché of the agent who opened up to a stranger with a sawed-off shotgun.

But he was somewhat surprised to see that Will Chan and Jenna Duffy had arrived together. She had been coming in from Boston, and he from Miami.

"Hey," Will said, offering his hand. "Will Chan, and —"

"Jenna Duffy," Jackson said, shaking hands with both, and opening the door to allow them to enter. "You're just in time.

175

We're setting up the cameras for the evening."

"Well, that's handy," Jenna said with a mild lilt. She stepped into the room.

The group wasn't shy, Jackson realized quickly. Will and Jenna had teamed up at the airport when Will had heard Jenna giving a cab at the curb the address for the house on Dauphine. They had introduced themselves, and they were quick and easy to do so with the others. Everyone was ready to help them with their luggage as well, Whitney and Jake quickly seized on the fact that Will had come equipped with some of his own microphones and recording equipment.

"Let's get these two in rooms, first," Jackson suggested.

"There are two nice ones left in the middle section," Whitney said. "Jake and I are just up the stairs — we grabbed a couple of the good rooms Jackson and Angela vacated."

"We'll stick together," Will said. "Won't we?" he asked Jenna.

"Ah, yes!" she said, smiling pleasantly. "I think I like having someone else close in this house."

Jenna looked just like the American stereotype of the Irish; she was five foot five, with bright auburn hair, styled in a soft pixie cut that framed her oval face nicely. Her eyes were bright green. Will Chan was tall, and he seemed a perfect mixture of all the races that had gone into his makeup; he had pitch-black, dead-straight hair, cropped short but not too short, almond-shaped dark eyes and a sculpted face that seemed to speak oddly of Greek in his distant heritage. He was of a sturdier build than Jake Mallory. The Indians, Chinese and English had settled Trinidad, and they had all settled in the body that was Will Chan.

"Take ten, and then we're all back here," Jackson said.

He waited, watching Angela, who wound up with nothing to carry, as the others all headed up the stairs with the newcomers' belongings.

She turned to him suddenly. "You're making me uncomfortable, you know," she told him.

"I don't mean to, but . . ."

"But what?"

"I just keep thinking about Shirley Jackson's *The Haunting of Hill House*," he said. "The character of Eleanor has led a hard life, and she's literally sucked into the legends of the house."

"Oh, low blow!" Angela protested. "Very

low blow! I liked being a cop. And, yes, I lost people, but I loved them very much . . . that you would compare me!"

"I'm sorry. It's just easy to be swayed by legend."

She shook a finger beneath his nose. "You are a liar, Mr. Crow."

He was taken by surprise. "I haven't lied to any of you," he protested.

"Omission can be a lie, and you haven't told any of us anything about your past, and you must think we're all dense if we believe there isn't a reason that you were chosen," she said.

"Maybe I was chosen to be the skeptic," he said. "You all have leanings toward — well, you all are ready to believe in ghosts. I'm a 'show me' type person. Show me the ghosts, and I'll believe."

She crooked a brow. "Sometime, you *will* tell me the truth."

He turned, hearing footsteps on the main stairs.

"Okay, we're all ready!" Whitney said.

Jackson moved over to the display of screens Whitney had set up in the grand ballroom. One mirrored the movements they were making; another showed the empty hallways and another showed the upstairs hall. While

Whitney took one of the cameras — attached to an incredibly long extension cord — and headed toward the hall to reach the kitchen, Jake bounded back up the stairs. "I'll give a call and a wave," he said.

Will positioned himself in front of the monitors.

"Yep, good," Will said. "Whitney, wave at me when you're down in the basement, too, and it's all set up. Let me know that the camera is good, and that you're fine, too."

"Of course, I'll be fine," Whitney said.

"I'll go with Whitney," Angela said, "and give her help if she needs any."

She seemed concerned about the basement, Jackson thought. But then, she'd dug a skeleton out of the floor there.

"No, you stay. I'll give her a hand. That camera looks heavy," he said. "Angela, would you watch the screens?"

"Sure," she said slowly, looking at him. Will and Jenna remained to watch the screens as well.

He carried the camera, and Whitney followed, laying cord out as close to the wall as she could, lest one of them trip over it.

They went the length of the house and down to the basement. He turned on an overhead bulb to light up the vast basement area as Whitney set up, and they waved.

"We're here — how's the angle?" she called out.

Jackson looked at her, surprised.

She grinned. "Mics — right there, see, at the bottom of the camera, right above the tripod."

"Excellent," he murmured.

"You look good!" he heard Will call to him.

"Yep, they're all working," Angela said. "Hallway, hallway, hallway, hallway, ballroom and now basement. All are a check."

"Okay, then, we're heading back," Jackson said.

Whitney preceded him, and together they walked back to the ballroom where the others were waiting, watching the monitors.

Nothing was happening.

"I'll stay up for a while and keep an eye on things," Will said.

"And when you tire out, just get me, and I'll take on a few hours," Jake told him.

"Cool," Will said.

"Get me about four in the morning. That's when I woke up when I was working as a nurse," Jenna told him.

"Well, that's great then — we'll make it through the night," Will said.

"I thought you had tape for when we were all sleeping," Jackson said.

"Hey, we do," Whitney said, "but if one of us is willing to be up, that's better."

"Okay, well, if anyone gets too tired, just let the tape roll," Jackson said.

"I'm going up to sleep. If you want me or need me, just come get me," Angela told them.

"We will," Whitney assured her. "But the film thing is what Will and I are supposed to do, so . . . I guess we'll figure it out as we go along, right?" she asked Jackson.

Jackson smiled. "Yep, I guess we'll figure it out as we go along." He was surprised to realize just how much he liked his team, though he had just met Jenna and Will. And it was odd. He hadn't quite reached his thirty-fifth birthday; Angela was thirty. The others were in their mid-twenties. But he and Angela were still the "seniors." And the "kids," as they had called them, seemed to have figured out the pecking order already. "Good job, kids," he said. "Angela, I think that means we're supposed to get our sleep."

She laughed. "Hey, it works for me."

He reached for her hand. She took it. "Okay, then, we're leaving the whole thing in your hands, kids. Is everyone's door to the balcony locked?" he asked.

He was answered with a sea of nods.

"Okay, I'm setting the alarm after Angela

and I go up and make sure that ours are locked as well. We'll see you tomorrow."

Good-nights were exchanged. He and Angela headed up the stairs, down the halls and to their respective rooms. At the door to hers, he paused. "You're sure you're going to be comfortable sleeping in there?" he asked her.

"I need to be sleeping in here," she told him.

"Okay, then, Mom," he teased. "Good night."

His room was next to hers. He'd hear her if she made the slightest noise. And he was still loath to leave her there.

He would have to.

"Good night — and I'm fine," she assured him.

"Make sure your door to the balcony is closed," he reminded her.

"I will," she promised.

"I'm right next door if you need me," he said.

"I know. And I'm glad," she told him.

She kissed his cheek. He was surprised by the gesture, though it was smooth and fluid.

"Thanks," she said huskily.

Then she walked into her room. She didn't close the hallway door.

Jackson went into his room. He found the

remote control that managed the house on the table next to his bed.

He opened his bedside table, making sure his Glock 22 was exactly where he had placed it. The pistol hadn't moved.

They'd been vigilant about the house, so he hadn't expected it to. But it was true that they were working for Senator Holloway. A man with a reputation like diamond. And threats that cut like one.

Thoughts raced through his mind as he lay down; he willed them to stop so that he could sleep.

The room didn't seem to offer any late-night sensations. Disappointment pricked at Angela.

Sleep claimed her quickly and she found herself in the midst of a dream.

The children were there again. They were at the foot of her bed, as they had been. Percy and Annabelle. Percy trying to make his younger sister stop crying.

And then, *he* came into the room.

Madden C. Newton.

He had mutton chops on his cheeks with the customary clean-shaven chin. He was a man of approximately forty years, about five feet five inches in height, traces of gray showing in the slightly curly hair he wore to his shoulders. He was neither compelling nor unattractive; his eyes were almost color-less.

"Children!" he said, smiling.

They were still hugging one another.

"Sir!" Percy said, stepping back just slightly as Madden C. Newton entered the room.

"What a polite child!" Newton said, feigning delight. "What a lovely child. Polite and caring. Which leads to the question. If your sister was in danger, how willing would you be to protect her, boy?"

Confused, and dreading what he began to sense was to come, twelve-year-old Percy still managed to say, "I would die for her, sir!"

"And so you shall!" Newton told him.

"Sir?" Percy said again.

And that's when Madden C. Newton pulled the ax he carried from behind his back and showed it to the children. The blade glittered in the light of the kerosene light that glowed within the room.

Young Annabelle was the first to realize that the man could seriously mean to use such a weapon against them.

"No, oh, no!" she cried. "Mommy, Daddy!" she cried hysterically.

And Newton laughed. "They're a bit tied

up right now!" he said, laughing again at his own joke.

"Annabelle, run!" Percy advised. He shoved his little sister toward the door, but Newton was blocking the way. As she tried to escape, he swung, and with a vengeance. The little girl was caught directly in the throat with the blade.

Percy began to scream.

Madden C. Newton stepped forward.

Percy tried to run. He did run. He ran from place to place within the room, trying to get to his sister, trying to evade his attacker.

But in the end, there was nowhere to go.

Madden C. Newton raised his ax. And he struck hard.

In a sea of blood spatter, Percy fell dead. His eyes still open. Staring.

And panting, Madden C. Newton said, "Delicious!"

And began to lick the blood as it dripped upon the floor.

Angela awoke. The room was cast in the soft and shadowed glow of the moon. She had never closed the drapes. For a moment, she thought that she saw Madden C. Newton there, clutching the child he had murdered.

And despite herself, despite her training,

despite the Smith & Wesson .22 within reach in the bedside table, she began to scream.

A terrible, high-pitched scream that tore relentlessly through the night.

CHAPTER EIGHT

Jackson Crow had bolted out of bed before.

And still, he was pretty certain he had never bolted out of bed quite so fast.

He was at Angela's door in a split second. When he arrived, there was nothing there to cause such alarm.

Well, nothing other than Angela, jackknifed up to a sitting position. She was just staring — as if a thousand aliens were attacking.

"Angela?" he said, his voice low, gentle.

At first, he received no response.

He walked into the room and sat on the side of the bed, but she didn't seem to see him. He set his arms on her shoulders; her body was like ice.

"Angela," he said very quietly.

She blinked, and turned to stare at him.

Her eyes touched his, and she recognized his presence there, gasping softly, and flushing so completely, he could see the change

187

in her color despite the dim light.

Little blonde princess, he thought. *What could have made her scream as she had screamed?*

"Oh!" she said.

"Oh?" he repeated.

"Did I do something that woke you?" she asked him.

"If you call screaming like a banshee something that might wake me, yes," he told her.

"I'm so sorry."

She was trembling. He was almost overcome by the desire to draw her against him, hold her, and tell her that everything was all right. He had to maintain the appropriate distance, and remember that he was the head of a team. But it was difficult. She seemed to warm beneath his touch, and her skin was like silk; her eyes were on his with tremendous trust, huge and blue, and golden-blond tendrils of her hair swept over his fingers like moonlit temptation. If he wanted to, he could draw her to him, and feel far more of the woman beneath the thin cotton knit of her nightshirt. She was dressed so appropriately for sleeping in a house with others, and yet, he wasn't sure that any outfit could have made her more sexually alluring.

"You don't need to be sorry," he told her. She was leaning toward him. He was in a pair of long flannel pajama pants himself, and shirtless, and if she came against his chest, he wasn't sure he could control the sheer physical reaction that was sure to arise — *no pun intended,* he mocked himself.

"How stupid!" she said, angry with herself then. "I've had nightmares before — we all have them. I've never screamed like that — I'm not a screamer, really."

She was drawing on anger, trying to shake off the trembling that still had a hold on her.

"What was it?" he asked her.

"A nightmare, that's all," she said.

It wasn't all.

But before he could question her, he heard footfalls as the others came running down the hallway, then Jake burst in first, followed by Will, Jenna and then Whitney.

"What's happened?" Jake demanded.

"Oh, Lord! I am so sorry," Angela said.

Jackson knew he had to be grateful for the arrival of the others. He leaned back; the moment of longing to just drag her into his arms — comfort her — and then turn it all into something else entirely wasn't quite tamped, but he was under control.

"Angela had a nightmare," he said.

"A nightmare?" Will asked, puzzled and curious.

"I've never done anything like this before, really," Angela apologized.

"Oh, Angela! Please, you don't need to apologize!" Whitney said, coming to sit by her on the other side of the bed. "I was in a bed-and-breakfast once in England, and I dreamed that the neon lights flashing out on the street were alien ships making a landing. I screamed my fool head off — and nearly got my boyfriend arrested for assault. It was a small place, and everyone heard me . . . at breakfast the next day, you should have seen the way everyone looked at us!"

"So everything is all right?" Jake asked, clearly concerned about Angela.

"Fine. Honestly. I'm just humiliated that I've woken everyone up."

"I wasn't actually sleeping," Whitney said.

"I was," Jenna said, but she smiled. "It's okay, I worked E.R.s at all odd hours — I can get back to sleep. I hope you can, too. Want me to come in here and stay with you?" she asked Angela.

Angela shook her head. "No, I'm fine. Humiliated. Mortified. Besides that, I swear, I'm fine."

"Well, good night then. I'm heading back to bed," Will said, yawning. "And feel free to scream anytime, seriously, anytime you need us!"

"Absolutely. Preferably not tonight, but absolutely," Jake teased.

"You're sure you don't want me to stay?" Jenna asked.

"I'm positive. Everyone, please, get what sleep you can before tomorrow. Go, shoo, go back to bed — and thank you!" Angela said.

The four left, heading back down the hall. Jackson heard Jenna and Will saying goodnight to Whitney and Jake as they continued to the front; he didn't know if they'd whispered anything else to one another.

Angela looked at Jackson again. They were still nearly touching. Nearly. Not quite.

"So what really went on in your *dream?*" he asked her.

She looked away from him, evading his eyes. "You know how dreams are, they're fresh the minute you wake, then they fade."

"Not a nightmare that makes someone scream like that. I don't think you should be in this room," he said.

"I'm not leaving," she said stubbornly. "There's something here that I'm going to be able to feel, to sense . . . It's important that I'm in here."

He sat back, folding his arms over his

191

chest. "Remember what I said earlier? Didn't you ever read the Shirley Jackson book or see the movie? Eleanor goes quite crazy and kills herself to get to stay in the house," he said flatly.

"Stop using that reference!" she told him angrily. "I'm a together person. I hunted down the bad guys, remember? I'm not going to go crazy. Of course, sometimes I get the impression that you do think I'm crazy already," she said, grimacing.

He laughed. "I don't think you're crazy. All right, a little crazy. But I guess we all are. And the thing about that movie — the idea was to find out if anything paranormal existed. So, if ghosts are playing some kind of dangerous game with you — even if those ghosts are in your mind, or your dreams — this could be dangerous for you."

"Like I said, I need to be in this room. And, yes, it was really terrible, and I screamed, but I can take care of myself, you know."

"I wouldn't say that you have to vacate this room — except for tonight. We really have to get started tomorrow, and you need sound sleep, real sleep — without dreams."

"I don't feel like picking up and moving right now —"

"Just go over to my room. I'll finish out

the night here," he said firmly.

"No, really, I don't want to put you out like that!" she told him. She jumped up suddenly. There was enough moonlight to filter through cotton. He could see her far too clearly, and the mystery of what he couldn't see was beyond compelling.

"You wouldn't be putting me out," he said, frowning. "What are you doing?" She had begun to tug at the large, antique dresser that stood against the wall.

"Help me," she said.

"Okay, now I am starting to think you're crazy," he told her.

She turned to him, laughing. "That's a door behind it — see the outline in the wallpaper? The door has to connect to your room. We'll just open the door — and then we'll be no more than a few feet away from each other."

He frowned, studying the paper behind the dresser. She was right. It was cleverly aligned, and it looked as if it was just the place where two wallpaper sheets met, but it was a door.

He quickly went to her side, curious that the dresser had been put there. He pushed with Angela, and the dresser slid across the hardwood floor.

There was a doorknob; it had been hidden by the dresser.

He turned the knob and opened the door; it opened an inch before crashing into the dresser that leaned against the wall in his room.

"I'll be damned," he said.

"Come on. We'll move the dresser in your room," she said.

She was already out in the hall, heading into his room. She flicked on the overhead light and the sudden illumination was brilliant. She was already shoving at the dresser in his room. She might be a crack shot, but she needed his help. He supplied it. She threw open the door, and he realized he could actually see her right from his bed.

For joy.

Nothing like seeing the vision that was already starting to slip into his mind and libido like the sweet scent of honeysuckle on the air.

"See?" Angela said, delighted.

"Great!"

She ran over to him, clutched his wrists and rose on her toes to plant a quick kiss on his cheek. She slid against the naked flesh of his chest as she went down on flat feet, and for a moment, she paused, her gaze connecting with his.

And he knew that she felt it. Whatever it

was exactly. The strange force that was simply nature, that drew one person to another. Older than the hills.

She stepped back, awkward, and, in his mind, more charming. "Thank you," she said. "I mean, this way, I stay in the room, I'm all safe and sound, anything I hear, you'll hear, anything that happens, you'll know. You can even see me breathe," she said.

"I know."

She stepped back again. Almost as if she didn't trust herself.

"Good night and thank you. Thank you. Really."

He smiled at last, amused at them both, even if he had just cast himself into an hour of torture. She had endured nightmares. The sweetness of his dreams and the events taking place in his imagination would be no less agonizing.

But he managed to remain where he was. Despite everything that begged him to forget that they were colleagues, a team. He'd spent his life being completely professional. He'd often made work his life.

A woman had died — it might be the same as if they were on a case in which a madman was terrorizing a community or crisscrossing the country in the midst of a killing spree.

But he wasn't on vacation, and he wasn't on leave anymore. They were here for a reason.

The only reason at this moment seemed to be the one that begged him to step forward and grab her and drag her back with him to his bed, and to forget the world as they went at it like a pair of rabbits.

But she turned then, racing back to her bed and plowing into it, pulling the sheets around her. "Sleep well!" she called. "Thank you. Thank you, really."

"Think nothing of it," he said dryly.

He walked over to turn off the light, and then went back to crawl into his own bed. If he closed his eyes, maybe . . .

No. If he closed his eyes, he'd start the dreaming while he was awake, and that wasn't going to be a good thing at all.

And so, he watched her.

He just watched her breathe.

"Gran-Mama!" Whitney said enthusiastically, greeting the woman who was not behind the counter in the store, but who had been helping a group of tourists as they perused the shop.

"Whitney, child!" the woman said happily, stepping forward to greet Whitney. Angela loved Mama Matisse's look. There was something special about her appearance. Her hair was graying, but there were still strands with dark glossy pigment. She had one of the most arresting and fascinating faces Angela had ever seen, with high structured cheekbones, emphasized by her lean physique, a straight nose, generous lips and brilliant dark eyes. Her hair was in a neat queue, and she wore a flowing cotton dress in a multitude of colors.

"You met my friend Angela Hawkins yesterday," Whitney reminded her.

"Of course, I remember. I'm not daft, child!" Mama Matisse said, taking Angela's hand. "I like what Whitney has said. She just called you her friend, and not her coworker. Whitney has no friends who are not good people."

"Thank you. It's a pleasure to be here," Angela said. "I really wanted to see your shop."

Mama Matisse did not let her hand go. She held it, studying Angela's eyes. "You are a special friend. I feel your energy," she told Angela.

"Thank you very much," Angela said.

She quickly understood the power of the woman and of the place. The shop was beautiful and fascinating. The place was filled with exquisite artwork, books and posters, and more. It was all laid out in a fashion to draw the eye. There was a table filled with gris-gris and gris-gris bags, another held potions and oils, another had wellness spa packages. There were the usual voodoo dolls, but she noted that many of these were different; they offered pins, but the dolls were marked in different areas on their bodies. The area of the heart said, For Matters Involving Love." The area of the head and neck were labeled, "For Help with Troubling Questions."

"So, what can I do for you, little one?" she asked, still looking at Angela, but obviously addressing Whitney. "I already answered questions for your group."

"We're trying to understand more," Angela said. "And, frankly, you have greater insight than anyone else we've met. I was hoping you could tell us a bit more about your own opinions, and about the people who are involved."

"Like I told you, I was glad to perform a banishing spell — a dangerous thing, if it was not done correctly," Mama Matisse said. "But that was my only time at the house."

"Regina had many red candles, and I think she might have been performing other spells at sometime."

Mama Matisse shook her head. "I knew nothing about red candles. But I'm not surprised if Regina did play at magic. She wasn't a happy woman. But then, I am one of those who isn't madly in love with Senator Holloway, so perhaps she wouldn't have told me about all her unhappiness."

"Mama Matisse," Angela said, "you're the first person I've met who doesn't like the senator — other than a few fanatical groups."

Mama Matisse shrugged. "When there is a storm, I want to see a man in the ghetto — in the midst of the crack houses and the poor, picking up. I mean, really, digging in, picking up — not posing. Yes, in ghettos, you will find the crack houses. You will also find the poor, who have no chance. I believe in a man who picks up the pieces, who works with his hands, and doesn't pay others to do so. And when there is an oil spill, I want to see that man walk among the fishermen. I want to see him with volunteers, cleaning the birds with his own two hands."

"Perhaps he was terribly busy, trying to deal with those who must find the massive machinery needed to stop a spill," Angela said.

Mama Matisse shrugged again; she wasn't

going to argue. "You have come to me for my feelings — I am giving you my feelings, that is all. But I haven't cared for those, either, who only clean the shoreline and the birds when the television cameras are rolling. I give you my opinions on this, nothing more." She smiled. "Come. We can talk in my office. Sandra is here, and she can manage the customers. Sandra?"

She raised her voice slightly, and a young woman disengaged herself from the couple she had been helping. She smiled at Mama Matisse and waved at Whitney.

"We will be in the back," Mama Matisse told her young clerk.

The girl nodded, and walked around to the counter and the cash register. Not even a voodoo shop was immune to thieves, but, then again, thieves plagued many churches, and every different kind of house of worship that existed.

They passed through the main body of the shop to an area that was apparently a little place of worship for the true believers. There were floor mats in the room, and against the one wall, a voodoo altar. There were several statues there — many of them of saints — along with a skull mask, African tribal pieces and an arrangement of coins and small wrapped candies.

"Loa," Whitney whispered to her, referring to the little statues and those in other forms she didn't recognize as well.

"You wish to understand our religion and our ritual," Mama Matisse said when they reached her office. It had all the right equipment for an office, handsome filing cabinets, computer, printer, a state-of-the-art calculator and a beautiful, handcrafted desk along with cushioned chairs to sit before it. It was also a personal place. Mama Matisse had a wealth of pictures of children, grandchildren and great-grandchildren on the bookshelves near the desk, along with an assortment of her own reading material. She had a number of books on spiritualism, a Bible, and then a host of mysteries and thrillers. Clearly, Mama Matisse liked to be entertained.

"I would love to know more," Angela said.

"All right, I'll give you a quick course," Mama Matisse said, her voice all business. "Are we different from our roots in Africa? Yes, definitely. The religion came from Africa, mainly to Haiti, and there it began to combine with the white man's religion. But, in voodoo, we don't see a devil the way that the Catholic religion sees a devil. We have a spirit, Kalfu, who controls the malevolent spirits of the night. It's not a black-and-white world where there is evil and good. Voodoo is a path that teaches us what we need to know, and when one worships correctly, it's a beautiful path that leads us to be better in life."

"I understand," Angela told her. "From what I've learned about the world, most religions teach us to be decent to our fellow man. But people have and do practice black magic."

Mama Matisse waved a hand in the air. "Like all religions, voodoo can be and has been used by men and women of tremendous evil purpose. Papa Doc, the Haitian dictator who ruled with an iron hand, and his Tonton Macoutes or 'bogeymen,' was a cruel voodooist twisting the religion to keep his absolute control of the country. Under Papa Doc, every man with him became a zombie. The toxin of the puffer fish is used when those who practice black magic wish to 'kill' a man and bring him back to life. This is not voodoo. Voodoo is filled with the great God and spirits like saints who come to us and help us through all problems in life and society, and those who practice the voodoo we teach and are looking for what is positive in life and nature. But, remember, like a *cult* arisen from a Christian religion, people twist what they believe for their own ends, and they will try to use black magic.

You have the Bokor, and they are those who take voodoo, tempt evil and twist others. Remember, too, voodoo in Hollywood has brought about ragged creatures that burst forth and rise from the dead, rotten and decaying, and voodoo in Hollywood gave rise to the little dolls that we prick with pins to cause affliction. Yes, I sell voodoo dolls, but you'll note that mine are to find answers and peace, not to rip at a man's leg and cause him to break it or lose it in an industrial accident or the like. If someone uses black magic with a ten- or twenty- or even hundred-dollar voodoo doll and it does something to someone, it's because that person has managed to slip into the mind of the enemy."

"We've thought about that. A prophecy can be self-fulfilling?" Angela asked her.

Mama Matisse nodded gravely.

"So Regina Holloway had a banishing spell done at the house, by you, and yet she was buying voodoo paraphernalia elsewhere as well, that's odd, don't you think?"

Mama Matisse hesitated, and then said slowly, "I don't know. Regina Holloway didn't come to me for any kind of potions, spells or purifications." She was quiet again, but Angela didn't speak, certain that there was more she had to say. And finally, Mama

Matisse added, "She did come to me at the shop once."

"She came to you?" Angela asked softly.

Mama Matisse seemed to be looking into the distance, and envisioning the time she spoke about. "She was bereft, the poor woman. She loved her son so much. Everyone knew that a piece of her died with that boy. So . . . so she came here one day. She was heartsick. She had been everywhere. She had been to her priest, but she was willing to try anything. She wanted me to intercede for her, to speak to a saint or a loa, and beg to know that her boy rested with the angels."

"And you spoke to her, and said something that disturbed her?" Angela asked.

Mama Matisse nodded without looking at her. She was seeing the past. "Regina sat before me, here in the office, and I told her that certainly, everyone knew, whatever they believed, that the goodly on earth rested in the Heaven of their choice. She was upset, and she said that if she just knew, she could be a wife again. She believed herself to be a very bad wife. I said that she was just a hurt wife, and she said that she was pushing her husband away, and she wasn't giving him comfort — he, too, had lost a son."

"She was suffering so badly," Angela murmured.

Mama Matisse seemed to be hesitating again. Angela fell silent, letting Whitney speak.

"Gran-Mama, please, if there is anything you can say that will help us, you must tell us what you know," Whitney said.

"I *know* nothing," Mama Matisse said. Once again, Angela held her breath, waiting.

This time, Whitney wasn't subtle or delicate. She sat back, laughing. "Gran-Mama, spit it out, please, will you? We won't repeat anything you say, if you don't want us to — not even to our colleagues. God knows, we're careful enough about what we do. Please, tell us what you *think,* or what you believe, or what your intuition told you."

Mama Matisse said, "Well, perhaps I am biased. I just didn't feel that the marriage was as wonderful as everyone said. You see, Senator Holloway came here to get her — with his trio of bulldogs. The chauffeur, that fellow named Grable, he was pleasant, looking at all our books and talking with Sandra. The bodyguard, he just stood with his arms over his chest. The third fellow, Martin Du-Pre, he was anxious. The senator was on a phone call, and Martin kept watching him, and me — this is when Regina Holloway and I came out of the office and back to the front. I think that DuPre thought that the senator was talking to someone he shouldn't have been talking to while waiting for his wife. And I think that DuPre is more suspicious or superstitious than he'd like to be. He seemed to be afraid that I had told Regina Holloway something that she shouldn't have known."

Angela frowned. "You think that Senator Holloway was having an affair?" she asked incredulously.

Mama Matisse shrugged then. "His wife is a lost soul, and he's a man in power. Perhaps not an affair. Perhaps he just saw another woman. Perhaps I am wrong. But I liked the senator less that day. He hung up, and came to his wife, and he was caring, but I think that he just wanted her out of the place. He wouldn't want people saying that his wife was trying to commune with the dead through a voodoo priestess. He came to her and held her, and he was dismissive. He barely glanced at me. He said, 'Pay the woman, Regina, and let's go, please.' You could see that he was contemptuous of the shop, and of voodoo."

Angela tried to reconcile everything she had heard about the senator with this new information. It was possible that a good man could do bad things. His wife had been beyond consolation, and he had been trying to hold to himself, to his career and a semblance of life.

He was human. No man was perfect; no politician could keep every promise, be it to his family or to his constituency.

She started to rise.

Mama Matisse stopped her. "May I have your hand, child?" she asked.

Angela settled in the chair again and reached across the table. She held Angela's hand for a long moment, hers so lean and brown, showing the signs of her age, Angela's like snow against it. Mama Matisse closed her eyes for a moment, and then opened them. "You are strong," she said, "and you are smart, but you've suffered tragic losses in your life, and they have left you open to many things. Good things, and bad things, if you don't learn to buffer your heart. You have great power within you because you have a great heart, and you see the suffering of others. Spirits guide us . . . they may be mischievous, and they have messages. You may listen to the messages, but you must never cross the line.

"The world is filled with ghosts, ghosts of times that have gone by, and the images in time and space of those events that were cataclysmic, tragic and even joyous. And spirits remain in the in-between world because they cannot or will not leave, because of what they know, or what they, in their wisdom, hope to prevent." She paused for a moment, looking at Angela. And Angela felt that the woman was reading everything in her soul. Mama Matisse *knew*. She knew that Angela *saw* things, or dreamed them, but even in dreams, saw them clearly as when they had happened. For a moment, Angela felt a chill. And then, it seemed that warmth and power came into her hand, the hand that Mama Matisse held, and began to travel all the way through her. "You must be strong, and you must also trust in others," Mama Matisse told her, "because no man — or woman — can take on the burdens and the tragedies of the past without the strength and vitality of life around them."

Mama Matisse released Angela's hand. She had finished; she had said all that she had to say. She arose, arrow straight and thin and with incredible dignity. "Now, if you ever need me, you come back. With or without Whitney, and bring any of your friends. Don't worry if you believe in voodoo or do not believe in voodoo. It is a religion, as many others. We all see our paths in different ways. A spirit may go by many names."

Angela and Whitney stood with her.

"Thank you, Mama Matisse," Angela said gravely. "I will come back."

Mama Matisse flashed her a quick smile. "I'm glad, and I believe you will. Now, Whitney, child, give your Gran-Mama a hug, and be on your way."

A few minutes later, they were out of the shop and on the street. "Well?" Whitney asked Angela. "Do you think that maybe he was having an affair — and that maybe Regina found out about it, and that was the last straw, and so she killed herself?"

"Whitney, we looked at the balcony, and we studied pictures of Regina's body *in situ,* and it would have been impossible for her to propel herself so far — backwards! No. She didn't commit suicide. It was murder," Angela said.

"But Jackson isn't pulling the police in to point that out yet," Whitney said.

Angela shrugged.

Whitney studied her for a moment. "You've seen something in that room," she said.

"Sadly, I'm not seeing anything that will help us — not yet," Angela told her.

"But you've seen something," Whitney said, her tone matter-of-fact. "Let's go and get in somewhere off the street. My friend owns a place just down a few blocks. Nice quiet courtyard at this time of day, and best pecan coffee you've ever tasted."

Whitney did know the little nooks of the city, certainly better than Angela did. In a matter of minutes, they were sipping really delicious coffee and dining on her friend's shrimp po'boys, definitely some of the best Angela had ever tasted.

"Gran-Mama was really impressed with you," Whitney told her. "And the way she held your hand . . . Gran-Mama can read people. She knows that you have what is called 'the sight.' "

"Well, not really," Angela began to protest.

But Whitney laughed. "Why would you deny something like that? Mine is so limited. That's why I became so fascinated with all the things you can find with film and sound equipment. Oh, I have a sense of things. To most people, I'd be impressive. But I have a feeling that your sixth sense is way superior to mine."

"Well, I'd never say that," Angela told her, shrugging and smiling. "We're brought up to deny the unusual, and we get to be very good at it."

"But don't you think it's obvious? Adam brought us together so that we would support one another. Adam sees ghosts, you know. Well, he sees one ghost. His son, Josh. He couldn't see his son for years, and then, finally, he did. And it's the greatest comfort in his life."

"He sees him?"

Whitney grinned. "Yes, which of course, is strange to people who don't know what he does — Adam didn't have a real gift. Josh did. Josh was killed in an accident, but he handed on something very special to the friend who was with him. She was the first person Adam worked with, I'm pretty sure. And that was several years ago now. Anyway, at first, Adam began really discreet investigations. He kept a very low profile. But people in power began to know about him, and he knew about people here and there and he called on them when he needed them. I guess he decided to try putting together an actual team, a unit to stick together, and go about on some of these unusual investigations."

Whitney spoke in a straightforward manner — as if Adam Harrison had been a contractor who had been doing piecemeal jobs, and then had decided to open his own company. Even working with police who knew a great deal about her, she was still certain that they looked at her as an anomaly fairly frequently. Even when she went through the academy, she was teased, some of the recruits tried to pick on her, but some friends also let the too-obnoxious know that she had suffered a loss, and she was tough and they might not win a fight with her.

She wasn't so sure about that; she was tough. She worked hard, and she maintained her strength with cardio equipment. But she didn't know how many of the really huge guys she'd ever take down through sheer brute strength.

"Well, this is an unusual situation," Angela said.

Whitney was relentless. "So, what are you seeing in the room?"

"It's not like a vision in a crystal."

Whitney waved a hand in the air. "I'm not expecting one. What are you seeing?"

Angela sighed. "Children — a little girl, Annabelle, and her older brother, Percy. They were among the first victims of Madden C. Newton."

"Your face turned green," Whitney told her.

"Green?"

"Yep, an ashen green. So — I imagine

you're seeing them dead?"

"Worse — I see them getting dead," Angela told her.

"Hmm," Whitney said thoughtfully.

"What's hmm?"

"The children aren't evil spirits, and they should be resting in some form of gentle afterlife. Of course, you're seeing a 'residual' haunting — something that must happen over and over again. If the children are active —"

"The children *are* active," Angela said.

"But —"

"Percy has stood over my bed."

"Now, that's interesting. I wonder if Regina Holloway saw the children," Whitney mused.

"Maybe."

"Maybe she was gifted. Or not. Maybe she was susceptible," Whitney said.

"To the suggestions of others?" Angela asked.

"That's always possible."

"But who would suggest she hurl herself off a balcony?"

"Someone human," Whitney said. "Or —"

"Or what?"

"The strongest ghost who ever existed."

Angela laughed suddenly. "Okay, so, we both agree that your great-grandmother is an exceptional woman, and she said that a banishing spell done correctly would allow for ghosts to move on. Which is it? Ghosts exist, but they don't believe in banishing spells, or they don't really exist, but someone suggested to Regina that there was a ghost in her bedroom, and so she saw the ghost of a little boy, and he was so strong he hurled her over the balcony?"

"That's what we're supposed to find out," Whitney leaned across the table. "So, how did you really find the skeleton in the basement?"

Angela looked back at her new friend and sighed at last. "I thought about the killer, and I thought about the victim, and I *imagined* a scene between the two of them. My skeleton would have been Newton's first victim — in New Orleans, at least — and he would have been testing his skills along with the logistics of committing murder. Easy. Have the man in the kitchen, get him ahead of him on the stairs and bash his head in with a prestashed spade or the like. Get him down — and finish the job. The sound couldn't possibly have carried, and since the basement is part of the foundation, he had plenty of dirt down there, and he could also hide the stench down there. Fill the place with some kind of herbs while the soft tissue rotted and then the skin mummified around the bones until it became earth to earth as well."

"The basement may give us more than any other room," Whitney said.

"Hey, by the way, did you pick up anything unusual on your cameras, or on tape?" Angela asked her.

Whitney smiled, just like the Cheshire cat. "Oh, yes," she said. "Will and I will show the film tonight. And roll our recordings. Oh, yes, we've begun."

CHAPTER NINE

The Church of Christ Arisen was an impressive building, mid-1800s, handsomely whitewashed and gleaming in the sun. It was on St. Charles, set back about forty feet from the road, and commanding half a block.

Jackson was driving Jake's car, and he pulled to the side of the road to stare at the building. Jake, at his side, was reading from the most recent file Jackson had acquired from Detective Andy Devereaux. "The main body of the church dates back to 1840 and was originally constructed by the Baptists," Jake said. He looked up from the paper and pointed. "Main building there, and the add-ons, either side, were built in the 1900s. The Baptist congregation moved into a new location, and in the 1970s, the place was a trendy nightclub. The nightclub was purchased by the Church of Christ Arisen in the mid-1990s. They've owned it since. The church has a bishop, currently Richard Gull, and he deals with all tenets, all legal matters and everything having to do with the church along with a council of five members, but their identities are known only to members of the church."

"Why?" Jackson asked him.

Jake looked at him. "Why? I don't know. I'm reading from a file!"

"Yeah, sorry. Go on."

"The bishop lives in the building to the left. The building to the right houses members of the church who are downtrodden or need a place to stay," Jake read. "Hey, and Detective Andy scratched in some notes on the side. Says here, 'Downtrodden seem to be female. Nothing to prove. No one talks.' "

Jackson had seen his share of cults, and they tended to have one strong central figure. Jim Jones. David Koresh. A host of others. Charismatic men who preyed upon the weak and needy, and promised them something far better than the struggles and misery they faced in their lives. They must have spent half their time laughing in their sleeves, since they brought women into the flock to have their choice of wives or lovers, and get away with multiple relationships in the name of God.

"Okay, so Richard Gull is over here — and his little harem is over there. And the main body of the church separates the two. Interesting." Jackson opened his door.

"Hey, hey, hey, what are you doing? I thought we were just going to ride by and see the place," Jake told him.

"I'm going to see it closer," Jackson said.

"No, wait. Stay here. I'll take a closer look. Come on, Jackson. You look like the wrath of God, come to take them all down. I'm just a young man in need of spiritual guidance."

Jackson weighed Jake's words; he was right. He was wearing a tailored shirt under his jacket, even if it was a casual leather jacket. Jake was wearing a sweatshirt emblazoned with the New Orleans Saints logo.

"Just get whatever information they give out and get back here," Jackson told him.

"Will do," Jake agreed.

He watched the traffic and then sauntered across the street to the brick path that led the way to the church. It was ironic; an old Jewish cemetery sat on the corner of the street, nearly blocked out by a large sign that advertised:

The Church of Christ Arisen — we are the way. Respect life, all life, respect your fellow man, and our God will show you the way. Bishop Richard Gull, Sunday sermon. If you would believe, you are welcome here.

The church door opened before Jake reached it. From his position in the car across the street and slightly down, Jackson saw Jake offer the young woman who opened the door one of his devilishly charming smiles. She looked uncertain for a moment, but she opened the door wider, and Jake walked on in.

A few minutes later, he left the church and returned. Jackson reached across the car to open the door for him. "I was about to sound the cavalry horn," he said.

Jake laughed. "I was gone ten minutes, total."

"And what did you discover?"

"I have some leaflets," he said, pulling printed material in sleek leaflet form from his jacket pocket, "and, drumroll, please . . ."

"Jake," Jackson said flatly.

"There were three young women in there, cleaning. It's modern inside, lots of hard, stern benches, an altar, a big cross hanging above it."

"That's the drumroll?" Jackson asked.

Jake laughed. "No, no. There was something interesting about the young girls who were doing the cleaning."

"*Oh?*"

"All three are pregnant."

"And how young?"

"I'm not certain about that. One might be fifteen or sixteen. I think I could guess the baby's daddy on the three. On the side of the altar, almost as big as the cross, is a portrait. In big letters on a brass plaque below, it has the name Richard Gull. He has a good face. Graying hair — and I can see how he might have an allure. He has something else."

"What?" Jackson asked him.

"Charles Manson eyes," Jake said. "The church is a cult massacre waiting to happen."

Jenna had found a stash of floor pillows in one of the closets, and she had arranged them before the screens in the ballroom. She had also taken the dust sheets off the furniture, and somehow, with the camera equipment, their jackets hung on the pegs on the rack just inside the front door, the cushions and the now-uncovered furniture, the house seemed comfortable.

Almost like being at home — someone's

home, anyway.

Coming back in with Whitney, Angela was glad to be greeted by Jenna and Will, who had been industriously moving about the house — and keeping an eye on the cameras and the equipment, and going through the digital film from the night before.

"This is super creepy," Jenna said with enthusiasm. "Lemonade, guys? Iced tea? I made popcorn. I'll just go get it."

"You made popcorn?" Angela asked her incredulously.

"Hey, it's kind of like sitting around at a friend's house to watch a DVD," Jenna defended herself.

"I think it's great," Angela assured her.

Will asked Angela about her trip to the voodoo shop, and Angela told him that she felt she'd learned a great deal. When Jenna returned with a tray filled with popcorn bowls, glasses and pitchers of iced tea and lemonade, Angela was telling Will that Mama Matisse was not madly in love with the senator.

"That's putting it mildly," Whitney said. "I think she considers him . . . not quite as honest and straightforward as he seems."

Will laughed. "That's just being a politician!"

"I don't know what to think anymore,"

Angela said. "When I spoke with Senator Holloway, I believed that he was truly bereft over the loss of his wife. It really seemed that he had loved her."

"My great-grandmother thinks that Holloway was guilty of something. Perhaps having an affair — or not an affair, but that he'd at least gone out and had a one-nighter somewhere," Whitney said.

"That would make him an adulterer, not necessarily a murderer," Jenna pointed out.

"That's true," Angela agreed. "But we can all figure that out when Jackson and Jake get back. Right now, we've got the popcorn, we've got the refreshments, let's see some movies!"

"All right, roll 'em!" Will said. He pointed to the screens. "Jenna and I went through them individually, but it's kind of cool to watch them all at once, because mostly, nothing is happening."

"Should I turn out the lights?" Whitney asked.

"It's daytime. You can't turn off daytime," Will told her.

"I can pull the drapes."

"Hey! Just roll it, please," Angela said.

The four of them folded themselves in various positions on the cushions, cool glasses of tea and lemonade in their hands, and the popcorn set on the floor before them.

Will explained that they were watching time elapse at a high speed.

He hit the control to slow it down at one point. Up in the left-hand screen, she saw Jackson come bursting out of his room and to her doorway. His dark hair was tousled; the light in the hall reflected off his deeply bronzed and well-muscled chest, and his expression bore a look of confusion and concern.

Will looked at her. "What happened?" he asked.

Angela felt that her few years of maturity on the others faded; she was blushing, she was certain.

"Hey, that's none of our business!" Jenna said.

"No, no, no! Nothing like that," Angela said.

"Like what?" Whitney asked, laughing.

"I had a nightmare, and I woke up screaming," Angela said.

"Yeah, when the sound is up, you can hear the scream," Will said sympathetically.

Angela glared at him, and then at Whitney and Jenna. "Well, then, you all know that Jackson came rushing to my defense."

"I wonder if he'd look quite like that if he

came rushing to my defense!" Whitney said lightly.

"The big chief looks really good shirtless," Jenna teased.

"Charming to watch the pretty people do weird things in the night!" Will said.

"Oh, Lord, please — children!" Angela said firmly.

"Did you change rooms?" Jenna asked, no longer teasing, but looking at her with concern.

She shook her head. She hesitated, but after her conversation with Whitney that morning, she was certain that they'd all had some kind of brush with the paranormal.

"No, I think that I need to be in that room. But the dream was horrendously grisly, and it did shake me up. We discovered that there's a door that connects the two rooms, so we opened it. It was the only way not to have Jackson take charge as head of the team and tell me it was too dangerous for me to be sleeping in there," Angela explained.

"Dangerous? Do you think that some manifestation in the room might be responsible for Regina's death?" Jenna asked.

"No. I really don't. What I — what I see is a pair of children, victims of Madden C. Newton," Angela said. She frowned suddenly. "And — and Newton himself. Newton attacking the children. Annabelle and Percy. The nightmare had Newton in it. It was horrible. The terror those poor children felt was just beyond imagination."

"And beyond the grave," Jenna said, still watching her, troubled.

Will was thoughtful. "Those murders happened. We know that they were real. And you have the ability to see them, but . . . from what I understand, the Holloways claimed they didn't believe in ghosts."

"There was an article in the paper — way back, when they first bought the place. Senator Holloway said it was a beautiful place and should be brought to life again," Whitney said.

"I'm guessing he didn't mean like this," Jenna said.

Will shrugged, drawing his knees to his chest. "Actually, Angela, you're *seeing* things because you have an extraordinary sixth sense. I'm not sure that it's not something that maybe everyone can tap into — we just don't know yet. I wonder what Regina saw. I mean, was there someone in there? Was she tricked into believing that someone was in there? Other than the fact that her neck was broken and her skull was crushed, Regina wasn't torn up. I mean, she didn't struggle with anyone. How did she wind up out on the balcony?"

"It might have been that someone was there that she trusted," Jenna suggested.

"And she might have had that *illusion,*" Will said. He reached behind Whitney's ear and produced a dollar bill. "Illusion can be everything."

"That was just a silly parlor trick," Whitney said.

"All illusions carried out by magicians are parlor tricks. That's the point — illusions can be very real," Will said.

"But an illusion didn't push Regina Holloway over the balcony," Angela said. "Still, I do believe that what we have in the mind can be just as powerful as something hard and tangible. Maybe we're looking for . . . I don't know. Illusion, ghosts — and a live person somehow pulling strings somewhere." The film had continued running as they talked. She gasped suddenly, and pointed at the bottom middle screen to images from the basement.

"What the hell is that?" she demanded.

"Oh, that's what we wanted you to see!" Will said, pleased.

They all stared at the screen. Will stopped and started the film, bringing the image back to the beginning of movement.

There was nothing. It might have been still footage. It was just a picture of the basement at the bottom of the stairs.

Then, subtly, it seemed that a shadow grew. Small, barely discernible, and then growing darker and larger.

It appeared as if some great, hulking beast in a cape might be there.

And then, the shadow dissipated. And they were just staring at the basement once again.

Angela's call came while they drove from the Church of Christ Arisen to the CBD.

"I've got a new spin for you," she told him.

"And what's that?" he asked her.

"I'm glad I went out. Mama Matisse was willing to spend the time talking to us. She is the first person I've met who isn't so fond of the senator. She believed that he was having an affair," Angela told him.

"Really? That is a new spin," he said, glancing over at Jake. "We have our first suggestion that Senator Holloway was involved with another woman," he said. "What made her think so? And is that why she doesn't like him?"

"I don't think so. She didn't think that he put enough hands-on work into it all when the city was in trouble. You know how some politicians hand-wash oil-laden birds when the cameras are rolling, and disappear right after? Well, that's what she thinks of him. I don't know — it seems to me that his grief for his wife is real."

"So, why does she expect an affair?" Jackson asked.

"Well, Regina had been to see her, and the senator had picked her up. And he was dismissive of the shop, of voodoo, of Mama Matisse, and he was on the phone with someone while waiting for her, and got off quickly when he saw her. Not much evidence, I agree. But an interesting angle. We have all believed that the senator was as pure as snow, a man to be pitied. He might just be an extremely fine actor, which does go hand in hand with politics," Angela said.

"Well, thanks. I'll keep that in mind," Jackson assured her. "We're on our way to his offices now. I'm hoping to have some conversations with his crew — while they're split up."

"Hey, by the way. There's something else you've got to see," Angela told him.

"And what's that?"

"A shadow."

"A shadow?"

"It's really strange. It's a shadow we caught on film in the basement."

"Does it — do anything?" Jackson asked.

"No, it appears, and it disappears. But it's really quite amazing."

"A ghost? Something's got to be down there to cast a shadow." Jackson knew that there was skepticism in his voice, and he never quite understood why he would mock anyone. He did believe in the possibilities; he'd also seen way too much done by shysters. It all came back to two basic concepts — energy didn't die, and the human spirit's need to believe there was something beyond the rigors and pains of life on earth. He'd seen too many organizations — such as the Church of Christ Arisen — that could take beautiful tenets and twist them into something that was mind controlling, greedy and cruel.

"I don't know," Angela answered slowly. "You'll just have to see it yourself," she said. "Good luck."

"Thanks. And you all be careful," he told her.

"Of course," she said. He heard her click off the connection and he slipped his phone back into his front shirt pocket.

"That's the building," Jake said, and Jackson, driving, nodded, and started looking for a parking space on the street. The building had a garage, but he preferred being on the street. Somewhere, not far, the sedan that was driven by Grable Haines had to be parked, awaiting the senator's whim.

He found parking and they both exited the car. "Well, boss?" Jake asked.

"Find the chauffeur," Jackson told him.

"Aye, aye, sir," Jake said. Hands in his pockets, whistling softly, he started off.

In the building, Jackson discovered that the senator's offices occupied a suite on the fifth floor; he went up the elevator. He thought the building was probably built around 1900; it wasn't ornate, nor was it ill-kept. It was an everyman's building if he had ever seen one.

He entered the suite door, and found himself in a vestibule. At a chair in front of a bank of computer screens on a plain wooden desk was Blake Conroy. He smiled as Jackson entered.

"Hey, there. So you've come to see the senator's New Orleans offices," he said. He'd been well aware, apparently, that Jackson had been on his way up.

"Yes, I thought I'd have a word with him here, get an idea of his situation when he was in town. I can see that no one could sneak up on him here, not with you on guard."

"No, sir," Blake said, pleased. His bald

head shone. He was dressed in his customary nondescript suit, but his tie was loosened.

"But you weren't here the day that Mrs. Holloway died," Jackson said.

Blake flushed. "The senator wasn't taking any appointments that day. We all thought that he was perfectly safe. He came in, and locked up. And Lisa Drummond was here, of course, and she could press an alarm button at any time. The senator is no slouch himself — he has a Glock in his office desk, and he knows how to use it."

"Interesting. But he still needs a bodyguard?"

"Yeah, out in public. He'd never want to be seen carrying a gun."

"No, I don't suppose that would be good for his public image," Jackson agreed.

Blake shrugged. "It is Louisiana, but . . . no, he doesn't want to be seen carrying a gun. And in public, with those crazies out there, you never really know what might happen."

"This is your usual position, though, huh?" Jackson asked him.

He nodded. "The senator wants to be a man of the people — but not a stupid man. And Lisa is a real secretary, you know? She's not a judo expert or anything of the like. So she wouldn't be much help if someone did try to get in to hurt the senator. Unless they're just going to lock up and work on paper — bills, committee work — I'm out here."

"How often are you off?" Jackson asked him.

"Not often," Blake told him. "Maybe a few days in a few months, that's all."

"But you happened to be off that day?"

"Yes, the senator had cleaned his slate so that he could work on a few speeches and read over some committee bills he and others were working on," Blake told him.

"So, shouldn't his aide have been with him?" Jackson asked.

"Naw, the senator needed time alone to think. Sometimes, having an entourage can get old, you know?"

"What about his secretary?" Jackson asked.

"You're about to meet her, aren't you?" Blake asked in return.

"Was she working with him then?" Jackson asked.

Blake frowned. He might have gotten punched one too many times as a fighter. He was truly puzzled.

"Hey, you'll have to ask about that. I'm not even sure. I didn't work at all that day

— I didn't see the senator until they called me. Just ask her — she keeps a regular schedule of everything. I mean, if she can't remember, she can just look at her schedule. Although, to be honest, I can't imagine anyone forgetting what they'd been doing that day. It was a horrible day," Blake said sadly.

"Thanks. And, hey, it's really great, you know. The way you all get along."

"We all?" Blake asked.

"You, Martin DuPre and Grable Haines."

Blake shrugged uncomfortably. He might not be the sharpest knife in the drawer, but he wasn't stupid.

"Yeah, we get along all right."

Jackson laughed. "That didn't sound convincing."

"We all really love the senator. Grable, he's a cool guy, but he's had his problems. He likes to gamble, and he's definitely a ladies' man. Girls just like him. All he has to do is grin. Maybe I am a little jealous, but, hey, he's fine. We have to kill time together sometimes, and it's cool."

"What about Martin DuPre?" Jackson asked him.

"Well, he's an aspiring politician himself, you know?" Blake said.

"You don't like him."

"I never said that."

"But you don't."

"I take my orders from the senator. I don't like Martin DuPre thinking he can snap his fingers at me. I tell him that. And I've told the senator that. Otherwise, well . . . I guess he's a little too Goody Two-shoes. He's with the senator, or he's at home on some online course about how to speak with proper diction, how to market, how to win the love of a crowd. He's a bit much for me, that's all."

"Different personalities," Jackson sympathized.

"Yeah. And you're going to dig into all our pasts, right? Because Senator Holloway is so torn up about Regina. If you haven't found it yet, you will, so I'll just give you the scoop on me. I did three years in juvenile for manslaughter. I killed a guy in a fight. It really wasn't my fault — other than I let the fight happen. Knocked him flat, and he came at me with a knife, and I didn't let him kill me. So, you can look into me all you want, and you won't find anything more. I paid for my sins, that's for sure. But I'm not worried about you or anybody else, because I found my peace."

"I'm glad to hear it. How?"

"I found God. I'm a born-again Christian, sir, and I let anyone know it."

"Well, Blake, it's a very good thing for a man to find his own peace. So, tell me, though, seeing as how you have found your own inner peace, how do you feel about the Church of Christ Arisen?"

Blake stared at him, shaking his head. "Those people are listening to demons, that's all I can tell you. Christ loves every man, and he comes to every man in a different way, and he doesn't hate those who are confused or haven't found their way. And Christ does not say that a man should sleep with children, and he sure doesn't say that a man should do injury to any other. Those people are just wacko, and they hate everyone. My God teaches love — theirs teaches something I don't begin to understand."

"You never had any trouble with Regina or David Holloway over religion, I take it?" Jackson asked him.

Blake grinned. "Regina and me, we loved to argue! She was a good Roman Catholic, and I used to tease her about getting guidance from mediums and tarot card readers. She told me her beliefs, and I told her mine, and we'd have a good time arguing now and then. David Holloway is a moderate himself, and he'd always just shake his head. The senator, he always said that debate was good for a man, as long as a man remembered that we were in the U.S. of A., where every man and woman was entitled to his own beliefs — as long as those beliefs did no harm to others."

"And you don't believe that the Church of Christ Arisen means no harm to others?" Jackson asked.

"They haven't been caught on anything yet, but if you call brainwashing children harm, well, then, I think they cause a lot of harm. You might want to look into them," Blake said. He cut himself off abruptly.

"Was there any trouble between them and the senator that we might not know about?" Jackson asked him.

He looked uncomfortable. "No. Nothing I know about."

"And the Aryans?"

"Assholes," Blake said gravely. "And I mean that in every Christian way possible."

Jackson grinned, but he didn't leave. "There is something that you're not telling me," he said. "Come on — no man can lead a perfect life."

"I think the senator tried," Blake said. "I think he tried. I really can't say anything else except that I heard him talking to Du-Pre one day, and it sounded . . . financial."

"DuPre needed money?" Jackson asked.

"I don't think it was for DuPre," Blake said.

"Are you talking blackmail?" Jackson asked.

"I'm not talking anything," Blake said firmly. "Anything I have is a vague notion, and could be entirely wrong. You got questions — ask the senator."

He indicated the door beyond the vestibule.

"Please, sir, go right on in. I don't think that I'll warn Lisa. I think you should meet Miss Drummond all on your own," Blake said.

Jackson arched a brow.

But Blake wasn't going to tell him anything more; if there was something going on between Senator Holloway and his secretary, Blake was going to flatly give him away. He did apparently love David Holloway. He might throw out a few hints, but . . .

"You said that you wanted to know all of us who were close to the Holloways," Blake said.

"That I did. Thank you."

Jackson opened the second door, and walked in.

There was a woman at a large desk, offering the usual: computer, medium-size screen, a picture frame, intercom and an appointment book by the side. The desk spoke of hard work.

The woman, Lisa Drummond, he assumed, wasn't what he had expected. She wasn't in her twenties, or even in her early thirties. She was attractive, but nearing forty, thin, with a short businesslike haircut to her light blond hair and an attractive, if not beautiful, face. From the pictures he had seen of Regina Holloway — in life, not once her skull had been shattered and her neck broken — she had been far more attractive than the secretary.

"Hello, what can I do for you?" she asked Jackson, smiling, but studying him carefully. Senator Holloway might have a bodyguard, but this woman was looking out for him as well.

"You're Lisa Drummond?" he asked her.

"Yes?"

He smiled, offering her his hand. "I'm Jackson Crow. I'm working on discovering the truth behind Mrs. Holloway's death."

"Oh, yes, of course! How do you do?" she said. She seemed pleased to meet him, and slightly nervous at the same time.

"Fine, thanks," he told her. "I was wondering if I could get a minute or two of the senator's time," he told her.

She frowned. "I thought he went out to

see you," she said.

"Yes, he did, and we were grateful."

"He just hates that house, you know."

"I can imagine," Jackson said. He waited politely. She kept staring at him.

"Do you think it's possible for me to see him again now?" Jackson asked.

"Oh, let me just ask," she said. She didn't use the intercom. She leaped to her feet. She was slim with the right combination of business and femininity in a two-piece suit and white blouse. She wore heels, and her legs were nicely formed. Of course, the idea that the senator might have had an affair was definitely making him take note, even though an affair didn't have to be with a man's secretary.

She disappeared into the office. Jackson heard the two of them talking. Lisa had an edge of fear to her voice. The senator's replies were low — so low Jackson only knew that he was replying because of her responses. He couldn't make out Lisa's words.

The door to the inner office opened. Lisa looked at him nervously, patting her short hair. "Come on in, Mr. Crow, please," she said.

Jackson walked on in.

"Jackson," the senator said, standing. He

offered his hand. "So, you've come to see my New Orleans offices."

"Yes, I just wanted to ask you a few more questions, if you don't mind," Jackson said.

"Of course, I don't mind. I've brought you here," the Senator said. "I pestered the right people to get Adam Harrison to find someone to do something about this situation. I'm here to serve you in any way. Please, have a seat."

Jackson sat across the desk from the senator. Lisa Drummond hovered nervously by the edge of his desk.

"Can we get you anything, Jackson? Coffee, iced tea? Something stronger?" the senator asked.

"No, I'm fine, thank you," Jackson said.

"Thank you, Lisa," Holloway said. His tone was gentle. His words were dismissive.

With no other choice, Lisa smiled and walked slowly out of the room.

"What can I help you with, Mr. Crow?"

"I understand that Regina went to see a voodoo priestess," Jackson said.

He saw the man's expression change, his easy composure vanish and his muscles harden. Holloway waved a hand in the air. "I can't possibly explain to you how deeply my wife felt the loss of our child. She was inconsolable."

240

"You didn't like the idea of her consulting outside religions?" Jackson asked.

"Religions? You mean *voodoo?*" Holloway asked.

"It is a religion."

Holloway sniffed. "Yes, and that heinous Church of Christ Arisen is supposedly a recognized religion, too. You know, you can register online and become a minister of something or other overnight. I believe in our great Constitution, friend, but, sometimes . . ." He paused. "I should be politically correct. But right now, here's the truth. I think that so-called voodoo might have finally warped Regina's mind. That's what I want to know. Ghosts, voodoo, belief in hokum. Belief that ghosts exist, maybe. She was a sensible, intelligent woman once. And now . . . well, that's why you're here. You tell me, where do we draw the line on our freedoms — and *insanity?*"

"In New Orleans, and in most of the United States, the real practitioners of any religion abide by the laws of the nation. Any religion, *established* religions, creates offshoot fanatics, Senator Holloway," Jackson said mildly. "And it was my impression that you believed that your wife had been murdered — that she hadn't committed suicide."

241

"Even if it was suicide," Holloway said, his head lowered, "I have to know. I just have to know the truth, that's all. Hell, if you tell me that the house is full of ghosts, I don't think I'll buy it, but I'll have nowhere else to go. Half the city believes that she was killed by ghosts. I just have to know."

"We're following every lead and every possibility, Senator Holloway. I have one other question for you, for the moment," Jackson said gravely.

"Yes, fire away," Holloway said.

"Were you being blackmailed by anyone?"

"Blackmailed?" Holloway repeated, staring at Jackson. "No!"

Jackson nodded. "Okay, then were you cheating on your wife?"

"I think it's ridiculous if we all go down there," Whitney said. They were watching the screen, and watching nothing at all. They were back to real time, and they might as well have been looking at still pictures.

"Why?" Will asked her. "There's safety in numbers."

"It was a shadow. Just a shadow," Jenna said.

"It actually takes a solid object to cast a shadow," Will pointed out.

"Right, so a shadow might have been a

ghost," Whitney said.

"I don't see a solid object that could have created the shadow so . . . yeah, why not? It could have been a ghost," Will agreed.

"I know what she's saying," Angela said, interrupting the argument at last.

"You do?" Will asked, surprised.

Angela grinned, nodding her head. "A lot of people are shy. If you were shy in life, and — if ghosts do indeed exist — might they not be shy in death, too? If we all bombard the place, nothing will happen. That's what Whitney is saying. One of us should go down, and someone else could linger in the kitchen, and someone else keep watch on the screens."

"Precisely," Whitney said. "And we should do it before Jackson comes back."

"Hey, he's on this team, head of this team!" Jenna said. "He's obviously sympathetic to what we're doing."

"Yes, but we know how he feels about people playing games, and pretending that they see things they really don't," Whitney said.

Angela glanced at her, bemused by the young woman's perception.

"And he's worried about our safety," Will said.

Angela uncurled her legs and rose. "I'm

going down. Will — you wait up in the kitchen, and that way, you're not even a few seconds away. Jenna, Whitney, you two man the screens. Or 'woman' the screens, you know what I mean."

"All right," Will said, rising. "I know about illusion, but trust me, that shadow on the screen was no trick, right, Whitney?"

"I swear we didn't alter the film. We didn't play with it. It wasn't a trick," Whitney said.

"Maybe our fearless leader is right," Jenna said nervously. "Maybe safety comes first."

"We're here to investigate. We have to investigate," Angela said.

"But . . ." Jenna said, still sounding unhappy, her voice trailing.

"But what?" Angela asked her.

"You found the body down there. Or the skeletal remains. You might be susceptible," Jenna reminded her.

"All the more reason I should go," Angela said. "Come on, Will, let's do this."

Will rose and walked with her through the hallway to the kitchen. He paused, waiting by the top of the stairs. She met his eyes.

"I'm here. I'm right here," he told her.

"A ghost isn't going to hurt me," she said gently.

She walked down the stairs to the basement level. The ground she had dug up —

with assistance from Jackson at the end —
remained disturbed. There were still pegs in
the ground with tape wound around them
to preserve the area in which they had been
digging.

She decided to sit cross-legged on the
floor near the location. She closed her eyes.

Her ghosts came to her in dreams; she was
learning that. Dreams that could come
when she let them, whether she was sleeping or awake.

She had to let go of reality, and remember
the past.

She sat still, just breathing, thinking about
some of the yoga mantras she knew.

This was not, however, she told herself
dryly, a state of Zen.

She opened her eyes, and she nearly froze.

A single, naked bulb allowed for light in
this area of the basement. It cast shadows
into the corners and over the relics of life
gone past, the everyday things that were
part of the humdrum — tools and mops and
sweepers, cleaners, more.

Shadows were creations of light. Light was
energy. Life was energy. Death somehow
changed energy.

She saw him at last. A man dressed in a
waistcoat, frock coat and stovepipe hat,
looking nervously at her from the shadows

cast beneath the stairs. He looked at her, as if he was afraid of her reaction to him.

Tentatively, he stepped out.

It's all right, she said silently. *It's all right.*

She didn't know if she was trying to assure him, or herself.

Her eyes were open, she realized. She was staring at him, really seeing him.

And then . . .

She realized that she was surrounded. Men and women in Victorian attire were all around her, looking down at her. And there were more people, she realized. A man who might have been in Edwardian attire. A youth in a T-shirt, a fellow with shaggy hair, who looked as if he might have just walked in from the street . . . except that he hadn't.

She was certain a woman touched her cheek.

These are his victims, she thought. *These are the victims of Madden C. Newton. He killed them all, some here, some elsewhere, but he buried them down here, and most had their bodies discovered, but some did not, and perhaps they have lingered, trying to help those who had not escaped the heinous man's hold in death.*

The light, the one bulb in the room, suddenly burned with a brilliant explosion. The entire room was suddenly aglow; dust motes danced like silver in the bursting-nova gold that seemed to glow.

"Angela! Angela! Angela!"

She heard the cry; for a moment, she didn't realize that it was coming from the great ballroom. Whitney and Jenna were shouting to her.

"Angela! Get the hell out of there!"

CHAPTER TEN

Senator David Holloway lowered his head and looked to the left.

That was usually a sign that someone was going to lie.

"No," he said, and the sound of his voice was a rasp. "I wasn't having an *affair.* I loved Regina."

Jackson sat still for a minute. He leaned forward then, keeping his voice low and evenly modulated. "Sir, a man can love his wife and find a time when he needs the solace of another woman."

Holloway looked up at him. Jackson noticed that he had a pencil in his hand and that the pencil was about to snap.

The senator stared at Jackson and spoke with a harsh voice of authority. "Mr. Crow, I did not have an *affair.* I was there for my wife every second that she needed me. My God! I lost my son, too, that day. But I understood. I understood a mother's love. I had my constituents. I had a world in which to immerse myself. My wife had always been that, an amazing and brilliant aid to a politician, and a wonderful mother to our son. She was lost but, I'm telling you — I was there for her. And I want you to find out what happened, and I guarantee you, it had nothing to do with me having an *affair!*"

"Thank you, Senator Holloway. I'm sorry. I apologize. I needed that from you. You asked for a thorough investigation, after all. Had she started to believe in ghosts? Did someone get into the house and kill her? Or did she kill herself because she could no longer bear the pain of her life?"

Holloway stood. The pencil snapped. "She didn't kill herself because of me! She didn't kill herself. She might have been . . . scared to death, and if so, it's because that damned house is tainted. Something is there. You need to find it."

Shakespeare rattled through Jackson's mind. *The lady doth protest too much, methinks — except that it was no lady speaking, it was Senator David Holloway.*

He kept emphasizing the word *affair.* Jackson was pretty sure that meant that he hadn't engaged in any sexual activity that had meant anything to him at all.

He wondered how Lisa Drummond would feel about the denial, if, in fact, she was the woman with whom he had had an affair.

Jackson stood. "Thank you for your time, Senator Holloway. Please understand, I wouldn't be asking you these questions unless we needed to find the tiniest detail, and when we talk, little things may come out."

"Of course. But if you think that I'd have harmed my wife in any way because of an affair with another woman — it's ludicrous."

"Probably. But, Senator Holloway, did it ever occur to you that someone else might have wanted to keep your wife from ever letting the world know it — if she had *believed* that you had engaged in an affair?" Jackson asked him. He didn't expect an answer. He just reached out and shook Holloway's hand. "Again, thank you for your time."

He headed out of the office, waving a cheerful goodbye to Lisa Drummond, who stared back at him, pasty white and unresponsive. He paused outside with Blake Conroy.

"Where would I find Martin DuPre?" he asked.

"Out, somewhere. He was running errands for the senator," Blake told him, grinning as he studied Jackson's face.

250

"Ah. So, would Grable Haines take him around town when he's out doing errands?" Jackson asked.

"Sometimes," Blake told him. "Not always."

"Very helpful. Thank you, Blake."

"No, I wasn't trying to be evasive," Blake protested.

"And I wasn't being sarcastic. Thank you. See you," Jackson said. He ignored the elevator and headed down the stairway. Faster than waiting, he thought.

Outside, he noticed a flyer taped to a street lamp. It drew his attention. Fight for Our America! the headline read. It went on, "We work against affirmative action, and for the people of this country. Join us tonight as we rally. Aryans for America."

He stepped closer to read the address.

"Hey, I'm over here, boss!"

Across the street, he saw Jake lounging against his car.

He walked over to him. "Well?"

"Well, driver boy is in a car just around the corner," Jake told him. "Want me to show you?"

"No, I'm assuming you already had a chat, and that you made it sound like you were both just gofers, waiting to do as you were told."

Jake grinned. "You bet. Couldn't think of a better angle."

"Did you get anything?"

"Actually, I did," Jake told him.

"And?"

"He's in trouble."

"How?"

"Gambling debts," Jake told him.

Jackson angled his head to the side, arching a brow. "And he just told you all about this?"

"We got to talking. The day Regina was killed, he was at the casino. He was sure that he was in the right poker game. He wasn't. He had thought that he could dig himself out. The senator was a good guy, he said, and would have loaned him the money he needed — but he wasn't going to get it."

"And why not?"

"Regina Holloway," Jake said. "Regina liked him fine. He swears that she really liked him. But she wanted him to grow up, work hard and pay his debts, instead of falling back on the senator."

"So, what's the situation now?" Jackson asked.

"He's fine. Holloway gave him the money, and he's supposed to work it off, hanging in extra hours, driving some other people around for the senator, that kind of thing."

"So, Senator Holloway paid the debt for him after his wife died?"

"Yeah. Grable said that he didn't even ask again. After Regina died, he just called him into the office, told him he'd pay the debt once and only once, and after that, God help him, because he wouldn't do so again."

"Good work," Jackson said.

Jake grinned. "It's all in knowing how to play it. Don't you agree?"

"More or less," Jackson said. "So, the kid had motive."

"Yep. What did you get?"

"Well, let's see — I think that the senator did sleep with another woman, and I think that the other woman was his secretary, Lisa Drummond. She's not a femme fatale of any kind, but she was there, that's what I'm thinking. And she cares about the senator."

"Hmm. A man with a secret, and it seems that it was actually a secret. But the senator is the one who brought us all in. Even if he was sleeping with another woman, he might have loved his wife."

"I agree."

"So where are we?"

"With a pack of motives. Turns out that our bodyguard, Blake Conroy, has a juvenile record — killed another kid in a fight. But he's a born-again Christian, and he admits to lots of religious debates with Regina Holloway. Oh, and let's see. He doesn't like Martin DuPre very much, but he thinks that the chauffeur is okay."

"And what's the story with DuPre?"

"Didn't talk to him. He wasn't there. Seems like he does a lot of running around. Errands, you know."

"Yes, he's got a busy life. That's one of the things that makes Grable Haines very unhappy. He gets to chauffeur Martin DuPre around town."

"But the chauffeur is here now, and DuPre isn't," Jackson said.

Jake shrugged. "I don't know where DuPre is now. Grable has got his paper. He's just sitting in the car. Tonight, he has to take DuPre around town. He said that he was taking some folks to a restaurant on Chartres tonight. One of the big new tourist places."

"What people?"

"Grable didn't say — I don't think he knows. He says that when he's out with DuPre, the man lords it over him. He says that Senator Holloway never acts that way — like they're all just servants. But Martin DuPre loves to play the big man, and that he wants to *be* Senator Holloway."

"Is it jealousy? Sour grapes?" Jackson asked.

"Could be. Could be that the guy is an ass, and that's why everyone dislikes him."

Jackson laughed. "Got it. I don't dislike you because you're male, female, black, pink, Christian, Jewish — I dislike you because you're a total jerk. Hmm. Then why does the senator keep the guy?"

"Maybe he's good at errands," Jake suggested.

"Any errands."

"Whatever those errands may be," Jake agreed.

Jake's phone rang. When he excused himself, flipped it open and answered, he frowned. He glanced quickly at Jackson, and tried to look away — a sure sign that the conversation had something to do with him. "It's all right . . . We're on our way. And I won't say that you called."

Jake turned. "There's been an incident at the house. Apparently, they got some ghosts in the basement on tape. They manifested for Angela."

Angela had felt it; against the brilliance of the light that had come into the room, there had been a ray of darkness. A ray of something that had nothing to do with light, and

255

everything to do with an aura of darkness and evil. The light had been something with an incredible strength; something that seemed more powerful than anything else. But the light had hurt the darkness, and that which had remained shadow and issued a silent scream of rage, trying to grow, to fight against the dazzling brilliance.

She had felt it just as she had heard the others screaming.

But nothing had happened. The door at the top of the short flight of stairs had burst open, and Will had come rushing down, screaming loudly. She had run to him, and together, they'd vacated the basement, running back up to the kitchen. There, daylight streamed through the windows and French doors to the courtyard. Whitney and Jenna had come rushing in, and they had all just stared at one another.

"What happened?" Jenna demanded.

Angela, surprised, looked at her. "What do you mean, what happened? You all screamed at me to get out."

"There was light — so much light. Something like moving shadows at first, and then a burst of light so hot the film almost seemed to burn, and then we could see you, and there was like a — a black thing coming right at you!" Whitney told her. "You were all alone down here — and there was a giant black shadow!"

"The light suddenly burned brilliantly — and then . . ." Angela paused. "Let's go see what you've got on film."

"Wait!" Will said, staring at Angela. "I've been here — I haven't seen anything yet, either. So, first, you tell us — what did you see?"

She was shaking inwardly; she had felt the malevolence, and she remembered coming home after dinner with Jackson, looking at the house, and thinking that, somehow, *evil* still managed to dwell within.

She had felt it again. Just then. Down in the basement. Evil had been the darkness against the light. Something that hadn't been able to bear the fact that —

"Oh, no, what did you two see?" Angela asked Jenna and Whitney. "What did you see that made you start screaming to tell me to get out of there?" she demanded.

The two women looked at each other before looking at her again.

"A . . . giant shadow, I guess," Jenna said. "And we were all up here. All of us. Except for you, and you weren't the one suddenly causing the light and shadow. Angela, we saw it!"

"Like there was someone there, and someone who cast some kind of massive — I don't know — it was like *black,* rising against all that light," Whitney said.

"Coming toward you," Jenna said gravely.

Angela looked at Will, frowning.

Will said, "Hey, when they screamed, I went flying down the stairs to get you."

"What did you see then?" she asked.

"You — all I did was reach for you," Will said.

"Okay," Angela said, looking at Whitney and Jenna again. "Coming toward me, and doing what?"

Once again, the two looked at each other.

"It was — bad," Jenna said.

"Bad?" Angela asked.

"I was afraid that . . . it was going to try to envelop you in some kind of darkness," Whitney said.

"At first, it seemed that everything was so beautiful!" Jenna spoke over her. "And then that darkness started rising against the light. I was just terrified for you. I didn't see burning red eyes or a horned devil or anything . . . just darkness. Malignant darkness."

"So, what did you see?" Will persisted.

Angela hesitated a minute. "All right, but then we see what's on the film. I'm going to tell you what I saw and felt, but . . . you repeat this to anyone — anyone! Including Jackson and Jake — I'll . . . well, I'll just call you all liars," Angela said. "I can easily say what I saw and felt around you because you — you all know that there are things that we can't really explain. But with Jackson in particular, I like to say what *was* — the facts — and that's it."

"Please!" Whitney begged. "We won't repeat what you don't want us to repeat, but please just tell us!"

"I saw . . . people. I think I saw the fellow who was killed here. The man who had owned the house, and sold it to Madden C. Newton — Nathaniel Petti. I believe that we dug Nathaniel's bones out of the ground the day I came. He was standing beneath the stairs, and he seemed — shy. Then . . . I felt as if there were others, and I saw a host of people. There were women in long, Victorian skirts. Men in waistcoats, vests . . . bleached-cotton shirts. They appeared to be milling around me, but they weren't frightening. They seemed kind and oddly grateful and resigned, and even hopeful, if that makes sense. Then the lightbulb flared. And then, at the exact time you started screaming . . ."

"What?" Whitney nearly shouted.

"I felt the same thing you did," Angela

said, and sighed softly. "I don't even know how to describe it. It was as if someone was absolutely *hateful.* I was afraid. I admit I was afraid. But then Will rushed down, and . . . nothing. Now, let's go and see the film."

The other three nodded gravely. They walked back into the ballroom and Whitney picked up one of the controls, running back the film to the point where Angela had come down into the basement.

She saw herself walking down the stairs. And then . . .

Nothing.

She was just standing there.

"I don't see —" she began.

"Wait for it," Whitney told her.

There was a subtle darkening in the room. It didn't become gray at first, but rather silver.

Then, coming, there was a brilliant flash of light; she could see the lightbulb, and it was evident that the illumination came from the bulb, but if so, it was part of the biggest power surge known to man.

Once again, the film had caught what seemed like dust motes, crystallized and beautiful, floating within the light.

And then . . .

Slowly, subtly, but then evident; a shadow

seemed to loom up from the ground, twisting into the brilliance of the light, just behind Angela. The shadow seemed to have tentacles or bony fingers that reached out . . .

Reaching toward her.

The front door burst open and a fresh breeze of cold air swept through the room. Then, they all screamed and spun around to see that Jackson and Jake had returned.

Will let out a hoarse laugh at himself while the others quickly rose. Jackson, sliding out of his jacket, stared at them all, not as if they had lost their minds, but with a tense expression of concern and displeasure on his strong, bronzed features.

"What's going on?" he demanded.

"We caught some kind of phenomena on camera. In the basement," Whitney explained quickly.

"And you didn't call me?" he queried.

Whitney flushed. "I called Jake. I didn't want to alarm anyone or make them rush through anything they were doing, but I thought someone should be aware of what was happening here," she said.

"You should have called me directly," Jackson told her.

Whitney looked away uncomfortably. "I

thought Jake might have been a bit more discreet. As I said, I didn't want you all dropping everything to run back."

"Let's see what you've got," Jackson said brusquely.

Will picked up the remote. They all stood, watching the film unfold again.

Angela looked at Jackson, trying to read his expression.

"Interesting," he said.

"Interesting?" Jake exploded.

Jackson looked at them all, one by one, as even and nonplussed as ever. "I'm afraid that a scientist would come in and say that the light was caused by a power surge and that the shadows might have been caused by any number of things. Something in the room falling or adjusting."

"Nothing fell," Angela said flatly.

"She was alone!" Whitney protested.

"And there was no breeze in the basement," Will said.

"It's an old house, on an old foundation, and the basement is foundation," Jackson said. "Old houses shift. Gravity and physics."

"So — so you don't believe we caught anything?" Whitney said incredulously.

Jackson smiled at last. "I never said that. I'm telling you what a scientific mind might do with that film."

"Then?" Will began.

"I'm saying that no one goes to the basement alone. I'm saying that there may be some kind of — some kind of something in this house. I think that Angela is our catalyst, and that we need to watch out for her." He stared at Angela. "And what did you see?"

She looked straight at him. "Light and darkness. Shadows moving. Maybe my mind was playing tricks. They seemed to take the form of people. Something happened, but in truth? I don't know exactly what."

"And you're all right?" he pursued.

"Absolutely fine," she assured him.

"So, what do you think?" Jenna asked him.

"I think that we may well find strange phenomena in this house," Angela said, looking at him earnestly. "There's history here. History leads to many things — like skeletons in the ground in the basement. As many times as this house has been redone, I wouldn't doubt that a psychotic killer like Madden C. Newton might have found a few other hiding places for his victims. There could be more skeletons to be found. Do unusual and unexplainable things happen? Yes. Did a ghost kill Regina Holloway? No. In my experience, spirits remain behind to help the living — not murder them. I think someone human had something to do with that. Does it all combine with the house? Perhaps. That's why we're here. We're investigating. Any other questions?"

They were all staring at him. It wasn't with malice. They were eagerly awaiting his answer to Angela's question.

"No," Jackson said. "No questions. We've barely brushed the surface here, but we have a great deal more to go on than we did when we got here. First, Senator Holloway, despite his squeaky-clean image and the fact that we believe he did love his wife, was most probably having an affair — one that was well covered up by his staff, if they were aware. A complete cover-up."

Angela stared back at him, surprised. It seemed he had almost forgotten what had gone on in the house, and what they had caught on film. His sudden turnabout was a little disconcerting.

"The affair was most probably with his secretary," Jackson continued. "We know that everyone pretty much hates Martin DuPre, and that Regina Holloway was standing between the chauffeur, Grable Haines, and a loan from the senator to pay his gambling debts — a loan that he has now received. And we know that the bodyguard, Blake Conroy, killed a man when he was young and has a sealed juvenile record. Oh, and it also looks as if the Church of Christ Arisen is one man's method of acquiring young women as sex slaves. Was that person really Martin DuPre — or was the senator using Martin DuPre to get to young women? One way or another, the people around the senator are involved in the organizations he supposedly hates, and we need to find out how and why — if the senator is aware, or if he isn't. Personally, I think the Church of Christ Arisen is a slimy cult created for a few men's benefit, but how it could fit into a murder at this house is something I'm not beginning to see yet, nor do I see the Aryans finding a way to sneak into the house — or for having a motive for murder, but we won't let them out of it yet, since those are the two main groups against the senator. There we stand. Putting it all together is what we're here to do. And along that line —" he turned and stared at Angela "— you and I are going to dinner," he said.

"Don't worry about the rest of us. We'll just eat sandwiches," Jenna said lightly. Jackson ignored her. He was still looking at Angela. He had been so matter-of-fact about the real and factual information he had acquired that day.

He hadn't denied them all, but neither had he seemed to take their findings as much that was important. They had something on film. They really had something on film, and she believed that even the most skeptical scientist of all time would have difficulty explaining it all away.

"Something did happen, Jackson," she said.

He just nodded.

He knew there was more, she thought. *He knew.*

He intended to interrogate her, she was certain.

"Dinner?" he asked politely.

"You're the boss," she reminded him.

"Good, we'll head out fifteen minutes, say? I want to take a run by the museum on Royal Street, too — and see if they have anything on the house. And you," he said, and turned at last to Jenna. "I think you might want to go out. You and Jake are just about as white as the newly driven snow. I noticed a billboard while we were out today. The Aryans are having a meeting in a rental hall over on Carondelet Street tonight. I think you two should attend."

"What? Not me?" Whitney teased.

"Apparently, he's not sending me, either," Will said.

"Oh, don't worry, your assignment will be *really* exciting," Jackson teased in return.

"Oh?" Will said, sounding dubious.

"You're going to go and watch the comings and goings at the Church of Christ Arisen."

"Isn't that almost like sending us to the Aryans meeting? Can't wait," Whitney asked.

Jackson grinned. "Almost, but not quite." He turned away, obviously intending to head upstairs to his bedroom. He started down the hall to take the middle staircase, but came back. "Keep the cameras running. And remember, no one in the basement alone. And, for that matter, no one in the house alone. All right? Everyone with me?"

They all nodded, and he started back down the hall, whistling.

When he was gone, Whitney said, "I don't care what living people might have been involved, there is something in this house."

Jenna spoke up suddenly. "I know what you saw, Angela. I've seen it before. I've seen it in the hospital. I've seen the light. Somehow, you released a lot of those people. They've moved on. That's what the light was. They've moved on to heaven or whatever one might call the phase we reach after we've died in this physical life." She

267

stopped, looking as if she was hesitant about saying more.

"I'd like a drink," Will said. "Anyone with me?"

They headed to the kitchen, Jake joining them. For a minute, they were all silent, except for Will, who was delving into the refrigerator and sorting out who wanted what. Angela was going to ask for iced tea, but she was uneasy about what had happened, and uneasy about going to dinner with Jackson. She opted for a beer, as did the others. She tried to sip it, and drained half the bottle in a single swallow.

Jake was looking at her sympathetically. "Don't look like that — kid," he teased. "He's really not out to put you through the nth degree."

"Huh?" she looked at him.

"He's following Martin DuPre," Jake explained. "DuPre's got some fancy dinner tonight."

"Oh. Well, that's good," she said.

The five of them wound up gathering around the table; it was a nice moment — a strange moment of bonding. "Jenna, go on," Angela said.

She took a long swallow of her beer. "I had a patient one time, a really nice old man named Jeter Miller. He had cancer, and he was dying, but one day, he went into cardiac arrest. The doctors worked on him, but he died. I had been his nurse. He'd been such a nice old fellow and he might have had six months, maybe a year, to go — I was sorry. Well, I wound up in the hospital morgue with some paperwork the night of the day when he had died, and I happened to be alone in the fridge — that's what we called the body storage — when he gripped my hand. I can tell you, I was so terrified that my scream came out as a squeak." She paused, taking a deep breath.

"He wasn't really dead?" Will asked.

"Oh, no. He was dead. And don't stare at me like that. I don't share this story often," Jenna said.

"I'm sorry," Will said. "I didn't mean to stare at you in any way that wasn't full of trust and sympathy, believe me."

"What then?" Angela prompted her.

"He just wanted to talk to me. He said that his business partner had messed with his IV, bringing on the heart attack. The man had killed him to keep Jeter from telling his son — from whom he'd been estranged until recently — about the will that left his half of the business to him. To make a long story short, there wouldn't have been an autopsy because he was a stage-4 cancer patient and he had died in the hospital. I started making a squawk about the situation, there was an autopsy, and it was proven that the partner had poisoned the IV. I went back down to the morgue, thinking that I'd been crazy the first time, but that I was going to tell the corpse that everything was okay, and he thanked me with tears in his eyes, and told me that he'd just been waiting to thank me, and then . . . well, I saw light. I saw light the way that we saw it today. So, Angela, maybe by freeing Mr. Petti when you found his skeleton beneath the floor, you let them all go where they needed to be."

"Thank you," Angela said. She reached across the table and squeezed Jenna's hand.

Jenna took another very long swallow of beer. "And now, you all think I'm crazy."

"None of us, honey!" Whitney said, lifting her beer. "To us," she said softly. "The ghost-files team. The Krewe of Hunters. Or, whatever they want to call us."

"The Krewe of Hunters? I like it," Will grinned, lifting his beer bottle as well. "Indeed, to us. And a sworn promise. None of us will ever think the others are crazy, and we won't be afraid that the others think we're crazy. We all know that we're delightfully different, and that's that!"

They clinked bottles.

"What do we think about Jackson?" Jake asked. "What do we think he thinks?"

"He thinks he's boss," Angela said.

"He *is* the boss," Jake punctuated his remark with a chug.

"Technically, Adam Harrison is the boss," Angela corrected.

"Whatever, he's in charge of the team," Jake said.

"He's a good guy," Will said. "And we shouldn't be lying or hiding things from him. He isn't saying that it can't be — he's just saying, *prove it.*"

Angela stood up. "I'm going to get ready for dinner," she said. "Have fun storming the castle, everyone."

She turned and started out of the room. Whitney tossed a cardboard coaster at her. "If it's a really fancy place, bring us all doggie bags!"

Angela turned back to her, laughing. "Okay, maybe I came out ahead tonight. Maybe not . . . Time will tell," she said.

She left them sitting in the kitchen, grateful for the friendships she seemed to be forging with them.

Up in her room, she paused. The door that separated her room from Jackson's was not closed tight, but it was closed. He evidently wanted his privacy.

Prime time, Angela thought.

Yes.

Dusk descending again, and it was that time that Regina had died, and a time when it seemed that the past liked to replay, almost like a play, but sometimes, the characters changed the lines. She had to be crazy, she decided. She had been terrified in the basement that afternoon — it had just been for split seconds really. Then Will had come down, and the world had begun spinning back to normal again.

What would have happened if she hadn't left the basement?

She didn't know. She hadn't been afraid of the manifestation she had seen that had appeared as the strange light in the film. Not at all. But she had felt that there had been something behind her. Something evil. Something ready to pounce on her.

Ghosts didn't pounce. They didn't have much physical power. Ghosts did exist in this house. Maybe Jackson knew it, and maybe he was right that a real, living, flesh-and-blood human with strength had to be involved as well.

She sat on the bed, half closing her eyes. "Annabelle? Percy?" she called softly.

For a moment, there was nothing.

Then, in her mind's eye or in real life, the little boy appeared. A moment later, she saw his sister peeping out from behind him.

They weren't real. They weren't solid. She could see the wall behind them.

But they were there.

"Please, miss, he's a very bad man," Percy said to her.

"You mean Mr. Newton? Madden C. Newton. He was terribly cruel to you," Angela said.

Percy winced. He lowered his head, and then nodded. Then he looked up at her again. *"But they keep coming. They come to this house, and something happens, because he gets into their minds, I think."*

"He's a very bad man," Annabelle said, still clinging to her brother.

"He was a bad man," Angela said. "But you were very good children. There is a better place for you, where you can find your parents."

"No," Percy said, looking at her gravely. *"I have to stay. I tried to help the lady. But she didn't see me, and she saw what they wanted her to see. She couldn't hear me, but the bad man made pictures with the light, and she saw what he wanted her to see."*

"Percy, I don't understand. What bad man?"

"He knows the house. He has come to the house. He came when the nice lady lived here. I wanted to help her. I tried to help her. She couldn't see me. She saw what he wanted her to see," Percy said.

"Angela!" There was a tap on the dividing door. It opened, and Jackson was standing there, impossibly tall and lean and solid and *alive.*

She looked at Percy and Annabelle, who faded away.

She turned back to Jackson, worried that he would have heard her conversation and become certain that she talked to herself.

But Jackson's keen, dark blue eyes were riveted on the spot where the children had been standing.

He had seen them, she thought. *He had seen the children!*

But he looked at her then and said casually, "Ready to go?"

"I just need a minute to change my clothes," she said, and closed the door between them.

CHAPTER ELEVEN

Angela walked along beside Jackson in silence, wondering just how they appeared to others, she so blond, and he so dark.

It was a beautiful season to walk in the city of New Orleans. A night with a soft breeze and enough warmth to make that breeze like the soft, comfortable touch of a warm and gentle hand.

But one of her favorite things about the city was the variety of people and colors to be found there, nationalities and backgrounds all mixed up to produce the most interesting and handsome human beings.

She didn't ask Jackson if he had seen the children in the room. If and when he wanted to say something to her, he would.

He seemed distracted as they walked, and still, he looked at her now and then, as if he remembered she had been in a dangerous position, and the fact didn't please him.

"Jackson?" she asked.

"Huh?"

"You've had strange experiences. I know you have. Anyone that Adam brought into this has had some kind of — strange experience."

He looked down at her. She thought that he would instantly deny her. But he didn't. "Dreams," he said. "But dreams may simply be projections of our minds, utilizing what we know and making sense out of it."

"All right. So . . . ?"

"All right — I'll tell you this." He looked pained for a minute. "I thought I saw one of my coworkers, Sally. She came to me in a dream and told me where the murderer was holed up. I made it there in time to save two lives, but found . . . well, that Sally had died. It shook me up pretty badly, but I know how Adam Harrison knew about it. He likely wondered how I'd gotten there, either through a brilliant burst of insight, or something that was paranormal. And I don't know which myself at times, really."

"You're still a skeptic."

He hesitated. "I believe in God, or a supreme being, and I believe our role in life is to live with kindness to others, and I believe monsters should be brought down. Maybe I do believe in something beyond, but I've also seen enough fakers, quacks, and criminals to remain a skeptic. Okay?"

She lowered her head and smiled. It was actually quite a lot from him.

"It was lovely of you to think of adding a trip to the museum on to dinner like this," she said, her tone light.

"I'm glad you think so."

They walked down Royal Street toward Canal until they reached the museum. Jackson swore softly. The museum would be closing in fifteen minutes, per a sign on the door.

"We can come back," Angela said.

"Well, let's see what we can see in fifteen minutes. At least, I'll get an idea of what we might be looking for when someone can get back here. There's a library of archives here somewhere that might give us something."

A pleasant woman in her mid-sixties with elegant silver hair and a sweet manner refused to take Jackson's money for entrance. "You haven't time to see much," she said. She brightened. "But, hopefully we'll whet your appetite. Oh, and the new exhibit is opening tomorrow, so I know you'll want to come back."

"It doesn't open until tomorrow?" Jackson asked her.

The woman pointed to curtains in the back. "No, I'm sorry, we still have it all under wraps."

He nodded. "Of course."

"We have a lot on Madden C. Newton, the murderer," she said. "And that house." The woman shivered dramatically. "It's downright scary. Creepy. And, in the news again!"

"So there is a lot on the house?" Jackson asked.

"And Madden C. Newton. We have his death warrant in the display."

"But we can't peek tonight?" Jackson asked, giving her a charming smile.

"I'm so sorry — they're still finishing up, and they'll be doing so tonight. But if you take a quick walk-through of the rest of the museum, you'll see that we've arranged a chronological history of the city. The new exhibit will focus more on the past scandal, murderers and mayhem."

Jackson thanked her. There was only time to get the layout of the place, really. Angela appreciated all that she saw — the stories were told with various tableaux featuring historical characters, while there was reading material on the walls between each episode of history.

Angela tried to pull back; she wanted to at least take a look at all of the tableaux. She felt as if she sped through history —

nearly three hundred years in three hundred seconds.

And while she was there, she had a feeling that she would find something important in the museum. That she would find something that would give her a clue in the mystery of the house.

Jackson dragged her back to where heavy canvas draperies enclosed a large section of the back. A banner over the drapery announced, "It's here! Meet the real monsters who called the city their home throughout history, and learn how history dealt with real monsters."

"Tomorrow," Jackson said glumly.

"Hey, we're on a mission tonight, remember?" Angela said.

An announcement over the loudspeaker reminded guests the museum was closing.

"Hey, I really love it. I'll come back here."

Jackson ignored her for a moment, looked around, and stepped up to the heavy drapery. He pulled it back to take a peek inside.

There were display cases at odd angles and a worker in a lab coat was still busy washing the floor. He looked up at them.

"Museum is closed."

"Sorry," Jackson said. He nodded and gave up. "All right, Angela, I guess we are on to the next part of our mission tonight.

Let's go — it is getting late. Are you hungry?"

"Definitely. And when work combines with a good restaurant, it's better than work combining with —"

"Bones in a basement?" he interrupted.

"Sure. So, we're . . . trying to see what Martin DuPre might be up to?"

He glanced down at her. "Neither Blake nor Grable like the man — while they don't seem to have a problem with one another."

She was silent for a minute, and then said, "I'm just not sure what we're actually supposed to interpret. The senator apparently had an affair with his secretary. Maybe he's still seeing her — now that his wife is dead. However, he is definitely grieving his wife — no man could be that good an actor, not even a politician. The Aryans and the people belonging to the Church of Christ Arisen are apparently really, really messed up, but it's not against the law to be messed up. No one likes Martin DuPre, even if they pretend to around the senator. So, where do you think that leaves us?" she asked.

"Closer than we were yesterday," he said.

They neared the restaurant. To Angela's surprise, he suddenly steered her around the block in another direction.

"Okay, what are we doing now?" she asked.

"Avoiding Grable Haines — he's hanging out by the senator's sedan just down from the entrance. We're going to go around the block."

They reached the restaurant, coming in from the far side of the car.

"Slip in, quick!" Jackson said. "I can see DuPre. They must have stopped for a drink or something, because they're just coming now, from where they parked."

"What?" Yet she quickly stepped inside.

The restaurant was situated in a building well over a century and a half old despite its modern decor. The place was jumping, an obvious indication that the food was very good — or that it had somehow become the trendy place to be. She waited in a group while Jackson spoke with the pretty girl at the front podium.

While they waited for a hostess to bring them to their table — on the far side of an elevator shaft that brought diners to an upper level — Martin DuPre arrived with three other men. At first, they didn't see Jackson and Angela, and they were close enough in the milling group that awaited tables for Jackson and Angela to hear their conversation.

281

"Why, DuPre!" a squat and rotund man said to Martin DuPre, "this does seem to be the happening place for an evening meal. I hope you have the rest of the evening planned out as well."

"Of course!" DuPre said. "Gentlemen, this is my city. I know my way around. When we've finished eating, we're headed to Bourbon Street. And I've made reservations there, too, just to make sure that you are entertained this evening."

"Sounds good to me," a taller man said. "So, you know the best on Bourbon Street? Isn't that strip clubs for college kids and the like?"

"Not if you know where to go," DuPre told him.

"I'm game for anything," said the last of DuPre's trio of guests. "All business, you know, and a man gets a little crazy. With a new baby in the house, I don't get out that much anymore. Nothing like a good business meeting — on Bourbon Street."

The conversation made Angela acutely uncomfortable — a group of middle-aged lechers.

"Sad, huh?" Jackson whispered to her.

"I guess . . . I guess some people have to pay. Or want to pay. Anyway, yuck. So much for a really nice dinner," Angela said lightly.

"But they'll notice us soon enough. Won't that make DuPre get as far from us as possible?"

He brought his fingers to his lips and whispered, "Shh."

She moved closer to him. She meant to just whisper right away, but she found herself hesitating for a beat. His tailored shirt was crisp and clean. He smelled of shampoo and woodsy soap or aftershave, delicious. She found herself fascinated again by the bronze tone and texture of his skin, the sleek darkness of his hair and the brilliance in the back of his dark blue eyes.

"What did you do? Pay the hostess to get the table next to his?" Angela whispered to Jackson.

He grinned and whispered back, "Not the table next to theirs. I want to be behind, out of sight."

"And how will you manage that?" she asked.

"You'll see," he told her.

He had definitely done something right. DuPre and his party were seated first; they wound up at a table around the elevator shaft from DuPre and the other three men, out of sight, and yet, in a position where it seemed that anything said at DuPre's table was amplified.

Angela leaned toward Jackson. "Can they hear us so loudly, too?"

"I'll have to bump into him over there to find out," he said.

He opened his menu. Angela heard the men talking about oil interests. There was something that had to do with an inspection, and DuPre assured the men that he would see that everything was fine. She picked up her own menu, listening. The squat fellow had a booming voice. He could be overheard the best.

"Well, I'm glad that Holloway has sent you out with us tonight, DuPre. David is a good fellow, but he's been in the midst of too much tragedy lately. Not that I don't sympathize with him, but . . . the man has forgotten what a good time could be," he said.

Angela was pretty sure that it was the tall thin fellow who spoke next, his voice lower. "Hey, I understand the man. He's a politician, so when Regina was alive, he felt right in doing whatever he needed to do to get people moving in his direction. But now she's gone. He needs his time of mourning. Then he'll be all right again."

"He scares me," DuPre said, speaking low, and yet the near whisper carrying. "He's brought in a team to investigate the house, he's so convinced that Regina didn't kill herself. Supposedly, they're from the government. I think they're just a bunch of charlatans, ghost hunters. I think he wants them to prove that there's some kind of presence in the house that killed his wife. Or maybe he's just trying to appease the constituency."

"Well, now," the taller man boomed. "That's understandable, too. He can't take the guilt that something he might have done caused her to take the header, you know? Frankly, I think Regina was a little off from the get-go. Might have been the death of their boy. That can do it to you. But I heard she had some kind of voodoo priestess in there — and a Catholic priest," he said.

"Maybe the voodoo worked too well," the squat fellow said, laughing at what he thought was his own great joke.

Their waitress appeared, smiling, and suggested the grouper almondine. They both agreed on the fish. Angela found herself noting that Jackson did have a knack for following and listening to people without being in the least obvious. He was pleasant with their server, not hurrying her along, but speaking easily in a manner to get their order in quickly — and the waitress on her way.

Angela leaned toward him. "So, despite his public image, you think that Holloway used to take guys like these out to a place *he* knew on Bourbon Street?"

"Doesn't mean he got in on the action," Jackson said softly.

She nodded.

He caught her fingers across the table. "Let's face it — being a politician usually means making a few compromises. I've seen it with the best of men — and women. That's why it's way more fun to be an investigator."

She liked the feel of his fingers touching hers. They somehow seemed incredibly intimate in the crowded restaurant.

But he eased back. They were listening.

Angela didn't really understand much of the conversation. It continued along the lines of oil, oil equipment, and the inspections that were needed for a rig. They were seeking some kind of permit, and it would need an inspection, and Martin DuPre was assuring them that they would pass their inspection and get the permit they wanted.

She watched Jackson as he listened. And then, they might have heard the key words in what Jackson seemed to be searching for that night.

It was the squat fellow with the booming

voice who spoke. They could hear him slap DuPre on the shoulder. "I say there, young fellow. When your boss gets tired of all the kissing baby butts and stuff that goes on, you're going to take his place just fine! You know how to get things done."

She looked over at Jackson. He returned her look with a grim smile, and lifted his wineglass to her. She returned it, set her glass down and leaned closer to him. "So, he's a butt-kissing, lying-ass, deceptive little goon. But does that make him a murderer?"

Jackson leaned closer to her.

"No, it makes him a butt-kissing, lying-ass, deceptive little goon. But it's good to get a true picture of those around the senator, and have a feel for what they would and wouldn't do."

"Sounds like the little rat would do about anything."

"Precisely," Jackson said.

Martin DuPre said, "Gentlemen, shall we move on?"

Angela whispered again, "Are we going to Bourbon Street?"

He grinned. "Are you game?"

"We're going to a strip club?"

"Let's see."

He motioned to their waitress and quickly paid the tab. They waited until they saw the men exit, and then they followed behind.

"Thank God for the foulmouthed fat man," Jackson said. "We can follow them easily."

"Cruel!" she said.

Jackson shrugged. "His weight is fine. His attitude is enough to make your skin crawl."

She didn't reply. She thought that she was coming to like him so very much because his words were true — and simply him. Nothing mattered to him about a person other than what was inside them. He had no patience for the manner of big-money oilmen Martin DuPre was entertaining.

She wrinkled her nose. "Oil."

He glanced down at her, grinning. "Ah, well, it's apparent, my dear, that you're not from this area. Oil is half the livelihood. And there are good men working in it — good men who aren't graft-laden and trying to go the wrong way. We need solutions in the future, yes. But oil money isn't necessarily evil."

"Did I sound like that? I guess I did. I don't know enough," she admitted.

"We'll all have to find solutions in the future, but it's careless overseeing and major problems in regulation that cause the problems — as with everything." He stopped, distracted, staring ahead of him.

"What?" she asked.

"There's someone else following Martin DuPre."

"Who?"

He pointed to a young woman who was about half a block ahead of them and half a block behind DuPre and his crew. She was young — maybe eighteen or nineteen — and had a small pudge, apparent because she was otherwise slim with long blond hair and a delicate face. She had paused for a moment to look in a window as DuPre and the men stopped at a corner for a car to go by; when they moved, she moved.

Jackson whistled softly.

"Do you know who she is?"

"I do — and I don't."

"What?"

"She's a member of the Church of Christ Arisen. She opened the door for Jake to go in and pay them a visit today."

Jake was glad to see that the meeting to recruit new Aryans was not going to be a huge success.

There were not quite fifty people in attendance. He stood by Jenna, responding with applause and enthusiasm to all the speeches given about maintaining the country for the "rightful" owners, and keeping a pure race.

He thought that Jenna was going to explode. Her fair skin was darkening to blood-red hue, and she held his arm, her nails digging into his flesh.

"Have you ever heard anything so insane?" she whispered to him. "The rightful owners! Is he forgetting the Native Americans — those people the *white* settlers basically stole all the land from? My God, I don't think I can sit through this. What is the matter with them? Don't they know that the days of slavery are long gone, and that we have laws guaranteeing equality?"

She was growing louder. He pinched her.

"Ouch!"

"You're going to get us thrown out!"

"I think I want to be thrown out."

"We're here to observe."

She tightened her lips and held silent. He smiled, feeling her beside him. Another outburst couldn't be too far behind.

And once again, it wasn't. "Oh, please! How can they do this here? New Orleans has come a long, long way and it's the most amazing city in the world for people from everywhere, of every color and sex and even sexual orientation, and there's still French spoken, and Spanish, and —"

"Shut up, please!" Jake pleaded.

She fell silent again. He was glad that the people who had come out were excited about the speakers — who were actually good at spouting rhetoric — because they didn't seem to notice Jenna's outrage. A young fellow was up at the microphone then saying that the world was what it was — a mess — and that there were all kinds of people in the world, and everyone had a right to be in the world, and they, too, had the right to seek the pureness of the Aryan race. They asked nothing of anyone else, they sought to hurt no one — they wanted their right to assemble and seek the life — the pursuit of happiness they had in mind for themselves.

To that end, they had to be very selective in voting for their representatives.

He began to preach a rabidly conservative doctrine — one that would leave even a staunch Bible Belt Republican squirming in horror, much less a moderate of any party.

Jake turned around to take a look at the others in the room, and he nearly jerked Jenna's arm.

"What?" she gasped, but she followed his gaze.

There, seated in the far back of the room, was the bodyguard. Blake Conroy.

■ ■ ■ ■

The pretty little pregnant girl followed Martin DuPre and his group.

Jackson and Angela followed the pretty little pregnant girl.

They made the turn off Chartres to head up to Bourbon, all keeping their respective distance. At Bourbon, the blonde girl paused. She seemed infinitely sad.

"Go talk to her," Jackson told Angela.

"Talk to her? What do I say?" Angela asked him.

"See if she's lost, or if she needs help. I'm going at DuPre and his group. I'll wait for you in front of the cowboy bar with the mechanical bull."

"You think that DuPre and his friends are going to go ride the bull?" Angela asked.

"No, it's next to a club that's behind a courtyard there, and supposedly offers the best and most expensive *dancers* in the city."

"Oh."

He gave her a little shove. Angela glared at him, and went over to the girl. Bourbon was already growing busy and loud. Rock ballads streamed out into the street from a variety of clubs, all trying to be louder than the next. Hawkers were handing out flyers, urging patrons to come in and enjoy their entertainment and their most incredible cheap drinks.

The girl stood near a hot-dog cart, staring after the group that had joined in the throng walking in the street, blocked off for pedestrians only.

"Excuse me," Angela said. "You look lost. Can I help you? Are you looking for a certain place?"

The girl stared blankly at her for a moment. Then she flushed. "I — no, I'm not lost. I live in the city."

"Oh, well, I'm sorry. I didn't mean to pester you. It just looks as if you're a bit tired and disconcerted, and . . . pregnant," Angela said.

The girl's flush became brighter.

Angela offered her a hand. "I'm Angela Hawkins. Are you sure you don't need any help?"

The girl shook her head. "No, no, I just have to head back uptown. I shouldn't have been down here."

"Can I get you a ride? Get you into a taxi? Where do you need to go?"

The girl looked down Bourbon Street, and then suddenly sagged against Angela. "I guess I don't feel very well."

Angela looked down the street. There was

a restaurant on the corner one block down, on Royal. It had a bar, but it was a far quieter place, more for dining than drinking.

"Let's get you some water."

She led the girl, who leaned on her heavily, to the restaurant. The seating was open, and she led the girl to a secluded table near the rear. She ordered water from the waiter, and suggested the girl might like soup or gumbo or something with substance.

"Oh, no, I couldn't —" the girl said.

"Please," Angela insisted.

In a few minutes, the waiter had them supplied with water, and the girl had a salad and soup coming.

She stared at Angela then with huge brown eyes. "Thank you!" she said. And she flushed. "I'm Gabby Taylor."

"How do you do?" Angela said pleasantly. "I guess you don't come to this area often," she added.

The girl shook her head. "Well, I did. Once. But that was before . . ."

"Before?"

"I'm a member of a church," she said primly.

"Oh. I see. No drinking?"

"Or dancing. We . . . we try to serve, you see."

"Serve who?"

She was shocked. "Why — God, of course!"

"How are you serving him?" Angela asked.

"Well, by . . . not drinking or dancing and serving —" The girl shifted in her seat.

"Serving who?"

Gabby looked down at her folded hands.

"Are your parents here, in the city?" Angela asked.

"I don't see them anymore," she said.

"Why not? They must be thrilled about the baby."

Gabby winced, fixing her gaze on her hands once again. "They don't know about the baby."

"Most grandparents would love news of a baby. Did — did they throw you out of the house, or . . . or what?"

"No, no — I belong to the church," she blurted.

"And the church doesn't want you to see your parents? Oh, Gabby! That doesn't sound very good."

Gabby looked at Angela and there were suddenly huge tears in her eyes. "I believed . . . I believed that they were right. I believed in . . . serving."

"Serving how?" Angela couldn't quite prevent the sharpness that came into the question. "Every church, temple and so on that I've ever heard about preaches love — love between parents and children as well as God!"

Suddenly, the tears began to drip down Gabby's cheeks. "I thought . . . I don't know, it all seemed to be all right, but I can't just give . . . we were all supposed to love one another, but it doesn't feel right. Tonight, I had to see . . . I had to see what he was doing."

"He? The baby's father? Is he the head of the church?"

Gabby shook her head. "I — I'm sorry. I can't tell you."

"It's my opinion that you should go home. To your parents. Do they know that you're still in the city?"

"They tried to get me away from the church," Gabby admitted. "But it was against the law for them to harass me or the church. I am eighteen."

Eighteen, pregnant and learning that the promised land was not so ideal, and that she had human emotions and needs that went beyond promises of redemption for her devoted duty to — to whoever was pulling the strings.

The soup came. Gabby wiped her cheeks and started to sip it. She was starving, or so it seemed. Angela tried to be patient, letting her get down a good portion of food before talking to her again.

"Gabby, are you married to the child's father?"

"Oh, yes! Well, not in the eyes of the corrupt law — but in the eyes of the church."

"Hmm. Does the baby's father have other wives?"

Gabby's eyes widened.

"He does. And you've realized that when you love someone, you don't want to share. And, tonight, you've also realized that the man you thought you loved is someone different entirely?"

"He has to — he has to keep the job he has. It's — it's just part of his — job," Gabby said.

"That's a crock!" Angela said flatly. It was confusing. His job was part of his job? He worked for the senator — and for the church. But his work for one or the other was felonious. If the senator had asked him to get involved with the church, the man had certainly taken the task to heart! But . . .

What if the church was his real passion and his work for the senator something he was doing because of the church, as Gabby suggested?

She hadn't meant to speak so quickly, or

so coldly, but it turned out to be the right thing. The girl sat back, folding her hands in her lap. "It is a crock, isn't it?" she whispered.

"Gabby, any organization that wants to cut you off from people who love you can't be offering you the best that is out there. I know how easy it is to get caught up in wanting to belong, to feel important, to be a part of something. But it sounds as if this hasn't been a great experience. Tell me, do you love your parents? Did you love them before all this came about?"

"Oh, they wanted me home, they didn't want me out with some of the people I was hanging with . . . I guess I was smoking a lot of pot . . . a few other things," she shook her head. "So, at first . . . well, I did quit the pot."

"Since you're pregnant, that's a very good thing. Tell me, do you want the baby?"

"Oh! I — I — I, yes. I do want the baby."

"Gabby, go home. Go to your parents. They are probably praying every single day that you will come home."

"Just — just go home?" Gabby whispered.

"Just go home. Do you want me to come with you?"

Gabby smiled suddenly. "No, I can do it." Her smile faded. "Do you really think that they'll take me back now I'm coming back with nothing but . . . a baby?"

"They'll love you, and they'll love the baby," Angela assured her, hoping she was telling the girl the absolute truth. But Gabby hadn't left home because of abuse. She had done so because she had been young and impressionable. Her parents had come for her.

"I'm going to do it," Gabby said. "After tonight . . ."

"Gabby, is Martin DuPre the father of your baby?" Angela asked.

Gabby stared at her and gasped. But then she shook her head. "No, no, no. I really can't tell you the father of the baby. I really can't. Please. Believe me."

"Why?"

Gabby was growing agitated. "I — I don't know. There were a lot of maybes."

She was lying, but she was terrified to admit that the father was Martin DuPre.

It came back again to one question. Did Senator Holloway know that his aide was associated with the Church of Christ Arisen? Not just associated — heavily involved? And if so, how involved was he?

"All right, all right, Gabby. It's all right. I don't know why you're so afraid, but if

299

you're going home, that's what's important."

The girl stared at her a long time, and then smiled. "Angela Hawkins. I know your name. You're investigating the Madden C. Newton house. The senator's house. *Are* you a ghost hunter?"

"How do you know my name?" Angela asked her.

"It was in the newspaper — you dug a skeleton out of the floor."

"I see. Of course," Angela murmured.

Gabby suddenly looked frightened again. "You can't say that you met me — please, you can't say that you met me!" She looked as if she was going to rise and run out of the restaurant.

And right back to the church.

"Please don't worry. I won't say anything about meeting you, honestly. I'm going to put you in a cab right now, and send you home, and we'll never say that we met at all, okay?"

She nodded. "I should call them." She laughed bitterly. "But I don't have a phone anymore. They don't believe we should have phones."

"How did you get here?"

"I walked. It's only a few miles."

Angela reached in her bag for her cell

phone. She handed it to Gabby. "Call them," she suggested softly.

What followed tore at her heart. She could vaguely hear the answer at the other end of the line. When the young woman first heard her mother's voice, tears sprang into her eyes again. "Mommy?" she asked after a moment.

The woman's joy at the sound of her daughter's voice was now more than audible, even across the table. Then Gabby talked and cried, her words disrupted, but her emotion totally comprehensible. "I'm coming home, Mommy. I'm coming home. Now."

After a moment, wiping her face again, she handed the phone back to Angela. "I don't have any money. But I'll get a real job, and get it back to you, if you lend me the money for the cab."

"I'm going to pay this bill and take you outside and put you in a cab," Angela said firmly. "Come on. It's going to be a wonderful night for you, I promise."

She wanted to get the young woman into a cab for home before Gabby could change her mind. She threw money down on the table for the food, and hurried out with her, holding the girl's hand all the while. She saw an empty cab headed down Royal and quickly hailed it.

Gabby clutched her hand suddenly. "Why are you doing this for me?" she whispered. "You're so kind! I'm just a stranger, I just . . . you must have really, really nice parents!"

Something seemed to catch in Angela's throat. "I did," she said quietly.

"What happened to them?"

"They died. Now, please, go home, and appreciate yours. Give me the address and get in."

She wanted the address. She didn't intend to betray Gabby, but she knew she needed the address. The girl's home was in Metairie. She gave the driver a ten-dollar tip to make sure that he got her there safely.

She watched as the cab went slowly down Royal.

Then she turned back toward Bourbon Street.

She didn't find Jackson in front of the cowboy bar, though she did wind up in a friendly crush of drunks coming and going. She saw the courtyard he had been talking about, and wandered to the gate. There were tarot readers set up in the courtyard area, and beyond, she saw a small walk-by bar that advertised quick, cheapie, frozen drinks, and beyond that, in oddly subdued neon lettering, a sign that advertised: Discreet! The Finest Dancers in All New Orleans. Men And Women Welcome.

She had a number of friends who would walk into any strip club, totally intrigued, amused and unashamed.

Sadly, she wasn't one of them.

But then, it was worse just standing there on Bourbon Street with the crowds sweeping around her. People were mostly young and fun, but smiling back and laughing casually at the "Oh, baby, baby!" calls that were coming her way was getting to be a bit much for her.

She slipped past the tarot readers headed for the strip club in back. Luckily, as she did so, her phone rang. She glanced at the caller ID. It was Jackson.

"Where are you?" Jackson asked without greeting her. "I thought you'd be a few minutes — it's almost an hour."

"Long story. You're not going to believe what I have to tell you. But where are you?"

"Watching Lovely Lola Lolita on the pole."

"Great. I'm downstairs."

"Okay, I'm coming for you."

A moment later, he emerged out of the darkened doorway. He offered her a hand. She arched a brow. "It's not that bad!" he called to her.

"Can't wait," she muttered, and went forward to take his hand.

A hostess with enormous breasts and tassels on her nipples was in the shadowed hallway when they entered. She was wearing something like a slinky harem skirt, and she had a smile as big as her breasts. "Welcome back!" she said to Jackson. "And this is your lady! Now I understand how you might want to enjoy our entertainment together!"

Jackson pulled her close. "Oh, yes, there's just nothing like watching a good dancer together, isn't that true, sweetheart?"

"Um, sure," she managed to mutter. When the hostess turned to lead them in, she jabbed him in the ribs.

"Ouch!" Jackson was taken by surprise.

The hostess turned back.

Jackson smiled at her. "Sometimes," he said, "she likes it a little rough, you know?"

The hostess laughed. "Oh, honey, we see everything here. Come on back in, you two!"

CHAPTER TWELVE

"Bastard," Angela whispered, smiling around her clenched teeth. If he wanted to play it this way, she could pitch in easily enough. With her arm slipped around him, she came up on her toes and whispered against his ear, "Is there really anything we're going to gain by being here? I can leave you on your own, you know. Let you get to know some of the girls up close and personal." She couldn't help herself. She nipped his earlobe.

He glared down at her as she slid back down, looking up at him. Then he laughed. "Okay, I deserved that one."

She wished that she didn't like him, and his sense of humor, his sense of being, *him,* quite so much. She had learned about loving and loving could be so much pain.

They were led to a table. It was in the back, and behind Martin DuPre and his group.

Jackson thanked the hostess and they took their seats at a plush, black, circular table.

Angela quickly noted that Martin DuPre and his party were closer to the stage where a scantily clad woman — a very beautiful one — was doing amazing calisthenics on a pole.

"Well. This is really comfortable," Angela said.

"DuPre and his group have already had about twenty lap dances," Jackson said.

"And you've just been sitting here?" Angela inquired sweetly.

"Hey, I'm working," he told her. He leaned toward her. "So?"

"So, I honestly think that I did a very good deed — and found out more about Martin DuPre than you did," she said.

"Tell me."

She quickly gave him a version of her time with Gabby.

He listened with grave intent.

"So," he said when she had told him about her time with Gabby. "So . . . Martin DuPre, aide to the senator, is a member of the Church of Christ Arisen. There's an oxymoron for you."

"Jackson, I really think that he's the father of her baby."

"And you want him to provide child support?" he asked.

"Naturally, he's going to owe child support," Angela said indignantly. "But she may not want it. Once Gabby is away from the Church of Christ Arisen, she may discover that she never wants to see anyone who had anything to do with it ever again — even the father of her child. And, after tonight, I think he's . . . I think he's slimy enough to have done anything," she said.

He didn't seem to notice the woman on the pole. He was deep in thought. "He's a slimy bastard. But did he kill Regina Holloway? And if so, how?"

"We both looked at those crime scene photos," Angela told him heatedly. "She was thrown. Or pushed. There was weight and impetus behind whatever happened."

"I'm honestly not sure if the senator suspects that DuPre is part of the church that is always spouting against him. And I'm not sure that being a total ass makes a man a murderer."

"He seems the best suspect to me so far," Angela told him.

He didn't reply. A waitress came by. She was almost as scantily clad as the stripper at the pole.

They ordered drinks, and the waitress moved on.

307

They sat in silence for a moment.

"Jackson?" Angela said.

"Yes?"

"What did you see tonight?" she asked quietly.

She was almost certain that he understood her question from the beginning.

"A lot of lap dances," he said.

She shook her head. "In my room. Or, really, in Regina's room."

He was quiet for a minute, and she thought that he would evade her again.

But he didn't. He looked at her, blue eyes nearly as dark and compelling as a stygian mystery.

"I saw them," he told her.

"Them?"

"The children," he told her.

She felt as if her breath caught, as if her heart stopped for a moment.

"You see . . ."

"I see what you see, frequently," he said, and then looked toward the stage again. "I see what we conjure in our minds, what remains behind — what is there, what is heart, what is soul, what remains to help us, when we desperately need help."

She was almost afraid to speak again.

He had sounded so casual. And yet, he had made an admission she thought that he rarely made.

"There he goes again," Jackson said softly.

Angela saw that the dancer who had left the stage had approached the group in front of them, and Martin DuPre had his money out. The beautiful stripper walked toward him and took the offered bill. She crawled over his lap. She twisted and shimmied. He didn't touch her.

"You do know that this is a really weird situation for me?" Angela said to Jackson.

He squeezed her hand across the table.

"Sorry, we can go. I have what I need to know," he told her.

"The bastard is living a double life. He's a member of the Church of Christ Arisen, while pretending to be the senator's staunchest supporter. He's planning his own political career on the senator's back. He's a lecher — a man who wants continual entertainment and stimulation. He'll leave here — and go seduce another innocent. All in the name of God, of course. How has the senator been so stupid and blind?"

"I don't know," Jackson said. "But . . . I believe the death of his son certainly contributed to the fact that he leaned on others — and never became suspicious of certain behaviors."

"He's disgustingly creepy!" Angela said,

indicating Martin DuPre, who now had his face buried between the stripper's breasts.

"That's more than a boy being a boy," Jackson said. "How the hell has Martin DuPre gotten away with leading such a double life? Convincing the senator that he's his most loyal proponent, cutting side deals and being a biggie in a church — and I use that term loosely — that considers the senator's entire platform to be blasphemy?"

"Jackson, Gabby is afraid of him," Angela said.

"She was following him — but you think that she's afraid of him?"

"She wouldn't tell me who the father was, but, in that conversation, it was apparent. She was afraid. We really have to find out more about that place. And we have to let the senator know that we know all about Martin DuPre," Angela said.

"Not yet," Jackson told her.

"What do you mean, not yet?" Angela asked indignantly.

"We have to figure out what the senator knows, what he doesn't know and if he has been involved in all of this in any way," Jackson told her.

"I am so confused — how could the senator be involved in a church that protests and pickets his platform?" Angela asked him.

"I don't think he's involved in the church. And I think DuPre will be out when the senator finds out that he is. But DuPre is dirty to the core. And whether or not the senator makes use of that, I don't know. Maybe he managed his gleaming image for so long because he's had DuPre doing what he can't be seen doing."

"Like killing his wife?" Angela asked.

Jackson shrugged. "We know someone was in with her. Someone who had access to the house. Someone who came and went without setting off any kind of alarm," Jackson said.

She saw him change subtly. There was a slight tensing in his features. "Come closer, hold my hands — whisper to me," he said.

She frowned, and then saw what he had seen.

They had been noted.

She was grateful for the shadows. She inched closer to Jackson, lowered her head and kept her eyelashes low. Martin DuPre had looked back and seen them.

He forgot about his lap dancer, pushing the stripper away. He rose, thought to excuse himself to his buddies and headed toward them.

"Closer," Jackson said, his right arm coming tightly around her as he cupped her chin with his left hand, bringing his face just inches from hers. "He's coming, right?"

"Right."

"Giggle."

"What?"

"Giggle."

She let out a small string of husky laughter.

DuPre actually stopped for a moment. She knew that he was staring at them, even while she murmured something else unintelligible to Jackson. Jackson seemed to sense that DuPre was close behind them, but in the shadows, apparently determining whether to accost them or not.

"I think we need to take this back to some privacy now," Jackson said, his voice rising just slightly, a sensual burr as thick as molasses in his tone.

"Yes, now. Now," she replied, keeping her voice low, breathy and urgent.

DuPre backed away farther. Jackson rose, catching her hand and drawing her up against him. "What's he doing now?" he whispered, nuzzling his forehead against hers while they stood in the body crunch.

"Still staring," Angela whispered.

"I knew you would love this place. Beauty is beauty, and movement, well . . ." Jackson purred.

"Yes."

"I'm burning up," Jackson said.

She kept her voice low, and very dry. "Yep. I'm just a hunk, a hunk of burning love."

His smile then was real, even as he asked again, "He's still watching?"

"Yes?"

He nuzzled her impossibly close, and kissed her. It wasn't a stage kiss. It was a full, passionate, filled-with-tongue kiss, and despite herself, she was swept away by it, forgetting their real mission, and simply luxuriating in the rampant wall of heat provided by the muscled hardness of his chest and the lava-flow sweetness of his kiss. She closed her eyes, stunned and seduced in one, and feeling a tidal wave of arousal sweep over her, something that the eroticism of the most accomplished dancer couldn't begin to create.

He broke the kiss, his lips a bare half inch away.

"Is he still there?"

"What?"

"DuPre."

"Oh!" She almost jerked away, but she held her ground. She brushed her lips against his teasingly, whispering all the while. "No. He's gone back to his chair. I think he's still looking."

"All right, then. I think we'll notice him."

He pulled around to his side; they were ready to leave. But as he did so, he looked out to the tables closer to the stage.

"DuPre," he said, not loudly. He lifted a hand to wave.

DuPre lifted a hand as well. He stood, walking away from the group to join them. Onstage, a new girl — Angela was pretty sure she had been announced as Cherry Candy — was winding lithely around the pole.

Martin DuPre looked at the two of them as if seeing them for the first time. He grinned wryly. "Wow. Imagine the two of you here. I didn't even know you were a couple."

Jackson laughed, pulling her close. "There's nothing against fraternizing on our team, we're really kind of a special unit."

"Yeah, ghost busters," DuPre snorted.

"Imagine *you* here," Angela said.

"Part of the job, I'm afraid," he said. "David Holloway is kind of a loner, a family man, but to most people, this is good clean fun. Oil guys," he said, indicating the three men at his table. "They don't get out that much . . . They're just having fun." He looked at the two of them, with another smile. He was convinced his story was

314

totally plausible, but then he seemed to think that theirs was, too.

"Sorry, still can't imagine the two of you here," DuPre said.

Jackson pulled her closer. "Well, this one, she's a wicked little hellion when she wants to be. It just increases all the good stuff when you get home, huh, honey?"

She kept her smile in place, staring at Du-Pre, and feeling like a fool.

"It helps Jackson along a lot, you know — keeping things going, and sometimes, you know, a working guy can be just a little worn-out," she said sweetly. She felt Jackson tense, though there wasn't a single change in his face.

"What can I say?" he asked. "She's insatiable."

"Wow," DuPre said, looking at her. Her arm was around Jackson's waist, his was around her shoulder. She gave his midriff a solid pinch. He flinched, but again gave no sign.

"I have to take her to the S and M clubs sometimes, you know?" Jackson said.

"Wow," DuPre repeated, looking at her with new appreciation.

"And we've just got to get home now — honey," she said to Jackson.

"Yes, we do," Jackson agreed. "Seize the

moment," he told DuPre.

"Well, good to see you two out and about and enjoying the city. Good night," DuPre said.

"Good night!" Angela said cheerfully. Jackson waved.

And finally, they were out, and back on Bourbon Street where the bars remained crowded, the music was cacophony and life seemed to scream out loud.

Angela pulled away from Jackson and glared at him. "An S and M club?" she demanded.

"Hey! You implied that I was impotent!"

"You made me out to be an animal," she said.

"Technically, we're all animals," he reminded her.

"Oh!" She stared at him with aggravation and started walking. "Hey, I think it's better to be a wildcat than a limp rag!" he said, humor in his voice as he walked after her.

She turned back, not sure what she was going to say, but it was going to be fierce. But she saw the amusement in his eyes. He lifted his hands. "Hey, it's all in a day's work," he said lightly.

She burst out laughing. His smile deepened; she waited and he stepped forward to start walking with her again.

"And quite a day's work," Angela said. "You know, I'm worried. There has to be a reason that Gabby was so terrified of me saying anything to anyone. She didn't want me to tell anyone at all that I met her. But she's going home. What if she is in danger? I doubt if her parents are prepared to protect her if someone really lethal is out there."

"You have her full name and address?" he asked.

"Yes, I made sure I gave the cabdriver the money and her address," Angela assured him.

"Let's get back to the house. I'll put a call through to Andy Devereaux and see if he can, at the very least, make sure that a patrol car keeps a close watch on the place."

She nodded. They kept walking. Close. When a staggering group would walk by, Jackson either caught her by the shoulders or slipped an arm around her, drawing her close — and away from a potential human gridlock.

When they reached the house, Whitney was there to open the front door. "You're not going to believe what happened tonight!" she said excitedly.

"What?" Jackson asked tersely. "Was there something that happened at the Church of

Christ Arisen?"

"No," Whitney said.

"Not unless you count Whitney singing every Beatles song known to man as something happening," Will said, coming up behind her. "Nothing. Door didn't open or close for three hours. We came on back."

"Then what?" Angela asked.

Jake and Jenna had been seated in front of the screens, all rolling real time in the house. They were twisted around now, watching the others at the door.

"Guess who was at the Aryans meeting?" Jake asked.

"Blake Conroy," Jackson replied.

"Wow, how did he know that?" Jake asked, staring at Jenna.

"Process of elimination," Jackson said dryly. "We were watching Martin DuPre. I saw Grable Haines lounging by the car about a block down from the restaurant. He didn't look like a happy camper, but bored as he might have been, I don't think he went anywhere else."

"Was the car still there when we left?" Angela asked him. She felt absurdly guilty; she hadn't even looked.

Jackson nodded. "I'm imagining that Haines had orders to stay put until Martin DuPre called him. So, our friend Blake

318

Conroy was at the Aryans meeting. Interesting. Did he see you? Did you speak with him?"

"We did," Jenna said.

"Jenna nearly caused us to be lynched first," Jake supplied.

"I did not!"

"If comments like 'these are the most racist assholes I've ever seen' aren't inflammatory at such a gathering, I'm not sure what would be," Jake said.

"No one heard me but you," Jenna dismissed his remark with a shrug.

"So what did Blake Conroy have to say for himself?" Jackson asked.

"He said that he had come to see what was going on so that he could warn the senator," Jake said.

"And what did you think about that?" Jackson asked.

"It was hard to tell if he was lying or not," Jenna said.

"Come on — you can read people. What did you *feel?*" Jackson asked.

"I honestly didn't know," Jenna said. "He walked right up to us, and it looked as if he was feeling the same way. As if he'd read my mind."

"Do you mean that you think he has some kind of telepathic ability?" Jake asked.

319

"I'd say he can really *read* people, and because of it, he's probably really good at manipulating them," Jenna said.

Jackson nodded. "Excuse me, I have to make a call to Andy Devereaux. Angela, why don't you fill them in on our evening. I think we have the trump card tonight," he said casually, and left them, pulling his phone out as he bounded up the stairs.

They all stared at Angela, waiting. "Well, it was . . . interesting," she said. And she told them about Martin DuPre and his group at dinner, and how she went after Gabby Taylor, what she learned from the girl, and that Martin DuPre had taken his business pals down to the strip club for lap dances. Both Jenna and Whitney found the latter amusing, and wanted to know if she had enjoyed a lap dance, too.

"Hey, hey. Business here," she said. "I'm worried about Gabby, but Jackson is calling Andy now to see to it that a patrol car drives around her house."

"I don't understand — shouldn't someone let the senator know right away that his right-hand man is practically a pedophile?" Jake asked.

"Jackson wants to lie low for a while."

"Because none of them are what they seem — and they all have the wool totally pulled over the eye of the public — the vot-ers!" Jake said.

"Minus my great-grandmother," Whitney said.

"Well, the thing is, the senator might want to just turn his head while Martin DuPre handles situations that could look a little on the sleazy side," Angela said. "After all, it's not illegal for adults to enjoy adult enter-tainment. If DuPre is taking some kind of kickback for getting business situations solved without the proper safety precau-tions, then he is engaging in a criminal of-fense. But we don't really know that. And, to say that David Holloway was having an affair — it's not like such a thing hasn't hap-pened before. Especially not in politics. Not only that, but suppose we prove that Martin DuPre is a horrible person — he still hasn't done anything illegal. Gabby Taylor fingered him as the father, but I'm not sure what that means yet. It's slimy and horrible, but other men have impregnated women, and they've been wretched about it, but I don't think people go to jail for it anymore. She is eighteen, and she joined the 'church' of her own accord. She slept with him — and, ap-parently, she did so by choice. I'm pretty sure she had to be major league brainwashed in one way or another, and it's as sleazy, slimy, contemptible as possible, but I'm not sure anything he did was illegal."

"Unless there are underage girls in that place," Jake said.

"Yes, that would be illegal," Angela agreed. "But the point I'm making is that it won't get us any closer to the truth about what happened here, so . . . we'll try to dig further. DuPre saw us at the strip club tonight, so he knows that we saw him there. He *doesn't* know that Jackson recognized Gabby Taylor from when she let you into the church, Jake, and that I followed her, and that she talked to me."

"And none of this has anything to do with a haunted house," Jenna said quietly. "And yet, somehow, it must."

"Maybe none of it has anything to do with anything," Angela said. "Anyway, kiddies, I've had it. I'm up to bed. See you in the morning."

They bid her good-night and she walked up the main stairway to traverse the middle wing and head to the back of the house.

She paused halfway down the hall, trying to see if she felt anything. The hallway was shadowed, and for a moment, the house felt oppressive. None of it made sense. The children were trying so hard to warn her about something, but she didn't think that the danger was in the house. Nor was she really afraid, though, after the experience in the basement, she didn't particularly want to be there alone. It was a good thing that Jackson had suggested that none of them do it.

"You all right?"

She jumped at the sound of Jake's voice, and then realized that it was coming from the camera and microphone set up in the hallway.

"Sorry! Yes, I'm fine. Good night," Angela said, laughing at herself.

She walked around the ell to the room she had chosen. Regina's room.

She stepped in and turned on the light. The room was a room. Walking over to the connecting doors, she saw that hers was closed over, but not shut. Jackson was on the phone; the low tone of his voice was audible. His door was ajar as well.

It was a surprise to realize that she wanted the door open a bit more before she indulged in a long hot shower before bed. That night, she didn't know why, she was feeling nervous.

Opening her door a bit more, Angela turned and walked to the bathroom, and then happily slipped into the shower and turned on the spray. The bathroom had been redone using elements of the past; there was a beautiful claw-foot tub along with a shower stall. There were dual sinks set into marble, a door that closed off the toilet and a beautiful wooden cabinet that stretched over the sinks and had a large oval mirror in the center. She set about brushing her teeth and washing her face, and then stepped beneath a deliciously hot and strong spray of water.

Moments later, feeling warm and fresh, she stepped out. While drying off, she suddenly felt as if she was being watched. She froze, looking around the bathroom, but there was nothing there.

Then, as she turned, she saw there was something in the mirror. She thought it was her own face at first. And then she realized that there, in the steam, was another face. It was that of a young woman, one with haunted, red-rimmed eyes.

The lips opened, as if they would issue a scream. But no sound came; the face began to decay as Angela watched, frozen in fear. It rotted dark and black, and the soft tissue of the eyes disappeared, and the black sockets seemed to stare back at her.

A choked-out cry escaped her as slowly. Even the skeleton disappeared, and all that was left was the steam-filled mirror.

"Angela!"

She was barely in a towel, but Jackson burst through the bathroom door and stared at her. He was wearing pajama bottoms and nothing more — and carried a big gun, his Glock 22.

He looked around the bathroom and quickly lowered the gun.

"What?" he asked her.

She swallowed hard, thinking that, even if he did *see* things at times, he might think that she was definitely a loose cannon now. She held the towel to her and figured there was still nothing to say but the truth.

"There was a face in the mirror."

That was the truth, but probably not the best way to express it. His expression was somewhat open for a change, and seemed to say, *Of course there's a face when you look in a mirror — your own.*

"It was a young woman," she said. That still didn't seem to help. "It wasn't me, Jackson. There was a face in the mirror, staring at me. Not my face. Another young woman. Please, stop looking at me like that. You admitted that you saw the children. There are spirits in this house, ghosts, souls — energy! — whatever. But . . ."

"But you're all right?" he said.

She nodded, wincing. "Look, I'm sorry,

sometimes these things still startle me."

He shook his head and said huskily, "You don't have to be sorry."

"Thanks."

"Well, I'll open both doors all the way so that you can get some sleep. And you're welcome to scream anytime."

"I'm really not a. . . ." She paused. She didn't know what to say. "I mean, I'm not a damsel in distress in any way."

"I didn't say you were. If something happened to me, I'd like to think you'd be there," he said.

She smiled.

"You like it rough, remember?" he teased her.

They stood there for a minute, she in her towel, and he in his pajama bottoms and Glock. The night seemed to have gone still. She waited, thinking that the time was right. He was going to take a step and come to her. She could still remember the way it had felt when his lips had come down on hers in the club, when they had played the couple looking for a little titillation before heading home . . .

"Scream anytime," he said again.

She nodded, not trusting herself to speak.

He turned and walked away, and she was astounded by the disappointment that flooded through her.

"Jackson?"

He turned back. She walked out, just holding the towel against her. "Who do you think it might have been?"

"Pardon?"

"In the mirror. Who do you think it might have been?"

He shook his head. "I don't know. You have the book on Madden C. Newton. Read through, and find out about his victims. It wasn't Regina Holloway, was it? That would be nice — if you could just have a conversation going with her, she could tell us what happened."

"I keep wishing we would see Regina. If she was murdered, she might well — linger," Angela said.

"If this group is really able to communicate with those who have gone, you'd think someone would have seen her," Jackson said.

"I've thought about that, too," Angela said. "She might be here — unless she did commit suicide and doesn't feel wronged anymore. But I don't think that's it — with Regina, I think that maybe she knew her son was in the world she had entered. She wanted to be with him."

"Maybe," Jackson said quietly. "Maybe."

"Anyway it wasn't Regina," she said. "It was someone much younger. A girl — a girl about Gabby Taylor's age."

"Then see what you can find in the book," he suggested.

He turned away again.

"Jackson," she said.

He stopped. She walked straight to him and set a hand on his chest. "I don't like it rough. Oh, I'm into energy and passion, but not pain. I don't think I'm particularly strange, but I do like to think that I'm exciting."

He looked down at her, and after a moment, smiled slowly. He tossed the Glock 22 on the bed and slipped his arms around her, tearing away the towel between them. He lifted her chin and kissed her lips long and with a lingering pleasure. Then he broke away. "Well, you know, you did take me to that club because you needed to get me riled up. So impotent, you know. But guess what? You're far more tempting in a towel than anyone I've ever seen on a pole."

"Is this allowed?" she asked, wondering that it could be so easy to stand here with him, wanting him, when it had seemed that desire had died along with the man she had once loved. He was nothing like Griffin. He was himself. But he might have in every quality something of what made him what he was that was something she subconsciously searched for in a man. Something in his inner strength, and more, his ability to deal with all that was horrible and cruel in the world, and to maintain honor, compassion and humanity.

And it might have been the way he wore his pajama bottoms. Or his naked chest. She wasn't sure right now. It certainly had to do with the way she felt, crushed against him.

"Not this room," he said softly. He released her to retrieve his gun. Catching her hand, he led her through to his room. The towel remained behind on the floor.

He slid the Glock into the drawer of the bedside table and turned back to her.

There was a moment when he looked at her, and Jackson looking at her was more seductive than the touch of any other. He seemed to drink her in, and as he did, she came alive before ever stepping back into his embrace and savoring the power of his arms as they came around her. Their lips locked passionately again, and she became instantly and desperately immersed in him, in every sensation that his touch brought.

She was never sure how they stumbled down upon the bed, but once there, they became a tangle of limbs, arms and legs, so eager to brush and touch one another that they seemed a stream of fluid motion. He was a practiced and courteous lover, natural and easy in all his movements, and with every caress. His fingers moved eloquently along her spine, cradling her buttocks to bring them flush to one another, and he was unhurried, careless of his own arousal as he kissed her shoulders, explored the line of her back and cupped, cradled, teased her breasts, bathing them with the wash of his tongue, edge of his teeth, and searing liquid caress. She moved against him as well, in wonder at the wall of his chest, at the feel of him, so responsive to the lightest pressure of her fingers, to a subtle kiss pressed here, there and everywhere upon him. Eventually she curled back into his arms, and he was inside her, and for moments then, she just felt riveted by the pleasure of him a part of her, so intimate and sexual. Such sweetness could not last too long, for the urge to move was strong, the urge to increase the friction and the madness rising within her.

And he knew how to move.

If there were ghosts in the house then, they were silent and discreet.

If there was a world beyond the bed, Angela didn't really care.

For infinitely miraculous minutes, there

330

was nothing in the world but being with him, feeling the sleek slide of his body against hers, the remarkable intensity of his sex and the very simple wonder of being so excruciatingly intimate together. Rising and falling, arcing and writhing, rolling and even laughing breathlessly, and finding the rhythm again. He held her above him, and his eyes caught hers, and his hands slid along her breasts and torso, and then they moved again, and she lay beneath him, and everything seemed to spin and turn in the sweetness of the shadows of the night. He caught her to him in a wild deep thrust and the shadows were illuminated in a burst of light as she climaxed, and felt the shuddering spasms of his body against hers before they collapsed together on the sheets, sleek with sweat, desperate for air, their hearts pounding a staccato beat in the night.

She lay against him then, feeling the air cool.

"Do you think this is . . . well, I'm not sure if it's good business," she said softly.

He rose on an elbow, amused as he looked at her.

"This isn't business," he said.

She laughed softly, amazed by the deep, deep blue of his eyes. "I'm not going to the strip club every night, you know."

"Aw, come on."

"Well, it was worth it. But the team —"

"It's my team. It's a new kind of team. We report to Adam before anyone else. Adam didn't give me any rules."

"Yes, but in other units —"

"This isn't another unit. It's my team. And I say it's all right."

She smiled. His fingers stroked her cheek in a long and hypnotic movement.

He kissed her lips and drew her against him. "Have to prove myself," he said. "I mean, if you're up to it, wildcat."

If she hadn't been, the way that he could touch and kiss, he would have easily persuaded her.

Angela was still sleeping when Jackson woke. He eased out of bed, looking down at her, and it seemed impossible that the passionate creature who had ruled his senses, his libido, and the entire night could appear so pure and innocent by the light of day. With sun shining in on her, the line of her back against the cool beige of the sheets curved like alabaster, the kind of beauty sculptors longed to capture.

He headed into the bathroom, closing the door quietly. While he shaved, showered and dressed, he came to terms with a number of things in his mind. He had seen the children; he had seen the little boy and the little girl in the room just as they had lost their ghostly nerve and faded into dust motes. He knew that Angela had something that was far more acute than whatever power he possessed himself, and he worried about her.

Now, by the light of a brand-new day, there was the earthly — and the unearthly — that must be tackled and solved. Odd. Now he had to question himself. He still wanted to fight the belief that ghosts existed — and that they could manipulate the living.

Somehow, he thought, the key now was to get to know the girl Angela had befriended last night, Gabby Taylor.

She was still sleeping when he emerged, and he decided not to wake her yet.

He called Andy Devereaux as he headed out of the room and down the stairs to the kitchen.

"Devereaux. That you, Crow?"

"Yes, morning, Andy."

"Morning. I've had a car keeping an eye on the girl's house through the night. You want to come down to the station and I'll give you anything I can. I'll tell you, we have the United States Constitution, and the

Church of Christ Arisen has a lawyer who seems to have memorized the thing and every damn law that has to do with the country, religious freedoms, personal freedoms, you name it. If we ever get what we need to shut the place down, it's got to be legal. In other words, I can't break into that church and arrest anyone without a warrant and a reason."

"I know that, Andy," Jackson assured him. "Yes, I'll come down to the station. But the girl and her family are all right — no one bothered them during the night?"

"Nothing happened at all," Andy assured him.

"And your officers were careful?"

"Absolutely."

"All right, thanks, Andy. I'll be there in a bit."

"I'll be waiting."

In the kitchen, Jackson discovered that Jenna was awake and sipping coffee while reading the daily paper.

"Are we getting that delivered?" he asked casually.

"Jake said that you mentioned we should get the paper to keep abreast of things happening in the city."

He nodded and joined her. She set the paper down and looked at him. "Jackson, what do you think can possibly make people — so bad?"

"They're not all bad, Jenna. Most people are basically good."

"But some are purely evil."

"Seems that way."

"I was watching those people speak at that Aryans thing last night, and I was just horrified."

"They have freedom of speech, Jenna. Freedom to think whatever they want, and to try to persuade others to their way of thinking. Yes, for most of us, it's hard to fathom."

"It's evil."

"Sadly, while I do believe in the basic goodness of humanity, there are, and always have been, those among us who might be described as evil," Jackson agreed. She was thoughtful and, apparently, still distraught over the meeting.

"Martin DuPre doesn't look it at first. He just looks like a man. But he's evil," Jenna said.

"Evil, good, godly — that's for another world to judge, so it seems," Jackson told her. "In this world, we have to catch what is *illegal*."

"I understand that." She hesitated. "Jackson, all of us know that there is something more."

"Yes," he said, looking at her gravely.

"Well, it scares me. I think that we are in our spirit form — our souls, or whatever — what we were in life. Good or evil. Okay, yes, there are shades of gray. But there is also evil that's almost pure."

"Perhaps."

"Something *evil* is in this house," she told him. "Well, we all saw the massive shadow thing in the basement. It scared the hell out of me, seeing how close it was coming to Angela. I don't know what to think about the whole thing. But it worries me."

He stood and walked over to her, patting her shoulder. "That's why we stick together in one way or another, always, Jenna. No one in this house alone. I'm heading down to the police station. Call me if anyone needs anything before I get back."

"Do all we all stick here for now?" she asked.

"For now. I'll have our next plan of action when I get back," he assured her.

At the kitchen door, he hesitated. "When Angela wakes up, ask her to start reading her book again, see what she can find in there."

"Will do, boss," she said.

"Are you the only one up?"

"No, Whitney went for a jog. She'll be right back. And Will is on his way down to cook breakfast. Sure you don't want to wait for that?"

"Save me something." He hesitated again.

Jenna looked at him and smiled. "I'll watch out for Angela," she said. "She's the most perceptive of us all, so don't you be worrying. I'll look out for her."

"And yourself," he said.

She smiled. "Of course. But I'm doing all right here, though I do feel that we need to be together, as a team. Angela has a real gift, Jake is amazing —"

"You all have something special," he said.

"But you bring out the best in all of us, Jackson. I believe you have far greater talents than you want to let us know about, but one that you have that is especially great is your ability to create a team. I feel like part of a team. Anyway, get going!"

He smiled, walked over to her and planted a fatherly kiss on the top of her head. "Thanks," he said, and left her, heading out. He hesitated at the door, and then took the keys to Jake's car. Out back, he used the remote to open the gate, and brought Jake's little Honda out to drive to the station.

Where Andy Devereaux waited.

"I'm sorry. I know how busy you are," Jackson told him.

"Well, it is New Orleans, but you might inadvertently be doing me a big favor. The two main groups that seem to be against the senator are the Aryans and the Church of Christ Arisen, and both of these organizations are bones in our throats, you know?" Andy said to him.

"I sent Jake and Jenna to a meeting of the Aryans last night," Jackson told him.

"Yeah?"

Jackson grinned. "According to Jake, our Irish girl almost got them lynched — but what's interesting is that Blake Conroy was there as well. He came up to them after the speeches, and said that he was there to look after the interests of the senator. Know what was going on, I guess."

Devereaux looked at him a moment and shrugged. "There are folks out there who are politically correct sometimes because it's what the world expects them to be — doesn't mean they don't have deep prejudice inside. And then, maybe he was telling the truth. Who knows?"

"At the moment, I agree. Here's what's more serious," Jackson said, and he described what had gone on when Angela and he had followed Martin DuPre.

"That's all crazy," Devereaux said. "How could DuPre work for the senator, and be part of the group ripping him to ribbons?"

"Either he's in the Church of Christ Arisen to spy for the senator, or he spies on the senator for the Church of Christ Arisen. I couldn't hear everything last night, but it sounded like he was making some under-the-table compromises with the oilmen," Jackson said. "So — there's that. And then there's the girl. She was terrified — of something or someone — according to Angela. And Angela wouldn't have said that if it weren't entirely true. And that concerns me. Have you heard about anything — anything at all — that had to do with suspicious disappearances and the Church of Christ Arisen?"

Andy groaned. "I know your girl — Gabby's — folks. They came to us. We had a car escort them to the place, but here's the thing. Constitution. That place has all the right paperwork. And the girl, Gabby, is eighteen. So when she said that she wanted to stay with the church and be left alone — she had given herself to God, *and* DuPre, apparently — there was nothing that we could do for them."

"Is there anything you can do if the girl talks about the church — and DuPre?"

"We can get a search warrant. But, come on, Jackson, you've been in the law-enforcement game long enough, and on a federal level. What can I arrest one of those elders or priests or ministers or whatever for? Having consensual sex?"

"It's statutory rape if the girls aren't old enough," Jackson said.

"Yes, but you know that we can't just burst in and demand to know the ages of everyone living at the church or working there," Andy said.

"If I get the girl to talk — that should allow for a warrant," Jackson said.

"Yes, possibly, but it's interesting that you're saying that, since you don't even want the girl to know that we're trying to watch over her and her family," Andy reminded him.

"Well, obviously, since she's terrified, we're going to have to take it slow."

"You don't want to warn the senator about the bastard right away?" Devereaux demanded.

"No," he said, and hesitated. Everyone — except for Whitney's great-grandmother — seemed to think that David Holloway walked on water. Now, Jackson wasn't so sure. But he didn't know how Devereaux would feel if he cast aspersions on Hollo-way.

"I want to explore a few possibilities before we report anything to Holloway."

Andy studied his face and nodded. "All right. I'll play this your way. But this is my city. I'll bend over backward for you, Crow, but don't mess with me. This is my city."

"Not a chance I'd mess with you Andy — I need your help."

"All right."

"I need to know if anything bad ever hap-pened to any of the young women there. Have you had a chance to put together that list of missing women I asked you for? I'd like to see it and learn the particulars. I need to know why Gabby Taylor is so terrified."

"I'll get a clerk on it right away. We'll find plenty of missing women, you know. Notifi-cations about missing women from across the country come just like popcorn. Filter-ing them is going to be the problem."

"I'd say you're looking for young women between the ages of thirteen and twenty-five, maybe as old as thirty, but I'd say younger," Jackson told him. "Often, the younger, the more easily influenced, maybe unhappy with some aspect of their home life. Cult leaders can usually speak ex-tremely well and they can sway those who are unhappy with themselves for one reason or another. A girl who feels she's been rejected, that her family doesn't understand her, or, perhaps, someone who has been floundering — maybe failed out of school, that type of thing. Do some cross-referencing — and see if you can find cases in particular where the parents felt they were losing the children; if they felt their daughters were girls who might have felt lost, alone, misunderstood. They might have been on drugs, though I don't think the victims targeted would have been thieves or dealers."

"All right. I'll get the word out to all our precincts. This is different, I usually have a crime to solve. Now, I'm looking for a crime that might have happened and a phantom girl out there somewhere. Hell, Jackson, you don't think we don't have enough crime in NOLA, we have to go looking for it?"

"Thanks, Andy. I'll get on the federal info systems as well, but I'm looking for just about anything, and just about anything won't show up on the ViCAP system."

"You think they murdered someone at that church?" Andy asked him. "Aren't we stretching it a bit?"

"What else, except the fear of a brutal death, would make a young woman so terrified in life? One more thing, Andy. Did anyone ever corroborate the whereabouts of Senator Holloway and his staff at the time of Regina's death?"

"You've seen the paperwork. They didn't need alibis. The coroner's office couldn't find the least sign of a struggle," Andy said. "Regina Holloway was dead and buried when Senator Holloway started raising his questions. And he didn't bring in the police again. He called someone he knew up in Washington, you all came in, and the chief asked me to make sure you were given full cooperation. Maybe Senator Holloway will be able to accept his wife's death if someone will just say that a ghost caused her to die."

"Thanks, Andy. I think."

"Do you want me to go after their alibis now?" Andy asked him.

Jackson said, "I'll get my guys on it in a subtle manner first. If we hit any stone walls, I'll call you."

"If you get anything on the Church of Christ Arisen, I'll be anxious to get a call, too."

Jackson thanked him and headed back to the house.

It was just after nine.

Angela hadn't been certain just how she was

going to feel about the night when she woke up in the morning. She hadn't slept with another man since Griffin had died; she had never fallen into an intimate relationship easily. It was too . . . intimate.

And there was the fact that they were working together. She'd never considered sleeping with a colleague before. But this had seemed . . . right. It had been what she had wanted.

And waking up, it seemed like something she wanted all the more. She wasn't sure where it would lead. And she wasn't even sure that their team would prove to be something that was viable and useful. That it would be continued after this assignment.

She lay awake for a while, aware that Jackson was gone. What next? She had become obsessed with law enforcement *after* Griffin had died; she couldn't fight disease, but it was possible to fight criminals. Sadly, though, talking with ghosts wasn't as easy.

But now . . .

That seemed all right. Taking the logical path and hoping that illogic would hop in to help was the right way to go.

She closed her eyes. The children in the room made sense.

Who the hell was the girl in the mirror?

She rose and headed back to her own

bathroom. She showered there, creating whirls of steam, but the girl did not reappear in the mirror.

Had she imagined her? Maybe she was susceptible to imagination, too, just the same as anyone else.

Jackson had suggested she start reading the book on Madden C. Newton again.

Showered and changed, she headed back downstairs. She'd left the book in one of the kitchen drawers.

Will was in the kitchen cooking breakfast with help from Jenna, who was slicing and dicing for him, while Jake set out glasses on the table. Just as Angela reached the kitchen, they heard a screech from the grand ball-room entry.

"Whitney! What the hell?" Jake said, hurrying out. Angela followed him, while Jenna and Will came running after her.

"What? What?" Jake demanded.

Whitney had just brought out a cushioned rocking chair to set before her bank of screens. She pointed to one of them. "It's in the basement again. It's in the basement!"

They all stared at the screen. Something large and dark that filled the basement like a giant wave reaching over had appeared. It undulated and writhed, and seemed to darken.

"Let's all get down there," Jenna suggested.

"Yep, great, let the big bad black thing eat us all up together!" Jake said.

"We have to find out what it is," Whitney told him.

As she spoke, they all spun around, hearing the key twist in the lock. Jackson was back.

"Look!" Whitney told him.

Jackson walked over to the screen. They turned back to it.

The black cresting shadow-wave was gone.

"It was there! We all saw it," Whitney said, irritated.

"What?" Jackson asked.

"My old shadowy friend from before," said Angela.

"All right, Jake, come with me. Jenna, stay with Whitney on the screens . . ." He paused. Then said, "What the hell is that burning smell? Handle that, Will. And Angela . . ."

His eyes touched hers, and she saw that he was hesitant about her.

Sleeping with the boss maybe wasn't such a great idea.

"I'm coming with you," she said.

"Angela, I'm not sure we should bring you. If there is something —"

"Then I need to be with you," she said. "I'll hold your hand."

He looked at her a moment then, and despite the fact that not a flicker of emotion registered on his features at her quip, she almost smiled. He was weighing his feelings for her against the fact that it was important that they do what they had come to do. Yes, she was most vulnerable and susceptible. And, yes, that was both good and bad. He'd been a good field commander, always, she thought. But he'd also seen his coworkers dead in the field, and one way or another, the decisions he made were going to be hard.

But she was right this time, and he knew.

"Okay, young lady, give me your hand when we head down," he replied lightly.

None of it meant anything then. She, Jackson and Jake went down to the basement. But nothing seemed to be there, and though they waited, walking the perimeter, exploring various objects that had been stashed there, nothing happened. Calls to the crew at the screens to ask if there was anything on them brought disappointed and negative replies, and eventually they came back up.

Despite Will's lament that his breakfast had been ruined, everything he had cooked tasted delicious, and when they complimented him, Jenna wanted them all to know that it had been her swift chopping and dicing at his commands that had made the omelets what they were.

"So, what's the agenda?" Jake asked Jackson.

"Gambling," Jackson said.

"Cool. On Uncle Sam's dime?" Whitney asked, pleased.

"No. On your own," Jackson said, laughing.

"I'll last about two minutes," Will said.

"Three of us will go. We need to chat up a few of the waitresses — and the croupiers. I need to know if Grable Haines was really gambling all day when Regina died."

"I'm good at talking to the crowd at a craps table," Jake said.

"I knew you would be," Jackson said.

Jake laughed. "Is that a compliment?"

"Talking to people is a strong point. I meant what I said. Actually, though, I'm going to take Jenna and Will to the casino. Jake, you're going to head back to the Church of Christ Arisen and appear to be really interested. Angela and Whitney, go back to the museum on Royal Street, and go through the new exhibit. It will have opened. See what else you can find out about the house and anything else that we don't know already about Madden C. Newton's reign of terror here." He hesitated, and then said, "Angela, study all the pictures you see of any of the characters involved in Newton's day, all right? Oh, and no one comes home alone — we'll meet at Café du Monde at, say, 3:00 p.m."

"We're all on it," Angela told him. "Whitney, make sure that your cameras are set for while we're gone. I'll get everything cleaned up and we'll be out of here."

She didn't really have to handle it alone; they all hopped up to put the salt and pepper, hot sauce, ketchup, butter and jelly away. The dishes arrived scraped at the sink, and Angela quickly rinsed them for the dishwasher and scrubbed the few pans Will had used.

She didn't need to see Jackson to know that he was near. He slipped an arm around her. "Are you good?"

She turned; they were alone in the kitchen. She had to grin.

"I'm imagining that should be for you to judge."

"I'll hold all I have to say on just how good for later. I mean . . ."

"No regrets," she assured him.

"But besides that," he asked, dark blue eyes intently on her then, "last night . . .

whatever you saw in the mirror . . . anything else?"

She shook her head. "No, and I actually tried this morning. I'm sure you would have told me if there had been any kind of problem, but Gabby and her family are fine, right?"

He nodded.

"You're sure?"

"I went and talked to Andy at the station this morning," he told her.

"I'm still worried."

"So am I. But I'm going to trust Andy Devereaux and the police to keep an eye on her. There's not much else I can do at this moment."

"Have the bastard arrested."

"On what charges?"

"There has to be something."

"Probably. When we dig deep enough. But if murder is going to be among those charges, we have to play it all by the book."

The casino wasn't rampantly busy, but even at noon, the play for the day was heating up.

Jackson left Will and Jenna to walk around together and headed straight for the craps tables; Will would get into a poker game in the next few minutes, while Jenna would sit

350

in for a few rounds of roulette and peruse the slots.

He found that there were three active craps tables, and he decided to play each of them. At the first, he struck up a conversation with one of the croupiers, and he talked about how much he loved the game, but remained a conservative player. He mentioned that he knew people who had gotten into trouble at craps. One of his was a local friend, who bet with bookies, but sure loved casinos as well. He described Grable Haines. He played that table for a while, hoping for a response, but none was forthcoming.

He bought a hot dog, and tried to engage the vendor in conversation to see if he knew anything, but the man behind the machine just looked at him blankly when he mentioned the senator's and Grable's names.

Before going to the second table, he worked a few slots and struck up conversations with a few of the cocktail waitresses. He tipped well, and they were happily chatty, and he finally found a girl who knew Grable, liked him a lot and was pretty sure she remembered the day that Regina Holloway had died; it had instantly been on the news.

"Yeah, I think Grable was here. You might

check at the craps table over there," the girl told him.

He started at the second table by playing it wild. Luckily, his ridiculous bets on playing the eleven all came in, so he was flush enough to keep up his chatter. And at that table, he struck gold again.

Though the croupiers were working, and certainly knew that their pit boss was near, they were fine with casual conversation. Necessary to keep up the camaraderie that kept folks gambling.

"Grable?" the croupier to his left said at his inquiry. "Yeah, hope he's doing okay. I haven't seen him in here since the day Senator Holloway's wife died. Nice guy, Grable. He was in here that day, all day, which I think really disturbed him."

"You mean later, because he was playing and having a good time while the senator's wife was dying?" Jackson asked.

"Yeah, poor fellow. He had been winning, too, I think," another one of the dealers added.

"Sad day, sad thing," Jackson agreed.

It was Jackson's turn for the dice; he played out a winning streak, and left the table. He saw Will sitting at a poker table, and nodded to him. Will finished out his game.

"So Grable's game is craps?" Will asked.

"Yes, and he was here just like he told us."

"So, you think he's clean?" Will asked.

"I do. Someone had to have had the time to get into the house and out of it. Regina died right at dusk."

"According to the coroner's report," Will said. "Right?"

"Right," Jackson agreed.

"Probably no more than thirty minutes before Senator Holloway found her body."

"Or . . ." Jackson said thoughtfully.

"Or?"

"Senator Holloway didn't *find* her body. He knew exactly where it was because he caused it to be there."

Angela was glad that she and Whitney had been chosen to go back and view the new exhibit at the museum — not that they'd had a chance to see any of the old exhibits, yet, really. It was an easy walk through the Vieux Carré, and they window-shopped as they strolled to it, stopping at Community Coffee for a pecan-flavored roast of the day, and admiring some of the clothing and hats in boutiques, and the Blue Dog art by Rodrique as they passed the studio shop.

She had always loved walking in the city; the air of fading and decaying elegance was poignant and beautiful, and still a part of day-to-day life. Someone was always repairing something, and someone else was planting something beautiful to flow over a railing, flowering vines or other such visual treats.

They reached the museum and paid their entry. The silver-haired woman was there, and she was delighted to see Angela back. Angela and Whitney exchanged a few casual words with her while she extolled the virtues of the excellent if small museum.

"Didn't you see most of the museum already?" Whitney asked her.

"No — it was like being in a film that was sped up ridiculously. Mostly, Jackson stared at the sign that said the new exhibit would open tomorrow."

"Okay, then we'll be real tourists," Whitney said.

The first part of the exhibit was a display on the city when the French first arrived, and brought them through the great fire that raged through the city and brought down a huge percentage of the original architecture, a second fire that had been another kiss of death, and into the Spanish period, when most of the buildings still standing had been built. Crime had been high on the busy waterfront, with beggars, murderers and thieves haranguing those on ships as well as the wealthy landowners. The exhibit touched on the cruelties of the slave trade. One area focused on the legend of Madame and Dr. Lalaurie, who, according to oral tradition, had brutally operated on and tortured slaves, detaching and reattaching limbs, and leaving behind slaves incarcerated in a basement, whose screams for help created ghost legends. Those poor souls were only discovered after death. The exhibit had a disclaimer, reminding everyone that the story was oral legend.

Sex and scandal were not overlooked, even before they reached the new exhibit.

Models had been made of Gallatin Street, and Storyville. Long before the days of Storyville, Gallatin Street provided base, cheap pleasures for river men, sailors, and whoever dared wander there. But in 1897, Sidney Story, councilman and respected individual, became horrified by the amount of prostitution in the French Quarter and introduced a Control Measure. It didn't actually make a decent thing of prostitution, but it sent one of the world's oldest professions down to one section of the city. Prostitutes were banished to an area that was bordered by Basin, Iberville, St. Louis, and North Robertson streets. There, a new era of raunchy entertainment began. Small houses, or "cribs," allowed for even cheaper entertainment. Larger houses and mansions allowed for a higher class of debauchery, and there, music began to play. The bordellos contributed to the development of Dixieland jazz.

Poor Sidney Story must have been mortified when it became known as Storyville, which reigned supreme in sexual entertainment for twenty years, until the federal government decided that it was far too well-known — and that it corrupted the soldiers and sailors based there. Storyville was closed, and now existed no more.

Moving on, Angela discovered that Abraham Lincoln, as a young man, had seen the slave markets in New Orleans, and some of what he had seen had cemented his determination that slaves must be freed.

"You know, he's known as our most psychic president," Whitney said. "He believed in destiny, and foretold his own death in a dream."

"Do we ever really foretell anything?" Angela asked her. "Or do we create our world ourselves with the way we view it?"

"I don't think he created John Wilkes Booth in Ford's Theatre!" Whitney said.

"Good point," Angela told her.

They entered the new exhibit, and the very first display there was on the Madden C. Newton house. They walked straight to the model of the home, as it had been when Madden C. Newton had carried out his reign of terror.

"Look — the one ell is still divided here," Whitney said. "When the house was built, that was actually a separate building."

"One of the reasons all those people are shown marching on the house is that he didn't get rid of a corpse fast enough — people smelled it, they figured out that he was responsible for the disappearances, and the police burst in on him," Angela said.

"Oh, Lord. It is amazing, how very, very bad human beings can be."

Angela walked over to read the page on the exhibit. There were drawings, and one photograph of Madden C. Newton in court. She had seen him in her dreams; of course, there had been a picture of him in the book she owned, so she might have sent the image to her imagination.

"He looks like any man," Whitney said.

"Not really. Look at his eyes. The bastard was demented," Angela said.

They both fell silent, reading, and then wandered apart in slightly different directions.

"Hey! Come over here," Whitney said after a minute.

Angela walked over to her. The man's death warrant was on display, along with a newspaper sketch of his public execution — a hanging.

"Ugh," Whitney said. "The body was left to hang there for three days. No one knows exactly when he was cut down. There had been orders for the disposal in 'an unmarked grave purchased by the city,' but no one seems to have recorded the plot number."

"Interesting," Angela agreed, walking over to read along with Whitney. "You would have thought that they might have burned the bastard alive and thrown his ashes to the wind."

"Too medieval!" Whitney said, laughing.

Angela walked back over to look at the model of the house, noting the difference in the architecture now, with the entire structure pulled together as one.

She went through the entire exhibit again, but it didn't give her anything new on Madden C. Newton. She saw pictures of many of his victims — Matthew Brady and other photographers at work during the Civil War had made portraits common and possible by then. She was most touched by one certain portrait; it was that of a family, husband, wife, son and daughter.

She knew the children. They remained in her room.

"That's them, isn't it?" Whitney asked her.

"Yes."

Whitney was quiet for a minute. "Jenna is certain that you — that you managed to release people from the basement when you found the skeleton of Nathaniel Petti under the floor. I wonder why the children can't move on. Their bodies were discovered long ago — they were buried with their parents."

"I don't know, I think they're trying to tell me what happened. But I'm not sure if they mix up what happened to them with what happened to Regina. They want me to know something, and they just haven't managed to do it yet."

"Why do you look so perplexed?" Whitney asked her.

Angela turned to Whitney. She grimaced and decided that they had agreed just to say whatever they were thinking — if one of them was slightly unhinged, certainly, they all were.

"I saw another face in the room. When I was drying off after my shower, I looked in the mirror — and there it was. A woman's face. I was hoping that maybe I'd see who she might be while we were here."

"Why, was she scary?" Whitney asked. "I'd love to really *see* the way you do. There's something special about you — it seems that specters *want* to be seen by you."

"Sure, it's endless fun. They tap on the shoulder, scare me to death and disappear!" Angela said. She looked at the model of the house again, and then down the aisle at the extension of the exhibit. She felt that she should be *seeing* something here and now, but she didn't. She glanced at her watch. "Time to meet up to head back, so it seems. Are you ready?"

"Yes," she said, starting ahead. Then she stopped suddenly, looking at the last bit of the exhibit, around the corner before the exit. "Oh!" she said.

Angela walked around to join her.

On the wall, a black silhouette against white, was a simple scene of a hanging. Because of sound systems throughout, they could hear the sound of a rope scraping against a scaffold. The man at the end of the rope was Madden C. Newton; it was a giant cutout from a sketch they had seen earlier.

A sign above read: The Wages of Sin And Wicked Evil!

Madden C. Newton had deserved his death; in Angela's mind, he had deserved far worse.

But there was something about the silhouette on the wall and the sound piping through that was unnerving. As she stared at the wall, she almost expected the image to turn to her; she thought that she would see his eyes, the terrible eyes that she had seen in her dream.

In her mind, she could almost hear the children screaming again. . . .

The children had found a certain justice; their killer had been caught, tried and executed. Yet they remained behind.

And the other woman, the one who had stared at her in the mirror . . .

She had looked through all the pictures. There was no image of that woman here.

"Let's get out of here," she said, and she left Whitney still staring at the wall, and hurried to the exit.

CHAPTER THIRTEEN

When Jackson arrived with Will and Jenna at Café du Monde, Jake Mallory was already at one of the outside tables, his long legs stretched before him. It wasn't busy, but there were people coming and going. A musician played out on the street, doing a decent rendition of a Billy Joel tune. Tourists walked by him, some dropping money in his open guitar case. Across the street, in front of Jackson Square, a girl painted in silver portrayed a statue, much to the amusement of a number of children gathered before her.

Cars moved along on Decatur Street, occasionally horns sounded with impatience.

Jake stood and waved, seeing Jackson. They came over to join him around the small circular table. Jake dragged another chair over so they would have room when Angela and Whitney arrived, and then plopped down again. A waiter was quickly there, and they ordered their cups of café au lait or iced tea or coffee, along with two orders of beignets.

"Well, this will be my third. I'm imagining that I'll be a bit wired tonight," Jake said.

"How did it go? You were back quickly," Jackson said. The weather was still pleasant. It would hold another month, maybe, and then the dead heat of summer would set in.

"Badly," Jake said. "Someone there was onto me."

"Oh?" Jackson said.

"I knocked at the church door, just like yesterday. A young woman answered — another young one. I don't know how young. Too bad she wasn't obviously under-age and pregnant; I could have called the cops. I started out saying that I'd been in the day before, and that I was interested in the church. And before I knew it, a fellow in something like a friar's cape came out and told me that he knew my kind, I had Satan in my soul, and I wasn't for his church. I tried to argue with him, but I had the feeling he was armed beneath his cape — and I wasn't. So I got out."

"That's an interesting development," Jackson said.

"They may not have 'made' Jake," Jenna suggested. "It might all be over the fact that

Gabby Taylor disappeared. I mean, they may not know anything about who he is — but they may be suspicious of him because soon after he showed up, she disappeared."

"True," Jackson said. He slid his sunglasses down his nose; he could see that Angela and Whitney were walking down St. Ann Street toward Decatur; they would be with them any minute. He smiled, watching the two. So striking in their different ways, Angela a snow princess, and Whitney exotic with her honey skin and dark hair. They paused at the light, talking to one another, and he was pleased to see that they might have been friends since childhood, they seemed so comfortable together.

They were a team. A good team, he decided. For a minute, he felt an edge of fear. It was impossible not to remember his last team. Good people, also. Three of them dead.

They had to be vigilant at all times. They had to have one another's backs at all times, and they had to learn to trust one another, and no one else. Of course, no one came into this without knowing the risks. And still, he knew that he was responsible, and he wouldn't relive the past.

"Jackson?"

He started and looked at Will.

"Yes?"

"How are we ever going to get closer to Blake Conroy? Or, for that matter, what can we do about Martin DuPre and the Church of Christ Arisen?" Will asked. "It's the hardest thing in the world to do nothing. We could at least confront the senator with what we know and get the slimy bastard out of politics."

"We will, we will, all in good time," Jackson assured them.

He stood as the two women arrived, and they weaved their way through the other chairs and tables to reach them. As they sat, Whitney said, "Oh, that feels good. We've been walking for hours now!"

"How was the exhibit?" Jackson asked.

"Interesting," Angela said.

The waiter reappeared with their beignets and drinks, and took drinks orders from Angela and Whitney.

"Did you gain anything from the museum this time — anything we hadn't known?" Jenna asked, blowing at some of the sweet powdery sugar from the beignet that had fallen on her skirt.

"Well, we gained a really creepy look at a picture of Newton's hanging," Whitney said.

"And we learned that no one knows what happened to his body," Angela said. "It was left hanging for days."

"Very much like the pirate days. Hang the fellow, and gibbet him!" Jake said.

"I'm glad that's outlawed," Whitney said emphatically.

Angela seemed thoughtful and pensive. "Anything else?" he asked.

"They have an interesting model of the house as it was in the 1860s. And some photographs from the time or newspaper reprints of the photographs," Angela said. He looked at her, hoping there was more. "I think it will help us, when we're working in the house in the future. How was your day?"

"Productive," he told her. "We have an alibi for the chauffeur."

"Can we really have an alibi for anyone?"

"Unless he was in on it with the senator, and the senator *did* throw his wife over the balcony," Jackson said.

"I still don't understand why David Holloway would call us in to investigate what happened if he had been guilty in any way," Jenna said. She dusted her skirt again. "My Lord, these things are delicious, but that sugar is everywhere."

"Blow on it," Will teased. "It's just an illusion. It will vanish in the air."

"Sugar doesn't really vanish," Jenna argued.

"And dust motes are in the air whether we see them or not," Will told her.

"Oh, good God, you're not going to pull a rabbit out of my ear now or anything, are you?" Jenna asked.

"No, no rabbit. I can produce a few other things if you like," Will told her. "I've worked many a horrible magic show with lights and projectors. It's far easier than you might imagine to create the illusion of magic." To prove his point, he reached into the air, and suddenly, there was a handkerchief in his hands.

He was good, Jackson thought.

Angela jerked forward suddenly in her chair, staring at Will.

"It's just a handkerchief. Clean, even," Will said.

She grimaced, shaking her head. "What if . . . what if Regina Holloway didn't commit suicide — exactly. What if she saw something that got into her mind, that made her run out on the balcony?"

"You're saying that the ghosts did kill her?" Whitney asked, confused.

"No . . . I'm saying, what if . . . well, we've been talking about the Church of Christ Arisen. They use *brainwashing* techniques, really. So . . . oh, God, I'm not even really sure of what I'm saying. What if she was told over and over again about the ghosts, made to think that they weren't only real, but that they were vindictive. And what if some kind of illusion was used on her?"

"It's a good theory, but she didn't go over that balcony of her own accord — unless she managed to *hurtle* her own weight backwards," Jackson said. "But . . ."

"Maybe," Jake suggested, "she was lured out to the balcony by that kind of trickery, except she was starting to catch on, or she saw something . . . and then she had to be helped."

The waiter arrived with the two cups of café au lait for Angela and Whitney.

They all fell silent until Jackson had paid, and the waiter went away.

"That adds another element of the possible to the scenario," Jackson said. "I've seen people do amazing things to others by the power of suggestion. Let's face it, the house is big and old, and has an unbelievable history, and . . . maybe Regina even had a touch of the sixth sense herself."

"The ghosts in the bedroom never harmed Regina," she said with absolute certainty.

"I didn't say that," Jackson assured her. "Here's the thing, though. Perhaps she was inundated with tales about the house — true tales, actually. It would take a staunch soul not to be a little afraid that there might be ghosts lurking there. And someone would know about the children who were murdered, and that Regina had just lost a child. It would have been easy to prey on her mind with subtle suggestion."

"And then something was done to convince her that there was the ghost of a child in the room. And that ghost lured her to the balcony," Angela said. "But how could someone have created an entire image in her mind that would do what they wanted it to?"

"Illusion," Will said. "Smoke and mirrors — and projectors."

"But there's nothing in the house. The police haven't found anything, and we haven't found anything at all," Jake said.

"We've actually found a lot in the house," Whitney corrected.

Jake stared at her. "There's something else in the basement," she said. "We've seen it. We've all seen it on the screens. And it's real. It's something," she said with determination.

"Back to the basement then," Jackson said, rising. "Everyone finished?" . . .

Three hours later, filthy and exhausted, they stood together in the basement. They'd tried digging.

They'd all expected Angela to be some kind of a divining rod, but she just didn't have a sense of where another body could be. They had found nothing, though they had broken up a great deal of concrete.

The basement wasn't giving away any of its secrets.

Now resting on shovels or picks, they continued to watch her movements. Except for Jackson, who was sitting on the stairs at a slight remove.

"This isn't working," he noted.

"Angela, nothing?" Whitney asked.

She had to laugh. "Whitney, I wouldn't stand here as everyone dug and destroyed the flooring if I had something to say!"

"I know that there is something down here!" Whitney said.

No one argued with her.

"Maybe we need to give it a rest," Jake said. "We'll all be going to bed with Bengay on our shoulders and backs if we don't quit for a while."

"I guess," Whitney said, defeated for the time. "All right, well, I'm going to take a shower and go to bed."

"Sounds like a remarkable plan," Will agreed.

"I'm in on that one," Jenna said. "Maybe

I'll dream up a solution." She smiled at Angela. "Or maybe you will."

Angela lifted her hands. "I'll try, guys. But . . ."

"But it doesn't work that way," Will said softly, putting a hand on her shoulder. "It's all right, the answers will come."

Jackson stood suddenly. "Well, I'm for the shower, a night's sleep, and then I think I'll try a different angle."

"What's that?" Jenna asked him.

"The attic," he told her. "Jake, I'm going to put you on the computer, following links for me. There's something fishy about Gabby Taylor, the Church of Christ Arisen and, of course, Martin DuPre. Check out social networking sites, too — they probably have some social networking going, particularly since they're targeting kids — Twitter or Facebook, or something. Andy Devereaux should have sent me some info by now, and following it up on a few of the federal sites can give us some more information that might be pertinent. For tonight, let's call it quits."

He started up the stairs for the kitchen. The others began to follow him, but Angela suddenly found herself unwilling to go. "Wait!" she said.

They all looked back. "I think — I think

that Whitney is right."

"Okay?" Jackson said.

"The shadow . . . the shadow that everyone sees . . . it's not like . . . well, it's not like a *ghost* or an image or remnant, revenant . . . that we *usually* see or feel. It is something evil," Angela said. "Yes, we've all said that it's different, but I mean *really* evil!"

"All right," Jackson said. "Agreed. I saw the film and I trust you all. But where does that lead us right now?"

"I think we're looking for Madden C. Newton," she said.

"But he was hanged," Will said. "I thought we were looking for more *victims*."

"Hanged, but no one knows what happened to his body," Angela said. "I think that his body is here. It makes sense. When did we see it coming after me? When it appeared that other souls were finally able to leave. The *victims* might have been waiting for one another, and Newton tried to keep them here, but the power of that kind of light is too strong. He couldn't. But maybe he's still trapped here, and that's the *shadow of evil?*"

"It makes perfect sense," Whitney said.

"Where?" Jackson asked. "We've been digging for hours."

"I don't know," she said, frustrated.

Jackson walked back down the stairs and came over to her. He smiled, setting his hands on her shoulders, then wiping at a smudge on her cheek. "Why don't we sleep on it and get back to it tomorrow. Right now, I think we should just all clean up and order pizza. We'll see what we can find in the meantime on the film."

She nodded. Frustration filled her; she felt as if they were so close. But when she looked into his eyes, she knew that he was right. And she also knew that she wouldn't go through the night alone, worrying about that shadow of evil. She would be with him.

"Come on," he said gently.

He took her hand and they headed up the stairs to the kitchen. The others followed. "Shower," Will said.

"Shower," Jenna agreed.

"Long bath," Whitney said.

"Oh, yeah. Long, long bath," Jake said.

"I'll call the pizza place down the street and order three pies, a meat, a veggie and a cheese?" she asked.

"Sounds like a plan," Jake said.

"I'll ask for delivery in an hour?" she asked.

"Say, an hour and a half," Jackson said.

They parted to head to their respective rooms.

"An hour and a half for delivery?" Angela said to Jackson.

"Well, you know me. I don't last that long," he teased.

They made it through the doorway into his chosen room before they started taking one another's clothing off, with little concern for subtlety. Jackson kissed Angela's lips while they were half in and half out of their shirts, and then pressed his lips against her collarbone.

She pressed her mouth against his shoulder. "Oh, ick!"

"Ick!" he protested.

"Spiderweb. I think I ate it."

"Oh, come on, a little web won't kill you," he murmured in return, sliding his feet out of his shoes. He wrenched his way out of his tailored shirt, finding her mouth and heading in toward the bathroom as he did so. His dirty shirt fell to the floor along with hers. Their lips were still locked as he angled her toward the bathroom door, and into the handsomely restored room. He opened the large shower-stall door while she wiggled out of her sandals and sent her shirt and jeans down to the tile, grabbed him by the waistband and slid her fingers beneath his belt line, rubbing her fingertips along his abdomen as she worked his belt buckle. He shoved off his jeans, drew her to him and kissed her again, feeling the length of her body naked against him, and relishing the feeling while his sex rose swiftly to the arousal of her touch. The water steamed down, and they drew one another in and beneath it. The hot thunder of the pulsing water was deliciously sweet, and he just held her beneath it, his erection growing against her lower belly. They both reached for the soap. It fell to the floor, and they laughed breathlessly as they both reached to retrieve it, only to rise in one body locked once again. He came up the master, and stood her still while he lathered her, her skin becoming flush and slick beneath his ministrations. He pressed his lips to her breast, followed with the soap down her torso, and carefully knelt beneath the rampant spray, soaping her midriff, abdomen, navel, and down to her sex and between her legs, following the trail of the soap with his lips and the caress of his tongue. She gripped hard onto his shoulders, saying words incoherently against the force of the spray and nearly collapsing against him.

He rose slowly against her then, and her arms cradled his neck, and she tried to retrieve the soap from him. Her fingers slick and filled with friction, she began to bathe him in return, capturing his erection in her hands, and caressing it hard with the satiny fluid of the suds to create an urgently sensual tug and pull, meeting his mouth as she did so, then falling low against him as well and taking him into her mouth. Hunger shot through him like elemental electricity and he drew her up to him; they staggered together in the water for a moment, and he hiked her up against him, nearly slamming her against the tile wall, and as the heat and beat continued to rain down upon them, he raised her hips high around his and eased her down onto his sex, and the world seemed to take on the rampant beat of the water, swirling around them and into them like liquid fire. They moved swiftly together, and the need arising between them was equally urgent, and in a matter of minutes they were both clinging to one another as they climaxed violently, staggering against the tile then, and then laughing again as they tried to balance. Dirt and spiderwebs were gone, they rinsed off the sheen of the soap, and Jackson reached for the spray to stop it at last, and pull her into his arms for one last kiss with her body full against his, and still as hot as the spray of the water.

"We should get out before we trip and kill ourselves," she said.

"True. Very true. It won't be a good thing if the headlines read, Ghost-busting Team Heads Die in Tragic Sex Accident in Haunted House," he agreed.

They emerged, reaching for towels, and finding that they drew together again then, enveloped in the towels, drying one another.

"Wow. You were right, we could have had the pizza in ten minutes," he said, holding her close.

"Well, speed does seem of the essence when you are facing death by slippery shower," Angela said.

She laughed at her own remark, and left her towel to fall behind as she headed out of the bathroom and toward the bed. She turned around to look at him, and she was natural, fluid in her movement, and so sensually easy with him. "Want to risk death by four-poster?" she teased.

"I've always lived an at-risk life," he said, and followed her out, catching her up at the end of the bed and crashing down on it with her, swiftly stoking her arousal once more.

Later, he nudged her. "Pizza in five."

"In five!" she exclaimed, bolting out of bed. "It can't have gotten that late . . ."

"Hey," he protested, rising with her. "I

had a lot to prove after those cracks you made about me last night!"

She shook her head at him, and raced through to the bathroom for a quick rinse-off, slipping by him before they could touch again.

The pizzas had arrived when Angela reached the kitchen with Jackson following behind her. Bottles of soda and a pitcher of iced tea were on the table, along with glasses, flatware, napkins, paper plates and a bowl of salad. They all slid into their seats.

"We really need to figure this out," Whitney said, dishing salad into paper bowls and passing them down. "I've been rerunning film from the basement. From the time we were down there, digging."

"What's on the film?" Angela asked.

"Well, us, of course. *And* the shadow. It seems to lurk by the far side of the twist in the ell — leading to your rooms above, and somewhere here, in the kitchen area," Whitney said.

"We'll take a look when we're finished here," Jackson said.

"I think that Angela has to be right. Someone must have brought the body back here to bury in the house," Jake said.

"We don't know that," Jenna said.

"But it makes sense," Angela said quietly. "One totally psychotic killer's body missing, and something in this house that just won't go away."

"Who would have brought him back here?" Jackson asked. "The answers might be in your book, Angela. At least, the answers to the past."

"I've read the book now, over and over. It's really just gory imaginings about the murders," Angela said. "I still have a log-on for Tulane, though. I can start looking back into some of the newspaper accounts from the day, and I can go back to the museum and go through their archives. Jake, hand me a piece with all the peppers and veggies on it, please."

Jake did so. For a few minutes, food traveled around the table, and was consumed, and they all commented on the fact that either the pizzas were really good, or they were really hungry.

When they finished, they quickly disposed of the boxes and paper plates, and headed down to the grand ballroom where Whitney reran the film. She sped through some, as they had been in the basement for a long time. But then she slowed the film. "Here," she said.

It did appear that there was something

dark rising in the room. Shadows formed along the baseboards, rising in jerking motion here and there around them, but falling again as someone spoke, raising a pick or a shovel, or moved back to one another.

"He was really a coward," Jackson said quietly. "In life, he was a coward. He had to isolate and control his victims. With an entire family, he had to separate the children from the parents, and he had to tie up the parents one by one because he couldn't control more than one person at a time."

He looked at them. "That's often the case with a serial killer. He gets his sense of power from disabling his victims. He makes sure that they're drugged or unconscious or securely tied up or shackled, and then he has the power. Life or death, except, of course, the end will bring death. That's why we saw the shadows rising over Angela when she was alone — and we see them rising and falling now."

"Does that mean that he might have terrified Regina Holloway, and that we might be wrong about a killer in the house with her?" Jenna asked.

Frowning, Jackson shook his head. "I don't think so. I don't think that the force needed to send her over could have possibly happened because of a ghost — or even fear of a ghost. We're still looking at two different situations. What we have to do is discover the link." He rose. "I've got to get some sleep."

"We'll take turn manning the camera overnight again," Will told him.

"Two and two," Jackson said firmly.

"Okay, Whitney, how about you and me on the first shift. Jenna and Will can take over at first light, and then we get to sleep until noon?" Jake suggested.

"Reverse it," Jackson said. "I'm going to need you on the computer tomorrow morning," Jackson told Jake.

"You got it, boss," Whitney said.

"Wait, I should be taking a turn at this," Angela said.

But Jake came to her and set an arm around her. "Oh, no. You old folks need your rest. We're fine on this detail. Go to sleep. You're our divining rod, Angela, remember? And Jackson is our mighty leader. Go on. Get some sleep. We can handle this."

"All right, then, kiddies, good night," she said.

Jackson bid them good-night as well, and they headed back up the stairs together.

"They know we're sleeping together," Angela said.

"Probably. I like to think that Adam didn't bring stupid people into our fold," he said, grinning.

She looked at him and smiled, and wondered how life could change so entirely and so quickly. But it had changed. And she knew that what she was sharing with Jackson was far more than the sexual attraction that was so strong, and seemed to be so natural and so easy. Maybe they were just a bit broken inside by the blows life had dealt them, and maybe that was just right. Maybe they were destined to heal together.

But that night, her sleep was disrupted by dreams. Scattered dreams and nightmares.

She saw herself walking down a long hall. There were doorways along the hall, and though she didn't want to open them, she had to.

The first doorway led to Regina Holloway's room. She saw the children, playing with their jacks on the floor.

Young Percy looked up at her. *"I wanted to help the nice lady. Honestly. I wanted to help the nice lady. I knew what they did with the one before her. I saw what they did."*

The door slammed shut, and she was impelled to keep walking.

She saw her hand as she turned the knob to the next room. When she opened that door, she saw Madden C. Newton. He looked at her; looked her straight in the eyes. He smiled slowly, knowing that she knew he saw her. "Evil begets evil," he told her.

He turned. There was an ax in his hand. Blood dripped from the blade to the floor. "Come closer, Angela. Come see what I've done."

She closed the door; she didn't want to see.

As she walked down the hallway, knowing that she would have to open another door, she heard Will's voice repeating the words he had said when they were at Café du Monde.

"Illusion. Smoke and mirrors. Smoke and mirrors."

She opened the next door.

She saw Madden C. Newton again, the ax in his hand. This time, the mutilated corpses of the children lay at his feet.

"You bastard, you're dead," she told him.

And he started to laugh, a gleeful laugh. "Evil never dies," he told her. "They say that it's love, but I tell you, it's evil that never dies. It follows me, and I live while the evil lives."

"Evil can die, and it will," she told him, but she was in the hallway, and he was in the room, and somehow, she could speak bravely because he was captured in the room. It wasn't the bedroom. It wasn't the basement. It was somewhere in-between.

But even as she spoke, fear slipped into her. She had been a cop; she *was* an agent.

But you couldn't shoot and kill a ghost.

She froze within her dream; a scream caught in her throat. There *was* someone behind her. She turned quickly, thinking there was no escape from the being in the hallway because she couldn't go into the room.

But when she turned, it was the girl. The girl she had seen in the mirror.

"He lets it live," she said. "He lets it live, and the evil is alive. Help me. God help us all."

Angela jackknifed to a sitting position, forcing herself to wake, forcing the dream to fade away.

Jackson's arm swept around her instantly, pulling her to him.

"What? What is it?" he asked her.

She was shivering, and she couldn't stop. "He's here. He's in this house, and we have to find him, we have to stop him before —"

"Before?"

"Before he stops us."

■ ■ ■ ■

Jackson sat with Jake in the kitchen, following various sites regarding missing young women, and cross-referencing them with inquiries that had come into the NOLA police stations.

"What about this one?" Jake asked, pointing to one of the pages he had just brought up. "Susanne Crimshaw, twenty-one. Last seen three months ago at her home in Grand Biloxi. She had a fight with her mom, and took off to meet up with friends in New Orleans, but the friends claim they never saw her. She withdrew a thousand dollars from her bank the day she left. There's no credit card trail on her after that, and her mother didn't report her missing until she'd been gone a week, since they'd argued, and Susanne left for her trip. Since she was twenty-one, and not speaking to her mom, the mother didn't realize she was missing until she didn't come home — and the friends reported that they hadn't seen her, and figured that she'd decided just not to come."

Jackson jotted down the case number, and they went back to work.

A Lettie Hughes had been reported missing the week before Susanne Crimshaw, but a follow-up report stated that she'd been found living with a junkie in Slidell. Shelley Dumont had disappeared, but her body had been discovered near the south side of Lake Pontchartrain; she had been shot in the back of the head, and her boyfriend had admitted they'd been involved in a drug deal gone bad.

They went through three more cases, and finally wrote down the names of Susanne Crimshaw and June Leven. June had now been missing four months. She had left New York City for Los Angeles to go to school out there. Due to a scandal at her college — a professor she'd been sleeping with had been arrested for statutory rape — her name had been in the papers, she had left town a marked woman, and her mother had received one postcard from her — postmarked from New Orleans — saying that she was miraculously on the road to recovery, and all would be well. She told her parents not to look for her.

Jackson pulled out his phone and put a call through to Andy Devereaux, gave him the case numbers and asked him if anything else had been discovered about either girl.

"They're both still MIA," Andy told him. "We had the pictures out on the media and in the newspaper, and received zero response. The patrol officers have all this, too, so if they saw them partying on Bourbon, we would have heard."

"If they recognized them, of course," Jackson said.

"Of course. Want me to put out a bulletin again on these two?"

"I would deeply appreciate it."

He hung up. Jake looked at him. "Did you see either of these girls when you were in the Church of Christ Arisen?" Jackson asked.

Jake shook his head and asked, "So what now?"

Angela came down as they were talking. She started to pour a cup of coffee, glanced over to where they were sitting, and at the picture up on the computer screen.

She dropped her cup and the coffeepot. Both shattered, but she didn't seem to notice.

Jackson and Jake leaped up. Jake pulled her away from the shattered glass. Jackson quickly ran his eyes and then his hands over the bottoms of her jean-clad legs.

She didn't even seem to notice them. She stared at the computer screen. She pointed.

"That's her."

Jackson looked back at the computer. The

picture of Susanne Crimshaw was up on the screen. She was a pretty young woman with a generous mouth, wide green eyes and tawny hair.

"That's her?" Jake asked.

"She's dead," Angela said. "I've seen her. That's the face in the mirror. She looks back at me, then decays and rots and becomes bone." She looked at them both. "She's here. She's here somewhere in the house."

Before either of them could reply to that comment, Jenna came running into the kitchen. "Come — come here quickly, all of you!"

Jackson grasped Angela's arm and they ran after Jenna. She led them up the stairs and she drew them all to her window.

From that vantage point, they could see the house next door, and, by craning, the front of the house.

At first, Jackson had no idea what she was talking about. And then, by twisting his neck and leaning, he could see.

Blake Conroy had just exited a car in front of the house next door. He looked around nervously, shifting the brim of his baseball cap back and forth, and then hurried to the gate, opened it and walked up the steps to the porch. He twisted a key in the lock, looked around once again.

And went into the house.

"Keep an eye on the front door, and the house," Jackson said briskly.

"Okay, and then what?" Jenna asked.

Jackson hurried down the stairs and to the computer. He keyed in the address of the house next door. It was owned by a business called Central Marketing. He keyed in Central Marketing and discovered that the business was a DBA of a company called H Family Associates. H Family Associates proved to be part of Genesis Urban Renewal, a parent company that had David Holloway as its CEO.

Jackson stared at the screen for several minutes. He ran up the stairs and to his room, slipped into his shoulder holster and took his service Glock from the bedside drawer. He slipped his jacket over his holster and the gun, and walked back to the hallway and called up to Jenna, Jake and Angela. "Hey!"

Angela appeared at the door.

"I'm going to pay a visit. Keep a lookout."

Angela nodded, and hurried back.

He exited the house, careful to lock the door behind him. And when he walked up to the neighboring house, he found that the man who had just entered had been careful enough to lock his door, too.

Jackson opted for a walk around the house.

It was a shotgun house — built long, with a front door and a back door that were in one even line, a technique that allowed for ventilation in the days before air-conditioning. A second story had been built on the rear portion of the older facade.

The back door he found was locked as well. He heard a sound behind him and instinctively set his hand in his jacket for his weapon.

"Stop right where you are!" a voice warned. "Hands clear from your pockets. Let me see them! Let me see them now!"

He wasn't about to be taken in such a manner; he drew his Glock as he turned.

He was facing Blake Conroy, who had a Smith & Wesson drawn on him.

"Looks like an impasse," Conroy said, eyeing him narrowly.

"I don't think so!" came a shout.

Both men looked up. Angela had the window to the Newton house open, her service weapon trained on Conroy. Jake was at her side.

Conroy began to swear. "What the hell are you doing, Crow?" he demanded.

"Trying to find out what you're doing in the house next door. Managed by a company that is, in actuality, David Holloway's."

Conroy's big, florid face became a serious shade of red and he lowered his gun.

"Holloway doesn't know that I'm here," he said.

"So what are you doing here?" Jackson demanded.

"I'm not — I'm not at liberty to say."

Jackson spun around as he heard the door open behind him. To his astonishment, Lisa Drummond, David Holloway's secretary, stepped out.

"Just tell him the truth, Blake. This is getting ridiculous," Lisa said. "Please, please, please, everyone. Put the guns down."

Jackson ignored the request. "Who else is in there?" he asked.

"No one — I swear," Lisa said.

"Tell you what," Jackson said. "Blake, hand over the weapon. Then both of you step ahead of me, and we'll walk on over to the Newton house and have a little chat. I like the idea of everyone telling the truth, Miss Drummond. I think that will be refreshing."

Conroy started to slide his Smith & Wesson into his shoulder holster.

"No, no. Hand it over," Jackson said.

"I have a permit," Blake told him.

"And I don't care. Hand it over."

Blake tossed the gun to the ground at Jackson's feet. Jackson reached down to retrieve it, never taking his eyes off him.

"Go. Angela?" he called, not looking up.

"Will is at the front," she assured him.

"Go!" Jackson ordered.

The two of them went ahead of him to the house. Will already had the door open. He backed away so that the couple could enter in front of Jackson.

Angela was down the stairs by then, and she still had her pistol aimed and ready.

"Blake, I'm sure you know your firearms. Angela carries a Smith & Wesson SD9 pistol, and so you know that she has a sixteen-plus-one capacity. She may look like an angel, but that's a gun that means business."

"I'm not going to pull anything," Blake said irritably. "I'm a Christian, and I've told you that."

"So what the hell is going on?" Jackson demanded.

Blake glanced at Lisa, who again seemed to explode with a combination of nervousness and fear.

"For God's sake, it's nothing underhanded. It's just . . . oh, Lord! We're having an affair, you idiots. It's nothing more than that. We're just keeping it secret be-

392

cause . . ."

"You're a born-again Christian? Isn't that . . . just wrong? Premarital sex?" Jackson asked Blake.

Blake looked away. "You don't understand. We love each other."

"I see. The rules apply when they work?"

"She had been sleeping with the boss," Blake said. "Before she learned the truth and goodness in life."

"From you, of course?"

"It's not adultery when she's with me," Blake said quietly.

Lisa looked at Jackson and didn't seem quite as nervous. "Yes, and you knew I'd slept with David. I could see that you knew it when you were in the office. But it ended. It ended when Regina died, but, still . . ."

"We couldn't tell him," Blake said. "We couldn't tell him because we didn't know how he would feel."

Angela hadn't put the gun down yet.

"So — so you two meet each other in a house *next to this one?*" she demanded.

"Why not?" Lisa asked wearily. "It's where I used to meet David. He said it was best to carry on in plain sight. He said that we could be in the house on business if we were ever seen — the house is up for sale. And he could keep an eye on Regina from here.

Oh, God, it was wrong, I know it! But he needed someone. He needed someone desperately, because she didn't care anymore. All she had cared about was that kid. David told me that she was shattered. He said that he couldn't stay married to her, but that he couldn't leave her when she was so badly hurting. He couldn't stand the pain, but he couldn't leave her alone. He could never really be with her again. But then, she died, and suddenly . . ."

"Suddenly?" Jackson asked.

Lisa shook her head. "I didn't know him anymore. He said that he'd never come back in this house. He asked me to wait, and I didn't tell him that I couldn't."

"Why not?" Jackson asked her.

"Because," she said. She looked over at Blake. "Because I was scared," she admitted.

CHAPTER FOURTEEN

Life really could be construed as the art of illusion by some people. Angela and the others sat around the table with Blake Conroy and Lisa Drummond, listening, and trying to make sense out of what they heard.

"All right, when did you start to see David Holloway as something other than your boss?" Jackson asked her.

"About two months after his son died. His holding company has actually owned the house next door for several years."

"What?" Jackson demanded sharply. "There's no information on the senator's holding company in his file, and the police didn't mention it. You'd think they would have, seeing as the house is next door to the house where Regina died!"

Lisa looked surprised, and then concerned. "Well, it's a company owned by a company, and I think there are other investors. The senator always wanted that kind of business interest kept quiet. Oh, it's not illegal at all! It's just all wrapped up in a lot of DBAs — doing business as, you know."

"It's illegal if he conceals his financial matters," Jackson said.

"It wasn't relevant to Regina's death!" Lisa protested. "If Senator Holloway had thought that the police needed to know, of course he would have mentioned it! It's a moneymaker — they rent it to groups, and, recently, with all the film activity in New Orleans, they rent out to movie and television producers as well. He asked me to meet him there one afternoon, and it was actually very innocent, I was just going to pick up some papers. But he was so down! He said that he liked being here because he was near Regina, in case she should need him, but then, he started crying, and he told me that she didn't need or want him, no matter how he tried. She wanted their son back, and that was all that she wanted in the world. I guess it was my fault. I was just trying to comfort him, and one thing led to another, and . . . we started seeing one another," she said flatly.

"But then you stopped."

She nodded. "When Regina died, like I said. He'd been at the office that day. When I saw him again, it was as if he'd never really known me. I think, in his own mind, he tried to pretend that it had never happened."

Blake cleared his throat. "I have loved Lisa from the moment I first saw her. And I didn't know about the affair."

"No one in the office — or anywhere — knew at first. And to this day, Blake only knows because I told him about it," Lisa said.

"So, I'm lost now. Why are you afraid?" Angela demanded.

"Why am I afraid?" Lisa asked. "Regina is dead!"

"Why does that affect you? I'd think that'd be a plus. Or is it that you think David killed her himself?" Angela asked.

"I know that this house is strange. David became strange when he bought the place and stranger still as he spent more time in it. Once upon a time, he was a good politician. He was moderate, thoughtful, careful — brilliant. I loved working for him. I believed in him."

"But you don't now?" Jackson asked her.

She swallowed a sip of tea from the glass that Jenna had provided to her. "I don't know," she said. "It's nothing I can put my finger on, but . . . I'm scared. David became obsessed with losing her. He's handed a lot of his work and his business over to Martin DuPre, and I'm not at all certain that Martin is serving his best interests, but when I try to point something out to him, he just ignores me."

"We both go to work. We do what we do," Blake said. "And we don't tell him about us because he's ridiculously fragile right now. I know that when Regina died, he suddenly called Grable Haines into the office and told him to take the money he needed. Grable was shaken up because he said that the senator was so *weird* that he wouldn't have taken the money if he hadn't been desperate."

"I need to get back to the office," Lisa said nervously.

"And I need to get back, too," Blake said. "The senator said that he was locking up from noon until 2:00 p.m. for a break, but it's nearly two now."

Lisa looked at Jackson earnestly. "We want to get married, Blake and me. I'm joining his church. When the time is right, we're going to get married."

"Honest. Neither of us feels that we can leave him in the lurch," Blake said.

Jackson leaned toward Blake and asked, "Why were you at the meeting of the Aryans?" he demanded.

"That one was David Holloway, I swear. He wanted me to see what they were about, and who they were complaining about. I even talked to you when I was there!" he said to Jake and Jenna.

"Yes, but you might have noticed — talking doesn't always answer every question, does it?" Jackson said.

"Look, I've told you what I know at every point when you talked to me," Blake said.

Lisa looked at him. "You didn't tell them about me, did you?" she asked.

"No," he said, glancing at Jackson and looking a little uncomfortable. "I mean, you know — no. I never said that Holloway had been engaged in an affair with his secretary, or, she with me."

"If you have to go back to work, go back to work," Jackson said. "But let me make a suggestion. Lisa, you should just tell Holloway that you two are seeing one another and planning on getting married."

"I guess we should," Lisa said, looking at Blake.

"I don't know . . . I don't know if it's the right time," Blake said. "I know you're still suspicious of me — you have to be. I *am* the man's bodyguard. But I was at that meeting of the Aryans because the senator sent me. I swear it. I swear before God. He's paranoid. He brought you down here because no matter what he says, he's afraid of ghosts, and he's afraid of everyone around him."

Jackson listened to Blake gravely. "All right, then. Wait. But don't you think it might be worse if he finds out later, or by accident?"

"I think he needs to find some peace. I think he needs . . ."

"I think he needs to believe that he didn't cause his wife's death," Lisa said. "Please, I don't want to be caught like this. We have to go back now."

Jackson nodded, lifting his hands. "By all means, return to work."

Jenna rose. "I'll see you out," she said.

"One at a time, if you don't mind. I'll get the car out of here first," Blake said.

"I walk back," Lisa told them.

No one said goodbye and no one spoke until Jenna returned to the kitchen. "They're out. We're locked," she said.

"Well, that was intriguing," Whitney said at last.

"Very," Jackson agreed.

"So, Senator Holloway was having an affair," Jenna said.

Jackson nodded. "Actually, that's not half as important as the fact that Senator David

Holloway owns the house right next door to this one — and that he has, for years," Jackson said.

"But what does it mean?" Jake mused.

"I'm not sure yet. It may mean nothing, and it may put us back to square one. Or worse. Now we have the Aryans, the Church of Christ Arisen, a mistress, a bodyguard, a chauffeur — and an aide we know to be a lying lech, if not something much worse," Jackson said.

"I say we have to take down Martin Du-Pre. If we do something about him, the rest of the charade that is the senator may start to crumble," Jake said.

Jackson looked at Angela. "We have to talk to Gabby Taylor. She's home now. I believe that what is going on at the Church of Christ Arisen might lead us to the answers." He hesitated a moment, and then grimaced. "We need to keep making every effort to discover what we can in the house, but I think we also have to concentrate heavily on the church. The girl was terrified of what they'd do to her if they found her, and I don't think she's going to be that hard to find. You're the one who befriended her. I need you, and I need you now, no matter how you feel that you're treading on a fragile young woman."

Angela winced, but nodded. "Okay, so what are we doing?"

"Will and Whitney, stay on the cameras. We need to be watching closely for anything that's going on in the house while we continue investigating other leads. Jenna and Jake, I need you to go back to the Aryans — find out if Blake has anything to do with their membership."

"Gag, vomit," Jenna said, sighing.

"It's all in a day's work," Jake told her. "Don't look at me like that. It's not my fault you're whiter than the driven snow."

She cast him an evil glance. "All right, come on. We'll be able to find an address on the internet and if not —"

"Just give Andy Devereaux a call. He'll find an address for you. And tell him I'll be talking to him later in the afternoon." He rose as well. "I think that whether we're really getting to the truth or not, people will *believe* that we're getting close, and that could make them dangerous. Lethal. Right now, if the senator is as off his game as Blake says, he's not paying attention, and putting his life and his platform into the hands of Martin DuPre. Gabby Taylor could be in serious danger."

"So, you think that they kill young women who leave the fold — and might talk?" Jake asked him.

Jackson said, "I think that Gabby's fear says something. There are always going to be missing young women. Some will be runaways. And some will be cultists. And some will be dead. Come on, Angela, we're going to take a ride."

She nodded. "We know that they're killing young women. We know it. I've seen one in the mirror," she said quietly.

The Taylor home was a modest ranch, built in Metairie sometime in the 1940s, Angela thought. They had Jake's car — he and Jenna were walking to the Aryans headquarters, discovered to be in the CBD, not far from the senator's home office.

"Should we have asked Andy to send an officer with us — or better yet, come along as well?" Angela asked Jackson.

He shook his head. "If we can get her to tell us something, we'll have enough so that the police can bring DuPre in," he said. "Andy has patrol cars watching the house, and I let him know that we were coming by."

"All right. They may not let us in at all," Angela said.

"Won't know until we try," Jackson said.

Angela needn't have been worried. She

raised her hand to knock at the door, and the door swung open. A slim woman with whitening platinum hair and a kind face threw her arms around Angela. "Thank you! Thank you so much! You brought our baby home to us! Gabby told us all about you."

"Mom, you're strangling her," Gabby said, coming out from behind her mother. She smiled at Angela. She already looked like another woman. The look of absolute dejection was gone from her face, and she was prettier than ever.

"I'm fine, I'm fine, and I'm so happy to see that you're all doing so well," Angela said.

"Is that her?" came a booming male voice.

"Angela, this is my mom, Ellie, and that's my dad, Sam," Gabby said.

"And this is Jackson Crow," Angela said.

"Pleasure," Jackson told them both.

"Great to meet you," Sam Taylor said. He was tall and thin, too, and his face was haggard. Angela imagined he had suffered badly over the loss of his daughter. "We can never thank you enough. Never."

"Never," Gabby said.

"If there were only some way we could help you! We had a reward offered —" Ellie began.

"No, no!" Jackson said with a smile.

"We're actually government employees — your tax dollars at work."

"We wanted to make sure that everything was all right," Angela said.

Sam dragged his daughter into a hug. "Our girl is back with us. What could be wrong?"

A look of dismay and fear flashed across Gabby's face, but it was quickly gone. "We're going to be all right."

"We're going on vacation, tonight!" Ellie said. "Gabby wants to get away for a bit."

Jackson looked at them all. "We need to talk," he said.

Gabby lost her poise; it looked as if she might have fallen, had she not been in her father's firm grip.

"Gabby, we have to get that church shut down. There's something very bad going on there, and you know it," Angela said quietly.

"May we sit?" Jackson asked Sam.

"My girl just wants to get away from it all," Sam shook his head.

"She is afraid of people involved with that church," Jackson said. "We need her help. Desperately. Mr. Taylor, don't you want other girls to go home, too?"

He hesitated.

"I can't prove anything. I can't really give you anything that will help. And if you know

405

things and go into that church, they'll know that you learned about them from *me*," Gabby said.

"Let's sit. Please. I'll get some nice iced tea," Ellie said. She was obviously distressed, but she was a consummate hostess, and she seemed to realize that something worse could happen to her daughter now.

When they were seated in the pleasant family room and tea had been served, Gabby glanced uncomfortably at her father. "They really don't want to hear a lot of details," she said quietly.

"And you don't need to tell us any," Angela assured her.

"We just need to know about other people who were there. Other people who were there — and then disappeared," Jackson said.

"Gabby, how did you wind up being involved with the church?" Angela asked her softly.

The girl's breathing quickened and she glanced at her mother, flushing.

"It's all right, Gabby. You're home now," her mother said, her voice filled with tremulous affection.

Gabby looked at Angela. "Oh, that was easy enough," she said dryly. "I was with some friends on the riverfront one day, and we'd been doing a lot of smoking. Weed, grass, you know, right?"

"Yes, I know the terms," Angela said, trying not to smile.

"I'm sorry, Mom," Gabby said.

Her mother patted her knee. "It's all right."

"Please, Jackson needs to know everything you told me, and anything at all you can think of that might help," Angela said.

"I — I saw him — as if he were walking right out of the light! He was so — holy. He started talking to me, and he told me to come to the church and see him. And all night, all I could remember was the way he'd talked to me. And that light he'd had around him. When he spoke, his voice was musical. He was . . . amazing."

"And so you went to the church."

She nodded, shaking her head. "Once I was there, nothing else mattered. We were in a group discussion one night and he looked at me. And he told me that my time was coming. That night, I couldn't sleep. His words filled my mind." She hesitated again. It had to be hard for her.

Her mother squeezed her hand.

Gabby looked at Angela and Jackson again. "There was a knock on the door, and it was one of the older girls, and she said that he had been expecting me, but I hadn't come to him. She said that I was privileged . . . I would be one of his wives. I kept seeing his face and hearing his voice, and when I went to his room, he was waiting for me. Naked. And then . . . well, it wasn't every night. He has other — wives."

"And you weren't jealous?" Jackson asked her softly.

She studied his face and grimaced.

"No. Yes. I don't know. He taught me that it was right, that I was a holy vessel, and that he was chosen, and that made me chosen."

Brainwashing. Mind control. He seemed to appear in light.

"There are others in danger out there, Gabby. Two women disappeared, one was named Susanne Crimshaw, and the other June Leven."

Angela could see that Gabby recognized the names. "They were there," she said softly.

"Can you tell us anything about them?"

"June . . . June felt that she had sinned terribly, and hurt everyone around her," Gabby said. "She came into the church so hopeful. She was really beautiful. She had dark hair and bright, bright green eyes. And we knew that she was destined to be special.

But one of the council members came and took her one night, and I never saw her again. And then . . ."

"Go on, Gabby, please?" Angela prodded. "What about Susanne?"

Gabby nodded. She grew whiter still. "I heard her scream. And he said that Satan came from those who didn't give themselves totally over to God and the church."

"He. He *who*, Gabby?" Jackson asked. Angela saw that Jackson actually looked a little perplexed. "Richard Gull? The bishop of the church?"

She looked at him blankly.

"A friend of ours went into the church the other day. You must remember him. A tall, good-looking young fellow. He told me there was a picture on the wall, a big one, of a man named Richard Gull, who is the bishop."

Gabby shook her head. "Richard Gull is a saint now. He died years ago. That's what they told me."

"Gull is dead? The police don't know that," Jackson said. "Legally, he's still listed as the head of the church."

"I don't know anything about that," she said. "The church has a bishop, and he's the one who is in control of everything."

"And is Martin DuPre — the man you

were following the other night — the bishop now?" Jackson asked.

"Martin DuPre — he's Senator Holloway's aide, isn't he?" Sam Taylor demanded.

"Yes," Jackson said grimly. "Gabby, please go on. Is he the bishop now?"

"He — he's just the bishop," Gabby said.

"Gabby, is he the man you were following the other night?" Angela asked.

She nodded solemnly. "He's the one," she said.

Jackson stood up. "We do need to get your family out of here, Mr. Taylor. And I'd like it to be now — not later. I think we've been lucky that no attack has been made on Gabby yet, but I believe that the police have been careful, watching the house. I'm going to call Detective Devereaux now and someone in the federal government. We're going to get you out in a private plane, so there will be no paper trail.

"You heard a young woman scream, and that young woman disappeared," Jackson said. "Gabby, for your own life, and for the life of your baby, you have to be strong."

Gabby buried her head against her mother's shoulder. Ellie looked helplessly at Angela.

Angela looked at Jackson. "Everything is going to be fine," she told Ellie.

■ ■ ■ ■

Whitney stretched and yawned, then blinked furiously. She looked over at Will, who was glued to the screens as if he was in a trance.

"Nothing," she said. "Nothing at all."

"Nothing at all when Angela isn't here," he agreed. "She seems to tap into something.

"And why do you think that is?" Will continued. "For one thing, why would a ghost only appear at night?"

"Maybe they don't like a lot of activity. Maybe there's so much commotion during the day, that they don't really have enough strength to combat all the data coming in. Maybe they do show up during the day, when they get to be good at being ghosts."

Will looked at her with a dry expression. "If these ghosts have been around for over a hundred years, they ought to be good at being ghosts."

Whitney shrugged. "We're still forgetting the power of the individual. Maybe some are just more powerful, just as they were when they were alive."

"There's something that we're not seeing yet." He shook his head. "Are they illusions? Maybe even shared illusions at times. Or some form of energy left behind. And they're individuals. Good people, bad people, all kinds of people. But we don't believe that a ghost killed Regina Holloway, though we do know that ghosts remain in the house. So, a person killed her, but how? And what do the ghosts have to do with it?"

Whitney stood up. "I'm going to take a nap. I'm going to head up to my room and take a nap. I want to be on these screens tonight. All night."

"That house next door is very convenient," Will said.

"Yes, but they are separate houses, separate doors, separate walls."

"True. Still, a great place to disappear — if you need to get out of this place quickly."

A young man with crew-cut blond hair manned the desk in the small office of the Aryans headquarters and looked them both over when Jenna and Jake entered. The two held hands, and, Jake hoped, they looked like the *pure* all-American couple.

"Brad Telfur," he said, shaking hands with them. "I know you. I saw you at the meeting."

"Yes, it was our first time, right, honey?" Jenna said to Jake.

"Our first time!" Jake agreed eagerly. "We

were fascinated. I'm from here, you know. And I want to stay here. Love the city, but . . ."

"Well, I'm not from here, and I'm thinking there are a few other places we could live," Jenna said, rolling her eyes. "But . . . well, when we heard about the meeting, we thought there might be hope. You know, a strength for — for our kind."

"You have an accent," Brad said suspiciously to Jenna. "You're Irish?"

"I have dual citizenship," Jenna said. "*British* and American. I'm from Northern Ireland," she lied.

"You're *not* Catholic?" he asked her.

"No, no, white, Anglo-Saxon Protestant," she assured him.

"Well, good, sit down, please. Are you interested in joining us then? Can you fill out some information for our roster?" he asked them.

"Frankly, first, we'd like to find out a little more about your organization," Jake told him earnestly.

Telfur indicated seats in front of the desk.

"We don't do anything unlawful. We support the candidates who can keep control on the various situations in our city. We exercise free speech, and we support the NRA. We're backed by a huge system

413

throughout the country, really. We hold meetings, and we give speeches, and we try to educate people about the problems caused when we step outside our racial lines. We're social — look on the walls. Bowling. And over there, a picnic at the park. We have dances, of course, try to get all the young folks meeting all the right kind of other young folks!"

"May I?"

Jenna stood, anxious to look at the photos on the wall.

"Certainly!"

They pretended to enjoy the photos; Jake was stunned that many contained swastikas and other neo-Nazi paraphernalia. But one particular photo of a group at a picnic perplexed him.

He turned to look at Jenna, indicating that she should seize the young man's attention.

"Um, Mr. Telfur, could you tell me where this is?" Jenna asked, pointing at a shot near a waterfall.

"Well, of course," he said, striding over to Jenna.

Jake slid his phone from his pocket and quickly took a picture of the picture as they talked.

He turned back, hoping he'd been swift and subtle. Apparently, he had been. Jenna was gushing away about something in the photo she and Telfur were looking at.

"Mr. Telfur, I'm curious. I saw a friend at the meeting. A Mr. Conroy. Has he been with the group long?"

"Conroy?" Telfur looked puzzled. "I don't know that name. Perhaps he's a prospective member, too."

"Well, thanks," Jake told him. "Honey, we should get going."

"But aren't you going to fill out some of the papers?" Telfur asked.

"We need to discuss this between ourselves, but I'm sure we'll be back. Right, honey?" he asked Jenna, smiling broadly.

"Oh, absolutely," Jenna said.

He caught her hand, and they left together.

"That was fast!" Jenna said.

"You were enjoying yourself? You wanted to stay longer?" he teased.

She shot him a look that could have killed.

"No, but it was business. Though, I don't think that the kid working the desk — good old Brad — did know Blake Conroy."

"No, I don't think that he did," Jake agreed.

"So Blake Conroy was telling the truth?" she asked.

"I think."

"Then?" Jenna asked.

"Blake Conroy was telling the truth. But, I think we do have what we need," Jake told her. "I think that Gabby gave Angela the information we need to force the truth out into the open."

Jackson was deeply gratified that the federal and local authorities had managed to coordinate and get Gabby Taylor and her family out of the city.

But after Gabby had sat in the station for an hour, relaying every bit of information she could about the Church of Christ Arisen, Andy Devereaux sat in conference with Jackson and Angela for another hour, debating the course of action that needed to be taken.

"You can get a search warrant, at least. Try to find out what happened to those other girls," Jackson said.

"And we search the place — and find nothing. Where do we go from there?" Andy asked him wearily.

"I think we have to rattle the cage," Jackson said.

"Maybe it would be better to rattle it through Senator Holloway," Andy said.

"What if the senator is involved in some way as well?" Jackson asked.

"Why would the senator be involved with a church that hates him?" Andy said. "Hell, no. He'll fire DuPre's ass! Then, maybe, DuPre will get careless."

Jackson was quiet for a moment. "Remember, the Feds are officially leading this investigation," he said.

Andy sighed. "You don't think that the senator will know something is up with the place once we execute a search warrant?"

"He'll find out about DuPre — if he doesn't already know."

"And cover up anything he might have been in on himself," Andy said.

Angela suddenly sat forward. "Come on, please! It's obvious that other girls may be in danger. No matter what, that church has to be shaken up."

Andy looked at her. He reached for his phone. "I'm calling the D.A.'s office. We'll set the search up for this evening. I want it to be bedtime at the church. We'll try to see who is in what bed."

CHAPTER FIFTEEN

"Guess who is an Aryan?" Jake demanded as Jackson opened the door to the house on Dauphine.

"I'm going to say that it's going to have be the chauffeur — Grable Haines."

Jake was so obviously disappointed that Jackson was sorry he had guessed.

But Jake produced his phone, and a picture of Grable Haines at a picnic, laughing with a woman. He stared at the phone image for a moment, frowning as he looked at the woman. Her back was to the camera; she was speaking with Haines.

"Have you downloaded this yet?" he asked.

Jake looked at him. "I can see him clearly — it's perfect."

Angela moved and studied the picture. "I think he wants it blown up. Nice and big. He wants to see the woman in the picture."

Jake took the phone back and frowned,

staring at the image. "All right. I'm on it," he said with a shrug.

"I'm preparing for a long night," Whitney told them all. She'd entered the kitchen when she heard the noise. "We'll see what happens by darkness, because it's usually better at night. Or rather, it's better when Angela is in the house."

"Well, I'm in the house. And I guess I will be here. We aren't going when they execute the search warrant," Angela said.

"She talked! Gabby talked," Will said. "Fill us in."

Jackson and Angela told them about Gabby and her family, and everything that Gabby had said. The so-called bishop Richard Gull was not at the church, and the people had been told that he was dead. Gabby had heard a scream the night that Jane Leven had been "called," and she hadn't been seen since. The police had called the D.A.'s office, and a judge had agreed it was enough for a search warrant. She hadn't mentioned Susanne, leading Jackson to believe that Susanne had been murdered before Gabby had come to the house.

"So, they'll be going in tonight, just a few hours from now," Jackson said.

"So you think that Martin DuPre came in here and killed Regina Holloway," Jake said thoughtfully. "Why?"

"He might have had a few motives," Whitney said. "Maybe she was beginning to suspect something about him."

"Well, everyone around him was a conniving bastard of one kind or another," Jake said. "The picture is downloaded. And I know why you wanted to see it blown up," he added. He was still seated at the counter with the computer. "Come over here — it gets thicker and thicker."

They all gathered around the computer.

With the picture blown up and enhanced, they could see the woman's face.

Whitney gasped. "It's the senator's secretary! She's an Aryan, too! So she had an affair with the senator, and she was an Aryan, and the Aryans are against him, and now she's sleeping with the bodyguard, and he was at an Aryans meeting!"

"Here's a new scenario," Angela said. "On the other side of the coin. I'm not saying it's the right one — it's just a theory. Holloway is — is as corrupt as they come. He has sent his people into organizations for an agenda of his own, thinking that as long as it's not him, and his name is not mentioned, his people will take the fall when something happens."

"What's his agenda — that's the question," Jake said.

"Killing his wife?" Angela asked softly.

"But he brought us in," Jake said.

"I think he really saw ghosts," Angela said. "And if there were ghosts, he'd clear himself, clear her name . . . and it would become sad history, and he'd smell like a rose. Remember, his reputation was at stake when she died. People began to wonder what kind of a husband he might be for her to have killed herself," Angela said.

"I'm going to pay the senator a visit," Jackson said. "I'll catch him before he takes off for the evening."

"He might already be gone for the day," Angela said.

"I'm calling," Jackson said. He already had his phone out.

"I'll go with you," Jake said, getting up.

Jackson nodded. "Remember, no one in the house goes anywhere alone. Everyone hangs tight here until we get back."

"Right," Angela agreed.

The senator himself answered the phone. "Holloway."

"Senator, it's Jackson Crow. I need to see you."

"Well, I was about to head out. But I'm

sure I can arrange to meet with you tomorrow. Have you found out anything? Did a ghost kill my wife?"

"I need to speak with you. You may be able to help me."

There was silence on the other end. "All right. I'll meet you at the Community Coffee shop on Royal. Give me about twenty minutes."

"I need to see you alone, Senator. Without your chauffeur and bodyguard hanging around."

"No problem. I'm alone right now. Twenty minutes."

The senator hung up. "We won't be needing the car," Jackson told Jake. "Come on."

When they stepped outside, Jackson paused, looking down the street to the shotgun house next door.

"What?" Jake asked him.

"The gate was closed earlier."

"Was it?"

"I could have sworn." He pulled his phone out and called Angela, despite the fact that they were still right in front of the street.

"Jackson?" she said.

He paused for a moment, curious that the tone of her voice when she just said his name seemed to make him grow warm.

"Yeah, yeah, I'm sorry. I'm right outside.

Get Whitney and Will to rig one of their cameras to keep an eye on the house next door. I want to see who is coming and going all the time."

"All right."

"And you sleep with your gun handy, I take it?"

"In the bedside drawer," she assured him.

"All right. I'll be on my cell phone if you need me for anything."

"Absolutely," she promised.

He and Jake walked down to Bourbon and then Decatur.

"Politics really do suck, don't they?" Jake asked.

"Well, maybe the name of the game makes it hard. I like to believe there are decent people out there."

"But it's all based on lies. Even when a man — or woman — doesn't mean to lie, they make promises. And then compromises. So at what point does a man sell his soul? The real problem, as I see it, is that no one in Holloway's camp really knows how to tell the truth anymore," Jake said.

"That's why you watch the body, my boy," Jackson told him. "The little things, like the eyes. Sweat on the upper lip. You have to try to catch a liar in a lie, and see him try to weave his way out of it."

At the coffee shop, he ordered lattes, and he and Jake sat down to wait. He noted that the senator came down the street from Bourbon.

Holloway entered the shop and looked quickly around. Spotting them, he came to the corner table in the rear where they waited.

"Crow, Mr. Mallory," he said, greeting them. He was in a tailored shirt and jeans. Not in any official business wear.

"Casual day at the office, Senator?"

"I'm trying to tie up a few personal affairs. I'm due back in Baton Rouge next week," he said. He leaned closer. "So, what have you found out?" he asked.

"Martin DuPre is some kind of elder at the Church of Christ Arisen," Jackson said, looking at the senator.

Holloway's brow knit; he looked confused rather than alarmed, or about to make a denial.

"He's not. I sent him in a while ago to get friendly with the people there and try to find out what was going on. I was doing it in tandem with our work on the Aryans."

"How long ago?" Jackson asked.

"Maybe . . . seven, eight months ago," Holloway said.

"I thought I should warn you — he may

be arrested tonight. The police are going into the church with a search warrant. One of the girls who left the organization has leveled some charges."

He shook his head sadly. "Who would have ever imagined that DuPre would have fallen prey to that debauchery?"

He seemed sincere. "What did DuPre tell you about the church?" Jackson asked.

"He said he felt like an ass, but he'd get involved, and try to keep an eye on what they were going to do with their demonstrations, what manner of spin and propaganda they were going to use against me. Frankly, recently . . ."

"Did you send your secretary into the Aryans fold?" Jackson asked.

"My secretary? Lisa?"

"Yes, the one you were sleeping with," Jackson said.

Holloway's face reddened. "It was brief. It was stupid. It is over."

"Yes, and you were sleeping with her in the house right next door to the Madden C. Newton house — a place you own as well. You might have shared that information," Jackson told him.

The senator's face went nearly purple.

"It's just a rental property. I don't live there."

"But you did *sleep* there," Jake put in quietly.

Holloway sighed, looking downward. "I just admitted to the affair." He looked up at them both again. "All right, the truth? I called friends in D.C., and I'd known Adam Harrison, and something about some of the people he's used over the years. Dammit, don't you understand? Yes, I would go to the house next door. I was frustrated. I didn't know what to do. I loved my wife, but she wasn't a wife to me anymore. We talked about trying again, but hell, you have to have sex to have another child, and she cried rather than have sex with me. I want to believe that there were ghosts in the place and that she freaked out and fell."

"She didn't fall — she was pushed," Jackson said.

"How do you know that? The coroner's office did rule it a suicide."

"Your staff is involved with the places that you most fear, Senator. How much you knew and didn't know remains to be seen, since I don't think you're being entirely honest with me. But we now know that young girls have been dying — young girls involved with the Church of Christ Arisen."

"That has nothing to do with Regina," the senator protested. "I don't know what you

426

expect me to say. I'm not responsible for my staff!"

"Yes, Senator, you are. To what degree — we will find out."

"No. The police ruled it a suicide, but there are ghosts in that house. Regina fell from that balcony — and you can prove that *ghosts* caused her death. The police —"

"The police were wrong," Jackson told him. "And it will all come out. So, it's not looking good for you, Senator. Your aide got very involved in the Church of Christ Arisen, and your secretary, bodyguard and chauffeur are all involved with the Aryans. Frankly, no one surrounding you is legitimate in any way."

"My secretary, bodyguard — and chauffeur?" he asked blankly.

"Martin DuPre impregnated one of the girls at the church. Lisa Drummond and Grable Haines are in pictures from Aryans events. Blake Conroy was at the Aryans meeting the other night," Jake provided. "I know because I was there," he said.

"Conroy — I did send Conroy," the senator said. "But . . . Lisa? And Grable?"

"Where are they all now, Senator? Why are you alone? Isn't a bodyguard supposed to protect you on the streets?" Jackson asked.

"I haven't wanted people around me," Holloway said.

"You need to clean house," Jackson told him. "If we found these things out in a matter of days, your constituents are going to know everything soon as well. And when the police go into the Church of Christ Arisen, I can promise you that Martin Du-Pre will wind up on the cover of many a newspaper, along with stories about corruption in politics."

Holloway nodded jerkily. "I'll take care of it."

"Not for a while," Jackson said. "What would you like? I'll get you some coffee. We're just going to sit here awhile."

"Why?"

"Because we're going to wait for the police results," Jackson said.

The senator shook his head. "Look, don't you get it yet, Jackson? I sent Conroy to the Aryans, and I sent DuPre to the Church of Christ Arisen. I was trying to find out if they were related in any way, because they were the groups so against me. And I think I was right. I still need the proof. But I believe that the Church of Christ Arisen was an offshoot of the Aryans. A sect, if you will. If I didn't get people involved, I'd never know what was really happening. You've got to understand — if they started buying into the doctrine, I didn't know it. I swear I didn't know it."

Angela helped clean up after dinner, but she was bored and restless. She sat in front of the screens with Will and Whitney for a while, and kept an eye on the screen that now showed the shotgun house from the side. But there was no one there; nothing happened at all.

Eventually, she yawned. She wondered if the police had stormed the Church of Christ Arisen yet, and if so, if they had found anything.

"I'm going up to bed," she said.

"You're not going to wait until we hear back?" Whitney asked her.

"I have my cell phone, or you two can come and get me," she said.

Upstairs, she showered in her own room, both fearful and hopeful that she would see a face in the mirror. But she didn't. She went into Jackson's room instead and stretched out on the bed there. For a while, her thoughts were torn between wanting him to come back and be there beside her, and twisting and turning with the questions that continued to plague them and grow worse. They weren't getting answers — just more questions.

Eventually, she drifted, never sleeping soundly. Then, it seemed that she was wide-awake, and she wondered why. Jackson hadn't returned.

She realized that she had the sensation of being watched.

Carefully opening her eyes, she looked to the doorway that separated the room she stayed in with Jackson from the room Regina Holloway had chosen.

And there they were.

The children, and between Percy and Annabelle, the woman she had seen in the mirror. The woman who might have been Susanne Crimshaw. Whoever she was, she was dead, and though she hadn't died anywhere near the era the children had perished, it seemed that their souls transcended time and space, because it seemed as if they were together here now, no matter how many years apart their deaths had been.

The woman crooked a finger at Angela, asking her to come, to follow them.

For a moment, Angela just lay there, fighting a feeling of terror. But then she made herself get up and she walked to the specters who were beckoning to her. Susanne turned, holding little Annabelle's hand, and Percy reached out for Angela. "Where are we going?" she whispered to him.

"Up," he said.

They walked down the hallway together, and then up the stairs to the attic. Angela floundered for lights by the side of the wall, and the naked bulb sprang to life, casting light and shadow over the vast expanse of the room. "Why are we here?" Angela asked Susanne.

The ghost raised her arm, pointing, but Angela couldn't really see what she was trying to show her. Angela spun around. She saw a dressmaker's mannequin, a pile of old trunks, cases and boxes. She thought at first that none of it had been touched in ages — other than the fact that she could see that the dormer windows had been wired for the alarm system. With the one bulb casting an eerie light over the piles of the past, she found the place unnerving.

"I just don't see," she said softly.

She turned around again, assessing the area slowly. There seemed to be something sad and poignant about the dressmaker's dummy with the full soldier's uniform upon it; made and never touched. The giant wire-mesh crate that held children's toys from all ages seemed very sad as well. There were old wooden trains, dolls from a distant time, trains and tracks, an old stuffed rocking horse and more.

"I don't see," she said again.

She felt the woman's presence behind her. The pretty young woman with the blond hair, the huge eyes, and jeans and T-shirt from the twenty-first century. She felt as if she touched her shoulders, turning her again.

Angela was certain that the ghost of Susanne Crimshaw and her young friends from another age were urging her toward the trunks against the wall. She walked over to them, curious, and still uneasy and unnerved, but certain that there was something she was supposed to discover.

She turned, wanting to know which of the trunks she should be going through, but the ghosts were gone. But she wasn't alone. She heard her name called. "Angela! Angela!" Whitney was shouting her name, and the pounding of footsteps on the stairs told her that Whitney wasn't coming up alone.

"I'm here, I'm here — I'm fine," she said.

Whitney burst into view from the landing, and Will was right behind her.

"We saw you — we saw you walking down the hall, and up the stairs!" Will said.

"It's on film. You — you weren't alone," Whitney said, her honey-colored skin an odd, mottled shade of paste as she looked at Angela. "We — we were scared to death for you."

Footsteps sounded on the stairs again. It was Jenna, rushing up to meet them. "Is everyone all right? What's going on?"

"Angela walked here as if she was in a trance," Whitney said.

"And we were watching the screens, so we could see Angela," Will explained. "Wait until you see that film again," Will said, staring at Angela.

"It was Susanne Crimshaw," Angela said flatly. "She's here, and she's managed to make contact with the children. They're together, and they're trying to help us find something."

"So they brought you here," Jenna said. "They're gone, aren't they? I don't — I don't feel anything here."

"They're very shy ghosts, I'm afraid," Angela told her.

"Well, then, let's get started looking," Will said. "Pick a corner, everyone."

"It's huge — three wings of attic, just like three wings of house, and three wings of basement," Jenna said. "This house is huge."

"Yes, but the ghosts brought Angela here," Will said. "I'll take a quick walk through the place."

He headed toward the front.

Angela looked around. There were piles of lumber and pipe, there were ancient paint cans. All out in the open, and clearly, just what they appeared to be. She needed to be digging into the unseen — what might be hidden up here.

She started for a far corner filled with trunks, and started to open them. They seemed to be mostly filled with clothing and mothballs.

"Stuff from the 1920s," Jenna said, closing one of the trunks she had opened.

"I think I'm back in the 1860s or '70s," Angela said.

"Ditto," Whitney called.

The third trunk that Angela opened was different. There was some kind of mechanism in it.

"What's that?" Whitney asked her.

"I'm not sure . . . I have to get it out."

Will came back in. "That wing is like a big . . . like a shelter or something. Tons of bed frames."

"Slave quarters, probably, back in the day," Whitney said.

"Yeah, I guess," Will said, coming over to Angela. "Hey, it's a projector."

"A projector?" Angela murmured. "I wonder what it was projecting."

Will shook his head. "Whatever it was, it

was probably outstanding. I've used this kind in a magic show. You can project images into the air with it, the thing is amazing — and really expensive. Let's see what's on it — grab that roll there, in the tin can, on the bottom of the trunk."

Angela grabbed the film canister and handed it to Will. He quickly searched for an outlet. "They can work on batteries, too, but . . . I think the ones in this thing are dead now. There — there's an outlet."

He plugged in the projector and hit a button. "Turn off the big overhead bulb. Let the light in from the stairs and hallway."

Jenna obliged him. And there, in the murky light, a horrible image appeared. It was the image of a little boy — with an ax in his skull and blood creeping down his face.

They heard a faint sound. A whisper. And it, too, was horrible. *"Mommy?"*

"Damn!" Will exclaimed, and played with the machine, finding the volume control. The plaintive word became louder. The image moved, as if alive. *"Mommy?"*

"Mommy, it hurts. It hurts so badly. Help me, Mommy," the image said, staring at them with wide blue eyes.

"Oh, my God!" Jenna said, and jumping up, she turned on the light. "I'm sorry, I'm

435

so sorry! I can't stand it. That's horrible, so horrible."

Even with the light on, they could faintly see the projected image.

"Turn it off, Will, turn it off, please," Angela said. "We know what it is. We can show Jackson, and he can get it to the police. Now we know for a fact that someone was in here, that they were playing horrible tricks on Regina — a way to get her out on the balcony of her own room."

Will turned off the projector. He was quiet a minute. "Was that the little boy you've been seeing, Angela?"

"Yes," she answered.

"But you weren't seeing a projected image — you were seeing the real thing, right?" Will said.

"I wasn't seeing a projected image," Angela said.

"So . . . do you think that whoever saw the image also saw the real ghost?" Will asked.

"Not necessarily," Angela said. "There are all kinds of pictures at the museum — and pictures of the children can be found there. They're probably also available in old newspaper archives. No, I don't think that anyone had to have seen the ghosts of the children to pull this off."

436

"Who the hell could have gotten into the house so easily, and managed this stuff?" Whitney asked.

"Well, David Holloway, for one," Angela said.

Jackson's phone rang while he was watching the senator sip a second latte. It was Andy Devereaux.

"Well, we went in, and we have a couple of guys in for questioning," Andy said.

"Did you find anything? Anything at all to suggest that a murder — or murders — were committed there?" Jackson kept his eyes on David Holloway as he spoke.

"Nothing. There are a couple of girls here, and we're trying to question them. And I have two members of the church council, but no Martin DuPre, and they're saying that they've never had anyone who matches that description as a member of the church. I can hold all of them for about twenty-four hours, but after that, I'm going to hope that I can at least find proof of statutory rape, and that may be all that I have."

"Thanks."

"Come in the morning. Maybe you have a unique way of asking questions," Andy suggested. "Right now, I'm praying the girls quit crying, that I can find out a few real names, and get something out of the crew. The financial guys are going over the books. But I need more. And I'm going to have to bring your girl, Gabby Taylor, back to identify DuPre, if he's really the father of her child. Have you told any of this to David Holloway?"

"Yes, I'm looking at him right now," Jackson said.

"All right. Get here in the morning. I've got officers on the case, but this might be something you can handle with more intuitive questions. I haven't dealt with crazy cults before, though I have dealt with enough crazy teenage girls."

"Do your best, Andy."

Jackson hung up. Both Holloway and Jake were watching him.

"DuPre wasn't there. Do you have any idea where he might be, Senator?"

"I gave him the night off," Holloway said.

"Call him."

The senator did so. The phone just rang and rang.

Jackson wasn't surprised. "I doubt if he'll be reporting to work tomorrow, Senator."

As they sat there, Jackson's phone rang. It was Will. "We've found something," he said. "Are you still with the senator?"

"I am."

"Can you leave him?"

"If you're telling me I need to do so."

Will began to speak quickly, so quickly that he didn't understand the gist of what Will was saying at first. And then he did.

"You need to see this," Will said. "The question is — should you bring the senator with you or not?"

Together, they watched the image projected. Jackson stared at the machinations, and thought about the fact that the answer had been in a trunk in the attic, and he grew cold. The cruelty behind the creation of the image was staggering; that the person with the mind to instigate such brutal torture was still walking around free was chilling.

He watched Senator David Holloway watching the images of the bloodied child, pleading for help, saying that "it hurt."

He watched tears form in the senator's eyes, and then roll down his cheeks.

"Who would do this?" he whispered.

"Someone close to you," Jackson said, his voice harsh. He had to watch the senator's reactions. "Someone close to you who has access to the house. I'm sure the plan was to allow the projection to lure your wife out to the balcony — and to her death. But I'm thinking that though she went to the balcony, she wasn't ready to jump. That's why she was thrown at the end, despite this display of smoke and mirrors, as Will would explain it. You have to know who did it, Senator. Because someone did it because they wanted to drag you down, or because they thought that they were doing you a favor. Frankly, I think it's the first — your people are all involved in groups that do their best to tear down your campaigns."

The senator shook his head, stricken. "It's impossible. I knew nothing."

He looked lost. Far older than his years.

"Would you like some water, Senator?" Whitney asked him.

The senator nodded. He had been seated in the grand ballroom, where they could best display the recorded image that was so state-of-the art, it appeared three-dimensional.

The figure began to repeat the pattern. *"Mommy!"*

"Turn it off!" the senator begged. "Please! Turn it off."

Will quickly hit the switch.

"Think about it, Senator. If you can think of anything that will help us, we need to know," Jackson said. "If you have been involved in this in any way, we need to know."

"How dare you?" Holloway huffed.

"Senator, your people are involved up to the gills. What part you might have known about is still in question."

"I wouldn't have done that to Regina!"

"But, the question remains — were you being blackmailed for any reason? Did you want your wife gone — just not this way?"

"Bastard," Holloway told Jackson.

"Well?"

"You were supposed to find ghosts!" Holloway raged.

"Were you involved?" Jackson demanded.

"I've told you! Dammit — I've told you. Yes, I knew about my people going into those wretched communities — joining the Aryans and the Church of Christ Arisen. Well, I knew about DuPre and Conroy. If they took that to mean they should go crazy — it wasn't me. And I didn't kill my wife."

"It's all still looking so gray, Senator. Not at all good," Jackson said.

Holloway didn't seem to have anything else to say. He stared at Jackson a long time and spoke at last. "You are a bastard, Crow. An absolute bastard."

"Did you have my team come in just to say that yes, there were ghosts, Senator? To distract from your little Aryans involvement?" Jackson asked. "Did you think you were getting a team of paranormal experts who would *want* ghosts to exist, and play it out like a pack of innocent lackeys, swearing that there were ghosts?"

"You're an ass, and I'm innocent," Holloway said. "I did want you to prove there were ghosts. There are ghosts in that house — and ghosts caused my wife to die. Quit accusing me. Maybe I did want to prove it because I didn't want to live with the guilt of having caused her to commit suicide — but she didn't, and I didn't kill her. And if you'd let well enough alone, DuPre and Conroy would have gotten what we needed, and I could have shut them all down."

"It was all for the good of man, right?"

"I'm innocent of Regina's death."

"Yes, but you either killed other innocents — or brought about their deaths with you machinations, Senator."

"No. I can't be responsible for others turning homicidal!"

"We'll see, won't we?" Jackson asked.

Holloway stared at him, furious.

Jake cleared his throat. "Shall I drive you home, sir?"

Holloway just shook his head. "I'll go next door," he said hoarsely. "I'll just go next door."

"Walk him over, Will, please?" Jackson asked.

Will nodded and left with the senator.

"I'm taking the projector down to the police station with me first thing in the morning," Jackson said. "We have to keep investigating this house. Whoever used the projector seems absolutely confident in his or her ability to get away with what he's done. The damn thing has been here. He or she put it in a trunk and thought that would be the end of it — it might have been. Some buyer another hundred years from now might have discovered it."

"We can try to trace the purchase," Jake said. "It's a very expensive piece of equipment."

Jackson nodded. "Jake — first thing in the morning, start up with your computer magic."

"Yes, sir."

"It's the house — we've seen it. The answers are in the house," Jackson repeated dully.

"We'll find the truth," Whitney said. "I know we'll find it."

Jackson slipped an arm around Angela's shoulder. "We're going to get some sleep," he said. "We're going to try to get some sleep, anyway."

"Wait!" Whitney said. "What happened with the police search at the Church of Christ Arisen? What did the senator know — and not know?"

"They missed DuPre. No one knows where he is. The senator originally sent him in like I sent Jake in — for information. He did send Blake Conroy to the meeting of the Aryans, but didn't send either Grable Haines or his secretary."

"So he says," Jake added.

"So he says," Jackson agreed. "They have two council members from the Church of Christ Arisen at the station, and two of the young women who live at the church. They're all playing dumb — they won't even give their real names. I'm going to talk to them tomorrow, and if we don't get something quickly, we'll have to bring Gabby Taylor back, though she did sign statements about her time at the church. I don't think DuPre can stay underground that long. He didn't think he was caught, or in any trouble, and DuPre needs an income. If the church assets are frozen, he'll be in a desperate situation. Anyway, Jake, see what you can find out about that piece of equipment, and we'll call it a night. Oh, Whitney — how's the camera on the house next door going?"

"It's working fine. No one in, no one out," Whitney reported.

"Keep an eye on it — the senator is in it tonight," Jackson said. "And make sure this place is locked up tight once Will is back in. We still don't know the truth — whether the senator is involved, or whether his mental state caused him to be totally unaware of what people around him were really doing. The thing is, he did send Du-Pre into the Church of Christ Arisen. So, did he send his own people to join the Aryans as well? It's worse than ghosts — it's the living, and we have to find exactly what is what."

"Absolutely. And we'll watch the house. I'm going to be on it until four in the morning . . . Will is going to take over then," Whitney told him.

"Everyone stay vigilant," Jackson said. "I have a feeling things are going to come crashing down."

He caught Angela's hand, forgetful of everyone around them. It didn't matter anymore. She didn't say a word, and he didn't care what anyone thought.

"Good night, then," he said.

"Night, all," Angela told them.

"This is really quite sad," Angela said, as they left the group and walked up to their rooms. "All we've learned is that Senator David Holloway's entire life was a lie, and the main missing ingredient is just how much he knew about the lie he was living."

"And we can't solve anything else now," Jackson said.

She smiled at him as they stood in the hallway on the second floor, eyes brilliantly blue, a half smile curved into her lips. "We can solve one thing," she told him.

"Oh?"

"The fact that it was very lonely in that bed without you."

He wondered if he should feel badly that her words were a bolt of lightning ripping through him; if it was wrong that he could take such raw and carnal pleasure in being with her when they were sitting on a bombshell. And yet, the very history of the house reminded him that relationships were the essence of life. Angela had become a part of his life so quickly, something that he had missed, he thought, maybe always. He had become so focused on solving every dilemma out there.

"No reply?" she queried softly.

He drew her into his arms and kissed her gently, heedless of the fact that they remained in the hallway. Then he led her inside. "I hope that was an appropriate reply?" he asked her.

"Excellent, right to the point," she assured him.

He held her there for a moment, just looking down into the pool of her eyes, wanting to explain what he had never managed to get clear to himself. His hands were on her shoulders; his fingers delicately caressed, and he tried to form words, a sense of his feelings, the reality he knew, and why his skepticism meant so much to him.

"Jackson?"

He was quiet for a minute, and then, at last, he spoke. "I have Native American blood," he said. "And I have done a dream quest, and seen amazing things, but that's not what touched me, made me wonder what was real, and what wasn't. Once, when I was in my early teens, with my mom's family, in northern Scotland, I was racing on horseback with friends. They thought that I had beat the hell out of them — I'm a good rider, and I had a damn good horse — but I hadn't beaten them, I'd been thrown. I wasn't ahead of them. I was lying there with a concussion, a rib broken as well, barely able to breathe. A kilted man had come along on a black horse that looked like some kind of mixed-breed warhorse and picked me up. I barely understood the man, his accent was so heavy and his speech was so strange. I was going in and out of consciousness. When I woke up, I found that I had been deposited on the steps of my mom's ancestral home in the Highlands. And then . . . well, later I saw the man again. I saw him on the wall in the grand hall of my mom's family estate. The painting was of Ewan McKeough, head of the clan in the late 1500s. He was the . . . he was the man who rescued me. Now, mind you, half the area of Scotland was McKeough. I tried to tell myself that he had to have been a relative. But I've questioned the truth of it ever since — being a skeptic, because so many people are willing to believe anything."

"You've known," Angela said quietly. "And you've known that you've had the ability to see beyond what most people see."

"My real ability is to bring out the strongest reactions in gifted people like you," he told her.

"And you can bring out abilities in me?"

"All kinds of abilities!"

She smiled and he closed the door firmly, turning to her. "Tonight, I'm thinking that I'll bring out a few of your other abilities. Hmm . . . somehow, I just feel I'll help you along without the benefits of a strip club. I mean, if you don't mind. And, then again, feel free to strip. . . ."

CHAPTER SIXTEEN

Warmth enwrapped Jackson as Angela lay in his arms. Hours of night had passed when they had been engrossed in one another, in sensation, in need, whispers and laughter, tenderness and volatility, and he had dozed and woken, and been pleased just to lie beside her. He breathed in the sweet clean scent of her hair, and felt the softness of her flesh beneath his fingers. There was even a time when he wondered at what he felt; *she* had known what it had been like to really become involved with another person, to lie comfortable and sated, happy to share time and space, wake together, share the simple pleasures of being together. He had spent his life restless and ever ready to move on, the world on his mind the second hunger was spent. He didn't know why; something had happened to him those years ago on the Scottish cliffs, and he had become obsessed with the mind, with what was real, and what was illusion in the thoughts of man. And from there he had come into the Behavioral Science Unit, and the criminal mind had become his passion. There was always another case, and those working with him seemed a little bit hard and jaded as well, all fighting demons in their own minds. Work had been good; there had been times of escape, and he had always thought of himself as a decent man, a decent human being, but he might have been wrong. He hadn't known the pain she had known. And he had never known the simple pleasure of sleeping beside someone, waking beside them and wanting them again.

Angela had her own demons — so many tragic deaths in her past. But she had learned to control the emotions that coiled around them. He didn't think he was *emotionless,* but he had never let feelings slip beneath the surface. He knew damn well that he couldn't solve the world's problems, but the demons in him kept wanting him to do so. The loss of his teammates might have been part of it, he knew. They were ghosts that now lived in his heart. He'd never imagined that a woman could bring so much to his soul without even knowing the full damage that dwelled there now.

He wanted suddenly just to go somewhere

with her and enjoy music or art, or a horseback ride through a beautiful forest, and not wonder about anything except the beauty around him and the wonder of his companion.

Then he started as there was a pounding at the door, and it burst open.

"Sorry, sorry!" Will said. "But there's someone prowling around the house next door."

Angela had been sleeping so soundly she was barely aware of the pounding of the door. She finally forced her eyes open to find that Jackson was already in his jeans, just sliding into his shoes. "What's going on?" she asked him. He gave her a quick kiss on the forehead. "Will was just here."

"Here? Damn — I heard some kind of pounding, but I didn't see Will."

"They've picked up something on the cameras. It's not clear, but there's someone next door, slinking around the house. Will is staying here; he's downstairs watching the screens with Whitney. Jake is coming with me — we're going over. Jenna tried to get the senator on his cell phone . . . He isn't answering."

She nodded. "All right. You go ahead, I'll hurry."

"We've got wires. Will is going to know where we are and what's going on. It might be nothing."

"Someone slinking around a yard is nothing?" she asked dryly.

"No, it might be another excuse. Like it's the bodyguard, and the senator called him. Everyone seems to have an answer for everything around here," Jackson said.

She was out of bed, even as he left, closing the door behind him. She quickly slipped into jeans and a T-shirt and scrambled for her sneakers. As she pulled them on, she looked up.

They were there again. The twenty-first-century woman, Susanne Crimshaw, and the nineteenth-century children, Percy and Annabelle.

"I can't come with you," she said. "Something is happening. We may be finding the answers."

Susanne shook her head. Percy broke free and walked to her. He shook his head. *"No, no, it's in the wall. It's in the wall."* They were not images made by a projector; they were real ghosts in the house, and they were trying to help her.

"What's in the wall?" she asked him.

She turned around, frowning, staring at the end of the room. This room met the ell in the house. It was part of the original kitchen structure that had been added to the main house.

She gasped suddenly, staring at the wall, at the way the panels joined.

On the outside, it would look as if the house were now one big horseshoe. On the outside, it all blended together perfectly. But now, she wasn't sure if the space in the rooms inside was as large as the space as viewed from outside. There had to be some type of secret room or crevice.

She looked at Percy again. "You might have told me before."

The little boy shook his head. *"I tried to warn the lady. But she didn't see me. She saw the images, but she didn't see me."*

Angela jumped up and walked to the wall, studying the paneling. There was space, she decided. Space between this room and the twist in the ell. When the buildings had been joined, they hadn't been flush. The architect who had drawn the plans for the renovation had cleverly hid the gap between the two buildings, but it was there.

Behind the wall.

She quickly wondered if whoever had designed to kill Regina Holloway had come across the plans and seen that there had to be a gap in there. Outside walls were flush, but the gap didn't allow for more rooms to be built, though on one of the ells, they might have been widened.

But they hadn't been.

She started to press on the paneling. Nothing happened. She wondered if she was being absolutely ridiculous, listening to a ghost while something tangible was happening downstairs.

"Thank you, Percy," she said, and told him gravely, "I just have to see what's happening downstairs. I have to make sure that I'm not needed."

He clung to her hand. *"You see me, you hear me, please."*

She walked to the door, wishing that this room wasn't on the far side of the ell. "Will?" she called.

"Angela?" His voice came from the microphone at the camera.

"Yes, what's happening next door?"

"I don't know yet. Jake and Jackson are walking the perimeter . . . they're out of camera shot right now."

"Please," Percy said. She looked down. It was amazing — she could see the little boy. She could *feel* the warmth where his spectral hand touched hers. "I'm so afraid for you," he told her.

"Then help me!"

455

He looked at her solemnly. *"The wall. They come through the wall,"* he said. *"They use the wall."*

Jackson and Jake scaled the brick wall that separated the properties, landing silently on the earth on the side of the brick barrier. Jackson motioned to Jake, and Jake nodded, heading around the front while Jackson came around the back of the house next door.

The shadows were so dense that night. He moved silently, and as swiftly as possible, scanning the foliage and brush that grew along the wall and was thick and heavy around an old, moss-dripped tree in the far corner.

When he reached the back door, he saw that it was open. Not ajar, just not tightly closed. It hadn't been jimmied; there was no sign of forced entry.

Inside, he could hear voices.

He waited, speaking softly into the tiny wired microphone he was wearing. "Someone is in the house, there are voices. No forced entry. I'm waiting for Jake . . . we're going to go in."

"I've got you, the line is clear," Will assured him.

A moment later, Jake came around the

other side of the house. Jackson drew his gun, indicating the door. Jake pushed it inward.

They entered by the rear door, and heard voices from the front. Silently following the sound, they moved through the house. Jackson motioned Jake to keep to the left; he stood to the right as they followed the shotgun hallway.

They crept along, holding back when they reached the front parlor. From his angle, Jackson could see Martin DuPre. He held a gun on the senator.

"You sent me in!" he accused David Holloway. "You sent me in, and I did what you told me to do. I infiltrated. I became part of them. It's what you told me to do. And now, you have to help me. You have to get me money. The cops are after me!"

"I sent you in to find out just what those people were really doing. I needed information to get them all closed down, and you know that we had a real agenda, and that I couldn't have my name involved with any of it. You became hypnotized yourself, trying to take everything for yourself, to have a good time — and you took it way too far, dragging all those girls off the streets."

"You knew!" DuPre cried, waving the gun. "You knew!"

"In your mind, DuPre, in your mind! My name could never be tainted by scandal! I didn't tell you to drag girls off the street and force them to sleep with you," Holloway said sharply. "What were you doing? Why are women missing, and did you kill my wife, you son of a bitch?" Holloway demanded in return.

Jake motioned to Jackson. DuPre had a pretty careless hold on the pistol he was carrying. Jackson couldn't get a really good look at it. The weapon appeared to be a small, snub-nosed six-shooter. It would certainly be lethal at close range, and DuPre looked like a desperate man. His customary meticulousness was gone; his hair was tousled, sticking up in all directions and his customary meticulous attire was wrinkled and stained as if he'd had to crawl through some muddy terrain to escape detection.

Jackson shook his head and brought his fingers to his lips, warning Jake to be silent. He was going to have to pick the right time to bring the man down, winging him but rendering him harmless. There were still a lot of questions DuPre needed to answer.

"I didn't kill your wife, Senator. *You* killed your wife. You still can't admit the truth! You broke her heart. You put her in that house. I was nothing but your patsy — every damn thing that I did was for you."

"You killed those girls," Holloway said.

"I didn't kill your wife! You made Regina think she was crazy, haunted by demon children. You killed the woman who didn't worship you as a god. Well I *became* a god, Senator. I learned I had it. I had more power than you, and I have the kind of power that I can make work again, work for real."

"The police are after you!" Holloway said.

"They'll know it was all you — when you're dead."

Jackson and Jake frowned at one another, hearing Will's voice come through their earpieces. "Someone else is coming, bursting through the gate. High speed. It's the bodyguard, the bald guy, Blake Conroy."

Jackson swore. He burst out from his hiding place, gun held between both hands. "Get down, get down!" he warned the senator and DuPre.

But the front door burst open as if a bull had come through. "Don't shoot, dammit, no, don't shoot!" Jackson cried.

But gunshots exploded.

"Ah, hell!" Will shouted.

Angela heard the shout and the sound

459

of gunfire.

She jerked away from her exploration of the paneling, and came running to the hallway, shouting to the camera and the microphone.

"What's going on, what happened?"

"Gunfire next door!" Will cried back. "Can't hear anything — it's mass confusion."

"I'm on my way!"

She raced into Regina Holloway's bedroom and grabbed her Smith & Wesson from the drawer, and then raced downstairs. The others were already heading out the front door.

Police sirens could be heard on the air.

They raced around to the gate. "Get back," she warned. "Stay flat against the wall, keep low!"

They obeyed and moved swiftly but carefully along the wall, then ran along the path to the house, and the front door.

"It's all right now," Jackson called. "Ambulances are on the way."

Angela frowned, and the others stayed back. She stepped carefully to the front, but Jackson called to her, "Stay back. It's a crime scene now."

She looked inside. David Holloway lay on the ground, moaning. Jackson was at his side, staunching the flow of blood that was oozing from a shoulder wound. Jake was next to a fallen Martin DuPre; DuPre wasn't getting back up, and no ambulance was going to help him.

Blake Conroy knelt on the floor, clutching his shattered hand, and blood dripped from it as well.

"I'm coming in," Jenna said. "I can help."

Jenna stepped into the house, rushing past Blake Conroy to assess the senator's more dire condition. She spoke to him quietly. "It's a shoulder wound. Looks like a through and through. Breathe easily, Senator. Jackson, apply more pressure. You'll be all right." She moved over to Conroy to examine his hand.

A moment later, the police cars arrived. Andy Devereaux stepped out of the first one, and hurried toward the house.

The ambulance came screeching to a halt.

For the next five minutes, there was mayhem.

But, eventually, Jackson, Andy and Angela stood alone on the sidewalk just outside the house. "We showed Holloway the projector and the images it had on its reels," Jackson explained. "And he didn't go home, he decided to sleep here. We had cameras rolling on the place. The best I can figure is that he did get hold of Martin DuPre, or DuPre figured out where he was and came after him. I don't think he intended to kill the senator, but we'll never know now. He wanted money. He wanted help to get out of New Orleans. But Blake Conroy burst through the door before we could defuse the situation. DuPre panicked and got off a shot when Conroy shot him — I shot Conroy's hand, trying to get him to put his weapon down," Jackson said.

Andy nodded, scratching his cheek. "Well, DuPre is dead. It will save the taxpayers a lot of money. He would have gone up for murder."

"He said that he didn't kill Regina," Jackson said. "He said that the senator killed her, that Holloway broke her heart."

"What does that mean?" Andy asked.

"Did you miss the part where DuPre died?" Jackson said, disgusted.

"Ah, come on," Andy interrupted. "Look, I'm an officer of the law, and I respect my office. I don't shoot to kill, and I bring a man in every time rather than shoot a bloody murderer, child molester and so on, but don't expect me to weep over this one, Jackson Crow," Andy said.

"It's not that," Angela explained quietly. "We still don't know what happened. Jackson's explaining that they were listening to DuPre when Conroy burst in."

Andy nodded. "Yeah, well, we'll have to piece together the rest." He stared at Jackson. "You'll have to come down to the station. We'll need a slew of statements. DuPre is dead, we'll have the bodyguard questioned at the hospital, and the senator won't be in shape for any information until tomorrow. But I'll need you, Jake and the nurse — she came into the house," he said apologetically.

Jackson nodded. "Right."

The ambulance was leaving with the senator on a stretcher. The EMTs were walking with Jenna, who was still holding Holloway's hand. The senator now had an IV in his arm and an oxygen mask over his mouth and nose.

Medical pathologists from the coroner's office had arrived, but they'd be working in the house for a while. Blake Conroy had already been situated in the back of another ambulance. He glared at them all with red, angry eyes.

Jackson glared back with anger.

Conroy suddenly jumped out of the ambulance, racing toward Jackson. Andy stepped between the men.

"You shot me!" Conroy accused Jackson.

"You shot me! The bastard was going to kill the senator. It was my job to shoot him."

"We had it covered, Conroy. And you killed the truth when you shot DuPre!" Jackson told him.

"Stop it!" Andy said. "We'll sort this all out at the station."

"I'm bringing charges against you," Conroy threatened Jackson.

"And you could be facing murder charges yourself," Jackson told him.

"He had a gun," Conroy said.

"Get back in the ambulance. Get back in the damn ambulance!" Andy said. "And get to the hospital . . . Charges are possible, Conroy, so cut the temper tantrums. And it's 2:00 a.m., dammit," he said irritably. "Let's move this. Move it!"

He got Conroy back to the ambulance. Jackson stood with Angela. She wasn't sure what to say. "Well, Martin DuPre did become a monster," she said quietly.

"It wasn't finished," Jackson said. "It wasn't finished. I still don't trust Conroy. Hey!" he called to Andy. "He's going to be in custody, right?"

Andy looked back at him, his expression tense. "He'll be at the hospital, and then down at the station."

Jackson nodded, then turned to Angela,

taking her shoulders. "All right, then, go back, you, Will and Whitney. Try to get some sleep, and we'll try to figure out if we can make any more sense out of it all tomorrow. Something still just isn't right."

"We can all come to the station," she told him.

He shook his head wearily. "That won't make sense, that's for sure. Get some sleep. Get in, lock up and get some sleep. At least I won't be that worried. DuPre is dead, and Blake Conroy will be occupied. Our time at the station will be as quick as I can make it." He gave her a pained and rueful smile. "And it had been one of my best nights, oddly."

She grinned in return.

"I can wait up."

"Jackson! You coming with me?" Andy scowled at him.

Jackson gave Angela a quick kiss on the lips. "Soon," he promised.

He got into Andy Devereaux's unmarked car with Jake and Jenna. Will and Whitney came over to stand by Angela.

"He's so upset," Whitney remarked.

"He wanted to know more from Martin DuPre," she explained.

"Well, he managed it in the best possible way," Will said. "He may have to be happy with that."

"Hey, handsome, you did all right, too!" Whitney teased him. "You caught DuPre breaking into that house."

"Yeah, I did, didn't I?" Will said. "Come on. Let's try to get some rest. My eyes are killing me from staring at those screens."

"I think a glass of wine is in order," Whitney said. "Then, maybe, my adrenaline will be down enough for me to sleep."

"Sounds good," Angela said.

They walked slowly back to the house, tired but wired. Angela decided that when Jackson returned and had gotten some sleep, they could start inspecting the walls. He'd been angry, frustrated and disconcerted when he'd headed toward the station; a dead man still lay in the house next door. Tomorrow would be time to tell him what discoveries they might make through the ghosts.

They walked into the grand ballroom. Will checked the door and set the alarms. "Should I forget about the cameras and film? I guess we are working on taxpayer money."

"Keep them up for tonight," Angela told him.

"Is it over? Is it really over? Did we solve it? No ghosts — just a very evil man?" Whit-

466

ney asked.

"Well, we know there are ghosts," Angela said. "But Jackson was right — evil is done by the living."

She headed into the kitchen, leaving them to do whatever their wonderful technical minds did with their technical equipment. For the moment, she slid her Smith & Wesson into one of the kitchen drawers.

She walked to the refrigerator and found a bottle of chilled Chablis. She took out the wine, opened the bottle and went to the cupboard for glasses. She noted that Jake's computer was on the counter bypass and she went to look at the screen.

He'd had a search engine at work. Jackson had told him to research the projector they had found. He'd gone to a number of sites, and she glanced at them curiously — the projector was in high demand by magicians.

She started backtracking through his system, and he'd been busy, using what codes she didn't know, but he'd done some hacking.

As she stood there, growing absorbed, little blips alerted her to responses coming in from the questions he'd been asking.

She clicked on the mouse, and it brought up another screen. It was listings of the trace he had made on the purchases of the projector.

She gasped suddenly.

"Will!" she called.

He didn't answer her.

"Whitney, Will! Come in here."

There was still no answer. She stepped into the hall, "Hey!"

A muffled laugh made her shake her head. Well, they were young, and the case was apparently over.

She walked down the hallway, aggravated. But when she reached the grand ballroom, she didn't see either of them. She walked around to look at the screens.

And when she did, she froze, berating herself for her stupidity.

One screen showed Whitney, knocked flat in the upstairs hallway; Angela couldn't tell if she was dead or alive.

Will could be seen in a like position on the landing of the central stairway, just above her.

They had all run out at the sound of the shots next door; they had run out, leaving the Madden C. Newton house open and vulnerable.

And they weren't alone.

She knew before she turned that someone was behind her.

She even knew who.

But the blow against her head took her down before she could turn to face their attacker.

Jackson gave his statement at another desk across from where Jake gave his statement. Jenna had come in after the fact, but she sat at another desk, telling the officer the senator's condition as she had seen it, and the emergency treatment she had helped administer.

Andy finished typing up the document, printed it out and gave it to Jackson to sign.

"Where's Conroy now?" he asked.

"Hey, there's an officer with him at the hospital. He'll be here with an escort, don't worry. He's not out on the streets." Andy chuckled. "He will need surgery on that hand."

"I shot for the gun," Jackson said wearily. "And I was a split second too late."

"Hey, the senator is still alive."

"Shots should never have been fired, period," Jackson said.

Andy shrugged. "But they were. And the senator is going to live, and a bad man is dead. Come on, Jackson, I can live with that. You're going to have to. Let's see, when it all comes out — that the senator's aide was in on fleecing and seducing young women in the name of the church — I'd say that fellow's career may be over, but then again, he may be so damn broken now he'd be no good in politics anyway. He had to have been slipping, to have ignored everything that was going on in his own house, so to speak."

"Come on, Andy. We can't let this go. We really don't know yet if the senator was heavily involved with those people," Jackson said. "Or . . . just how deeply others around him were involved."

"Fine," Andy said wearily. "But it looks like we did find out the murderer."

But Jackson had heard the conversation between DuPre and Holloway. And DuPre had denied killing the senator's wife.

"Anyway, we can meet in the morning and try to sort more out," Andy said.

"Is that it for now? Can we get back?" Jackson asked.

"You're free to go," Andy told him. "Just as soon as the others wrap up. The patrolman over there, Smith, will give you a ride back."

They left the station. Two blocks down, they passed a police car on the side of the road. There were two silhouettes visible.

"Stop, go back," Jackson said.

"Sir?" Smith said.

"Go back — there were two officers in that car, and they didn't look right," Jackson said.

Even Jake, next to him in the backseat of the car, looked at him as if he was losing it.

"Smith, go back, please."

"They're probably just on break."

"Please," Jackson said firmly.

With a sigh, Smith did as he was asked. He parked the police car and Jackson hopped out. He walked toward the car.

Both occupants were slumped over.

Dead.

The driver was a police officer.

The passenger was not.

Angela woke with her head pounding. For a moment, she was lost — completely lost. Disoriented, and in pain.

Then she remembered clearly what had happened. She was in Regina Holloway's bedroom, on the floor. The pain of rug burns on her flesh told her that she'd been dragged there.

Something was touching her foot. Whitney's body, she realized.

"It's time," she heard.

She looked up. Grable Haines was grinning down at her, a gun in his hand. "Ghost busters, busted! Cool. The legend of this house is going to grow and grow."

She stared at him, knowing that he wasn't alone when she heard the giggle behind him. It was Lisa Drummond, of course.

"Be careful. The ghosts will get you," Lisa said.

He laughed again. "I've got the gun. Ghosts don't get guns, I don't think."

"You'd be surprised at how powerful they can be," Angela said.

"Make her shut up, Grable," Lisa said.

He ignored Lisa.

Angela shook her head. "The senator is an amazing actor. I believed he was horrified by the images the projector put out. But he ordered the projector," she said.

"Right. Well, Lisa ordered the projector. But, yes, the sainted Senator Holloway knew. He wanted his wife to think that she was meeting her son. He thought that she would die happily that way. He never saw the images we created," Grable said.

"Everyone in this was a liar," Angela said. "And you should know this — I think the senator actually brought us in, knowing what would finally come out and planning on getting rid of DuPre and all of you, through us."

"Oh, no," Grable said. "You don't understand politics. The senator will come out of

472

all this just fine — after you're dead, of course. And we'll be just fine as well."

"Shut up, she doesn't need to know any of this!" Lisa said. "Everything will fall on Martin DuPre, and they'll think street thugs got hold of Blake and that cop. And everything went just perfectly, so let's just finish it."

"The senator will get you — just as he got DuPre," Angela said.

"We know what we're doing," Lisa insisted. "Oh, yes, we'll be just fine."

"No, you won't. Don't you see — the senator really has to clean house. And speaking of which, that leads to one more question — you obviously slept with everyone," Angela said to Lisa. "Which one are you really trying to be with?"

"Obviously, I'm going to be the next Mrs. Holloway," Lisa said with disgust. She didn't seem to mind explaining things to Angela, as long as she was the one doing the talking. "And once you're dead, taken by the ghosts, it will be clean and clear. Martin DuPre went insane. He was responsible for everything. And Blake is dead now, too. So we've survived, horrified and grieving."

"Why are you back here to kill us? That makes no sense," Angela said.

Lisa smiled. "I'm not a dumb blonde. I know all about Jackson Crow — and the members of his last team! They died. And now, he's lost so many people on this new team. His word will be worthless. Nothing he says against the senator will mean anything — because DuPre was the killer."

"They'll know we died after DuPre," Angela said.

Lisa shook her head. "Time of death is never that specific."

"Yes, it can be," Angela said.

"Get up!" Grable said. "The ghosts will be blamed for anything that doesn't fall on DuPre."

"Oh, please! You can't believe that! This may be New Orleans, and people love their stories and their legends, but they'll never blame it all on ghosts!"

"Don't kid yourself — when men can't find an explanation, they look to legend all the time, and to superstition!" Grable said. "You're just trying to waste time. And you're not going to do it anymore."

"You really are an idiot. Don't you see — you just told me. Holloway did want his wife dead. You carried it out for him. If he's really cleaning house now, he's going to have to get rid of the both of you, too. Lisa, you are never going to be Mrs. Holloway."

"You don't know anything!" Lisa told her. "Men love me. He loves me."

"Like he loved his wife," Angela said.

"Get up!" Grable ordered again.

Angela staggered to her feet. She could see that Whitney and Will were alive, thank God, but they weren't going to help her. They were still unconscious. Maybe it was best that way.

Standing was painful. Time. She had to play for more time, get them arguing, explaining again and again. Lisa liked to prove she was smart. She didn't want to be a dumb blonde. "You're crazy. You really are. Did Martin DuPre really kill the missing girls? Or did you? Was DuPre being set up and framed for everything? I'd say you could have done it, easily. Maybe DuPre was really the one being set up."

"Set up? The little bastard was going to ruin everything. He wanted to be the real messiah. He thought he was God."

"But did he kill the girls?"

"Get out on the balcony," Grable said.

"Wait. I'm going to die. I want the truth."

"All right," Lisa said, pushing past him. "You want it all? Regina Holloway went nuts with grief. The senator was desperate. First, Martin got him a girl, pretending in the dark that David Holloway was the 'bishop.' Then Martin took her himself. And then . . . well, Martin was the one who killed the girl. He got the bright idea to bring her here, and she started screaming, and he could hear that Regina Holloway was coming in the house — home early from some function or the other. He killed the girl to shut her up, stuffed the body down in the basement for the night, but then had to come back to actually get rid of the corpse. It wasn't so hard. In his mind, he'd become like a god, so he didn't owe anything to Holloway or anyone. He did it a second time — got carried away with one of the girls — when the little bitch got bitchy. Holloway needed to get rid of his wife anyway. So I talked him into a bit of a scheme that would just rid him of her. He ordered the projector, but he said that the house was creepy."

"Where did Blake fall into it all?" Angela demanded.

"Oh, well, he was the fool, you see. He fell for Lisa, and he believed everything that she said to him. He was set up to kill Martin DuPre," Haines explained.

"And both the girls are buried in the wall, right?" Angela asked.

"Weirdest damn thing," Grable said, grinning. "It was like someone showed me where to bury those bodies! But, you know, someone did show me." He started to laugh. "There's some old bones back there, so . . . hey, this is a murder house. Has been, always will be."

"You're crazy. Do you think that Jackson Crow is going to come back and let all this rest? Do you think that he won't tear apart the whole damn place? He'll find the bodies — and you'll be all who's left!"

"DuPre will be blamed."

She shook her head. "The projector," she said.

Grable's fingers twitched at the trigger of the gun. "Get out," he told her. "Get out."

"Sure."

"You go first," Lisa said, laughing. "Your ghost can wait for your little friends!"

"Stop it!" Grable said, angry. "Wait! The projector? What are you talking about?"

"We traced it," Angela told him. "The police will know that Senator Holloway — or someone in his office — bought the projector. You see, actually, I'm thinking that the senator didn't really know about it. Sure, his wife was making his life hell. But he didn't want anything like what happened to her happening. Let's think — I bet he also had ordered Martin DuPre bring women from the Church of Christ Arisen to meet with him, and that might have been why the first one had to die. And why the senator had to pay blackmail. Not his loan to you, Grable. But blackmail. Blackmail, because you figured out that DuPre was getting him a young girl. But what does that really matter now?"

"Oh, you are an ass! The senator knew about the projector. He knew," Lisa said, pushing forward. "He knew! He had to get rid of his wife, for his polecat future. Come on, think about it, Angela. He was a desperate man. But what he wanted was me. At the beginning, it was just an affair. And, at the beginning, he did just want the organizations infiltrated. The church was a group that splintered off from the Aryans. The Aryans didn't care enough about God — they were all about color and race! Holloway just wanted to find something that would bring them down at first, but he was always a dog. He loved listening to DuPre talk about what was going on. He loved women. But his wife was a worthless, sopping pile of tears all the time. I wasn't the first woman with whom he had an affair, but now, I'll keep him happy."

"But he used the women Martin DuPre cajoled into his sect. He slept with them. He pretended to be a bishop. He doesn't love you, and I just don't believe that the two of you can't see that he's going to have to kill you, too." She turned from Lisa to stare at Grable.

"Grable — you were seen at the casino the day that Regina Holloway died." She turned back to look at Lisa. "So, you were the one who ran the projector and killed Regina Holloway. She didn't just plummet over the balcony with fear — so you pushed her."

"Yes, I did. I was very, very good," Lisa assured her.

"You didn't answer me. Grable — what did you get out of it?"

He grinned. "Gambling money. And I'll just take your friend's computer."

"Please, Grable. You can't be that much of an idiot. We'll just look it all up again."

Grable looked at Lisa, uncertain. "We'll have to get to the senator. We'll have to finish him. And quickly."

"No! I'm going to be the senator's wife!"

"No, come on, Lisa! She's right. Don't you see — she's right! David Holloway did use Martin DuPre's association with the church — I don't care how it all started out! DuPre used the women, and the senator used them, too. God knows, maybe the senator killed them, and not DuPre — we only know what he told us. We know about

479

the bodies, but . . . what if we have been duped? What if the senator brought these people in on purpose — to expose all of us and get everything blamed on DuPre, and then us. He'd find a way to kill us, too. He got us to kill Blake . . . he can get someone to kill us. He manipulated everyone!"

"He's a politician," Angela said dryly, watching the pair.

"He loves me!" Lisa said. She was almost pathetic.

"I can help you," Angela told them softly. "I can help you get this all straightened out. Grable, you didn't kill anyone. Lisa killed Regina Holloway, and DuPre killed the young women. At least he killed the one — the girl he had here when he heard Regina Holloway coming home. Grable, you can make it out of all this."

"Grable knew the women, too!" Lisa protested. "Don't you understand — they were all involved. The people who weren't getting enough out of the Aryans formed the church, and there's always been the association! Grable knew the women. He helped get them around — he helped hide their bodies."

"I'd go to prison," Grable said dully.

"But you wouldn't get the needle," Angela said softly.

"Yes, yes you will, you'll die right along with me!" Lisa said. "You conspired! Conspired is the same thing — she's just trying to trick you!"

"And the senator has been tricking us both!" Grable said.

Tears suddenly trickled down Lisa's face. She believed.

"We have to kill the senator, too," Grable said. "And get far, far away from here!"

"That means we have to finish here!" Lisa said. "Get her out on the balcony, now, Grable!"

"Shoot me," Angela said. "I won't jump, and they'll trace the bullets. Go ahead. Shoot me."

"Damn you!" Lisa ran at her. Angela's head was still killing her; she wasn't prepared and she fell back, but when the woman pounced on her, she fought back. She managed to throw Lisa off, but she was weak, and Grable reached down for her, jerking her to her feet and landing a hard, bone-jarring blow to her chin.

"Get out on the balcony!" he roared.

She walked toward the balcony, praying one of them would come close enough.

If she was going over, one of them was coming.

She edged out just ahead of Grable.

481

But then she saw them. The ghosts. The two children flanked Susanne Crimshaw.

And the woman found a voice.

"Grable. Grable Haines."

He suddenly stood still, and turned around. A scream ripped from his throat.

He grasped hold of Angela's arm. "No, no, no!" he gasped.

"What?" Lisa cried hurrying after them. "What?"

She didn't see the ghosts, but the ghosts saw her. Little Percy raced toward her, ramming her. She was thrown against the balcony railing. She staggered for balance.

"Help me, Grable!" she screamed.

But he couldn't move; he was mesmerized. He shouted again; he started shooting wildly at the ghost.

He shot Lisa Drummond.

And Lisa went catapulting over the railing.

Grable started to shoot wildly again, but the door to the bedroom was thrown open and Jackson came rushing in. His gun was in his hand, and he shouted, but Grable didn't hear him. He started to turn the gun on Angela.

And Jackson shot him. Dead on, in the chest.

Grable grabbed at Angela again. They

started to fall, together.

She felt herself tip over the railing.

She imagined the hard brick below her.

Then she felt Jackson's hard grasp, catching her arm. She looked up, terrified that her fingers would slip.

He held on hard. She felt other hands. Ethereal hands.

And slowly, slowly, she was dragged back up and over the railing, and into his arms.

Whitney and Will were kept in the hospital for observation the next day; Angela insisted that she was not suffering any ill effects from concussion. She wanted to be with Jackson. They all gave their statements, which took hours.

The senator was arrested that night; they could only imagine the sensation there would be when he finally went to trial and his reign of complete corruption was uncovered. Angela had supplied the police with everything she knew after her exchange with Grable and Lisa, and Andy was working on getting Holloway to unweave the tangle he had created with all those around him.

He had thought that he could really be the puppet master; he had forgotten that he was working with people and personalities, and someone was bound to come apart.

Jackson was with Andy when they carried out their first interrogation with the man. He still thought he could pull strings, and talked without a lawyer.

It was almost morning when Jackson joined the other three.

So far, according to Andy and Jackson, Holloway was still trying to proclaim his innocence; he hadn't killed the girls — DuPre had done it — and Lisa had ordered the projector that had created the images that she'd intended to use to kill his wife. Jackson said it was probably the truth — Holloway was a man who liked sex with adoring women, but he didn't like dirty work himself. He wanted others to do the actual killing.

They weren't finished with the business of the house, though.

"We should sleep," Jenna said.

"Oh, right. While the questions still remain," Jake said.

They looked at one another. "Back to the house then," Jackson said. "I'll get Andy to send over a few of his men since we're pretty damned sure of what we'll find."

They were right.

They discovered the bodies of the two dead girls from the Church of Christ Arisen, and another skeleton. A very old skeleton

— that of Madden C. Newton. After his hanging, someone had brought him back to the house to inter him in the wall. Maybe they had thought that his body would be some kind of an offering to the victims he'd killed in the house. It was a historical mystery they were unlikely to solve.

But when they found his bones, a groan seemed to echo from the walls; a groan, and something like a cry of rage.

"These old places do settle and shake," Jake said.

They were all still for a moment then, because it seemed that the sound came again, and then, shadow filled the crevice in the wall despite the lanterns there, and a darkening shadow, huge and hideous, came for that shadow.

As the greater darkness enveloped the first, the horrible groan and cry of rage increased so that the whole house shuddered, and then, in a blink, it was gone, and all was silent.

"Maybe the real evil was Madden C. Newton after all," Angela said. "He's been the evil in the house all along, tormenting some people — and tapping into the evil to be found in others. Maybe he's been able to keep the essence of his cruelty alive, and to make it seep into the minds of some who come here. But no more. I think that whatever lurks in hell finally came for him. He managed to exert his influence over others, but we finally fought him on his level. He's been beaten."

They were all silent for a moment, wondering what they really saw, what was in the mind, and still, knowing somehow that it had been Madden C. Newton, and he was gone. Only the crumbling bones of the man remained.

"I'm going to call Devereaux and get him over here, no matter how tired he might be," one of the officers said.

Andy came back with crime scene techs and a medical examiner from the coroner's office, and the day was spent again with the police. That night, exhausted, the team slept over at the beautiful Hotel Monteleone, where they would stay until it was time to leave the city.

But the next day, Angela wanted to go back to the house — with everyone. Will and Whitney had been released from the hospital, and they were all together again.

She urged Jackson that they go.

"Why?" he asked.

It was Whitney who answered him. "My great-grandmother is coming over, and we're going to try to see that the children meet their parents."

The house was still officially under criminal investigation, and yellow tape covered the entire end of the block.

But Andy Devereaux gave them permission. The six members of the team sat with Mama Matisse while she prayed to saints and gods, and incense burned in the air.

The children appeared, still holding hands with the specter of Susanne Crimshaw.

And then, they all saw the light. It was stunning, and it might have been a mass hallucination, except, in their hearts, they all knew that wasn't so.

There was the light, a shaft, a ray, a hallway. A woman came walking toward them. She was sad, but she smiled when she saw the children. She was dressed in Victorian attire, and she moved slowly at first, and then she ran, and she fell to her knees, taking the children into her arms. She stood then, and hugged Susanne.

Then, other images appeared. Instead of walking toward the light, they were walking *from* the light.

They remained at a distance; but Angela clearly saw a woman and a little boy. She knew the woman — she recognized her from the pictures she had seen. It was Regina Holloway, and Angela knew then that she had surmised the situation correctly. Regina had never haunted them because she had gone on. She had gone on to be with her son. But she was grateful to them, and she had come there, for just a shimmering instant, to say thank you. She mouthed the words; she smiled, and then she turned away, her son's hand held tightly in her own.

And the light faded from the room.

"It is done," Mama Matisse said.

And it was.

That evening, the kids headed out for a night on Bourbon Street.

Angela and Jackson did not.

They played in the rooftop pool for a while, and they enjoyed the carousel bar, and they dined on delicious room service. Jackson told Angela the story of his first strange encounter when he was a child, and he talked about taking her to Scotland. He talked about the guilt he couldn't help but feel over the loss of the members of his previous team, and she felt that she'd shared more of him than anyone had before. He had shared his heart and soul, and he had done so much to mend hers.

They teased, laughed, grew serious, made passionate love.

And then, early in the morning, Jackson's

phone rang.

He answered it. Angela listened lazily, half-awake.

"Who was that?" she asked when Jackson hung up.

"Adam Harrison," he said slowly, looking over at her. "We've gotten our next assignment," he said.

"Oh?" she asked.

But he took her into his arms.

"We don't start until tomorrow," he said, and he gave her a dazzling smile. She grinned slowly in return, and then she kissed him. Today, they were going to exercise a few of the amazing joys that came with being alive.

NEW ORLEANS RECIPES

TO FEED THE BODY. . . .
Jambalaya

First, according to every chef I know in Louisiana — it just can't be *real* jambalaya if it isn't prepared in a cast-iron pot or Dutch oven.

4 large yellow onions chopped fine
8 cups water
4 cups rice
1 bell pepper — chopped
(Optional for spicy jambalaya, add 1 to 3 chopped banana peppers)
4 crushed garlic cloves
20 green onion straws, finely chopped
2 lbs sausage (mild for non-Cajun spicy dish lovers, hot for the true experience!)
2 pounds cooked chopped chicken and/or pork
Salt, pepper, red pepper flakes, onion powder to taste

- Brown the meat and set it aside.
- Sauté the garlic, chopped onions, and bell pepper (and banana peppers, if you choose to use them).
- Return the meat to the mixture and add the water, and the seasoning to taste. Pork and chicken need to cook thoroughly, until completely tender.
- Add the green onions when the meat is cooked through, and then add the water and rice, bring to a boil, then lower the heat to a simmer until the water is gone and the rice is cooked.
- Eat and enjoy!

The more you create this dish, the more you'll learn about your personal tastes — just how spicy is spicy? Many of my friends in Southern Louisiana *must* have Tabasco sauce in every dish, including jambalaya. (And on their eggs in the morning, come to think of it!) They carry tiny bottles of hot sauce on them, just in case they wind up in an establishment that is lacking the proper condiments!

TO FEED THE NEED FOR LIBATION!
In the 1940s, tavern owner Pat O'Brien was sold some pretty badtasting rum. He had to find a way to get rid of it. He created the

first "hurricane," with plentiful shots of rum, lime juice, and passion fruit syrup. Today, it remains one of New Orleans' most popular drinks on Bourbon Street, and, naturally, they are still on the menu at Pat O'Brien's!

A good "hurricane," sworn to kill whatever ails you. . . .
4 ounces of dark rum
1 ounce freshly squeezed lemon juice
4 ounces passion fruit syrup

- Shake well with crushed ice; strain, serve over ice, or as is
- Garnish with a lemon slice, and/or orange slice, and add a maraschino cherry

ABOUT THE AUTHOR

New York Times bestselling author **Heather Graham** has written more than one hundred fifty novels and novellas, has been published in nearly twenty-five languages, and has over seventy-five million copies in print. An avid scuba diver, ballroom dancer, and mother of five, she still enjoys her south Florida home, but loves to travel as well. Reading, however, is the pastime she still loves best, and is a member of many writing groups. For more information, check out her Web site, theoriginalheathergraham .com.